The Promise

Drew lifted one hand and touched Mandy's cheek in what could only be termed a lover's caress.

Her eyes flashed, but she did not turn away. There was no mistaking what Drew Robelard was asking for. Worse yet, there was no mistaking what she ached to answer.

"I must remind you, Captain," she said breathlessly, "that I am engaged to a man you promised me you'd do your best to locate."

"I promised to find out how he met his end, Miss Henderson," he whispered in a voice husky with desire. "I never promised to step aside for him."

Also by Suzanne Ellison

Eagle Knight
Hannah

Available from
HarperPaperbacks

SUZANNE ELLISON

SUNBURST

HarperPaperbacks
A Division of HarperCollinsPublishers

This is a work of fiction. The characters, incidents, and dialogues are products of the author's imagination and are not to be construed as real. Any resemblance to actual events or persons, living or dead, is entirely coincidental.

HarperPaperbacks   *A Division of* HarperCollins*Publishers*
10 East 53rd Street, New York, N.Y. 10022

Cover illustration by R.A. Maguire

First printing: February 1993

Printed in the United States of America

HarperPaperbacks, HarperMonogram, and colophon are trademarks of HarperCollins*Publishers*

❖ 10 9 8 7 6 5 4 3 2 1

1

Mandy Henderson stared at the bizarre, shaggy beast tethered just inside the crude adobe walls of Fort Tejon, then closed her eyes and shook her head as if to clear the mirage. She'd been travelling most of the last forty-two days on a bone-thrashing stagecoach, the last lap of a seemingly endless journey that had started over three thousand miles to the east with a week on a dusty train. Was it any wonder, she asked herself, that she was starting to see things? She'd been told to expect the unexpected in primitive California—tatooed Indians, fist-sized hairy spiders, bright orange scorpions as big as her arm—but nobody had ever mentioned *camels*.

This one stood six or seven feet high, his woeful eyes peering out at her through incredibly long lashes. When the carrot-haired young soldier standing beside it adjusted the square platform-saddle and tugged on the girth, the camel moaned as though it were at death's door.

"What is *that?*" demanded the awe-struck small boy at Mandy's side. "Have you ever seen anything like it?"

Mandy patted the straw porkpie hat on his head, then gave him a quick hug. "No, I haven't, Percy, except in a book, but I told you right from the beginning that this trip was going to be full of surprises."

Percy warmed her with one of his rare, sweet smiles, then sobered as he met and held her gaze. "Surprises are lots of fun, but I'd rather find Rodney," he confessed in a low tone.

Mandy squeezed his hand. "So would I, honey. That's why I'm going to talk to the fort commander before we find a place to spend the night. I'd go crazy waiting till morning to find out if he's heard anything."

The boy's round brown eyes brightened. "Do you think Rodney might be at the fort by now, Mandy? Do you think we might actually see him tonight?"

For months Mandy had teetered between hard truth and tender optimism when Percy confronted her with such questions, and at times like these it was difficult to decide what course to take. As gently as she was able, she told the child, "I wouldn't count on seeing Rodney tonight, Percy, but there's a chance that the major will be able to give us some news." When his lips straightened into a thin line, she forced herself to add brightly, "Wouldn't that be wonderful?"

"I guess so," he agreed, his sad eyes revealing how unlikely he considered that possibility.

At the moment, Mandy wasn't feeling particularly

optimistic herself. At most of the Army posts they'd visited, some kind soul had rushed up to greet Mandy and Percy the instant they clambered down from the stage, but here at Fort Tejon, no one seemed to take much notice of a solitary woman and a very tired child.

Mandy had been told that the fort was only six years old, but the blistering summer sun had already given the handful of adobe buildings the weathered look of decades. Although Fort Tejon was the home of the illustrious U.S. First Dragoons, Mandy didn't think that the flower-flanked row of officers' quarters and spartan enlisted men's barracks could house more than a couple of hundred men.

At three in the afternoon, the post looked almost empty. Certainly there were no other women in sight, and no children except for some half-dressed Indian boys frolicking at the far end of the stables. A few settlers drifted in and out of the sutler's store near the corral east of the fort, and half a dozen soldiers lounged against the solitary window, surreptitiously eyeing Mandy as they pretended to enjoy the crisp, clean air and a few bright rays of sun. By the look of the grounds—peppered with mud puddles and deep wagon ruts even where the hard-packed earth was dry—it had been a rainy spring in California.

This beautiful small valley nestled high in the pines bore little resemblance to most of Mandy's dusty, grueling journey. She'd been told that the Army guarded a pass here in the mountains, a key connection between fledgling Los Angeles and booming San Francisco, as well as the first safe spot west of the seemingly endless desert which the pioneers crossed in their prairie schooners. It had been Rodney Potter's dream to replace those horrible Conestogas with a transcontinental railroad, a dream he'd risked his life for.

It's still his dream; he's still alive! Mandy corrected herself sharply. Somewhere . . . out there . . . she knew he was still alive.

A rush of tears momentarily blurred her vision, but she forced herself to straighten her perky green leghorn hat and march toward the nearest soldier, the fellow fussing with the camel. Mandy felt a curious empathy for the bizarre-looking creature, whose heartrending sighs reminded her of the way she'd spent too many of her recent nights.

Unable to stop herself, she found herself blurting out to the scrawny boy in the blue uniform, "Is it really necessary to pull his girth so tight? The poor thing sounds like he's in agony!"

The soldier, who couldn't have been more than twenty, whipped around sharply to meet his accuser, and his acne-scarred face reddened when he realized that he was being lambasted by a woman.

"Ah, don't pay him no mind ma'am!" he pleaded. "Old Hadj always talks like that when we're loading supplies. He thinks I won't respect him if he don't complain. Truth is, the girth don't bother him none. The weight don't neither. He can carry nigh up to a thousand pounds."

Weary though she was, Mandy forced herself to smile. She *had* been told to expect tall tales in the west, and even a Boston-bred lawyer's daughter could tell that this one was a whopper. "That's remarkable,

Corporal," she responded a bit more cheerfully, pleased that she'd learned enough about military protocol on her journey to identify his rank by the two yellow chevrons on his sleeve. After the redheaded soldier introduced himself as Corporal Johnson, Mandy teased, "I suppose he never eats or drinks or gets tired either."

Johnson laughed, thin shoulders shaking, then winked at Percy, who still clung to Mandy's hand. "Hardly never. When old Hadj here heads out across the desert, he packs grain and water for the horses, but he don't need nothin' but mesquite thorns and greasewood 'tween here and Fort Mojave."

At once Mandy's gray eyes brightened with interest. "Fort Mojave?" she repeated, smoothing a particularly aggravating wrinkle in her green poplin skirt. Little Percy said nothing, but his eyes grew owl-like behind his thick lenses, and his straight little mouth tightened. He knew where Rodney's last letter had been mailed as well as she did.

"This camel is going to Fort Mojave?" Mandy prodded.

"Yes'm." The soldier bobbed his head, then gave a groan that mimicked the crochety camel's. "Army mules usually carry supplies out there, but somebody decided it was time to try the camels as an experiment. The shipment from Washington ain't showed up yet, but at least Captain Robelard finally got here."

"Captain Robelard?" Mandy asked uncertainly. She was sure she'd been told that a major by the name of Larson commanded this fort. "Has there been a change of command?"

"Not recently, ma'am. Major Larson's been here since Christmas or thereabouts." It seemed to Mandy that the boy shed some of his rollicking southern accent when he mentioned the major. Vaguely it crossed her mind that he *had* been laying it on a bit thick. Perhaps his youthful guilelessness, or at least part of it, was also just for show. "Captain Robelard is here on special assignment from Washington to get all the facts on our camels."

Mandy's memory of the cavalier treatment *she'd* received from Washington in response to her inquiries about Rodney's whereabouts temporarily obliterated her sympathy for the camel. "The Army sent somebody all the way out here just to look at *this?*" she burst out. If they could spare a man to cross the country to look at a bunch of walking carpets, surely they could spare somebody to help her find a missing human being!

The young corporal flushed deeply while he scratched a pimple behind his ear. "Well, Old Hadj is the biggest, miss, but he's not the only one," he retorted a bit defensively, reaching out to pat the shaggy beast's neck. "We've got a whole corps of camels— nineteen at the moment—a regular scientific experiment, you might say."

Mandy decided to drop the subject; neither the captain nor the camels had anything to do with her search. She was more concerned with the fact that if Major Larson was new to the fort, he wasn't likely to know anything that would help her; he certainly couldn't have encountered Rodney here last fall. But she refused to allow this latest obstacle in her path to slow her down. The important thing was whether or not Major Larson would help her make inquiries.

As Mandy glanced at a pair of yapping mongrels dueling for a meatless bone, a striking specimen of military manhood rode into the stableyard and quickly dismounted. Clad in an officer's knee-length coat, he was at least a foot taller and a decade older than the homely young soldier who rushed forward to tend to his horse. With orders to double-grain the animal, the officer dismissed the recruit with a salute and a friendly grin before setting off on foot toward the main compound. It was hardly the smile Mandy would have expected from such an imposing figure, and she was surprised to see two deep dimples transform his square-jawed face into a ray of California sunshine. Although the officer had not even seen her, his warm smile brightened her spirits considerably.

"What's it like between here and Fort Mojave, Corporal?" Mandy asked Corporal Johnson.

She knew it was desert, of course, barren and bleak, the antithesis of the poppy-painted hillsides which guarded this hidden fort. And she also knew that after she'd exhausted every possible clue as to Rodney's whereabouts which might surface in this comparatively safe haven, she'd have no option left but to brave that deadly desert which had swallowed him whole, sifting through the sand until she stumbled across some trace of him. But she *would* find him. It was, Mandy repeated to herself almost daily, only a matter of time.

"They say the Mojave is the back door to Hell, if you'll pardon my language, ma'am," the corporal informed her as he threw another hundred pounds or so of supplies on the beleaguered camel. "I've been in Texas, New Mexico Territory, even down into Old

Mexico on a scouting mission once, and there's not one single inch of it that comes close to the horror of the Mojave."

Mandy swallowed hard. Suddenly she felt exhausted and unutterably depressed. Nevertheless, there was nothing that this young soldier or any other man could say to deter her from her goal. She would to find out what had happened to Rodney Potter! She owed it to her family, to Percy, and to Rodney himself. Mandy had lost too many of her loved ones this past year to give up yet another. And so had the sad-eyed, bespectacled boy who stood so solemnly beside her.

She glanced down at her fiance's young brother, who'd hardly left her side for weeks now, and noticed that he was no longer listening to the soldier. His big brown eyes were focused on something at the other end of the compound.

A group of Indian boys, shockingly naked except for tiny flaps of deerskin that hung between their legs, were chasing each other in circles while they used long bare branches to push a huge flat burl of oak around a clearing. Some of the boys were about Percy's size, but several were much bigger. One of them, a strapping teenager with an unusual white streak in his hair, seemed to dominate the game, attacking the oak burl as though his life depended on it.

As Percy studied the boys with obvious longing, Mandy wondered how much he missed his friends at the boarding school he'd abandoned so abruptly. It had been a terrible journey for a seven-year-old child, and she wished she'd been able to leave him safely behind.

Yet he was as determined to find Rodney as she was, and she knew he would have run away to join her a second time if she hadn't relented when she'd found him hiding on the train.

"Corporal, do you suppose it would be okay if my young friend here went over to watch the game? These Indians are, uh, relatively harmless?" After the horror stories she'd heard in Texas, it was hard to think of any Indian as totally benign, but even a lady from Boston could tell that those boys wouldn't be allowed inside an Army fort if the military had anything to fear from them.

The skinny soldier squatter down in front of Percy, plucked off his hat and ruffled his straight brown hair. "You want to go play some shinny?" he asked cheerfully, suddenly sounding like somebody's father instead of a green kid barely out of short pants himself.

Mandy could feel the strain in Percy's eager young body as he nodded vigorously, lifting his big brown eyes to hers to plead for a rare moment of fun after all the hard weeks of bone-shattering travel. "Could I, Mandy? Could I play for just a little while?"

Mandy wished she could have turned him loose, but the next few minutes might well be the most important of their entire journey, and she couldn't allow him to meet Major Larson looking like a ragamuffin. On the other hand, she could speak more freely without Percy by her side. And if the major did have news, especially bad news, she didn't want Rodney's little brother to hear it from a stranger.

"I tell you what, Percy. You can go over there and

watch the boys while I talk to the major. Just don't get dirty, and don't wander off. Is that a deal?"

Percy glowed and wriggled like a puppy. Dropping her hand, he seized his dusty lapels in a fair imitation of a dapper young man. "You bet, Mandy! I'll stay clean as a whistle!"

With that he darted away, leaving Mandy to set off alone to find the post commander. After Johnson told her a bit more about the fort and the area, he directed her across the main road to a bridge over a stream that separated the stables from the main compound. Headquarters was some distance beyond that.

As she sidestepped an enormous mud puddle, she mentally recapped her most persuasive arguments for Army assistance. Corporal Johnson had told her that Major Larson was a stern man but a fair one, which gave her a fighting chance but certainly no guarantees. She'd met "fair" men all over the southwest, in and out of uniform. Most of them had been sympathetic as well as patronizing, but all of them had told her to go home.

She had not listened to any of them. She would not listen now. She had come to California to find Rodney Potter, and she would not leave without him.

No matter what the cost.

As Captain Drew Robelard entered the drab adobe-walled office that served as headquarters at Fort Tejon, he smartly saluted Major Sherwood Larson. He'd known Sherwood for years and generally dispensed with such formalities when they were alone, but he always adhered to military protocol in front of the men. And at this time of day, there was a good chance that Sherwood's adjutant or aide-de-camp would be working in the office.

"At ease, Drew. Have a seat," the white-haired major declared at once, gesturing toward a rawhide-lattice chair beside the desk. "Harris is conferring with the surgeon and I've ordered poor Johnson to go load up that camel we're loaning to Ben Hayward's boys until they get their wagon fixed, so we should be able to speak undisturbed. What have you discovered so far?"

Drew knew he wasn't being asked for his preliminary report on the Camel Corps, although that was the official topic of this scheduled meeting. Unfortunately, Drew's secondary, and secret, investigation at Fort Tejon was going very badly. And while he was not a man who was easily embarrassed, he found himself a bit uneasy that he still had so little to report. Oh, he'd done his homework all right, checking out every nook and cranny of this post and every man who was assigned to it. But so far, he'd found nothing out of line.

"Sherwood, my preliminary review of the manifests has revealed nothing about the missing supplies, I'm sorry to say. Everything appears to be in order."

"Dammit, Drew, everything is *not* in order!" Sherwood corrected him. "Only a fraction of the supplies the Department insists it has sent through this fort seem to have reached the reservation. A few shipments have come up short even since *I've* been here. The Indians are dressed in rags or not at all. Any fool can look at them and see they're not getting enough to eat. And Anna, our Yokuts nanny, insists that some of them have been sold as slaves to the miners."

Drew scowled. "Do you have any evidence that there's an active local slave trade, sir?" he questioned. "I know there was some dissension when California was admitted to the union as a free state, but—"

The major laughed without humor. "*Some* dissension? Drew, the political bigwigs agreed to abolish slavery out here. Nobody asked the common people. Most of them don't even consider the Indians human enough to make decent slaves! Ever since the first settlers crossed the Sierra Madre they've been killing off Indians like any other game in the forest. In fact, some of the men get together on Sunday afternoons and go hunting for them just to pass the time!"

Despite his terse, controlled tone, the older man could not conceal his disapproval. "Drew, this Indian situation undercuts everything the Army's trying to do here. One of the ways we've been able to pacify these local Yokutses is by promising them protection from the settlers and those damn Mojave braves that come swooping out of the desert every now and then. If they're not getting enough to eat and their women are being snatched at sundown, why on earth should they stick around?"

"Do they?" Drew asked, lacking Sherwood's experience of seeing the nearby Yokuts reservation first hand. It was vital that he talk to Lieutenant Maynard Cox, the commander of the temporary dragoon detail that had been supervising the reservation ever since the last

Indian agent had been mauled to death by a grizzly last summer. The civilian Indian Department was supposed to be sending out a replacement, relieving the Army of its temporary obligation to step in, but the political problems of the upcoming and hotly contested four-way election between Douglas, Breckinridge, Lincoln and Bell had caused innumerable delays. Sherwood had been expecting a new agent "any day" for a matter of months.

In the few days Drew had been at the fort, he hadn't been able to come up with a justifiable reason to visit the reservation without raising suspicion; it was hardly the sort of place one went to make a social call. "Do the Indians stick around?" he repeated.

Sherwood lifted his hands in a helpless gesture. "Cox says it's hard to tell. He never sees the Indians all at once unless there's some sort of big powwow, and I guess he has trouble telling them apart even when they report for rations. But Anna knows most of them, and she insists that so many young men and women have been stolen that half the others are hiding up in the mountains."

Drew had met Sherwood's nanny, a silent, solemn girl who was not yet thirty but carried herself like an old woman broken by grief or time. She dressed like a white woman when she was inside the fort, but she always wore that hollow expression—a blend of defiance, fear, or just plain anger—which he'd seen before on the faces of members of other defeated tribes. He suspected she had access to information that could be crucial to his investigation, but since she'd never even acknowledged his existence, he knew it would do no good to question her.

"Do you have any reason to doubt Anna's word?" he reluctantly asked Sherwood.

"Her word?" the older man repeated. "Do I think she'd deliberately lie to me?" He pondered the question, then shook his head. "I doubt it. Do I think she'd believe a bunch of superstitious Indians who are tired of being hunted down like white-tailed deer? Certainly."

"Then unless her connections are completely fabricating their stories, there may be some truth to what she says. Enough that I should try to check it out even if it's not connected to our immediate problem."

Sherwood rubbed his shaggy eyebrows, then exhaled deeply. "Yes, I guess you should. But for God's sake, be careful, Drew! The Indians aren't the only ones who disappear in the gold rush country. There's a silver strike town up north that prides itself on burying a man a day! I'm sure it's an exaggeration, but just the same—"

"I'll be careful, sir," Drew promised. "And I'll get to the bottom of this mess, one way or another, before it gets out of hand."

It was the nearest he dared come to expressing what he knew to be Sherwood's fear, that somehow he would be blamed for this mess he'd inherited from his predecessor and retire from the Army with a blemish on his proud and spotless forty-three-year record. If Drew couldn't clean things up before the new civilian agent showed up, Fort Tejon would have to publicly air its dirty laundry.

Quickly the older man said, "We've got our work cut out for us in this new state, Drew, no doubt about it. But with so few men stationed at the post, and barely enough supplies to begin with, even when we get them all, it's an uphill struggle. And these ridiculous *camels*"—he spat out the word as though it were somewhat profane—"make it difficult for the rest of the Army to take us seriously. The First Dragoons, finest mounted unit in the whole U.S. Cavalry, humiliated with these odiferous, cud-spitting, walking carpets! Every time they show up at a city or fort the horses go wild and the cattle stampede. The women shriek and the children laugh! And the men . . . the men either swear at us or shake their heads. No matter what you unearth about those missing supplies, I should hope that your report on those damn camels will at least free us from—" He broke off, startled, by the timid knock on the door.

"Should I get that, sir?" Drew asked, partly out of deference and partly because he wasn't ready to discuss that part of his mission to Fort Tejon until he'd observed the camels on a long haul. When Sherwood nodded, he rose quickly to open the stout plank door, ready to dispatch the caller with a courteous promise to relay a message to the major. But the instant his eye fell on the young woman who stood beside the apologetic guard at the door, his right hand froze in mid-salute.

My God, she's a beauty. He was surprised to find any woman at the fort headquarters, since there was only one other officer's wife at the garrison beside Sherwood's, and no Indian or Mexican laundress would dare to approach the captain's office on her own. This lady—and she was definitely a lady—looked too independent to be anybody's wife, too patrician to be a

laundress, and too intelligent to be the kind of girl who
ogled Drew at the Washington social functions he was
so often compelled to attend.

She was dressed in a dusty green gown that drew
attention to her slender waist. The frayed lace at the
collar and cuffs had been carefully mended. Her light
brown hair was gently upswept beneath a leghorn jock-
ey hat that discreetly sported only a black velvet ribbon
and one emerald feather.

The woman herself was very small and as fragile-
looking as a china doll. Her high cheekbones were
delicate but well-defined and her mouth, gently
curved in a way that let him know that smiling usually
came naturally to her, now trembled with uncertainty
or fatigue. But it was her eyes that haunted him. They
were gray, big and solemn, full of hope and determination which almost, but not quite, masked her weariness and fear.

Drew was too new to the post to know which days
the stagecoach arrived, so he wasn't sure if she was a
local settler's daughter or a lone traveller passing
through. But he did know, with the certain instinct of
one who has learned to see trouble coming, that this
lovely creature had come to Fort Tejon determined to
find a solution to some terrible problem. Even before
she spoke, a hoarse voice within him vowed to help her
find it.

"Good afternoon, sir. My name is Amanda Henderson," she began in a steady voice which gave the
impression that her words had been rehearsed. Then,
abruptly, she glanced at Drew's shoulder, as if to confirm his rank. Surprise registered on her lovely face as
she discovered two gold bars but no major's oak leaf,

but she recovered quickly and asked in an even tone, "Captain, I wonder if I might have a word with Major Larson."

Drew knew perfectly well he should tell her that Sherwood was busy, but he'd be happy to relay a message or set up an appointment for some later time. Yet he found himself powerless to ignore the pain that shadowed Amanda Henderson's determinedly cheerful gray eyes, or the weary gratitude he read there when he heard himself reply, "Of course you may see the major, ma'am. Please come in."

As he stood aside and gestured toward the major, she lifted her green skirts a few inches and cautiously stepped across the threshhold as though it were a far bigger boundary than the one between the major's office and the splintered wooden porch. As Drew turned to face his friend, he was relieved to see a comforting blend of surprise, delight and concern flicker across Sherwood's face as he quickly rose.

"Major Sherwood Larson, at your service, ma'am," he declared, giving a small but courtly bow. When she curtsied with equal decorum, Sherwood motioned to Drew as he added, "And this is Captain Drew Robelard, currently assigned to Fort Tejon."

As she turned to face Drew, a whisper of afternoon sunlight crept into the dark little room, lighting up the sweetness of her full lips. When Drew smiled at her, she gave him a courteous nod, apparently oblivious to the impact she had upon him.

"My name is Mandy—I mean Amanda—Henderson, sir," she began in a decorous tone, addressing herself solely to Sherwood, "and I've just arrived from Fort

Wilmington. I started out in Boston almost six weeks ago and—"

"Boston?" Sherwood repeated incredulously. "Boston, Massachusetts?"

Good God, no wonder she looked exhausted! Drew thought with a shudder. It was a hellish journey for anyone, a trip no sane person would undertake if there was any way around it, and certainly not a journey for a woman travelling alone. And Mandy—how that sweet nickname suited her!—was definitely travelling unescorted. Drew was sure of it. Otherwise she would never have approached the headquarters of an Army post alone.

"Young woman"—Sherwood was almost speechless with shock—"please sit down. You must be—"

"Incredibly brave and determined," Drew cut in admiringly before Sherwood could demean her momentous achievement with too much concern.

Miss Henderson turned to face him, and this time a ghost of a smile did cross her weary face. "Why, thank you, Captain. Most of the terms I've heard from officers along the way have not been so flattering."

He grinned. "I'm sure they're just jealous because their own women aren't so courageous."

"Captain," Sherwood broke in, his terse tone reminding his friend who was the commander in charge, "do help the young lady sit down."

Mandy was only a few feet from the chair Drew had vacated, but he marched toward her quickly and pushed it an inch or two in her direction. Perching tentatively on the edge of the chair, she thanked Drew for his courtesy, but did not meet his eyes again. Instead, she directed her attention to the major, who resumed his seat behind his desk and watched her, steepling and unsteepling his gnarled hands.

"As I was saying, Major Larson, I came to Fort Tejon in search of information. Perhaps you can help me." Her voice wobbled on the last word, and Drew caught a glimpse of too much moisture in her eyes.

"If it is at all in my power, Miss Henderson, I will certainly do so," Sherwood quickly promised in his most grandfatherly tone.

She blinked a couple of times and Drew felt a surge of pride for her when she arrested the threatening tears. Some women he had known would have used those tears, even manufactured them if necessary, to tug on the old man's heartstrings, but this young woman was determined to take the high road to her goal. Drew considered handing her a handkerchief, but decided that she'd probably prefer to conquer her tears on her own.

"Major—" She stopped and swallowed hard as Sherwood, glaring at Drew in reprimand for his apparent thoughtlessness, took out his own handkerchief and leaned across his desk to hand it to his guest. Awkwardly she took the small embroidered cloth, but she did not dab her eyes. Instead she blinked a few times, valiantly struggling to regain her composure, slowly turning in her chair to face not Major Larson but Drew.

He had no idea why those glistening gray eyes had sought his own, but suddenly he forgot that a third party was in the room. He wanted to reach out and touch her shoulder, to offer some sort of warmth and consolation, but when she lifted her delicate chin ever so slightly, he forced his hand to remain at his side.

With sudden clarity he understood what she wanted from him, something that Sherwood, overly solicitous, had unwittingly denied her.

Believe in me, her aching eyes begged him. *Tell me I'm brave again; don't let me cry! If I give into the despair, I'll start sobbing and I'll never, ever stop.*

Drew hesitated for only a moment, then snatched Sherwood's handkerchief from her hand and dropped it on the desk. "Please tell us how we can help you, Miss Henderson," he suggested briskly, as though he had no time to waste on a woman's tears. "I believe you said you were in need of some information."

Sherwood's lips tightened in disapproval, but Drew was certain that Mandy understood the true reason for his stringent words and was grateful for them. Abruptly she straightened and tightened her lips. Her tears dried instantly as she turned back to Major Larson and started to speak again.

"Major, I'm looking for a man named Rodney Potter. He was scheduled to arrive here at Fort Tejon last November. I was hoping you might have some information about his whereabouts."

As Drew saw her small, perfect body grow rigid with anticipation, or dread, he felt a sudden surge of anger at the unknown Rodney Potter. How dare he put tears in this brave beauty's eyes! How dare he disappear in California, expecting her to follow him into the great unknown!

Sherwood considered the question thoughtfully, then slowly shook his head. "I'm sorry, Miss Henderson, but that name means nothing to me."

Mandy swallowed hard, then turned to face Drew

once more with those proud but wounded gray eyes. But now he could see no trace of the secret understanding he'd imagined between them just moments before; her thoughts belonged wholly to the missing Rodney Potter. "Captain Robelard? Perhaps you've heard something . . ."

Slowly Drew shook his head, desperately wishing he could help her. Such courage deserved to be rewarded. "I've only been here a few days myself, Miss Henderson," he was forced to admit. As she continued to stare at him, Drew struggled to find something to offer her. Used to thinking on his feet, he managed to suggest, "Perhaps if you'd tell us a little more about him . . ."

For the briefest of moments he was rewarded by the flicker of hope in Mandy's eyes, and perhaps a ghost of gratitude. Then she turned away from him again, eagerly leaning toward Sherwood her voice low but full of passion.

"Rodney—Mr. Potter—is an engineer, sir. As I'm sure you know, Congress has been debating the best location for the first transcontinental railroad line for some time now. Mr. Potter's company, the Sea to Shining Sea Railway, asked him to head a survey team along the thirty-fifth parallel to determine its feasibility." Nervously, she smoothed nonexistent wrinkles in her fraying skirt. "The last leg of their journey was from Fort Mojave to Fort Tejon. Mr. Potter left Fort Mojave in October with six other men. The Sea to Shining Sea Railway tells me that no one has heard from any of them since."

Over Mandy's head, Sherwood's eyes met Drew's with an expression that reminded him of the time in Fort Union when he'd heard the older man lament, "I think I'd rather take an Apache arrow through my own heart than write one more letter to a mother saying that her boy won't be coming home alive." Now Drew waited to see how Sherwood handled the equally arduous task of telling Mandy that she'd never see Rodney Potter again.

From the moment she'd revealed that Potter had disappeared in the desert, Drew had realized that Mandy Henderson had come west on a fool's errand. Men disappeared in California all the time. Sometimes it was by accident, other times on purpose. If a man attached to a formal expedition had disappeared—worse yet, if the entire *expedition* had disappeared—there was hardly a chance in the world that he would ever be unearthed, even by a determined young lady from Boston. She would take the news hard, but Drew was sure that it wouldn't come as a surprise to her, and she'd find a way to cope. In his opinion, Mandy Henderson deserved to hear the truth.

But to his surprise, Sherwood sidestepped the inevitable, tapping his lips with one thoughtful finger. "I do believe I recall something about a missing survey team in the notes left to me by my predecessor. But what it might be . . ." He stopped, flustered. "Miss Henderson, I'll have to consult my personal staff and also confer with my wife. She hears things . . . unofficially, you understand. Rumors and such. I never pay much attention to them, but Mrs. Larson is very good at keeping track of social details which perpetually elude me."

It hurt Drew to see the futile upsurge of hope that suddenly lit Mandy's tired eyes. Sherwood's feeble promises, however well intended, would do nothing to help this courageous, beautiful girl. It made no difference what Harris or Johnson dug up in the files. If by some unlikely miracle Rodney Potter was still alive, then he must not have made contact with Mandy because he *wanted* her to give him up for dead.

And Drew was every bit as certain that it was the one thing that Mandy Henderson would never do.

2

Anna knelt in the rich mountain soil and leaned forward to pluck the *loy-yo* at the base of the live oak, but she couldn't quite reach it. Heedless of the shriek of the red-shinned hawk circling above her, she stretched out flat and poked her digging stick a little farther up the slope. As she wriggled it deeper into the dirt, the hooked end seized the tiny fern securely, ripping it out of the ground with a satisfying jerk.

It took a few minutes to gather the other *loy-yo* roots in the area, longer yet to shake the soil off of her skirt. Mrs. Larson would not approve if Anna came into her house looking dirty. Worse yet, she would be upset if she knew that Anna had been collecting Yokuts herbs again for the purpose of doctoring the baby.

Mrs. Larson loved her grandson, but she did not cherish him the way Anna did. The baby was of Mrs. Larson's blood, but he was of Anna's heart. Anna knew that Jonathan had been sent to replace the little girl that she had lost to the white man's sickness. She had tried to explain it to Mrs. Larson once, but Mrs. Larson had looked quite alarmed.

"You're his nanny, Anna, not his mother," she'd declared a bit dramatically. "Your job is to take care of him while we live here. That's all."

"I will take care of him the best way I know how," Anna had promised. But she had learned that to Mrs. Larson and herself, this meant different things.

Last night Jonathan had cut a new tooth, although Anna was the only one who knew it yet. The last time that had happened, Mrs. Larson had told Anna to put a foul-smelling white man's lotion on his gums. It had not helped; it might have made things worse. But when Anna had rubbed the sweet juice of a *loy-yo* root on the baby's sore flesh, he had quieted at once. Mrs. Larson had still objected. She had insisted that he was a white baby and he would only be treated with white man's medicine.

Of all the white women Anna had known, Mrs. Larson was the kindest, and she had no wish to defy her. But her feelings for Mrs. Larson, and for her husband, were tepid compared to what she felt for the baby. It was his little heart that kept hers warm.

He needed fresh *loy-yo* roots to ease the pain in his gums, and Anna had none left in the small woven basket she kept hidden under the straw pallet on her bed. It would not be easy to sneak them into the house if Mrs. Larson was downstairs sewing, but Anna had done it before.

Actually, it would be easy compared to finding a way to keep the baby with her when the old major retired

soon. Anna was not yet certain whether she could convince the Larsons to take her with them, or whether
she could bear to leave her ancient great-grandfather
and her almost-grown son. She was only certain that
she could not, would not, live without the little one.

Captain Robelard offered Mandy his arm as he ushered her over the rough ground toward the private
quarters belonging to the major and his wife.

"I hear you're in California on a secret mission, Captain," she teased him, certain that this handsome man
had listened to enough of her troubles for one day.
"What did you have to do to earn this honor?"

"Secret mission?" he repeated, his blue eyes meeting
hers with quickly concealed alarm.

Mandy stared at him, wondering if that gangly corporal had been pulling her leg. "I meant the camels, sir.
I was told, perhaps in jest, now that I think of it, that
you'd been sent out here from Washington to see how
they're getting along."

A dimpled grin—part humor, part relief?—warmed
his clean-cut features. "Oh, I think *they* are getting
along fine, Miss Henderson. The problem is that they
aren't getting along with anybody else."

Mandy giggled. His joke wasn't that funny, but
she'd been so tense conferring with the major that it
was a relief to chat about something inconsequential
with an appealing man close to her own age. "Frankly,
Captain, I was surprised to find camels out here. I read
a lot about the government's projects, especially in
California, and I've never come across any mention of
them."

Drew—for some reason she couldn't think of him as Captain Robelard—laughed and patted her hand as though the two of them were on their way to the dance floor. "I think that's because a lot of the Army upper brass is embarrassed about the camels. Most of the men never wanted them here in the first place, and ever since they docked in Texas three years ago, nobody's been quite sure what to do with them."

"I'm not surprised!" Mandy replied with a chuckle. "I've never seen a stranger creature . . . or a noisier one! Do they moan all the time?"

Drew shook his sleek black head. "No, only when they're trying to make a point. Abu, the camel driver who came with them from Armenia, tells me that you can find a caravan of nomads in the desert just by listening for the chorus of camel groans at sunrise. I guess it's like a horse blowing up his belly to keep the girth loose. The camel figures if he complains enough, the load will be lighter. But I'm told that once the load's in place, a camel will march all day without a word."

"Corporal Johnson told me they can go for days without water."

"I believe Corporal Johnson is correct. But I haven't really seen the camels in action yet, at least on a lengthy journey. I'll find out a lot more when we take a trip across the desert."

"To Fort Mojave." It was not a question, and Mandy knew by the look on Drew's face that he realized she'd done her homework well.

"Yes, to Fort Mojave," he admitted slowly. Then, as he met Mandy's eyes with a searching gaze, he added in a low tone, "And yes, I'll make inquiries for you there if

Major Larson can't come up with anything for you before I go."

A whisper of relief—or was it some other nameless joy?—zigzagged through Mandy's heart. She'd finally found somebody who would truly help her on her search for Rodney. But she still couldn't rely on somebody else to ask the hard questions for her when so much was at stake.

Choosing her words with great care, she said, "You're very kind, Captain, and I greatly appreciate your offer. But actually, what I had in mind . . . that is, if it's not too much to ask . . ." She paused hopefully.

"Just name it," Drew assured her.

Mandy took a deep breath. "Captain, I'd like to go with you."

Drew stopped dead in his tracks. "Miss Henderson—"

"Captain, please! Unless Major Larson finds out something remarkable, I know I'm going to have to cross the desert sooner or later. Frankly, I thought I'd have to rely on local recommendations to find a scout to take me, but if the famous First Dragoons are—"

"Miss Henderson!" he burst out again, clearly dismayed. "You're not talking about hiring a hansom cab in Boston. Every man in this unit risks his life when he crosses the Mojave. Even if the hostiles between here and there were totally pacified, there are three thousand ways for a person to lose his life in that treacherous stretch of no man's land." His sensuous lips drew together in a straight, forbidding line. "Even if by some chance I would be foolish enough to consent to your request, I guarantee you that Major Larson would forbid it."

Stung, Mandy said, "How do you know that until you ask him? You said you've only been here a few days yourself, sir."

"That's true, Miss Henderson, but I've known Sherwood Larson for years. Some of his ideas about ladies are a bit old-fashioned, I'll grant you, but when it comes to crossing the desert in Indian country, I have to agree with him."

Mandy stiffened, wondering how she could have been so mistaken in believing that Drew Robelard was special, that he alone among all the Army officers she'd met on this endless journey actually understood what she had to do, even admired and respected her for it. Had she imagined that private moment of understanding in the major's office? Perhaps desperation was coloring her judgment.

"So much for all your kind words about my bravery, Captain Robelard," she retorted, too hurt to hold her tongue. "I wonder what you *really* think of me!"

Drew came to an abrupt halt, and studied Mandy's face for several moments in ominous silence. Somewhere behind her, she could hear the rat-a-tat-tat of a woodpecker on a nearby oak and the squeals of glee of the Indian boys playing shinny. She tried to focus on the sounds and not the silence; she tried not to meet Drew's piercing gaze. But he waited stoically until she bravely faced him and read in his eyes all the respect and compassion she'd imagined once before.

"Miss Henderson," he began slowly, "I have a great deal of respect for you. So much, in fact, that I think you deserve to hear the truth. I don't think there's a chance in the world that you're going to find Rodney

Potter alive in California. It'll be a miracle if you even find out how he died." Again he paused, his eyes on her quivering mouth. She had the eerie feeling that he wanted to take her in his arms . . . or maybe even kiss her.

He didn't. Instead he straightened and glanced at a well-kept house at the far end of the post where a gray-haired lady was sitting in a rocker on her front porch, chatting with another woman who stood on the steps as though she were leaving.

In a voice that was little more than a whisper, he added, "But I think you knew that long before you left Boston, and it doesn't have a thing to do with why you made this terrible journey."

Mandy swallowed hard. "I don't think I understand," she replied softly.

He lifted his hands in a helpless gesture. "I understand why you came to California, and I think you did the right thing."

Still she stared at him, curious, uncertain. "What do you mean?"

When Drew slipped both hands in his pockets, he looked more like a humbled teenager than a proud cavalryman. His words came slowly, as though each one were from the heart, and Mandy wondered what personal tragedy had lodged them there. "It doesn't have anything to do with logic, Miss Henderson, or hope or even courage. My father taught me young that sometimes there are things a man must do just to keep on living with himself." His tone was gentle now, as soothing as a goat's-hair brush stroking her sensitive scalp. "I imagine that sometimes it's the same for a woman."

Mandy gulped back the hard lump in her throat, touched even more by the kindness of his deep voice than by his caring words. How clearly this man saw through her! How willing he was to soothe her pain at the risk of revealing his own! What loss had Drew Robelard weathered in the past that made him understand the depths of her heartache? And made her want to share with him all the feelings churning in her soul?

"My admiration for your courage has nothing to do with the end result of your search, Miss Henderson," he concluded softly. "By the time you go back to Boston, you'll know that you did everything you could possibly do for Rodney Potter, and you'll be able to lay him to rest." This time he did reach out to touch her shoulder as he finished gently, "And isn't that really why you came to Fort Tejon?"

A shudder swept through Mandy, though she wasn't sure if it was triggered by Drew's insight or his unexpected caress. Surely it was the tenderness in his voice and not some manly magic, that jolted her so abruptly, that made her ache to lean against him and plead for his help in battling the world. But it was a luxury she didn't dare indulge. Suddenly she felt touched by a nameless guilt that made her edge away from the virile man who stood before her.

"If I have to go home without him, maybe I will take comfort in knowing that I tried," she admitted honestly. "But I'm not about to give up yet, Captain. I just arrived at Fort Tejon. I've barely begun to search for Rodney, and I still have no proof that he died."

Drew glanced away quickly, leaving Mandy to face her demons.

He's dead, Mandy, and you know it, said a voice within her.

But the other voice, the voice of a friendship that had lasted twenty-five years, insisted, *Oh, no, he's not! I just won't let him die!*

Mandy shivered. She couldn't look at Drew and believe that she'd ever see Rodney again. He understood why she'd made this grueling journey, but that didn't mean that he had any real hope that Rodney was still alive.

"Please take me to Fort Mojave, Captain," she begged once more, not sure she'd ever get another chance to speak to him so openly. His eyes, so full of tender warmth and respect, darkened as he pondered her request, but he did not refuse her outright. Desperation forced her to plead, "With or without you, I've got to go."

Mandy would have given a fortune to have seen into Drew's heart right then. His tense mouth told her that he was at war within himself. Clearly, he was a man who lived by the rules of duty, and he was no longer certain just where his duty lay.

For just an instant, his warm hand closed over hers as he whispered, "I can't promise to take you to Fort Mojave, but I swear I'll do everything in my power to find out what I can for you." Then, quickly, as if he were embarrassed by his fervent promise,—he lifted his elbow with courtly protocol and waited for her to take it.

When Mandy slipped her fingers around his muscular forearm, she felt transformed by a rainbow of hope and courage that obliterated the thunderstorm that had soaked her spirits just moments ago. She'd come to

Fort Tejon to plead for help, but she'd never expected to find it so quickly. She certainly hadn't expected to find Captain Drew Robelard dressed in shining armor, mounted on a great white horse.

At Mandy's request, Drew left her at the Larson's house and went to find Percy Potter for her. By the way she'd referred to the boy, Drew could tell that she loved him dearly, but he didn't get the impression that he was her brother, her nephew or her son. His confusion had reminded him that he still didn't know what her relationship to Rodney Potter was, either. But he sternly reminded himself that it didn't really matter: Mandy's feelings for the other man had nothing to do with Drew's vow to help her find him. It was something he simply had to do.

White boys, especially white boys in spats and black box suits, were rare in this part of California, so Percy wasn't hard to find. He was the small, slightly chubby, child standing just out of range of the Indians playing at the far end of the stables.

His eyes were wide with awe as he studied the long-haired, half-naked, tattooed Yokuts boys and he was too enthralled to notice Drew, even when he walked up beside him. Drew had spent enough years on the frontier to know that such fascination with Indians was short-lived in this part of the world. By the time a boy reached his teens, he saw nothing magical about the wild men who had once owned this land. But this child would probably still view a trip to a reservation as a spectacular picnic to boast of to his friends.

When Percy glanced uneasily toward the main office, as though he'd been keeping one eye on it for some time, Drew touched his shoulder and introduced himself. "Percy? I'm Captain Robelard. Miss Henderson asked me to tell you she's gone over to the major's house, but she'll come back to get you in a little while."

The boy straightened quickly and tugged off his round straw hat. "It's nice to meet you, sir," he declared with a stiff, tiny bow. Then he licked his lips and sighed uncertainly before he burst out, "Do you know if the major's seen my brother, sir?"

The words struck Drew in the hidden part of his heart where his own little brother still lived, the only place where Eddie had lived for almost thirty years. He hadn't been speaking idly to Mandy about understanding the need to lay a loved one to rest; he still took comfort from the knowledge that he'd done everything he could possibly do to save Eddie's life.

Thrusting aside the still painful memory of his childhood loss, he replied genially, "Well, Percy, the major didn't live here when your brother was scheduled to arrive, so he's going to talk to some other people who were. Maybe he'll find out something."

"When?" the boy pleaded, his brown eyes huge with hope and dread.

"Well . . . I'm not sure, Percy. Maybe tomorrow." But when the big eyes glistened, Drew found himself saying, "Maybe today."

The child stiffened with stout determination. "Thank you for the message, sir," he said, in a voice too old for one so young. "Does Mandy want me to wait here until she comes?"

Drew wondered how much of his life this brave child had spent waiting. For Mandy, for Rodney Potter, just for bad news? He replied gently, "Yes, she does. But if you get hungry in the meantime—"

"Oh, I'm fine, sir," the boy answered quickly, as though it were a memorized line. "I don't want to be any bother."

And how many times has he said those words? Drew wondered. In how many posts and how many towns? For the first time he felt a flash of anger at Mandy for bringing the little one with her. A California-bound stagecoach was no place for a child, especially a city boy like this one.

And then, abruptly, he realized that Mandy had surely brought Percy with her because she had nowhere to leave him. Which meant that there was nobody to take care of Percy if anything happened to Mandy. And Mandy had vowed to cross the treacherous Mojave with or without the First Dragoons.

"Percy," Drew asked thoughtfully, "Do you have family back in Boston?"

The boy's mouth tightened as though it were a subject he'd rather not discuss. "Not any more, sir. All that's left is me and my brother and Mandy."

"Then Mandy is . . . your sister?" Drew asked with sudden hope.

When the boy shook his head, Drew realized he was grasping at straws. Still he had to prod, "Or your aunt, perhaps?"

"No, sir."

"She's no relation to you at all?" he tried again.

"No, sir."

"Nor to your brother?"

"No, sir."

"Then why has she made this incredible journey just to find him?" Drew already knew the answer, but he had to hear it out loud before he could accept the obvious disheartening fact.

Percy shrugged, as though the answer were as clear as day. "Because Rodney would do the same thing if it was Mandy who was missing, sir. She's going to be his wife."

"You must stay for supper, Miss Henderson," Lucinda Larson ordered as she banged about the tin pans and delicate crockery with equal abandon, determinedly fixing her unexpected guest some tea. "My cook is out at the moment, but I'm sure you'll be quite delighted with her skill in the kitchen. I hardly know where anything is anymore. She does everything for me."

Mandy had found the slender older woman on her front porch, chatting with her neighbor and enjoying the afternoon sun while she pieced red and blue flowered strips into a Log Cabin quilt. As if in defiance of her role as the commanding officer's wife, she was quite casually clad in a plain brown checked dress which had been in fashion back east six or seven years before. Her hair was parted in the center and tucked into a snood, and her spectacles were twice as thick as Percy's.

Her plump neighbor, Betty Sue Harris, wore her hair the same way, but that was the end of the resemblance. Betty Sue was dressed in the height of fashion, and her face held none of the kindness Lucinda's

did. After she'd gone, Lucinda explained that Betty
Sue's husband was a brevet captain who served as
Major Larson's adjutant. "Her father is a congress-
man, and he makes sure Captain Harris's career pros-
pers or I'm not sure he'd be doing very well. But she's
the only other officer's wife at the garrison right
now," Mrs. Larson explained. "I'm grateful to have
her company. It's dreadful to be assigned to a post
where there are no other women or only young lieu-
tenants' wives who are intimidated by Sherwood's
rank."

After spending five minutes on the front porch with
Betty Sue Harris, Mandy had been quite certain that
she was not intimidated by anyone. She was a big-
boned woman who did not seem to believe that
silence was a virtue. She'd demanded that Mandy
bring her up to date on life back east, and expressed
her opinions on everything from politics to the current
laundresses's gossip at the fort. Mandy had been a bit
relieved when she'd finally announced it was time to
leave.

"Captain Harris shot a grizzly yesterday—he's the best
hunter at the fort—so you're in for quite a delicacy!"
Lucinda Larson gushed. "I don't imagine you dine on
bear meat much in Boston." Fortunately, she gave
Mandy no chance to reply before she galloped on. "I
remember those terrible New England winters. I grew up
in Maine. But in California we can grow vegetables of
some kind in almost every season. Well, not in the mountains, you know. The snow gets fierce in the high Sierra.
But here at Tejon Pass there's just enough snow to celebrate Christmas and still harvest cabbage on New Year's
Day."

She babbled on as Mandy relaxed in the stiff hickory chair by the table, grateful to be sitting in anything that didn't bounce her up and down and side to side. Although the major's quarters were undoubtedly the most luxurious of any on the post, Lucinda's kitchen was bare and primitive compared to Mandy's back home. A simple wash basin and smoky cookstove filled one corner; whittled wooden pegs on the wall up above served as storage for the cast iron skillets and pans. The rug on the floor was woven from some kind of dried grass or fronds, and the table itself was crowned by an incongruously delicate glass vase full of some kind of purple and orange blossoms which Mandy had never seen before.

"Oh, Anna, there you are," Lucinda said as a somber young woman slipped silently through the door and headed for the stairs. "We have a visitor."

Anna, whose broad, dark features and guarded eyes proclaimed her Indian heritage, was wearing a faded frock of indiscernible color and style. In one hand, nearly hidden by her limp skirt, she held a long stick that had a tip at one end vaguely resembling a shepherd's crook. Her eyes briefly met Lucinda's, but she didn't seem to notice Mandy at all. Wondering if perhaps she were shy, or simply didn't speak much English, Mandy smiled. "Hello, Anna. My name is Mandy," she said. "I'm from . . . far away."

Anna's chilly stare briefly impaled Mandy, effectively conveying that it wouldn't be a bad idea at all for the newcomer to go back where she came from. Stiffly she said to Lucinda, "The baby needs me now," then melted from the room.

Lucinda smiled apologetically. "Please forgive her,

Miss Henderson. She doesn't mean to be rude. She's just . . . well, she's an Indian, and I'm afraid she's not nearly as good with adults as she is with children." For a moment she looked almost wistful as she observed, "I don't know how she does it, Miss Henderson. She can't tell time by a clock, but she knows exactly when Jonathan will wake up from his nap every day. I bet he'll start crying before she gets to the top of the stairs." Within moments her prediction came true as an infant's wail floated down to the kitchen. An instant later it was silent in the house.

It was obvious to Mandy that gray-haired Lucinda, spry though she was, couldn't possibly be the mother of an infant, yet it hardly seemed prudent to ask what young mother was living in the house. After all, she'd come to Fort Tejon to take care of her own problems, not to make friends or ask nosy questions of strangers. Neither the baby, nor the hostile young woman who cared for him, were any of Mandy's concern.

But of course, it took no prodding at all for Lucinda to answer Mandy's unspoken question.

"Jonathan is my grandson," she proudly explained. "The most adorable child who ever lived."

"He's here for a visit?" Mandy guessed.

For the first time since Mandy had arrived, Lucinda's gnarled, blue veined fingers ceased to bustle about. The garrulous chatter died away, and a mask of grief closed over the grandma's softly wrinkled face. Then, just as quickly, it was gone.

"My goodness, no. Johnny lives here. His mother was my youngest, but she's gone now and her husband is, too. He served under Sherwood at Fort Union years ago."

Briskly she rattled the tea cups as she joined Mandy at the table. "Anna has a little boy, too. Well, he's not so little anymore. Salt Hair is sixteen now, which means he's nearly a man by Yokuts reckoning. But there's no woman alive who knows children better than Anna. That woman has a magic touch with my sweet grandbaby, I'll tell you that."

She paused to take a quick breath, then rattled on before Mandy could summon up a reply. "I don't know what we'll do without her when Sherwood retires someday. I'm tempted to try to take her with us, but I just can't see her fitting into a household anywhere but in the west."

"What kind of an Indian is she?" Mandy asked.

"She's Yokuts on her mother's side, and she grew up with her mother's people. I don't even know if she's sure who her father is. She dresses white just to make me happy, but don't let that fool you. Inside, she's Yokuts through and through."

Before Mandy could ask any more questions, Lucinda began to pour the tea, once more babbling with goodwill. "Well, it's quite a lovely spot we've got here, Miss Henderson, as you can see. You won't find a prettier fort west of the Mississippi," she insisted, as though Mandy were a tourist eager to take in the sights.

"Do enjoy your tea, dear, and make yourself at home. I know how dreadful it is to take that stage from Los Angeles. Now tell me all the latest news from Fort Wilmington. Has Major Rathmore's daughter convinced that darling Lieutenant Howard to marry her yet?"

"I'm afraid I wasn't there long enough to meet the

lieutenant," Mandy replied soberly, wondering how she'd missed him, since every other single officer on the post had found some pretext or other to make her acquaintance. Suddenly she realized that Drew Robelard was also a young, presumably single officer who'd instantly curried her favor. He seemed honest and honorable, but she had nothing but her own instincts, dulled by fatigue and heartache, to guarantee that Drew truly intended to help her track down Rodney.

"I did have the pleasure of meeting Major Rathmore," she told Lucinda, "but I don't recall anything being mentioned about his daughter."

Undaunted, Lucinda spilled out the entire tale of the shy young lovers as though Mandy had breathlessly begged to hear the story. While she prattled, Mandy's thoughts strayed back to Drew's regal face, graced with sympathetic blue eyes and a deeply dimpled smile. She couldn't forget the moment when he had promised to do his best to help her find Rodney, the moment when he'd swallowed up her hand in his own. Had she just imagined the depth of Drew's concern for her . . . or the power of his admiration? Or had he just been being kind?

Eventually it occurred to her that Lucinda Larson, in her own way, was also trying to be kind. As Mandy focused on the other woman's vibrant, horsey features, she realized that the major's wife was paying no more attention to her long-winded story than Mandy herself was. Her knowing eyes were studying Mandy, lightly skimming her face, then dashing off, in a way which hinted that she was deliberately giving her guest time to collect herself before bringing the conversation around to the matter at hand. Mandy was surprised she hadn't seen through the smoke screen of cheery conversation earlier.

"Now then," Lucinda said after she'd forced a second cup of tea on Mandy as the first hint of twilight shadowed the face of the afternoon sun. Her tone was quieter now, almost maternal. "Dear Captain Robelard says you have a problem Sherwood thinks I can help you with. It must be a grave one if he sent you to me."

When Mandy lifted her eyebrows in surprise, Lucinda laughed out loud, then smiled at Mandy with a gaze so warm that Mandy couldn't help but smile back. "My dear, when you've been married as long as I have, you'll learn what your husband means by what he *doesn't* say."

She set down her teacup and studied Mandy closely. Her bright blue eyes had taken on an expression that promised to get to the bottom of Mandy's problem and solve it no matter what the menfolk had to say.

"Now it's obvious, my dear, that a young woman travelling alone through country this bad in search of a man she hasn't heard from in six months must have a mighty fierce reason for making the trip." Her tone grew surprisingly gentle as she added, "And she must be desperately in need of all the help she can get."

As she reached one hand across the table to touch Mandy's wrist, Mandy fought against a new siege of tears. What had she done to deserve such kindness? Lucinda Larson was treating her as though they'd known each other for years. Already she felt as though they'd been chatting in this very parlor most of Mandy's life!

"Mandy—may I call you Mandy?—I know you're very tired, and whatever's weighing you down makes it hard for you to smile," Lucinda acknowledge with near-maternal tenderness. "I don't know if I can help you, though the good Lord knows I'll surely try, but in the meantime I insist you stay until we straighten all of this out. We don't have a spare room, but there's plenty of room in the one Anna shares with the baby."

As if the matter were settled, she continued without waiting for Mandy's response. "Would you feel better if you got some rest before we started working on your problem?"

At that point Mandy's long-banked tears did spill over, and this time she did not try to brush them away. "Oh, Mrs. Larson—"

"Lucinda."

"Lucinda," Mandy repeated gratefully as the last of her self-control gave way. "I'm so tired, and I'm so discouraged! My fiancé has disappeared. I'm his little brother's guardian now, and if anything ever happens to me there'll be nobody left to take care of Percy!"

She let the tears spill in earnest as she recounted the terrible months of waiting, the even more difficult weeks of travel, the gray pall of hopelessness that had clouded her life for so long. She didn't try to explain why Rodney was so important to her; most people assumed that she'd agreed to marry him out of genuine passion, and it was easier to let them believe that than to clarify the more complicated nature of her love for him, let alone her family obligations.

"If your husband were missing, Lucinda, if he'd just

disappeared, wouldn't you do everything in your power to find him?"

Lucinda straightened her old spine proudly. "Of course I would."

Mandy felt a gust of hope, the same gust of hope that had filled her when Drew had so gently patted her hand. At least, she thought it was the same kind of feeling, though when Drew had touched her she'd felt something more than relief, a powerful, nameless something she'd never felt before, but longed to feel again. Yet Mandy knew that this was no time to be thinking of flashing blue eyes and deep, beguiling dimples. No time to wonder if that black-as-night hair was as thick and soft as it appeared. No time to wonder. . . .

Forcibly pushing Drew from her mind, Mandy met Lucinda's kind, knowing eyes and pleaded, "Then you do understand? You will try to help me?"

The other woman leaned forward and took both of Mandy's hands in her own. "Mandy, if your young man is anywhere in the wild and woolly state of California, the U.S. First Dragoons will track him down and deliver him to you right here at Fort Tejon. I personally guarantee it."

She squeezed Mandy's fingers with the utmost of confidence, then leaned back and commanded, "Now then, dear child, start from the beginning. And don't leave out a single word."

Later that night, Drew Robelard leaned back on his wicker chair in the Prairie Schooner Saloon and studied homely Lieutenant Isley with feigned nonchalance.

So far Isley had given every indication of being exactly what he appeared to be: a lackluster but loyal quartermaster who couldn't quite stifle his resentment at waiting so many years for further promotion. But Drew was trained to look past the obvious and knew he needed to ignore the surface truths and probe the soft underbelly of the garrison until he found the source of Sherwood's problem, without calling attention to himself.

At the moment, the only man in the saloon doing that was a seedy looking character perched at the bar, telling tall tales to a group of young recruits who hung on his every word. Despite the warm spring weather, he was wearing a crude mountain man's coat of heavy furs which bunched around the mass of armory stuck into his buckskin waistband. Drew could see three cap and ball pistols, an unsheathed hatchet and two enormous but very dull knives, as well as a hickory bow and arrow and an old firelock musket lying on the section of the bar where the old geezer was swilling whiskey and holding court. They were all ancient weapons, probably picked up on various back country pilgrimages, but Drew always took note of a man who travelled so heavily armed.

"Summer of fifty-two, it was, when I was leading the cavalry through the buttes north of the mighty Rio Grande," the old blowhard bellowed in a voice that could be heard in the quietest corners of the saloon, "when them 'Paches came outta the mountains like demons from hell, deadly arrows hurlin' through the air. There I was, didn't have nothin' but my Bowie knife"—he pulled back his coat and pointed to the knife in question—"and the biggest one of all jumped off his paint and went straight for my gullet!"

Drew shut out the rest of the old man's prattle and continued his casual grilling of Lieutenant Isley, who seemed so delighted to have another officer's company that Drew almost felt guilty about the reason he'd issued the invitation to share a nightcap. The other junior officers had all gone to a private party off the post this evening, but apparently Isley had not been invited. The enlisted men were gathered around two pretty Prairie Schooner dancers, joshing a sergeant about his chances of persuading a certain local senorita to become his bride.

None of the married officers were in the saloon this evening, though Captain Harris's bagging of the bear had been a major topic of conversation among the other saloon patrons. Several unflattering comparisons had been made between the bear and the captain's wife. Drew wasn't sure if the jokes referred to her build or her personality, but he was sure that they would not have been made within the captain's hearing.

Drew wondered about Captain Harris, whom he barely knew as yet. Harris was Sherwood's adjutant, but his duties seemed to overlap with those of Corporal Johnson. Considering the difference in their ranks it seemed to Drew that there should have been a sharper distinction.

Both ostensibly handled correspondence and relayed Sherwood's orders, but so far Drew hadn't seen Harris in the office nearly as often as he had Corporal Johnson. Like most Army posts, Fort Tejon was grossly undermanned, so that didn't mean that Harris was shirking his duty. But it did mean that Drew needed to poke a bit more deeply into Sherwood's use of his personal staff, a delicate undertaking for a captain investigating the problems of a major, even an old friend.

Drew also intended to learn everything there was to know about Lieutenant Isley. As post quartermaster, the transfer of foodstuffs and supplies to the reservation would always pass through his hands until a civilian agent took the reins again. His job, among others, was to check and keep records of all shipping manifests. Nobody at the post was in a better position to steal the Yokutses' supplies. On the other hand, nobody would be more likely to bring suspicion on himself.

As a matter of course, Sherwood, as fort commander, periodically checked the quartermaster's records, which meant his personal staff also had easy access to them. It would be difficult, but not impossible, for Captain Harris or Corporal Johnson to doctor the books after they left Isley's hands. But Sherwood absolutely refused to believe that any of these three "loyal" men could be responsible. Only native prudence had restrained him from sharing his suspicions with them already.

Drew had no such loyalty. One of them, he was quite certain, was degrading the honor of his uniform and abusing helpless people. But the guilty party could not be working alone. Even if he'd bribed or impressed other soldiers into helping him move the goods out of the fort, he needed an outside man to sell and deliver them to the miners. Drew had come to Fort Tejon planning to start his search for suspects within the Army, but he was already wondering if it might be wiser to look for clues in the mines.

"So what's your off-the-record opinion of the camels, Lieutenant Isley?" he now asked casually, hoping to lead the pudgy lieutenant from the subject of camels to the subject of the missing supplies.

"I think they're God's punishment for all our sins," Isley retorted darkly. "They smell. They spit. They kick when you try to load them. One of them nearly took my arm off last year. I've still got the scars."

That piece of news surprised Drew. So far nobody he'd talked to except green-as-grass Corporal Johnson and Abu, the Armenian camel driver, had spoken of the camels with much affection, but nobody had accused them of willful savagery. "What happened? Were you loading him up?"

"I was trying to get him to kneel down so I could load him—a process which takes as long as packing half a dozen mules. He took umbrage when I asked him to hurry and sank those horrible fangs into my arm. I once wrestled with a wolf, sir, and I tell you a camel's teeth are considerably sharper."

Isley downed the rest of his whiskey. "The worst of it was when that crazy camel driver started sweet-talking that brute into letting me go, then insisted that I hand over my jacket and let that vicious camel tear it to shreds! He said otherwise the beast would track me to the ends of the earth. I replied that it would be much more sensible to just shoot the brute, but Abu stopped me just before I—"

He broke off, embarrassed, as Drew's eyes narrowed at his words. "I mean, I'm not a man of vengeance, Captain, and I would never wantonly destroy Army property entrusted to my care."

Drew nodded, feigning sympathy, but made a mental note to ask Abu about the violent incident. Then he asked pragmatically, "How do camels serve as pack animals on the desert, Lieutenant? That's the question I need to answer. Do they go lame easily? Do they need water? Can they really live on shrubs and thistles?"

Isley shrugged. "Well, they're indiscriminate about food, I guess. They'd probably eat rocks if there was nothing else available."

"And water?"

"Well, I guess they don't drink much," he admitted begrudgingly. "But the simple truth is, whatever benefits their eating habits might be to the Army are outweighed by the trouble they cause. It's hard to pack mules or horses anywhere near them. That camel smell drives 'em crazy, which is why we have to stable the camel herd so far from the fort. And camels are miserable to ride even when they cooperate, which isn't very often, and the *noise* they make when you load them sounds like a scene right out of hell."

The sudden burst of laughter over at the bar covered Drew's own chuckle at the total loathing in Isley's voice. Realizing that the guffaws surrounding the mountain man had grown so loud that further conversation was futile, he asked, "Who is this noisy fellow? Does he show up here often?"

Isley laughed without humor. "Unfortunately, yes. Big Charlie's a loudmouth, but he doesn't seem to cause much trouble. He just likes an audience while he brags about his exploits, and the men enjoy his tall tales."

"I take it you don't think he's much of a scout?"

"I doubt he ever was a scout," Isley scoffed. "Can you imagine anybody being foolhardy enough to follow *him* across the desert? Especially families with women and children?"

For no good reason a sudden image of Mandy Henderson and the solemn child who travelled with her filled Drew's mind. The journey she'd already completed was unbelievable, and the one she now proposed to make was simply absurd. Crossing the Mojave, with or without the Army, was just plain lunacy! Especially when the man she was looking for was surely dead.

But he didn't really *want* her to find Rodney Potter alive, he admitted to himself, embarrassed by the shameful discovery. He wanted that brave woman for himself. What did he have to gain by tracking down a rival?

It wasn't often that Drew worried about romance these days. He had almost accepted the likelihood that he, like lonely Isley, would spend the rest of his life as a bachelor. Army life was hard on a woman, and only a special sort of female could adapt to it at all. Drew had found one once, or so he'd thought, but she'd changed her mind at the last moment. He'd been crushed at the time but later he'd realized it was for the best. A woman who kept looking backward would never survive military life. Nor would she do much to warm her husband's heart or his bed.

Drew barely knew Mandy Henderson, but the thought of her warming his life was already as tempting as dawn on a bright spring day. She was forthright, courageous and strong. Yet there was nothing hard-edged about her. Mandy's strength came from desperation just as her love came from loyalty. He was jealous of Rodney Potter. What he'd give to have a woman like Mandy cling to his memory so long after he was gone.

He shook his head to clear the unsettling vision of feminine grace. Soulful gray eyes and soft brown hair. *Please take me to Fort Mojave,* she'd pleaded, oblivious to the dangers she faced in the fierce Mojave. *With or without you, I've got to go.*

Recalling his vow to help her find her fiancé, Drew now asked Isley, "Tell me, Lieutenant, have you ever heard of an engineer named Rodney Potter?"

Isley downed his drink and shook his head. "No. I've heard about the young lady who's here to find him, though. Major Larson should put her right back on the stage to Boston."

Drew was glad that Mandy didn't have to listen to that reply, or to the half dozen similar replies he gathered later from the other saloon staff and patrons. They all were sure that Rodney Potter had died in the cruel wasteland of the Mojave, and if the "pretty li'l gal from Boston" tried to cross the desert in search of him, she'd wither and die there as well.

It was an image which poisoned Drew's sleep when he finally turned in for the night at his room in the Bachelor Officers' Quarters. He dreamed of Mandy in her dusty green dress, faithfully dogging Big Charlie's footsteps as he brandished useless weapons and prattled to the buzzards which hovered above her pretty feathered hat. The sun shimmered against the sand while Mandy's gray eyes glittered with fatigue and fear.

Off in the distance, little Percy was galloping across the hellish Mojave Desert on a frothing pony, the shaggy gray pony Drew had cherished as a boy. "Don't die on me, Eddie!" he cried out as the pony stepped in a jackrabbit hole and went down, leaving the child to scramble on, barefoot and fatigued, over freshly laid railroad tracks. Tears streamed down his pudgy cheeks as he hollered over and over again, "Somehow I'll get to the doctor in time!"

But as he hobbled toward the next Joshua tree, its arthritic-looking arms reached out to shake him, and then the tree turned into Mandy. "You promised to help me find him, Captain," she accused the child, "and I took you to be a man of your word!" Little Percy tried to explain that he'd done his best, that he couldn't find a doctor who would come to Rodney, but Mandy kept shaking her head as though she didn't understand.

A moment later, a Mojave brave leaped from a coffin-sized hole in the ground to fling a Bowie knife at Mandy's smooth white throat. Just before the blade found its target, Drew woke up, drenched in cold sweat.

3

The sun was just coming up when Percy awakened. After spending so many nights in jostling stagecoaches and wayside inns, it took him a frightened second to remember that he'd finally reached Fort Tejon. Anna and the baby were gone, but Mandy still slept heavily, and he didn't blame her. He knew she'd never truly felt safe in most of the places they'd travelled, and as each day passed she'd looked more tired and wan.

Percy decided she wouldn't mind if he slipped out and got a start on the day as long as he didn't leave the post, didn't get dirty, and stayed out of everybody's way. He found no sign of the Larsons or Anna downstairs, but the cook, Isabel, was bustling about in the kitchen. He wasn't surprised to find a strange man laying a fire in the parlor. At every Army post he'd visited he'd seen soldiers work for extra cash as "strikers" for their officers. Back home Percy's dad had paid the servants to do daily chores like that.

Outside, Percy scanned the fort for signs of the Indian boys he'd played with yesterday, but all he saw was a wiry soldier carrying a folded flag toward the flagpole. Instinctively he headed for the stables across the tiny creek that rambled through the middle of the fort. It was clear and running fast, a sure sign that the mountain snows were melting. Percy got down to drink some of it, taking care not to get mud on his knees. He wished he could wear Yokuts clothes and get dirty like the Indians. Maybe someday he wouldn't have to look perfect all the time. And maybe someday he could have a horse.

What he'd do to whistle and have his very own pony come running! How he longed to feel powerful in the saddle, grown up and tall. He also longed to ride off across the desert and look for Rodney.

With a sudden shiver, Percy realized that he could no longer quite recall all the features of his brother's face. Desperately he tried to make the memory come into focus, but nothing happened. It had been too long.

He pushed away his momentary panic as he reached the stables, eager to pet the horses, but none of them seemed disposed to greet him this morning. They'd already been fed and were busily worrying a stack of hay. Struggling to get snatches of it from outside the fence were three scrawny hobbled ponies: one buckskin, one gray, and one black-and-white pinto. Percy wasn't sure who they belonged to, but they didn't look like the big Army horses.

Suddenly a very tall man mounted on a lathered sorrel called out, "You, boy! What are you doing over there?"

Percy blanched. He'd tried so hard not to get into trouble! But the big blond officer looked cranky and rushed. It was obvious that he'd pushed his horse pretty hard, and Percy wondered what thrilling Army business had required this tough-looking officer to cover so much ground before sun-up.

"I was just looking at the horses, sir," Percy said respectfully, wondering if he should mention that he was staying with the fort commander.

"This isn't a play yard for civilian children," the soldier chastised him as he dismounted and barked for a private to come get his horse. "You get on out of here."

The officer's long blue coat was just like Captain Robelard's, but his personality sure wasn't, Percy decided. He'd barely taken two steps back toward the Larsons' house when the big man barked again.

"You Indians! What do you think you're doing?"

Percy turned around, frightened by the thought of trouble with Indians. He'd seen all kinds in his journey. He'd been afraid of them most of them, but every now and then he'd seen some who looked afraid of *him*. The Indian boys slipping down the hillside didn't look the least bit scary because Percy recognized them. They'd all been playing shinny inside the fort yesterday. The one they called Salt Hair faced the officer boldly. Behind him stood his two friends.

"These horses are ours," Salt Hair announced as he slipped a rawhide bridle over the pinto's head and quickly unhobbled him. "We are going hunting now."

Glaring, the officer said, "Did you get permission to enter this post?"

"I come and go when I wish to see my mother, Captain Harris," was the defiant answer. As the three boys put heels to their horses, Salt Hair declared coldly, "I do not need permission for anything from you."

The officer fumed for a moment, then called for a soldier and yelled at him. "Three Indians just snuck in here and took off with their ponies, Private Dorn. The next time they could steal our horses instead. Don't let it happen again."

"Yes, sir," the brawny private promised unenthusiastically.

Captain Harris returned his half-hearted salute, then wheeled toward to the parade ground. As the bugler started to play reveille, Percy noticed that the cranky officer had broken into a dogtrot. He reached the flagpole just as the last note sounded.

"Good news, Drew!" Sherwood declared when Drew reported to his office right after reveille. "I've found you the perfect cover. You can nose around all over creation without raising a hair of suspicion."

Drew raised his eyebrows but kept his voice low. Corporal Johnson was usually somewhere near the office and was more than likely within earshot now. The carrot-haired corporal couldn't have looked more innocent and unassuming, but experience had taught Drew that innocence could be feigned. "I thought the Camel Corps was supposed to provide my cover, sir," he said.

"Well, of course it is. But after you've romped about on a few of these short trips and weathered that heinous journey across the Mojave, you'll have all the information you need to get rid of those godforsaken camels. The men will think you're shirking if you hang around, and the thieves will grow susp—"

He broke off as Corporal Johnson's tuneless whistle signaled his arrival. Johnson quickly saluted both officers, then slipped around the major's desk to pick up a record book of some kind before returning to the adjoining room.

"As I was saying," Sherwood continued when they were alone again, "this girl provides a perfect cover for your investigation. She'll need someone to drive her here and there, asking the local settlers if they've heard anything about her young man. At the same time, you can add some questions of your own and keep a sharp eye out for Army property and Indians that appear . . . well, even more skittish than usual."

Drew didn't really hear most of the major's words. Somewhere about the time he'd said "this girl" Drew had suddenly realized that he was talking about Mandy. *Assigning* him to spend hours and hours in her company, *ordering* him to protect her from herself! Granted, it would make his own work load easier because he wouldn't have to limit his search for Rodney Potter to his off-duty hours, but it wouldn't be easy to spend so much time with Mandy Henderson without revealing that she shook him to the core. Drew suddenly felt as jittery as poor Corporal Johnson, who was slipping behind the major again, silently this time, as though he didn't want to draw attention to himself.

"Of course I'd be delighted to help the young lady, sir. I should have some free time before we leave for Fort Mojave," Drew replied stoutly. "To be honest with you, Major, I made a few inquiries at the saloon last night, and nobody's ever heard of Rodney Potter or any other lost railroad engineer."

Sherwood mumbled "I'm not surprised," just as Johnson dropped a packet of letters onto the rough wooden floor. The corporal scrambled sheepishly to pick them up. Drew eyed him sharply. Johnson's interruptions this morning had been too pronounced to be accidental. What did he think they were talking about? What did he really want to hear?

Exaggerating his irritation for effect, Drew demanded, "What is the problem, Corporal? Can't you see we're in conference here?"

The boy's ears turned the same vivid shade as his hair, and his protruding Adam's apple jerked up and down as he swallowed. "I'm sorry, sir. I'm looking for something Captain Harris needs. I'll come back later, sir." He saluted sharply and scuttled away.

When he was gone, Drew asked, "Is Johnson always so . . . obtrusive? I haven't seen much of your adjutant, but your aide-de-camp always seems to be around."

Sherwood shrugged. "There's not enough room in the office for all of us without feeling cramped, so Harris often works at his quarters. He has no children and plenty of space. He also does some of his work at night so he can spend the daylight hours hunting."

"Hunting?"

"He's the best hunter at the post. The junior officers often pay him for fresh meat." He grinned. "Fortunately, he often gives it to me."

"What's his military record?"

Sherwood frowned. "No black marks, no commendations. He started Army life as a captain, Drew. Big connections through his wife. I'm lucky I get any work out of a man who earns his commission through politics or family."

"How are his office skills and his ability in the field?" Drew asked, wondering what else Harris might be doing while he wandered freely in the neighboring hills. A man who came from money was hardly likely to dirty his hands with petty theft, but his comfortable excuse to spend his days unsupervised in Yokuts country was certainly worth examining. "Is he much use to you?"

Sherwood paused a moment before he said, "To tell you the truth, I think Corporal Johnson does more than his fair share of the work, but I think of it as an apprenticeship. He comes from poor folks, no education to speak of, but he's learned a great deal in this office. He used to be my predecessor's striker before Major Berthold realized he was a real go-getter and could be put to better use."

Drew pondered the situation for a moment before he said, "He seems to be . . . everywhere. As your aide, he has easy access to sensitive places."

Sherwood looked surprised. "Surely you don't suspect him, Drew. He can be irritating at times, like a puppy who won't stop licking your face, but he's not brave or clever enough to dupe the Army. Besides, he fancies himself a great patriot."

"It's my job to suspect everyone, Sherwood. If you hadn't lodged this report yourself, I'd even be investigating *you*."

The major laughed, running a hand through his thinning white hair. "You do whatever you have to do to clean up this supply mess, Drew. And the same goes for Rodney Potter. Lucinda's given me my orders, and I'm supposed to pass them on to you. She wants the First Dragoons to raise this fellow at once. From the dead if necessary."

"I'll do my best, sir." He braved a smile. "I always obey a superior officer. *Especially* Lucinda."

Sherwood chuckled. "You're probably the only man on this post I'd let talk about my wife like that." They shared the laughter of old, familiar friends before he leaned forward and met Drew's eyes with new solemnity. "Seriously, Drew, you know that Potter's dead and so do I," he admitted with obvious reluctance. "Sooner or later, Miss Henderson and poor little Percy are going to realize it too. What I want from you is some kind of proof that headstrong girl can come to terms with. Something that will keep her from doing anything rash."

Drew nodded. "She wants me to take her to Fort Mojave, sir," he felt compelled to reveal.

Sherwood threw up both hands in exasperation. "I hope you nipped that notion in the bud."

Uncomfortably, Drew replied, "I made it clear what the Army's position would be, but at that point she threatened to take off across the desert on her own. And frankly, Sherwood, I wouldn't put it past her."

The old man stood up impatiently, prowling toward the tiny window that allowed the only hint of light. "Lucinda says Miss Henderson reminds her of Sara Beth, Drew," he admitted softly, referring to his late daughter for the first time since Drew's arrival. "She's always believed that if somebody had tried harder to help our little girl, she wouldn't have been so determined to cross that desert to reach her husband." He turned to face Drew directly as he added, "Lucinda begged me to make sure that Mandy Henderson doesn't suffer the same fate."

Drew was silent for a moment, honoring his old friend's grief. Sarah Beth had been killed by Apaches on her way to join her husband at Fort Defiance, and little Jonathan was all that was left to the Larsons of their beloved youngest child. Drew had been deadly serious when he'd told Mandy that Sherwood would never, ever let her cross the Mojave, and equally serious when he'd told the major that Mandy might be reckless enough to brave the journey on her own.

"I'll do my best to keep her out of trouble, sir," he said.

"That's all I ask," Sherwood answered. Then, recovering himself, he said more stoutly, "I'd like you to make some more inquiries this morning and report to Miss Henderson this afternoon. Convince her that you'll leave no stone unturned. Then arrange to take her out to the reservation tomorrow. It'll be a perfect cover for you to talk to Lieutenant Cox and you might turn up something about Potter. You never know."

"I'll make the arrangements, Sherwood," Drew promised, wondering how Mandy would feel about spending the entire day with him. Of course, a trip to the reservation wasn't exactly like going on a picnic, but there would be hours to talk, to get acquainted, to . . .

Bringing himself up sharply, Drew asked, "Should I take the boy along, sir? I'm sure he'd like to go."

Sherwood nodded. "Good idea. I'm sure a trip out there will be the highlight of his trip to California."

"I'll do my best to make it fun for him, sir," Drew promised.

"You do that." A tap on the door revealed young Lieutenant Markson, so Drew excused himself and turned to go. He was halfway out the door before Sherwood called to him, "Don't forget that Lucinda's counting on you to keep that little girl safe. And Drew—"

"Yes, sir?"

The old eyes grew sad with the memory of his own paternal loss. "I'm counting on you, too."

"Drew, come in!" Lucinda's cheerful voice echoed throughout the house moments after Mandy heard the firm rap on the front door. "How delightful to have you join us!"

Mandy, sitting upright in the woven-reed chair near the vague light from the window, had spent most of the day helping Lucinda with her mending. She hadn't expected to see Drew so soon, but on the other hand, she wasn't too surprised by his arrival. After breakfast Lucinda had spent at least an hour repeating, with notes and addenda, her ten-minute bedside chat with Sherwood the night before regarding Mandy's situation, then rambled on for another twenty minutes about the marvelous times the two of them had spent with Drew at Fort Union years before.

From what Mandy could gather, Drew Robelard had single-handedly fought off three or four thousand Apaches, rescued several hundred damsels in distress, and brought the whole Navajo nation to its knees before the rest of the Army had even put the New Mexico Territory on the map. Tracking down one solitary Bostonian who took a wrong turn somewhere in the desert would be child's play for such a paragon of virtue. He'd probably have Rodney home by sundown without even working up a sweat.

Mandy wasn't so optimistic, but she knew that things had started looking considerably brighter since she'd arrived at Fort Tejon. Part of that was due to the Larsons' extraordinary kindness, but a good deal of it was due to Drew. Mandy had every reason to feel grateful to him, but she was troubled by her suspicion that the quickening of her pulse when she heard his voice had nothing to do with his trustworthiness as an Army officer or his potential as a cross-country guide.

As Drew followed Lucinda into the parlor, Mandy felt a guilty pang as she realized that she was terribly glad she happened to be wearing a snug-fitting blue plaid dress, temporarily adorned with her second best tatted collar. Her light brown hair, mercifully clean now that she was settled in a place where baths were available on a regular basis—not that it was easy to haul in water to fill the big tin, but at least it was possible—was pinned back and hung in pretty corkscrew curls.

She felt like a young girl whose beau had come calling, Mandy realized, tongue-tied, as she watched the easy stride of Drew's long legs and the firm bearing of his muscular chest. Her hands were sweating so much that the needle she had been plying stuck to her fingers, and her throat tightened at the sound of his deep bass voice greeting Lucinda. Guiltily Mandy admitted to herself that she'd never felt like this with Rodney.

Of course, Rodney had never properly courted Mandy, either. He'd lived next door all her life, teasing her the first time she'd fallen for a boy, giving her a hug and a little squirrel he'd whittled from a stick when the same boy broke her heart. *If Rodney were here, would he tease me about my response to Drew?* Mandy asked herself. *Or would he be jealous now?*

Mandy loved Rodney dearly for his courage and compassion, but sometimes she found it hard to imagine him as her husband in a physical sense. She wasn't certain whether he still thought of her as a little girl or a robust woman who would soon become his wife. Although their last farewell had been tender, Rodney, always discreet and respectful of Mandy's feelings, had made no effort to alter their comfortable platonic relationship before he'd left for the west. After all, they'd both been in mourning at the time.

"Good afternoon, Miss Henderson," Drew greeted her formally, inclining his head in a stiff bow. He was wearing the same smart uniform he'd had on yesterday, but today his boots showed a fresh layer of dust. "I'm glad to see you looking rested."

Mandy swallowed her disappointment. Yesterday he'd called her beautiful; today she was just well-rested, like a hardworking horse who'd been properly curried. Reminding herself that her interest in Drew was strictly business, she invited him to sit down. "Mrs. Larson told me you were going to make some inquiries today," she said politely.

Taking her cue, Drew echoed her businesslike tone
as he replied, "Yes, ma'am. I've talked to the post
sutler, since he meets up with everyone in the valley,
sooner or later, and I've made the rounds to most of
the local business establishments. Last night I talked
to the saloonkeeper and an old scout who appears to
travel extensively through the desert. And I've also
asked every officer on the post if he's had any word
of your friend, and all of them passed the word
among the men and got back to me a short while
ago." He lifted his big hands helplessly. "I'm sorry,
Miss Henderson. I haven't been able to turn up anything yet."

Mandy digested this disheartening information in
silence. She hadn't really expected anything so soon,
and yet. . . .

"Thank you, Captain," she managed to reply in an
even tone. "I'm sure you did your best."

His eyes were bleak with a frustration she was
unable to interpret. With forced cheerfulness, he
announced, "The major would like me to take you out
to the reservation tomorrow, Miss Henderson. It's possible that someone there will know something."

"Do you mean the Indians?" Mandy asked, feeling a bit uneasy at the prospect of being a solitary
white woman surrounded by an Indian tribe. Or was
it the idea of spending a day alone with Drew that
sent the shiver from her nape to her toes? "Aren't
there . . . enough of them here at the fort to answer
your questions?"

Drew shook his head. "The Indians on the reservation generally stay there, or else slip in and out of the
hills. The ones who live around the fort tend to be more

Americanized. I'm just trying to cover all the bases, Miss Henderson," he explained, "and I got the impression yesterday that you didn't want to be left behind. But if you'd rather I go by myself—"

"No, Captain. I'd love to go with you."

Mandy flushed as she realized how eager she sounded. Under ordinary circumstances she would not have agreed to go anywhere with a man she'd only known for a single day, even an Army officer, but nothing about her trip to California had anything to do with her life back home. And so far none of her conversations with Drew had followed any of the rules. He forthrightly told her things that most gentlemen would have withheld from a lady, and she in turn had confessed private feelings she normally would have kept from a man.

Even during Drew's official report on Rodney, Mandy felt as though she were receiving a social call from a prospective suitor. Despite the grave formality of the handsome uniformed officer before her, she couldn't stifle the unfamiliar sense of excitement that made her blood pump a little too energetically through her veins. She felt as though her mother was about to pop in the door with her wonderful cinnamon crumb cake and ask Drew to stay for supper.

It was Lucinda, actually, who bubbled into the room with tea and sandwiches, followed by a silent, sullen Anna. The Indian woman made Mandy intensely uncomfortable, but she didn't feel it was her place to complain about the Larsons' nanny. This morning Mandy had found Lucinda's precious grandbaby in his cradle—not crying yet but wide awake—and she'd picked him up and started to rock him gently just as Anna sidled into the room. Without a word the Yokuts woman had snatched the child away, and Mandy had the distinct impression that she was looking him over to be certain he hadn't been injured by his brief moments in her loving hands.

For half an hour Lucinda held court in the parlor, giving Drew and Mandy precious little time to say a word to each other. The major's wife wanted to hear about every person Drew had encountered since he'd left the house the day before, every question he'd asked and every single answer. By the time she was done, Mandy wouldn't have blamed Drew if he'd thrown up his hands and bolted for the door. But he was all smiles for Lucinda until she bustled out of the room, leaving Mandy acutely aware of the contrast between her bubbling presence and their uneasy silence.

After an awkward pause, Drew said carefully, "I don't want to pry, Miss Henderson, but it occurs to me that perhaps I need . . . a little bit more information about your friend."

Something in his tone made Mandy stiffen. "What kind of information?" she asked coolly.

Drew leaned forward, elbows on his widespread knees, as though to better catch every word she uttered. "What can you tell me about his likes and dislikes? His strengths and weaknesses? His habits, his . . . well, shortcomings, if you will. Anything that might give me a clue as to what his intentions might have been when he left Fort Mojave."

"His intention was to chart a railway to Fort Tejon, Captain," Mandy snapped. "That's what he was told to do and that's exactly what he did."

Drew stood up abruptly, thrusting both hands deep in his pockets. "Miss Henderson, I'm not casting aspersions on your friend. All I'm trying to find out is—"

"He is my fiancé, Captain," she corrected Drew, suddenly realizing that she'd never clarified her official relationship to Rodney, an omission which now seemed somehow disloyal. "Rodney asked me to marry him before he left for California."

"I see," Drew replied, but his tone implied that he didn't much care for that piece of information. "And when did he plan to come back to Boston?"

"We were expecting him home for Christmas. It was going to be Percy's first holiday without his parents, and Rodney wanted to make sure that we were all together."

This comment seemed to raise Drew's concern. Gently he murmured, "Holidays are particularly difficult for a boy his age after he's . . . lost someone special."

Brushing away the memory of all she'd lost—mother, father, three brothers, even her lifelong grandmotherly housekeeper—Mandy declared stoutly, "Rodney is the only family Percy has left, Captain. Everyone else was killed in a terrible fire that destroyed the whole neighborhood. Percy was away at his boarding school at the time and Rodney was surveying a possible site for a railway in Kansas."

Drew was silent a moment, as though paying homage to those who had died in the fire. Then he asked none too subtly, "Is he often away? Does he wander around a lot?"

"About as much as an Army officer does, sir!"

Mandy tossed back with a spark of anger. "He's a hardworking professional, and he goes where he's told."

Drew whipped around to face her, his eyes smoldering but his tone stiff and calm. "All I'm saying, Miss Henderson, is that for some men, it's a lot of responsibility to take on a woman and a child. Are you absolutely sure that . . ."

That Rodney didn't run out on you?

Mandy heard the accusation as clearly as if he'd shouted it out loud, and it filled her with rage. Her voice was low but each word was clipped as she vowed, "Captain, I am positive that until Rodney Potter draws his last breath, he will move heaven and earth to get back to Percy and me!"

Drew said nothing in reply. Instead, he turned away, fists jammed in his pockets, studying the dingy window beyond which Percy played outside.

After a tense moment of silence, he said quietly, "I'm a soldier trying to do my duty, Miss Henderson. When I conduct an investigation, I have to pose a lot of hard questions to people who would rather not answer." Slowly he turned back to face her. "I don't know Rodney Potter, but I've known dozens and dozens of men with wanderlust. I have to follow my hunches, because sometimes they're my best leads."

Mandy rose and laid aside the shirt she'd been mending. "Captain, in most cases I'm sure that I would trust your instincts about men on the frontier. But you need to understand that I have known Rodney since the day I was born. All my life I've been as close to him as I was to my own brothers. And I *know*, without the slightest question, doubt or hesitation, that if there was any way on the face of this earth for Rodney to have gotten word to me by now, he would have done so."

Her forceful words hung in the air between them for several awkward moments until Drew glanced away. Stiffening once more with military courtesy, he suggested, "Please sit down, Miss Henderson, and continue your story. Anything you have to say about Mr. Potter's background may help me."

Mandy did what he asked, but she couldn't keep tension from threading itself through her even tone. "When I first went to break the news of the fire to Percy, I thought he was the only member of his family to survive," she told Drew softly as she resumed her seat and her sewing. "Several weeks passed before we learned that Rodney had left Boston early to visit friends on his way to Kansas and wasn't at home when the fire broke out."

Her gaze flickered nervously to meet Drew's once more, and she saw that his earlier anger had cooled to ashes. The silent compassion of his deep blue eyes told her that he understood the unspoken pain beneath her words.

"So this is the second time you've lost your friend, Miss Henderson?" he asked gently. "The second time he's been away on an assignment and you thought he was dead?"

Mandy twisted a stray lock of hair in a nervous gesture. "I . . . I thought he was dead, yes, but we weren't engaged at the time."

Why had she told him that? Mandy wondered. The puzzled look on Drew's face told her he was asking himself the same thing.

But out loud he merely asked, "So how did Percy come to be in your care?"

"My family has lived next door to the Potters for three generations, Captain," she said quietly. "We're as close as if we were true kin."

"You lived next door to him?" he repeated. Blankly he stared at her, surely realizing without being told that if the whole block had burned to the ground, then *Mandy's* home and family had most likely been lost in the holocaust as well.

She could see it visibly rocked him; his grief for her wrapped around her like a blanket, and genuine sorrow filled his eyes. He started to take a step toward her, then froze where he stood.

But his tone was infinitely gentle as he concluded, "So you have recently lost a great deal more than . . . a childhood friend."

Mandy swallowed hard and closed her eyes. In her travels, she'd told many people about Rodney's disappearance in the west. But she'd never told any of them about the terrible beginning to the whole event, and she didn't know why she felt the need to tell Drew about it now. She was embarrassed to let him see how great the hurt still throbbed within her, yet there was relief as well. Nobody else at Tejon knew the whole story. She hadn't even told Lucinda.

For several moments Drew said nothing, pondering what she'd confessed, as well as what she hadn't said. His eyes met Mandy's with new respect and new compassion. There was also a new intimacy that warmed her, frightened her, filled her with a compelling desire to draw him closer, to seek comfort—or something else?—within the shelter of his arms.

But Drew was no longer looking at her. He was turning to greet the eager child who'd just bolted in from the hillside, covered with dirt and leaves, his spectacles askew as his eyes shone with the joy of the great outdoors.

"Mandy! Did you know that Yokuts arrows come in two parts? Anna showed me how they—"

Percy froze when he spotted Drew. Practically saluting, he whisked off his cap and whispered, "Good afternoon, sir." His brown eyes grew huge with regret for his ungainly entrance.

"Hello, Percy," Drew greeted him warmly, earning another inch of space in Mandy's heart as he reached out to shake the small boy's hand as though he were a grown man. "I'm glad to see you're enjoying your time at Fort Tejon."

Percy blushed and stared at the big man's fingers which gripped his own. "Well, so am I, sir. I mean, everyone's been very nice to me. But I didn't come to California to have a good time, Captain. I came to find my brother." As Drew released him, the boy glanced nervously at Mandy, barely able to control his need to ask if she'd heard any news. When her blank face gave him no indication, Percy turned back to Drew and blurted out, "Have you found him yet, Captain?"

To Mandy's surprise, Drew swallowed hard before he answered. "No son. I'm sorry."

"You haven't found out anything?" Percy's eyes clouded with tears. "You haven't found out anything at all?"

Silence swept through the room as the tall soldier knelt down beside the boy until they were eye to eye, then spoke in a voice that was calm and quiet but vibrant with masculine strength.

"Not yet, Percy. But I swear to you"—he spared one glance for Mandy, as though to include her in his promise, before he reached out to squeeze Percy's little hand—"I won't give up until I do."

4

It was late in the day when Anna returned to the house with Jonathan securely wrapped in his cradleboard. She often took him for a walk in the afternoon when he couldn't fall asleep and started to get cranky. He loved to look at the dried periwinkle and abalone shells hanging from the tule sunshade, and the slow, rocking motion of her walk always relaxed him. Mrs. Larson had asked her to go pick up some sugar for the cook while she was out, so Anna poked her head into the parlor to report that she'd returned. She was instantly sorry, though, because Mrs. Larson was not alone. Captain Harris's wife was also in the room.

The two white women sat by the window, making use of the fading light, as they worked with bold, bright cloth and slender needles. Anna's mother had taught her to sew with a bone awl, sinew, and deerskin, but it didn't seem to be a skill she could use now. Secretly she longed to learn how to wield a white woman's needle; she wanted to make a pretty new dress of her own. But she could not bring herself to ask Mrs. Larson to teach her.

When Anna entered, a bright smile lit Mrs. Larson's face. "Oh, Anna, there you are. Where you able to get some sugar?"

Anna nodded. "I will give it to Isabel." She did not look at the other white woman; Mrs. Harris rarely acknowledged her.

But today she made it only two steps toward the door before Mrs. Harris boomed out, "Goodness me, Lucinda! Surely that isn't your grandchild strapped to that Indian's back!"

Anna stopped, wishing she'd escaped sooner but knowing it was too late now. "He is very safe and very warm, Mrs. Harris," she replied with all the white courtesy she could muster. "He likes to go outside this way."

"Only because he knows no better!" Mrs. Harris was an average-sized woman with a medium-loud voice, but her disapproval made her tone sharp as vinegar. "And I wasn't asking you, girl. You remember your place and don't talk back."

Anna looked bleakly at Mrs. Larson, who quickly said, "Anna is a wonderful nanny to my grandson, Betty Sue. As long as we live out here where there are no smooth city streets to push a carriage, I think Anna's improvised arrangement will have to do."

Mrs. Harris shook her head. "It's not proper for the grandson of the fort's commander to be gallivanting among the enlisted men like a papoose. They need us to set a standard for them, Lucinda. And you as the commanding officer's wife—"

She broke off as she saw Mrs. Larson's tense expression. Anna was not surprised. Mrs. Harris was a nosy woman, critical and sometimes mean, but she knew the rules of Army life better than Anna did, and Anna knew enough to know that a captain's wife didn't tell a major's what to do.

"Anna, you can take Jonathan on upstairs," Mrs. Larson said firmly. "I think it's time for his nap."

Anna fled. Mrs. Larson had defended her, more or less, but she had already forbidden Anna from doing many traditional things she wanted to do for Jonathan. She hoped carrying him in a cradleboard would not be another one.

The minute she entered the upstairs room, Anna knew that something was wrong. Her private cave, as she liked to think of it, had been invaded. The white woman from Boston lay in her bed. Anna reminded herself that Mandy had been given permission to sleep there, while Anna herself had been demoted to a pallet on the floor without any consultation. Still, it was a shock to find Mandy curled up there before supper with tears running down her face.

Anna was surprised at first, because she so rarely saw white people cry. This woman had seemed so strong and self-assured, so very, very white when she'd first arrived. Anna had been frightened that the Larsons had hired a white nanny. But now she knew that Mandy Henderson was just a sore-hearted stranger who'd come to California in search of a missing man.

She felt a sudden, unexpected kinship with the sad-eyed young woman who quickly sat upright, greeted Anna briskly and started to comb her hair. As Anna stepped past her and started to undo Jonathan without risking a single kind word that might be taken as "uppity," she realized that she and Mandy had both crawled into the same cave this afternoon to lick their wounds. It was too bad that it was impossible for them to give comfort to each other.

Drew was in a pensive mood when he finished supper. Knowing that sleep would be long in coming, he was grateful that he had a good reason to take a leisurely ride out to the camel corral a few miles away from the horses. Tomorrow he hoped to try out the camels in a new experiment, but first he had to run his idea by the camel driver.

"Evening, Abu," he greeted the squat Armenian who slept with his beloved herd and generally spent his evenings whittling stick figures as he sat in the dark near them. "How are your big friends tonight?"

Abu, wrapped in a bulky Yokuts rabbit-skin blanket to quell the brisk evening chill, flashed Drew a bright smile which revealed two straight rows of big, white teeth. "They are happy, Major. Happy that Washington has sent someone here to take them seriously."

Drew smiled, unsure how to reply. He doubted Washington would have bothered to send him if the camels had been his only mission. "I'm taking a lady out to the reservation headquarters tomorrow, Abu," he said. "Back east they told me that a pair of camels

could be hitched to a wagon and would perform as well
as two mules." He lifted his eyebrows skeptically. "Do
you have a team that can do that?"

"Of course, Captain!" Abu crowed, but not before
Drew caught the shadow of alarm that skimmed across
his bearded face. "Hadj and Ila would be delighted to
go."

Drew gestured toward the hulking beasts, surely the
most peculiar collection of body parts God ever put
together. "Which two are those?"

Abu hurried toward the corral and leaned over
the fence to gesture toward his pets. "Ila, she is the
pretty white one just going down on her knees. Hadj
is very dark, very big, and very strong. And he . . .
well. . . ."

"He what?" Drew prompted, suspicious of the way
the Armenian's enthusiasm had suddenly faded.

"He . . . uh . . . he is very intelligent."

"How can you tell?"

Abu laughed. "Old Hadj needs to be told only once.
He does not hurry, you understand, but he does not
forget."

Drew suspected that there was more to the camel's
"intelligence" than Abu was going to tell him, but he
decided to let it slide. "I want to see a team of camels in
action, Abu, but if there is any chance of an upset
which might disturb Miss Henderson, then I'd rather
take the fort's best mules."

"Never would my camels upset Miss Henderson!"
Abu insisted. "They will be calm and steady, and they
will never complain . . . as long as you and I are the
only men who will handle them."

Drew narrowed his eyes. "What difference does it

make to the camels how many men handle them?"

Abu spread his hands expansively. "The number of men? No difference, sir. The names of these men?" He shook his head. "Old Hadj, he never forgets."

Drew sighed impatiently and took the hook. "Who is it, exactly, that Old Hadj is not likely to forget?"

"Lieutenant Isley, sir," Abu confessed after a dramatic hesitation. "Once the lieutenant called him names and used the mule skinner's rope on his tender neck. Old Hadj—"

"I know. Old Hadj does not forget."

Missing Drew's sarcasm, the Armenian glowed. "I knew you would understand the way of the camel, Captain. Old Hadj will always be your friend."

As Drew said goodnight to Abu, he wondered if Mandy Henderson would always be his friend. He sorely regretted the way he'd let his jealousy color his appraisal of Rodney Potter this afternoon, and he was afraid it would take her a while to forgive him for it. But tomorrow would be another day, bright and clear, and he'd do his best to uncover a rumor on the reservation. Everywhere he'd ever served, the Indians had always known things that amazed him. Unfortunately, most of them were loath to share their knowledge with the Army.

As Drew rode back into the main stableyard and saluted the guard, he saw another horse trotting away from the compound. Quietly he said to the guard, "Who's riding out so late at night? Is there trouble I haven't heard of?"

"No, sir. No trouble. That's Captain Harris."

"Captain Harris," Drew mused thoughtfully, wondering if the man was running an errand for Sherwood, or whether he had some sort of evening rendezvous that might pertain to the missing Yokuts supplies. At this hour he could hardly be going hunting. "Does he often leave the fort so late at night?"

"I wouldn't know, sir. I'm usually not down here at the stables, but Private Banner is in the lockup tonight."

Drew was tempted to follow the vanishing horse, but such a move would be too obvious in front of the guard. If Harris did leave frequently after dark, he might well pay a stable guard for silence, which meant that any expression of interest on Drew's part might easily get back to him.

He decided that the best course of action would be to chat with the lonely young man for a few minutes while he brushed down his own horse, a fine big bay named Napoleon. The young soldier relaxed after a few minutes and shared his views on camels, none of which were complimentary. Drew was fairly certain he'd forgotten his questions about Harris by the time he put the horse away and headed back across the parade grounds.

Drew was halfway to his own quarters when he noticed a single kerosene light in Sherwood's office, a mere flicker in the darkness. Certain that his old friend had planned to remain at home this evening, Drew glanced at the posted guard, currently studying the far side of the building, and decided to move a little closer to the window for a surreptitious peek inside.

In the very back of the room, seated at the major's desk, a man in a noncommissioned officer's short waistcoat was methodically studying the pages of a small Army record book. His vibrant red hair was visible even in the uncertain light, but Drew was sure that the nervous motions of the young corporal's hands would have given him away even if he'd been wearing his forage cap.

Quietly Drew opened the door, making a mental note to ask Sherwood if he ever locked it. Despite the clumsiness of the big plank door on its half-rusted hinges, Corporal Johnson showed no sign that he suspected he had a visitor. Drew watched him for several moments before he spoke.

"Working kind of late, aren't you, Corporal?"

Johnson leaped to his feet, knocking the book and a pile of letters to the floor. He saluted and tried to right the mess at the same time. His scarlet flush was evident even in the eerie light cast by the kerosene lamp. It reminded Drew of how furiously he'd blushed the first time his father had caught him kissing a girl behind the barn when he was fourteen.

He returned the salute with a stiff thrust of his hand but did not suggest that the corporal take his ease. In general, he did not like using his rank to bully the men, but in this case he felt that it was crucial to keep the boy off center until he got some facts. "Are you in the habit of sitting at the major's desk?" he asked bluntly.

"N-no, sir," Johnson stammered.

"Rifling through his papers?"

"No, sir!"

"Reading his private correspondence like some thief in the night?"

By this time Johnson's ears had turned scarlet, too. "Captain, if I could just—"

"Explain?" Drew kept his tone severe. "By all means, Corporal, please do."

The boy's pose grew even more rigid, if that were possible. "Sir," he said, his high voice trembling, "this morning the major asked me to check on that survey crew headed by Rodney Potter. I found a letter that Major Berthold, who was the fort commander here before Major Larson came, had received from the Sea to Shining Sea Railway asking about Mr. Potter and a note which said that he'd told Captain Harris to answer it. But I couldn't find the captain's letter, sir. I was afraid"—his voice dropped as though he were about to confess to a murder—"that I'd misplaced it, sir. Or perhaps forgotten to copy it in the first place." His eyes all but begged for forgiveness for his heinous crime.

Drew stifled a great urge to chuckle. Having once been young and very gauche himself, he was certain that nobody could have feigned this youthful trauma, certainly not Corporal Johnson, whom nobody could accuse of being exceptionally bright. Compassionately keeping a straight face, he commanded, "At ease, Corporal."

Johnson clasped his hands behind his back, but otherwise stood as rigid as ever, his eyes still desperately begging for mercy.

"Corporal, was it Major Berthold's habit to order Captain Harris to write letters without checking on them later? Are you the only one who recorded such things in the log?"

At first the boy did not answer, and Drew could see that loyalty for his old commander vied with his desire to clear his own name. "Son," he said more gently, "you must know that Miss Henderson is desperate to find her missing friend. I've been assigned the task of helping her. If you know anything at all about Mr. Potter's disappearance, it is incumbent upon you as a gentleman to inform me."

It was a nice speech, and true as far as it went. Although Drew had meant it when he told young Percy that he would do everything in his power to find the boy's big brother, he didn't expect to find out anything worthwhile about Rodney Potter tonight from Corporal Johnson. What he suspected was that he might flush out some pertinent fact about the missing reservation supplies. Clearly, Sherwood's predecessor had been lax about certain aspects of Army business, and his personal staff, who apparently had the job of tidying up after him, might be in a position to fill in some missing pieces of the puzzle.

After pondering Drew's words, Johnson finally admitted, "Captain, all I know is that Major Berthold received a letter from the railway company around Christmas time asking if he'd had any word about their missing survey party. The next day Captain Harris wrote a courteous letter back saying he had no information."

Drew had assumed that Mandy was exaggerating when she'd said that the Railway had conducted only the feeblest of investigations; now he wondered if he'd misjudged her. "Did Major Berthold make any inquiries into the matter?"

"If he did, he didn't tell me nothing, sir."

"But you would have known," Drew pressed.

Slowly, the boy nodded. "Yes, sir. I reckon."

Drew felt a swell of anger on Mandy's behalf.

Why should a beautiful young girl have to cross a primitive continent to track down a man that his own company and the U.S. Army had virtually forgotten? Were those involved really that indifferent? Or did they, perhaps, have something they wanted to hide?

"Corporal," he said, "I want you to think carefully about the next question. I know you don't want to cast judgment on a superior officer, but there's something I need to know. Did Major Berthold often ignore matters of this importance?"

For several moments the boy was quiet. His face was still red and his eyes were miserable, and Drew wished he could have released him from his anguish. But he had a hunch that his own mystery and Mandy's might be related, and he couldn't afford to put personal considerations before his need to ferret out the facts.

"Captain, my mama taught me never to speak ill of nobody," Johnson finally muttered, as though he really meant it.

"And did she teach you to answer the direct question of a captain who finds you in a compromising position late at night?" Drew demanded.

The boy winced but he made his confession. "You know that Major Larson ain't never one to let nothing slide," he declared in a near whisper. "Major Berthold, he was different."

So Berthold had been a laggard, Drew thought. That would certainly account for how the thefts had gone undetected in the first place. He probably hadn't had his finger on a lot of things that went on around the post.

"I don't mean that he didn't love his country, sir," Johnson suddenly burst out with passion. "And he loved the Army, too. But he was old when he got here. His heart was giving out. And after he got word that his only son had died of cholera, he had nobody, sir, and he just sort of gave up." His eyes beseeched Drew for forgiveness, not for himself, but for the old man he'd once faithfully served. "Do you understand, Captain? If there was something Major Berthold should have done that he didn't, it was only because he was too tired by the end. Too sick at heart."

Drew pondered that report before saying, "Tell me about Captain Harris, Corporal. Is he also the sort of man who lets things slide?"

Johnson did not meet his eyes. "Major Larson seems to be happy with the work done in this office, sir."

"Whose work, Corporal? Captain Harris's or yours?"

The boy swallowed hard. "I just do what I'm told, sir. I follow the orders of my officers."

It was a safe and prudent answer, but the boy's need to hedge so carefully told Drew what he wanted to know. Harris might not be a crook, but he was certainly lazy. Behind the scenes, Johnson was running this show. Sherwood had alluded to the problem this morning, but it hadn't seemed to trouble him. Drew was afraid he'd have to bring the subject up again.

Sympathetically, Drew clapped Johnson on the shoulder. "I think Major Larson is very pleased with your performance, Corporal. You have nothing to worry about. There's no law that I know of that says a hardworking corporal can't put in extra hours after dark."

As he heard the boy's sigh of relief, Drew regretted how harsh he'd had to be earlier. But he had a job to do, and he couldn't afford to be too tender-hearted. More casually he asked, "If that survey team had come this way last fall, you would have heard about it, wouldn't you?"

"Of course," Johnson answered promptly, eager to cooperate on a question which did not force him to judge an officer. "Any visitor to Tejon is big news to all of us."

Drew nodded. Johnson had confirmed his own assumptions. "Well, corporal, go back to your work"—he glanced pointedly at the table in the far corner of the room—"over there, please. I'll see you in the morning."

"Yes, sir!" Johnson scrambled instantly toward the other desk, clutching both the record book and the jumbled pile of letters. Drew had opened the front door and was ready to leave when the high voice suddenly chirped, "Captain?"

"Yes?"

"About Mr. Potter, sir . . . While I was looking for that letter to the railway company, I found another one that you maybe ought to know about if you're trying to help that nice young lady."

"Oh?"

"It's a letter to the Department, sir, that Captain Harris wrote after three of our men were killed when the supply train was ambushed on the way to Fort Mojave in October."

Drew pondered the words. Same trail. Same month. Same cause of death? "Ambushed by whom? Outlaws? Indians?"

"*Kwanamis,* sir."

"*Kwanamis?*" Drew repeated, wishing he'd been given this assignment in New Mexico where he knew more about the local Indians.

"A gang of killer Mojaves, sir. Young braves who have to have 'visions' and kill warriors from other tribes to prove they're men. Even their own people are afraid of them, and they stay out of the way when the *kwanamis* go out to make war. They don't take prisoners, and they don't take booty. They just feel good about killing anybody they can find. I've heard they go clear into Chemehuevi country in the east, and last spring they went clear over to the coast to attack the Chumash."

Drew stared at him. "Corporal, Fort Tejon sits between Fort Mojave and the coast. Are you telling me that those killer Mojaves have recently come here to attack the Yokutses?"

"No, sir. Not recently. But what with you going out to the reservation with Miss Henderson tomorrow, you might want to remember that the *kwanamis* have been there before and"—a ripple of fear slithered across the young man's face—"sooner or later, they're bound to come back again."

It was midnight when Mandy woke up, nearly one by the time she gave up the pretense of sleeping. Exhausted though she was, she was too keyed up about the next day's trip to the reservation to relax. Or maybe, the voice of honesty forced her to admit, her restlessness had something to do with that virile man who'd taken Percy's hand so tenderly this afternoon. Angrily Mandy thrust away the suspicion, thrust away the guilt. Drew Robelard was a handsome man, a charming one . . . a man who made her feel alive. She hadn't had a lot of experience with men and she had been alone a long time. Wasn't it natural that she'd be flattered by his obvious concern?

You never noticed flattery before, another voice reminded her. *You have never trembled at the sound of a man's voice at the door.*

Impatiently, Mandy threw off her covers and quickly slipped into her tired green travelling dress. With a quick glance at sleeping Percy, she silently slipped down the steep staircase and out the front door, seeking the privacy of darkness.

At least, privacy was what she expected. But the moment she opened the front door, Mandy all but tripped over the Indian woman who sat on the splintery porch, her legs tucked beneath her as she cradled the baby in her lap.

Anna was crooning to Jonathan in a language Mandy had never heard before, a repetitive chime of syllables that made him gurgle with delight. The little boy reached up both tiny hands to grab Anna's long dark hair and pat her smiling lips.

Mandy was trying to decide whether to greet Anna, walk right on by or turn around and try to slip back up the stairs when Anna said sternly, "The major will not like it if you leave the house at night."

Mandy took a deep breath. It was the first time Anna had ever spoken to her, and it was hardly a conversation starter. Carefully she answered, "I just needed some air. I wasn't planning to go very far."

For a moment Anna did not reply. Then, without facing Mandy, she reiterated, "You should not leave the post alone. Especially in the dark."

Mandy hesitated, sensing some spark of genuine concern in Anna's dry tone. But why? The corporal had said the local Indians were not dangerous, and Anna herself was surely proof that the Yokutses were trusted here. Gingerly, she asked, "What makes it so dangerous outside the fort? I know someone shot a grizzly the other day, and there are rattlesnakes and coyotes and—"

"It is not the rattlesnakes I speak of," Anna warned. "*They* have always been here."

Still perplexed and uneasy, Mandy sat down on the rough porch steps beside Anna, who was tenderly rocking the baby now. The night was nearly silent. Here and there a dog barked; a cow lowed once or twice. The moon was barely visible, but there was no sign of rain.

"You are a white woman, city-bred, from very far away," Anna explained almost gently. "You do not see the trouble that could wait for you out there."

She lifted Jonathan up to her shoulder, pressing her cheek close to his as her long black hair brushed his face. She made no effort to hide the tenderness she felt for him, just as she made no effort to hide her obvious concern for Mandy.

Touched by Anna's surprising expression of compassion, Mandy said truthfully, "You are very good with the baby. I've been awake for an hour and I never even heard him cry."

Mandy caught a glimpse of Anna's shy smile before she lapsed into silence. It was a comfortable one this time, broken only by the neigh of a startled horse in the night.

They sat together, enjoying the peace, until Anna said, "I do not want to be the one to tell you this, but you will not find your man here. The soldiers do not know where he is, and the Yokutses will not say."

Instant hope clattered in Mandy's chest. "Are you telling me that the Indians know? Have you heard something? Anna, I would give anything—"

Anna hugged the baby closer, as if to ward off the chill, then spoke again in a whisper. "My people are afraid. Afraid of the miners who buy them as slaves, afraid of the settlers who kill them only because they want their land. No one at the reservation will talk to Captain Robelard. They will not speak to you."

Mandy's pulse began to hammer. There must be a reason she's telling me all this, she realized. There must be a way to make her help me. "Would they talk to you, Anna? Would they tell you what they know?"

Bleakly Anna met her eyes. "They say that I have begun to smell white. I am no longer one with my people." The words were quiet, spoken without great emotion, but Mandy sensed the great pain behind that grave confession. "But my grandfather still lives with his tribe. He will never turn his back on me."

It took all of Mandy's strength to restrain her eagerness, but somehow she managed to speak in an even tone. "Will you take me to see him, Anna? Will you talk to your grandfather for me? Please?"

"It will do no good to beg."

Desperately, Mandy asked, "What would it take to make you help me? What do you want from me?"

Anna brusquely shook her head. She almost looked offended. "The things I want are far beyond your power to give me." Her eyes darkened with unmasked sorrow. "Can you bring back my sister from the miners who stole her? Can you bring back my baby girl who died from white man's fever? Can you bring justice to the settler who shot my husband through the head?"

Mandy struggled to respond, but no words came forth to save her. She was shocked by Anna's abrupt confession, stunned by her own grief for the other woman's loss. Helplessly, she realized there was little she could do to ease her suffering.

"Mrs. Larson is a good white woman, but I know your heart in a way she cannot," Anna whispered, the shadow of anguish coloring her ragged tone. "She has lost many of her children, but she still has her man."

For a fraction of a second Anna's grave eyes met Mandy's with an empathy far greater than the kindest words of any traveller Mandy had yet met on the trail. It was a moment to be shared for only an instant. Then Anna stood up and turned away, silently slipping up the stairs into the pitch-dark house.

She hadn't promised to help Mandy find Rodney, but Mandy knew she wouldn't need to ask again. Come morning, she would find Anna perched in the wagon when Drew came to take her to the reservation. And if there was one tiny scrap of information to be found there, Mandy knew that Anna would place it in her hand.

5

Percy was almost as excited as if somebody had told him they'd found Rodney. Oh, going to the Yokuts reservation wasn't quite the same as going to an Indian village before white people had tamed it up some, but it was an Indian village nonetheless, and Anna had told him it wasn't too different from the Yokuts village where she'd grown up. It was a beautiful spring day, clear and crisp, and about the only thing that would have made it better would have been if he could have been riding beside Captain Robelard on a horse of his own.

Unfortunately, Mandy seemed tense today, almost snappy, and she wasn't snappy very often. She walked briskly to the camel-drawn wagon and held herself stiff while Captain Robelard dismounted, helped her climb up to the buckboard seat beside Abu, then got back up on his big bay horse. Nobody helped Percy as he jumped up in the back of the wagon with Anna.

He wasn't sure why Anna was coming along, but he was glad to have her company. She didn't talk much, especially to grownups, but she'd brought him some salt grass candy the night before and smiled at him in a way that made him feel good all over.

It felt funny to be pulled by camels. They were so much taller than horses or mules. The wagon jerked about a bit as they got started, but once Abu got them going in a good trot, or what passed for a camel's trot, the ride really wasn't too different from usual until they started down a steep grade. Percy hadn't been paying much attention when the stagecoach had tugged them up into the mountains on their way to the fort, but he couldn't ignore how high they were now that the wagon seemed to be plunging straight down.

It was a long ride, even with a midday stop, and most of the time Captain Robelard was up ahead of the wagon or circling back among the half dozen troopers who accompanied them. It wasn't until early afternoon that he trotted up to the front of the buckboard, just a few feet away from Mandy. She looked surprised and pleased to see him. Percy noticed that she smoothed out her pink ruffled skirt and sat up a little straighter right away.

"This is magnificent country, Captain," she said as the rutted road dipped through a grove of oaks. "Percy and I have travelled through so much desert that it's a pleasure to be in the mountains again."

"Well, they are beautiful, but they're deadly in the winter," the captain responded, looking rather serious. "I understand that the snow is quite thick through this

pass, and up in the Sierra"—he gestured to the east—
"it's impassable for months at a time." He turned to the
back of the wagon and asked, "Anna, isn't that so?"

"It snows," Anna answered stiffly. "If you are high,
you cannot come back down."

Captain Robelard didn't comment on that and neither did Mandy, but it occurred to Percy that if Rodney
had gotten caught in the snow, he might not have been
able to write to them. Of course, there was no logical
reason why he would have gone from the lowest desert
in the country up to the highest peaks, but then again
there was no logical reason why Rodney had disappeared in the first place.

There certainly was no logical reason for the abrupt
explosion of gunfire off to the right. Percy felt a sudden
lurch of panic as the soldiers, to a man, spurred their
horses in that direction the instant they heard the
sound. Captain Robelard was calling out some sort of
order in a scary new voice that was hard and dark with
command. A moment later two of the men dropped
back and galloped their horses up close beside the
wagon.

"What's wrong?" Percy whispered to Anna, instinctively taking her hand.

"I do not know, but the captain will take care of
it," she assured him. "See how the two soldiers came
right back? They are supposed to stay here and protect us."

Over the hill a musket boomed again, and this time
Mandy gave a frightened order. "Percy, get down and
don't move. Whatever happens, I want you to remain
absolutely silent."

Percy froze against Anna. The soldiers' horses were

prancing now, but the camels seemed grateful for a moment to rest. Abu began to speak to them in a soothing foreign tongue, and they didn't even stir when the musket boomed again.

Drew knew, even as he spurred Napoleon over the ridge in the direction of the gunfire, that he was overreacting. The gunshots were sporadic and fairly distant. But Mandy and the boy were on that wagon, and the knowledge that they could be subjected to danger alarmed him.

"Cease fire!" he hollered, identifying himself as an army officer to whoever was shooting. "Come out and let me see who you are!"

The firing stopped instantly, and an embarassed voice called out to him from behind a cluster of black oaks.

"Captain Harris here, sir. I'm just out hunting. I didn't mean to alarm you."

Drew felt a surge of relief as Harris extricated himself from the pines. He was on foot in a dirty uniform and looked surprised at all the uproar. So far Drew's dealings with his fellow officer had been minimal, but he was keenly aware that Harris was only a "brevet" captain, not a real captain at all, while Drew's title reflected a legitimate promotion. He'd be courteous if he could, but the bottom line was that he outranked Harris, and Harris was right at the top of his list of suspects.

"What are you doing so far from the fort?" Drew demanded. "There's plenty of good hunting closer in."

Harris looked disconcerted. "I'm afraid I've been trailing a valley elk that I wounded some ways from here. I've been following him for hours."

While that was certainly possible, Drew was still not going to overlook the fact that Harris was only a few miles from the reservation and might have some sort of surreptitious business here. Nor had he forgotten that Harris had left the fort after dark the night before. "You must have had an early start to get so far on foot," he observed.

"Oh, not so far, Captain," Harris assured him. "My horse is just over the next ridge. And I did have an early start."

"Must have been pretty early. We left shortly after reveille."

"A hunter who doesn't beat the sun up isn't likely to catch much game, sir."

"I guess not," agreed Drew, silently adding that a man who spent so much time off the post wasn't likely to get much work done, either.

By now he was certain that Harris was skirting the truth. Sweat beaded the other man's lip and he'd started to scratch the back of his neck. "Is there some problem at the reservation?" Harris asked.

Drew shook his head. "No. Your gunfire merely alarmed a young woman and child we're escorting out there."

"Ah, Miss Henderson and the boy. My wife has mentioned her unfortunate dilemma. Please give my apologies to the young lady, Captain."

"I will," Drew promised. "Good hunting."

As Harris saluted and disappeared into the tall grass, Drew made a mental note of the exact location of the cluster of oak trees. Sherwood had ordered him to take Mandy out looking for anybody who might have heard word of a survey party heading for California while he investigated the Yokuts problem, and this spot seemed as good as any to start his search tomorrow. Drew didn't know if there were any ranches or settlers in the immediate area, but he was quite certain it would be worth his time to find out.

Mandy was greatly relieved when she saw the first sign of blue coming over the hill, even more relieved when she saw that the horses were all trotting at a relaxed, unhurried pace. After an instinctive glance at Percy, who looked flushed with excitement, she slowly forced herself to unclench her hands, surprised to find that her fingernails had cut tiny half-moons into her palms.

It was a jolt to discover how very much the wilds of the west could frighten her. Was she merely responding to the horror stories of Drew and the major, she wondered, or was the simple truth of the matter that she'd been scared to death all along? Either way, it did not matter. She had to carry on. But now that she'd discovered her total vulnerability, it would be harder.

Drew trotted Napoleon directly to Mandy, his gaze taking in her wide-eyed distress. "It was only Captain Harris, hunting a valley elk. I'm sorry if the incident alarmed you."

Mandy swallowed hard and tried to look at ease. "I have every confidence in you and your men, Captain," she told him a bit shakily. "And Abu kept the camels quite steady indeed."

Abu beamed at her praise. "Think of how solid the camels would be in battle, Captain," he bragged. "Gunshots, earthquakes, grizzly bears . . . Nothing bothers them."

Drew tried to smile, but Mandy could tell it was an effort. "I'll include it in my report, Abu. I'll have a few good words to say about you, too."

As he turned his worried gaze back to Mandy, it suddenly occurred to her that Drew's concern for her well-being might not be entirely professional. It was a prospect that filled her with joy and dismay.

Drew stayed close to the wagon for the rest of the trip, which passed very quickly. In less than half an hour they spotted the smoke of the Yokutses's campfires, and ten minutes later the village itself came into view. Far down the valley Mandy could see the tiny houses—really just piles of brush on branches—with hosts of half-naked Indians wandering around. A lot of them seemed busy, but countless others poured out of the huts as the wagon approached the camp. Curiosity, or maybe fear, lit up their dark faces as they clustered together and stared at the new arrivals.

Still, the rest held back as a tall, slender man with brilliant colors painted on his breech clout marched towards the wagon as though greeting people were his job. He didn't look threatening, exactly, but he didn't look very glad to see them, either. His scowling demeanor made Mandy glad that she'd arrived with an Army escort.

Captain Robelard said to Abu, "Wait here till I call you." Then he touched his heels to his horse's flanks and loped up to greet the Yokuts watchman.

Mandy couldn't hear a word that either man said,

but she had no trouble hearing Percy whisper to Anna, "Is something wrong?"

"No. It is the watchman's job to greet visitors to the village in the Yokuts manner, but the Army men do not understand this. They always try to send him on his way."

Percy asked, "Haven't you explained it to them?"

She shrugged. "No one listens to an Indian."

When Mandy turned around to look at Anna, she was surprised to see that Percy was holding her hand. Now he looked at the Yokuts woman with big soulful eyes and leaned a little closer.

"I listen, Anna," he said sweetly. "And so does Jonathan. He loves you."

Mandy was touched by the smile Anna gave Percy just as Drew called out, "Abu! Bring the wagon in."

At once the camels lurched forward, rocking Mandy back against the hard wooden seat. Quickly she regained her balance and cast a nervous eye around the camp. The Indians were pressing closer now, staring at her as though she were a being from another world. One of the women giggled at her pink feathered hat, and another one tugged at her skirt as though it might be something she'd like to wear.

"Anna, how come they don't look like you?" Percy asked asked bluntly. "You don't wear Indian clothes."

Mandy, turned around and whispered sharply, "Percy, you don't ask a person why they look a certain way. It's not polite."

Anna ignored her. In her stiff and quiet way, she said, "I am half white, Percy, and I dress like a white woman because I work for people who are white. Mrs.

Larson would not let a true Yokuts woman take care of Jonathan."

Mandy heard the bitterness in her voice and wondered at its cause. Was it really Lucinda's alleged preference for a white nanny that galled Anna? Or was it her own mixed blood? So far she'd never heard Lucinda say anything but the nicest compliments about Anna's care of the baby. There was an underlying edge of discomfort in Lucinda's voice at times when she talked about Jonathan's dependence on Anna, but Mandy assumed it was because she was worried about his reaction when Anna went away someday.

"Look at that lady!" Percy squealed, pointing to a Yokuts woman whose face was black with some sort of earthy paint. Her hair was singed almost to her scalp. "Is she hurt? What happened to her?"

"Percy, don't point!" Mandy chided him, embarrassed by his naive display.

But Anna took his questioning with the same calm affection she always seemed to display toward children. "She is in mourning, Percy, because recently she lost her small son. Her hair is gone to show that she has no use for beauty when her heart is dead. When her hair was burned off, it was buried in the river so no one could use it to make her do evil."

Percy shivered. "Anna, does it hurt when they burn off your hair?"

She studied him sadly. "Not nearly so much as burying your husband or your little one."

Mandy felt odd emotions she could not place at first. Part of her was repulsed by the primitive ritual and wanted to whisk Percy away. But another part of her ached for Anna and felt her still-lingering grief. It was amazing that after all the pain she must have endured, Anna still had love to give to Jonathan. Mandy feared that if anything happened to Lucinda's grandchild, Anna's grief would be as great as if he were her own small son. She was also sure that it was this sort of native tradition that caused Lucinda to believe that Anna could never fit in as a family servant in an eastern city or even a civilized western one. Mandy's lifelong housekeeper had been a different social class from her family and had spoken with a strong Irish accent, but there had never been any doubt that she was an American.

"You still have Salt Hair," Percy said gently, squeezing Anna's hand. "I know he's almost grown up and all, but he's still your baby."

Anna found a smile for Percy. "He is no longer my baby, but he will always be my son."

Percy grinned, apparently pleased to have said something to make Anna smile. "Why didn't he come with us today, Anna? Doesn't he like to visit his friends?"

"I am the one he comes to visit, Percy. He lives here with his grandfather. But we will not be able to visit him today."

"Why not?"

"He is in the sweat lodge, preparing for his jimson weed ceremony."

"His what?" Percy wanted to know.

"Percy—" Mandy cautioned.

Again Anna ignored her. "It is a special ceremony for when a boy becomes a man."

"Really?" Percy sounded fascinated. "What does he have to do? When does it happen? Is that when he gets his own horse?"

"Salt Hair already has a fine pinto pony, but he will now get a *shaugh-num-uh* counselor, an old man who will guide him for the rest of his life. Salt Hair's *shaugh-num-uh* is my grandfather. You will meet him today."

Percy looked thrilled at the prospect, but the new information made him ask, "If a Yokuts boy doesn't have a grandfather, can he still have the ceremony to become a man?"

Anna nodded. "Any man who believes that the boy is worthy of the honor can volunteer to be his *shaugh-num-uh*. This is good, because nowadays we do not have many grandfathers left."

"No, we don't," Percy agreed, no doubt thinking of his own dwindling family.

As she heard the wistful tone in his voice, Mandy felt an unexpected ache for any one of her dear brothers. How she longed to see Rodney! She had done everything for Percy she could possibly do, but there were times in a boy's life when he needed a man.

There were times when she needed one also. Mandy told herself that finding Rodney would be the answer to all her prayers, but abruptly she realized that once she did, she'd have no further reason to spend time with Drew.

Embarrassed by the conflicting emotions that had so suddenly gripped her, Mandy turned away from Percy as she saw Drew approaching the wagon with a short blond man in an officer's uniform. He had narrow features that made him look somewhat like a weasel, and she found herself glad that he wasn't garrisoned at Fort Tejon.

"Miss Henderson, may I present Lieutenant Cox.

Lieutenant, Miss Henderson is visiting Major Larson from Massachusetts."

As Mandy and Cox exchanged proper introductions, she glanced at Drew, wanting to ask why he'd tried to give the impression that her visit to California was a tourist trip. Such journeys were not unheard of, but the rare ladies who undertook them almost always had a great deal of money and a healthy cluster of servants or slaves.

"It's a pleasure to meet you, Miss Henderson," Cox declared, his keen gaze making her feel as though she might not be entirely dressed. "I do believe you're the first lady ever to visit this reservation."

"What about Anna?" asked Percy from behind her. As he turned to Anna, he continued, "Don't you come out here all the time?"

Although Mandy agreed that Percy had a point, she knew this wasn't the time to explain modern society to him. She took his elbow and squeezed it hard in a bid for silence. "This is my ward, Percy Potter."

Through gritted teeth, Percy said, "It's nice to meet you, sir."

Cox patted him on the head in an offensively paternal gesture, then offered Mandy some tea. "As civilized as we can be in wild California," he said with an ingratiating grin.

"Perhaps later Miss Henderson would care for some refreshments," Drew interrupted. "Right now I believe she's eager to meet Anna's family."

Anna did not wait for further directions. She just took Percy's hand and started walking, as though she expected Mandy to follow. Mandy wasn't sure what to do; she'd intended to interrogate Cox right along with

Drew, and his casual dismissal of Cox's invitation to share with her whatever hospitality he might have to offer was certainly less than gracious, if not downright rude. But as Drew barked out a command for Private Gorton to escort Mandy through the village, his eyes warned her that he expected her to comply in silence.

Uneasily she excused herself and trailed along with Private Gorton after Anna, wondering what it would be like to enter an Indian village unescorted. Even with an armed soldier beside her, she felt vulnerable and exposed. There were Yokutses everywhere—scantily clad men, tattooed and painted women, children who were big-eyed, bone-thin and unclothed.

The central area was cleaner than the mess hall at Fort Tejon, and though the houses weren't exactly laid out in rows, there was an orderly sense to the way they'd been erected. One of the women who wasn't following their small entourage was using a dried willow branch, still thick with leaves, to sweep the central area around a communal fireplace. Three others were sprawled over a giant flat rock with several deep holes, pounding some sort of nuts with smaller rocks they held in their hands. Two of them spoke cheerfully to Anna in Yokuts, but the third glared at her and said an Indian word that sounded nasty.

Anna did not respond, but Mandy found herself feeling sorry for her anyway. It couldn't be easy returning to her home village leading a group of white people and looking like one of them. More selfishly, Mandy wondered if Anna's association with the fort might cripple her ability to find out things from traditional Yokuts sources. Hadn't Anna said as much last night?

A moment later Anna stopped in front of a long brush hut at the far side of the village. An old man was sitting cross-legged by the open doorway, working on the shaft of an arrow. Despite his palsied fingers, he was carefully placing feathers into tiny grooves in the gooseberry wood with the same precision Rodney used to draw his maps with pencils. As Percy's eyes opened wide behind his glasses, Mandy knew he was dying to ask if he could learn to do it, too.

It took all her willpower not to stare at the old man, who was by far the strangest looking person she had ever seen. Despite the warm sunshine, he wore on his shoulders a shawl that looked like duck skin, skin-side out, with the heavy down and feathers covering his bronze skin. Over that he wore several bead-and-shell necklaces. And in his earlobes, stretched out nearly to his shoulders, he wore giant willow-twig rings that were full of all kinds of odds and ends that Mandy assumed were Indian jewelry—abalone shells, snail shells, piñon nuts and brightly colored beads.

He said nothing at first, merely studied Anna with an aching intensity that reminded Mandy of how much she had once been loved by her own grandfather. She'd found him embarrassingly old-fashioned at times, but she'd cherished him nonetheless. She was glad he'd died long before the fire and hadn't had to endure that heartache.

She couldn't imagine that this old fellow had too many more years left on the earth. He smiled toothlessly as Anna knelt down behind him and spoke in Yokuts, apparently asking for permission to bring Mandy and Percy into the hut. The old man looked at them in uneasy surprise, but he immediately began to rise. It took him a long time to get to his feet, his bony knees turning this way and that, but eventually he managed. Then he made a loquacious but hearty speech of greeting that needed no interpretation and ushered them inside.

As Mandy glanced through the low branch doorway, she could see tule mat pallets against the far wall and beautiful baskets full of seeds and berries sandwiched tightly between them. A giant fire was burning quietly beneath the center poles, and something seemed to be cooking in the waterproof basket. A young girl was stirring the mush, but she vanished the instant Anna entered.

"I'll wait outside, Miss Henderson," said Private Gorton, gripping his musket firmly as he posted himself by the open doorway. "Don't hesitate to call out if you need me."

"Thank you, Private. I'm sure I'll be fine," Mandy assured him, hoping she sounded more confident than she felt. She tried to tell herself she wasn't afraid. Anna's grandfather was certainly a friendly sort, and nobody else had said anything threatening. Besides, if she couldn't cope with such tame Indians, how was she ever going to face the wild savages who owned the Mojave?

Still, Mandy's tension heightened as she ducked inside. Safe or not, this wasn't just a social visit. This old man was precious to Anna, and she had extended a fragile hand of friendship by bringing Mandy here. If Mandy offended Anna's grandfather, he wasn't likely to use his Indian sources to help her locate Rodney, and Anna would surely never speak to her again.

To Mandy's surprise, the second notion troubled her
more than she'd have expected. As she glanced again at
Anna, she tried to guess what that other woman might
be thinking. Until last night, she'd thought of her as
cold and unfeeling, but as she saw Anna's much-mend-
ed skirt spread over the tule mat on which she sat,
Mandy suddenly realized that lack of feeling wasn't
Anna's problem at all. She was filled with emotion and
wore that mask in self-protection.

At the fort, she'd always looked out of place with her
shabby clothes and cool demeanor, but Mandy had
assumed that since Anna was a Yokuts, she'd naturally
fit in here. It was a surprise to discover that Anna, free
of face paint and deerskin clothing, looked just as
uncomfortable sitting in her grandfather's hut as she
did gliding through Lucinda's parlor. With a sudden
sharp gust of understanding, Mandy realized that poor
Anna did not belong in either world.

Drew made sure his men were being fed and the
horses watered, then strolled over to reservation headquarters. As he settled into the small dark room that
Lieutenant Cox used as an office, he tried to tell himself
that he had no reason to dislike the officer. But he
couldn't seem to help his instinctive negative response
to Cox. He was a young man, slightly built, with close-
set eyes and sunken cheeks that gave him a cadaverous
look when he drew on his cigar. He never seemed to
look at Drew directly.

He certainly had stared at Mandy in a way that made
Drew's hackles rise. His decision to keep the two of
them apart had been instantaneous and instinctive. He

was quite certain that Cox was not the sort of officer to take a woman's inquiries seriously. Drew could get a lot more out of him by keeping the conversation "man to man." Mandy wouldn't like it, but she couldn't always have her way. He would simply point out to her that her first priority was finding out what had happened to Potter. Her own pride had to take second place.

While Cox hustled up some coffee, Drew studied the reservation headquarters. It was a simple building constructed of adobe bricks and pine, no better or worse than the buildings at the fort. Crude though it was, the building was a mansion compared to the spindly Yokuts dwellings.

"Major Larson sends his regards," Drew said as he handed Cox a copy of Sherwood's orders regarding his investigation. "He authorized me to carry back any report you might have that pertains to him. It's important that we keep everything we say to each other in the strictest confidence."

Cox shrugged as he sat down behind the crude table that served as his desk. "What's to report? The Indians still live like pigs and I still need a woman. I rather like the looks of that one you brought along with you."

Drew felt his fists ball up so tight he was afraid his knuckles might break. "The young lady is Major Larson's personal guest," he said stiffly. "She is engaged to be married to a Boston gentleman."

It went against his grain to make Rodney Potter seem so damn virtuous, and so damned alive, but it was either that or smash Cox's teeth out of his mouth. He couldn't imagine that the latter would help either his career or his investigations.

"Too bad," Cox said. "So what's she doing out here? This is no country for a city-bred female."

"I couldn't agree with you more," Drew commented, struggling to control his temper. "Unfortunately, the man in question has temporarily been waylaid and Miss Henderson is trying to . . . arrange a rendezvous with him."

Cox's eyebrows lifted. "You mean he skipped out on her?"

Drew ran out of fancy talk. "I mean he tried to cross the Mojave without an Army escort and nobody's seen him since." Briefly he explained the circumstances of Potter's disappearance. "The major has assigned me the task of trying to locate him."

Cox hooted. "Locate him? Hell's bells, Captain, the most you're likely to find are his boots and his bones, and that's only if the wolves and the *kwanamis* haven't taken off with them. If you want me to ask my Indians what they know just to make the major happy, I'll do it, but it's not going to change a thing."

Drew disagreed. It would change one thing. Once Mandy felt she'd exhausted every lead, she might be able to let Rodney go. That alone was worth every ounce of effort Drew intended to put into this project.

Knowing there was nothing more he could learn from Cox about Rodney, he now shifted the conversation to the real reason Sherwood had sent him here. "The major tells me that you feel these Indians aren't getting enough supplies."

"Now that's the truth. Any fool can look at them and tell that much. And they give me hell about it. I keep hammering at the major for more food and blankets, he keeps writing to the Department, and they write back nasty letters saying they've sent plenty."

While nobody could say that the lieutenant was voicing genuine concern for his Yokuts charges, he did seem to be taking their side in this issue. And it wasn't likely that he was involved with the thefts or he would never have reported the problem in the first place.

Carefully, Drew asked, "How long has this been going on?"

"Well, the agent kicked the bucket late last summer, and Major Berthold sent me out with the next load of supplies. I've been here ever since"—he sighed wearily—"but the Indians didn't start complaining until October. I wrote it down in my records if you want the exact date. I already gave all the information to the major."

"Thank you. I've seen it." It occurred to Drew that possibly a member of Sherwood's staff had seen it too, or even copied it for him. He made a mental note to ask. "So the Indians have continued to be shortchanged, despite your efforts to remedy the situation?"

Cox glared at him. "I don't like being stuck out here, Captain, but I'm doing my job the best I can. I take the men out daily in sweeps for those slavers or any sign of stolen supplies, and we try to stay highly visible to the miners. Just 'cause I'm no bleeding heart Indian lover doesn't mean I want to see these heathens starve."

It was an odd defense, but Drew didn't feel the need to challenge it. Aside from the fact that Cox had reported the problem, nobody involved in a court-martialable offense would risk speaking in such an undignified fashion to a superior officer. Cox was a man without much dignity, but he was also a man who had nothing to hide.

Cautiously Drew asked, "Is it possible, Lieutenant, that there's some discrepancy between what the Department sends to you and what actually arrives?"

"I'm sure of it," Cox agreed. "The thefts could be occurring anywhere up the line, but it's my guess that the supplies are getting as far as the post and somebody is making off with them once they're loaded onto the camels."

"Do you have any idea who that somebody might be?" Drew asked.

Cox was quiet for a minute as he drew on his cigar. Then he said soberly, "I'm not one to accuse a man without proof, Captain."

"But?"

"That foreign fellow. The camel driver? There's something funny about him."

"Funny?" Drew asked. "Funny, how?"

"Well, I don't know. Just think about it. He's the one who loads up those camels, doesn't he? And gets them to go from place to place? Our soldiers can't get near them half the time. How hard would it be to let one escape and go after it, unloading it in some convenient place?"

Drew could see a certain logic in the accusation, but his instincts told him Abu was just who he appeared to be. Cox might be willing to judge a man by his distant land of birth and his predilection for a misunderstood beast that the soldiers hated, but Drew needed far more evidence than that. If Abu looked "funny," it was probably because he felt so out of place. Sherwood said he never socialized with anybody. Nobody knew or cared where he spent his free time.

Drew wondered if the same was true for Lieutenant Isley.

As Anna sat down on a mat and waited for the white people to do likewise, she tried to look at the hut through their eyes. It was neat and clean—her young cousin was doing her job while Anna was away—but it was half the size of the Larsons' kitchen. It had taken Anna months to create the complexly woven baskets and mats that furnished it, years to learn the arts of working hides and weaving. But to white eyes, she was certain, they were worth no more than trash.

Mandy did not look at anyone, not even Percy, as she slowly lowered herself onto the largest mat, trying to keep her billowing skirt from skimming the dirt, the fire and the baskets. Percy, on the other hand, stared in fascination at Grandfather's earrings. Anna didn't want to think of his reaction to the abalone shell fragment that had adorned her sister's nose. She wondered if it had been removed when her sister had been stolen and sold into slavery. She tried never to think of what her life had been like after that.

Major Larson had made it clear that Anna would not have very much time to visit with her grandfather today. He'd also made it clear that he would hold her personally accountable if anything happened to Mandy or Percy while they were at the village. His distrust of her people still rankled.

But Anna could not rush her grandfather to meet the Army's time schedule, so she did not try to dissuade him from offering Mandy and Percy a traditional guest-welcoming meal of grass nuts and acorn soup. But after a few awkward but courteous exchanges that centered on Salt Hair's ceremony, she said, "Grandfather, this woman is looking for a white man who disappeared in the desert. He was not a hunter or a soldier." After she translated Rodney Potter's name into Yokuts, she explained, "He was trying to make a paper picture of the path from Fort Mojave."

Her grandfather listened carefully while Anna spoke. When she was done, his gaze fell on Mandy. "Granddaughter, tell my guest that I have not heard of this white man who calls himself Maker of Baskets, the kind made of clay," he answered thoughtfully. "I can ask the others if it is her wish."

Up until now, Mandy had remained quite still, but now she whispered, "What did he say?"

"He said he knows nothing."

Then Grandfather said, "We have not all been together since the last *lonewis*. If the Hiding Ones join us, they may know something."

Tensely, Mandy touched her arm. "Anna?"

"He says that when he sees the Hiding Ones at the dance of the dead, he may learn something about Rodney from them."

Anna did not want to think about the annual ceremony attended by every Yokuts in the valley. Since childhood, she had never missed it, but she was not sure she could bring herself to go this year. Even though her grandfather would be disappointed if she failed to attend, Anna did not want to leave Jonathan for five days. He would miss her terribly, and she would miss him. Worse yet, if he did not suffer, the Larsons might believe they could get along without her.

"Who are the Hiding Ones and when is the dance of the dead?" asked Mandy.

"Many of our people have been seized as slaves by whites. We have told the Army officers but they do nothing." Anna did not try to hide her bitterness or her fear. She had only told Percy half the truth when she'd explained why she wore white clothing. The whiter Anna looked, the safer she felt. Her sister had been dressed in deerskin when she'd been stolen years ago. "Some of the people from the other valley bands have gone into hiding in the mountains. They could know something we do not."

"You mean they could have seen Rodney?" Percy asked eagerly, unable to keep quiet any longer.

It hurt Anna to see the desperate hope on his young face. She knew how it felt to wait for someone you dearly loved who would never, ever come back.

"We do not think they went the same way as your brother. My grandfather is only saying that we could ask them what they might have heard when they come back for the *lonewis*."

"When will that be?" Percy prodded.

"Next month."

"Next month?" The little boy pushed his round glasses back up his nose. "You mean you can't find out anything till then?"

"My grandfather will send out messengers, and maybe we can find something sooner," she suggested, gently touching Percy's hand.

He did not look at all content. "But we can go to the *lonewis* for sure?" he pressed.

Again Anna had to disappoint him. The *lonewis* location was always kept secret from white people, and the Yokutses met at a new spot every year. One year a shepherd had accidentally stumbled upon the gathering with his flock, and the Winatun had ordered him held as a "guest" until the very end of the *lonewis* so the people would not be at risk if he told other white men what he'd seen.

Anna felt a sharp pang of sorrow as she realized that the day might come when she might not be trusted with the location of the *lonewis* herself.

Mandy left Anna's grandfather's hut furious that there were miners stealing Yokuts and forcing them into slavery, and angrier yet that the Army was not doing a thing to prevent it. She was appalled at how skinny the Indians were, how obviously underfed. She was also angry that Drew had not let her question Lieutenant Cox about Rodney.

She assured herself that any one of these reasons would justify the sudden hammering of her pulse when she first caught sight of Drew standing by the wagon. It could not be the long, lean legs clad in blue or those broad shoulders. And it certainly couldn't be the relieved look in his eyes when he spotted her. Had he really been afraid for her?

"I trust everything went well, Miss Henderson," he said as she approached him.

His eyes were bluer than she remembered them; his two dimples even deeper. He looked so glad to see her that Mandy had trouble remembering her earlier indignation.

"Anna's grandfather was a wonderful host," she told him truthfully. "Unfortunately, he didn't have any news."

Drew met her gaze as he slipped his hands chastely around her waist and lifted her up toward the wagon seat. "I'm afraid I came up empty also."

Mandy stifled a surge of frustration, then realized that it was not as great a sense of dismay as had filled her before. Suddenly she realized that it was hard to feel hopeless and alone when Drew was so close, so handsome, so enticingly virile. It was also hard to think about Rodney.

Shamed by the notion, Mandy gazed at the ground instead of Drew's handsome face. She tried to ignore the warmth of his fingertips as they crushed her corset, but they burned all too hotly against her covered skin. She was engaged to marry Rodney Potter, she told herself severely. It was inexcusable for her to savor being touched by another man.

Fortunately Drew vanished a moment later, leaving Mandy to sit stiffly in the seat beside Abu. He was busy straightening out one of the reins and speaking to the pretty white camel.

After a minute he turned to Mandy and asked, "You like your ride with the camels? They are better than horses, no?"

Mandy smiled at the old man. She couldn't bear to spoil his pleasure. "They did a fine job, Mr. Abu. I've never had a smoother wagon ride." It was not much of a compliment, since any wagon ride was horrendous, but it was the truth. The camels had done their job in a respectable manner. She wasn't sure they'd done it any better than mules or horses, but they had done no worse.

It seemed to take forever for Drew to pay the necessary homage to the Yokuts watchman and the others who clustered around him. By the time he mounted up and got the detail rolling, the afternoon sun had passed its zenith. Mandy hoped they'd make it back before dark.

Shortly after the wagon began to roll, Drew trotted up and asked Abu, "If you don't mind, I'd like to try my hand at driving the team. They're trained like mules?"

Abu looked delighted. "Oh, yes, they are trained very well indeed. If you are kind to them, they will be kind to you." He grinned as he stepped down and let Drew take his place beside Mandy. "Do you want me to sit in back or ride your horse?"

"Oh, I think you better stay nearby in case I have some questions to ask," Drew said calmly. Then, raising his voice just a little bit, he continued, "I hate to tie my horse to the wagon, though, since he hates being so close to the camels. I wish we had somebody else along who could help us out by riding him back to the fort."

As Mandy caught a glimpse of Drew's smile, she realized instantly what he had in mind. His kindness to Percy never ceased to amaze her.

"Captain Robelard?" Percy said eagerly from behind her. "I can ride a horse. I could help your horse go back."

Mandy was glad she wasn't facing Percy; she didn't want him to see her grin.

"Oh? Do you think you're up to it, Percy? Napoleon is a man's horse, you know. Soldiering is a man's job."

Mandy didn't need to turn around to know that

Percy's chest was starting to swell. His tone of voice told her exactly what he was feeling.

"I'm working hard to be a man, sir," Percy claimed. "Even though I don't have a *shaugh-num-uh.*"

"A what?" Drew asked, grinning in confusion.

"An old man who gets a boy ready for his manhood ceremony. You know, the way the Yokutses do."

"Ah." Drew nodded as he faced Percy directly. "I'm not sure you have to go through the same ceremony to become a white man, Percy. There are other things you can do."

"I'm ready!" Percy squeaked.

Drew grinned broadly, but to Mandy's delight he managed not to laugh. "Well, good. I guess the first thing you ought to do is ride my horse. Now he's awfully tired from the busy day he's had already, so don't push him. I'll be very unhappy if I see him moving any faster than a walk."

"Yes, sir," promised Percy, oblivious, Mandy was sure, to Drew's attempt to make sure he wasn't getting in over his head.

She waited until Napoleon's stirrups were shortened, Percy was mounted and Drew had taken the camels' reins. Then she asked Drew to tell her what Cox had said about Rodney.

"Frankly, Miss Henderson, he said that he hadn't a heard a thing. It was his opinion that between the wolves, the drought and the *kwanamis,* your search has come to an end." His tone was not cold, but neither was it particularly gentle.

Stiffening her spine, she asked, "Did you press him, Captain? Did you see if he'd talk to the Indians?"

"Miss Henderson, if the Indians know anything, I

assure you that you've got a much better chance to hear about it from Anna than from Cox. I doubt that the Yokuts tell him anything they don't have to."

"What does that mean?"

"It means he's not getting winded trying to improve their situation. They have no reason to feel much loyalty to him."

Mandy couldn't take much consolation from that chilly opinion. Unhappily, she said, "Captain, I believe you should discuss the Yokuts situation with Anna and her grandfather. Something is seriously wrong here."

"Oh?" Drew replied, arching one eyebrow. "Is there some specific problem, Miss Henderson?"

It wasn't easy carrying on a conversation in a jostling buckboard with a man who showed so little interest in her conversation, but Mandy was determined to speak her mind. "I should say so. These people are starving. They don't get a fraction of what they need to survive. And Anna says that when they leave the reservation to hunt, they're often attacked by local settlers and snatched to be sold as slaves."

His voice was low as he replied, "She may be right."

Mandy waited for him to promise to look into the problem immediately. When he didn't, she demanded, "Captain, why isn't Major Larson doing anything about this?"

Drew didn't look at her; instead, he snapped the camels' reins a little harder as though he hadn't heard.

"Don't pull on Ila's mouth," counseled Abu behind them. "She works best with a gentle hand."

"I'll keep that in mind," Drew answered drily. Another long minute passed before he responded to Mandy's question. "I'm sure the major is doing all he can. You must remember that the ultimate responsibility for the Yokutses' well being lies with Lieutenant Cox."

"That's supposed to make me feel better? Captain, you just told me that he didn't give a fig for their well being!"

"I didn't exactly put it that way. Cox is not particularly devoted to the Yokuts people, but he's doing his job," he replied without looking at her. "You must remember that I was sent here to study the camels, and Major Larson has a post to run."

Mandy colored, but she was too angry to hold her tongue. "I don't care what your official duties are, Captain, or his either. You both outrank Lieutenant Cox. If you cared at all what happens to these people—"

"Miss Henderson," he said sharply, "I'll see what I can do."

She took a quick breath. "You will?"

He spared her only a quick glance before he answered, "I'll look in to the matter unofficially. But I have my own orders to carry out in California and I won't be likely to finish my report if I spend all my time looking for lost people."

"Like Rodney Potter?"

This time Drew met her eyes and looked at her long and hard. "I was referring to the missing Yokutses whom you claim have been sold as slaves."

"But you don't really want to be bothered with them, do you, Captain? Or with Rodney, either."

"I would prefer," he said darkly, "to pursue the matter in my own way and discuss it with you later."

Then he did something that surprised Mandy so much she fell silent. He slid his gloved hand over hers, hidden by the folds of her pink skirt, and quickly squeezed her hand. Although it jarred her with a sharp, sensual awareness, there was nothing lover-like about the gesture. It was a warning, a plea, a command.

For the first time she realized that Abu, sitting so close behind them, could hear every word of their conversation. Was there something Drew wanted to tell her that he did not want Abu to know?

She willed herself to silence, determined to take up the matter with him later. She tried to communicate to Drew her understanding of his orders, but apparently he was taking no chances.

A good two minutes passed before he released her tingling hand.

6

While Drew readied the carriage the next morning, he sent Corporal Johnson up to the house for Mandy. The proper protocol would have been to collect her himself, but he preferred to take care of his own horses, or camels, as the case was today, and he preferred to go into battle well prepared. Today, he was headed for war, if not with Mandy, at least with himself.

Although he hated to admit it, Drew knew he was afraid to spend a whole day alone with her. He'd tried to remain professional and objective about his search for Rodney Potter, but the truth of the matter was that every day his feelings for Mandy grew more intense and more protective. Unless she treated him a great deal more coolly than she had yesterday, he was going to have a hard time keeping a crisp and courteous professional demeanor during the long hours they would spend checking out every sign of civilization in the vicinity of Captain Harris's "hunting trip" yesterday.

Worse yet, he didn't know how he was going to be able to keep from revealing his secret assignment to Mandy. He could have sidestepped the interest of any other female, but Mandy Henderson had proven herself to be a remarkably forthright young woman, not the kind to lay down the banner once she'd taken up a cause.

She might already have alerted Abu to some danger. Drew liked the friendly Armenian and didn't want to view him as a suspect, but Cox had a point: he was a logical candidate for the thefts and couldn't be disregarded. Yet a better choice might be a rootless soul like Big Charlie, who could easily have cultivated the contacts needed in the seedy underbelly of the state to sell Army supplies and slaves to miners. He certainly didn't seem to be long on scruples. Drew doubted it was Charlie, however. He didn't seem to have the brains to carry on such a complex operation, and he couldn't possibly get hold of the goods without the cooperation of somebody who worked in the warehouse, or at least had access to the paperwork. Brevet Captain Harris certainly fit that description, and his nervous behavior yesterday, not to mention his wobbly excuse for being so far from the fort and so close to the reservation, was troubling to Drew.

Still, he was working in the dark. All he had in his favor was the element of surprise, and Mandy might rob him of that if he didn't take her into his confidence this morning. She'd responded quickly to his cue on the wagon yesterday, but she might merely have been in shock because his action in taking her hand had been so surprisingly bold and familiar.

At the time, Drew had only wanted to hush her up before she'd spilled his plans. But now, as he remembered the feel of her pliant flesh beneath his own firm fingers, he realized that if she'd been some other woman, or a man, he would have found another way to give her a message. Because she was Mandy, it had felt remarkably natural to reach for her hand.

The problem had been letting her go, just as the problem now was getting her out of his mind. She had taken root there, like some wild desert weed, and she was starting to flower in the spring.

She looked just as pretty as the larkspur on the hills when she joined him at the carriage. She was wearing a snugly-tailored lavender frock that made her small waist look temptingly huggable, and her eyes sparkled with the brightness of the new day.

"Good morning, Miss Henderson," he said formally, tipping his cap. "Are you up for another adventure?"

Mandy gave him a glorious smile that sent his pulse racing. "I certainly am, Captain. How many ranchers do you think we can speak to today?"

"Well, the ranches themselves are pretty spread out," he explained. "We'll be lucky to reach the headquarters of one or two this morning. But the cowboys and shepherds out here rub elbows with miners and trappers coming across the desert, and they may have heard rumors that never reached the fort."

Drew deliberately busied himself with the already-adjusted harness while Corporal Johnson helped Mandy up into the carriage. He didn't want to touch her, or sit beside her, or find himself mesmerized by that beautiful smile. He'd had to act downright chilly to keep from flirting with her yesterday, and he was prepared to do the same today.

As he steered the camel team through the cluster of civilian businesses around the fort and headed north through the canyon, the oddly-groaning creatures raised a lot of interest. Twice horses veered to get away from them, and one mule team got so hysterical that Drew was afraid their driver couldn't hold them. Lieutenant Isley hadn't exaggerated the trouble the camels caused.

"It's odd, isn't it, Captain," Mandy observed, "that the horses are so upset by the camels and the camels don't even seem to notice."

"Abu told me they'd be calm and steady, and so far he's been proven right. But I can't ignore the effect they have on the other mounts. The presence of these camels almost constitutes a safety hazard."

"You worry a lot about safety, don't you, Captain?" Mandy asked.

"The Army is supposed to protect the civilian population, not cause extra problems. It's the duty of every officer to set a good example."

He tried not to look at Mandy, so pretty and glowing as she gazed his way. They'd always had someone else to keep their conversation from getting too personal, but Drew knew he'd have no outside help today.

"How did you happen to join the Army, Captain?" Mandy asked. "Was it always your plan?"

"It was my father's idea," he confessed. "He always planned to send me to West Point, and the day I graduated was his finest hour."

"Was it *your* finest hour?"

He risked a glance at her but resisted the urge to stroke one of her appealing corkscrew curls. "To be perfectly honest with you, I didn't care about the Army so much in those days. I was young and uncertain about a lot of things, rebellious sometimes, but basically I did whatever my father told me to do."

"And now?"

Drew smiled at her persistence. "I still follow orders, Miss Henderson, and I proudly wear the Army blue."

"So when did you experience your 'finest hour?'" she pressed.

If another soldier had asked the question, Drew's reply might have been the time he'd done himself proud in battle despite two excruciating arrow wounds. But this morning, with the vision of those scrawny Yokuts Indians haunting him, his memory of another incident was keener.

"I believe that my finest hour was in Dakota Territory in 1852," he told her truthfully. "I was trailing a pair of Lakota Sioux renegades that had killed a settler's wife and daughter. We stumbled upon a small encampment of Dakota—another band of Sioux—and the men with me, both Army and civilian, were crying out for blood. They called me a coward when I refused to authorize the slaughter of innocent people just because they happened to belong to the same tribe, and I nearly got killed by the dead woman's hot-headed teenage son."

He clucked to the camels, who were slowing down, then continued. "If we'd attacked that band, I have no doubt that dozens of settlers would have been killed in retaliation. Instead, when their chief found out what I'd done, he sent a personal envoy to thank me. Two weeks later his people brought in the two renegades all trussed up like Christmas turkeys. Alive, no less. He said we should be allowed to do the honors."

Mandy was smiling at him now, clearly understanding the subtleties of his victory. "What happened to the renegades?"

Drew sobered. "Miss Henderson, they were given justice."

"I'd really like to know."

He gave her a curious glance. "Why?"

"Because we always hear that the Indians are savages. When I looked at Anna's starving people yesterday, I started asking myself if we're ever savage in return."

Drew was silent for a moment before he told her the truth. "They weren't tortured, but they were hung at the fort. It was not a pretty sight, but they got what they deserved."

After an awkward pause, Mandy asked, "How do the Indians kill their victims?"

"You mean the Sioux?" Desperately he hoped she wouldn't make him share those gory details.

"No. I was really thinking of the Indians that live in the Mojave Desert."

Drew studied her in silence. How much could she bear to know? If he told her the truth, would she be haunted forever by nightmares of Rodney's death?

"I don't think the details matter," he finally replied. "Death is brutal. Death in the desert is doubly so."

After that Mandy was quiet for a while as she stared at the flowering countryside around them. Drew hoped that the kaleidoscope of spring hues would distract her from her earlier dark thoughts. It didn't look like a well-kept Boston garden, but surely she'd never seen flowers that looked any more beautiful.

As the terrain changed from semi-civilized to magnificently primeval, she finally mused, "I don't imagine death is any more pleasant for an Indian. Slavery in the mines is surely just as grim."

Drew knew what was coming and braced himself for a cautious answer that would satisfy Mandy without giving too much away.

"Captain, yesterday I asked you a question which you seemed to feel you had good reason not to answer. Now that we're alone, I want to know what it is you have to say."

"Thank you for keeping your peace in front of Abu," Drew replied as he clucked Ila and Hadj through a poppy-covered meadow. He did not refer to the way he'd touched Mandy yesterday or try to apologize. That part of their discussion was better left unmentioned. "Miss Henderson, do you have faith in my integrity?" he asked her slowly.

The surprise on her face made it clear that he'd taken her off guard; she seemed to struggle for an answer. Drew knew he didn't really know her well enough to ask the question, and yet he was going to ask her to take his word.

Slowly, Mandy said, "I trust you, Captain."

Drew's tense lips relaxed into a smile. He told himself he was only glad that he wouldn't have to reveal his mission, but he knew it was more than that. He was pleased he was developing a special rapport with Mandy.

Choosing his words with care, he said, "I share your concern about the Yokutses, Miss Henderson, and I am not at all indifferent to their plight. But I am not at liberty to answer your questions about their situation, nor am I in a position to pursue a zealous program of reform at this time. I can only tell you that it would be counterproductive for you to voice your concerns aloud to anyone."

Mandy stared at him as he reined the camels to a stop. "Counterproductive for whom?"

"For them. You could hurt them badly."

"I don't understand."

"I don't expect you to. I hope you don't. All I can tell you is that if you ask anyone else the questions you asked me on the wagon yesterday, their situation is likely to get even worse."

"They're in trouble, Captain," Mandy replied indignantly. "You're asking me to turn my back."

"No, I'm not." Suddenly his fingers were linked with hers. It wasn't something he'd planned; it just seemed to be the only way to underline his message. "I'm asking you to trust me to take care of it my own way. I hope I'll only need another month or two. If I haven't lived up to your expectations by the time you return to Boston, you can do anything you like. By then public outcry might be necessary anyway."

Mandy did not pull away from him, but neither did she move closer. Her face was a study in confusion. Or was it incipient sensual awareness? Drew felt a surge of need for her. It wasn't wholly unexpected, but the fact that he had anticipated it did little to help stifle his desire.

I want this woman, a voice within him whispered. *I want her far too much to keep on pretending otherwise.*

Mandy's eyes met his with an intense expression that he thought must reflect the same sort of longing. He tightened his grip on her fingers and moved the tiniest bit closer. He wanted to touch her face, to kiss her lips, to feel the clutch of her hands upon his shoulders. He wanted to—

"You're working on a secret investigation!" she burst out, abruptly shattering the spell. The magic he thought he'd seen in her eyes seemed to vanish. "The Army didn't send you all the way out here just to look at these camels. You're here to find out who's stealing Anna's people!"

Miffed by the broken mood and unwilling to reveal his secret, Drew replied stiffly, "I'm not at liberty to say." He knew it was time to release her hand, but he couldn't bring himself to do it.

Mandy sobered, but her eyes reflected hope and pleasure. He wasn't sure whether it was good news about the Yokutses or something else that made her look that way, but he hoped she was tingling with the urgent sense of longing that still enveloped him.

"That's all right, Captain," she assured Drew softly. "I understand."

She surely understood what was on Drew's mind as well when his grip on her fingers tightened. At once she glanced away from him, her body braced for flight. Drew knew she was trying to tell him that his attentions were unwelcome, but he couldn't seem to release her. He felt helplessly imprisoned by the power of his emotions.

"Miss Henderson," he confessed, desperately hoping he had not imagined that Mandy returned at least a fraction of his feelings, "may I say in all truth that you are a rare lady. A true gem."

Mandy swallowed hard, but she still did not look at him. Neither did she disengage her fingers from his own. In fact, for a long, tense moment, it seemed to Drew that she swayed ever so slightly in his direction, mutely urging him to pull her closer, begging for a further declaration.

An overpowering surge of need for this fine woman gripped him. He wanted to kiss her, to hold her, to make her admit that she quivered when he touched her, that she'd buried the past, that she was ready to forget Rodney Potter and let Drew Robelard make her his own.

But Mandy was not prepared to admit anything this morning. "Thank you for those kind words, Captain Robelard," she replied as she straightened regally beside him. "You are a fine gentleman yourself. A lady would never need to worry about her virtue in your company."

As the courteous words fell like stones in the silence of the meadow, Mandy's rejection of any further intimacy was unmistakable.

Drew's neck reddened as he released her hand.

The next few days were not easy for Mandy. She started each morning jouncing about in a camel-drawn carriage and spent her afternoons asking repetitive questions of settlers, miners, and cowhands. None of them had heard of survey party coming across the

Mojave. All of them had heard of some missing white man, but none of them had encountered Rodney. There were almost as many missing white men in California as there were horses.

It was a frustrating and hopeless endeavor, complicated by the presence of the charming, handsome fellow who spent each day at Mandy's side and often shared dinner at the Larsons' table. A hundred times she asked herself if she might have misinterpreted Drew's simple compliment their first day out in the carriage. Though he was always gallant, not once since that outing had he said a word which might be construed as romantic. Mandy knew she should have been glad that he never tried to take advantage of her unsettled situation, but somehow she was disappointed that he never paid court to her again.

The more time they spent together, the more the secret tension within Mandy heightened. In the privacy of her own sleepless bed at night, she could not pretend she was unaware of Drew's deep blue eyes and dashing dimpled smile. She could not pretend that she was immune to his strength, his determination, and his constant efforts to attend to her every need and comfort. Nor could she pretend that she ached for Rodney quite as keenly as she once had. If the truth be told, she had never truly ached for him as a man.

Mandy would never forget the night Rodney had asked her to marry him. He had not attempted to embroider their deep family friendship with false romantic notions, and neither had she. When he'd belatedly received word of the fire from a business associate in Kansas, he had rushed back to Boston on the very next train. She would never forget that he'd taken the time to come to her even before he'd headed upstate to see Percy.

When the landlady at Mandy's boarding house had told her the name of the young gentleman who had come calling, Mandy hadn't even bothered to comb her hair. She'd run all the way down to the parlor, unable to believe in the miracle. Until that moment, she'd been quite certain for months that Rodney was dead.

But there he was, carrying his theodolite, the one precious piece of engineering equipment he trusted to no one but himself. He almost looked cadaverous. His eyes were sunken pits of misery when she reached him.

He must have known everything by the look on her face, because all he said was, "Then it's true?"

Weakly, Mandy had nodded, quickly assuring him, "Percy was away at school. I've been to see him, Rodney, and he knows I'll take care of him, but I'm afraid he thinks you're dead. He'll be delirious with joy to find out we were mistaken."

Rodney took Mandy in his arms the way a brother comforts a sister deep in grief. His voice was hoarse as he'd confided, "I rushed back the instant I got word of what happened. From now on, I'll be taking care of you and Percy."

He stayed with her less than an hour because he was so desperate to console his lonely little brother. "I'd take you with me, Mandy, but I don't think it would be proper. We can't get married until a suitable period of time has elapsed."

That was the extent of their courtship. Mandy had agreed to start scouting around for a proper little house for Percy to call home when he wasn't off at school, and Rodney had kissed her on the cheek and said goodbye.

Not once, in all that had happened since then, had Mandy challenged the sincerity of Rodney's offer. She had not felt that he was doing her a favor, because he needed a mother for his brother as much as she needed a man. And they both needed someone from their former life to hold on to, someone to believe in. Getting married had seemed like the only reasonable thing to do. Mandy had no doubt that if Rodney's sister and one of Mandy's brothers had survived instead, they would have gotten married, too.

It had all made sense before she'd met Drew Robelard. Now she felt like a puppy chasing its own tail. How could she melt at the touch of another man, even for a single moment, when Rodney lay dead or dying? It was inconceivable. But as the days passed, it seemed harder and harder to deny.

"Tomorrow night we have that dinner party at Captain Harris's house, Percy, and I'm afraid it's for grownups only," Mandy said as she dug through her trunk for her best crimson dress, one she hadn't worn during the long months she'd been officially in mourning after her family's death.

Anna, who was busy changing Jonathan, glanced at the dress with an odd expression on her face but said nothing as she finished fussing with the baby.

"The next day we're going to talk to a settler up near Fishback Creek," Mandy continued. "He came across the desert right about the time Rodney did. Captain Robelard says we'll have to travel on horseback."

Percy was so jealous he could hardly speak. Despite Mandy's concern that he wasn't old enough to handle a gun, the captain had been teaching him to shoot in the thickly wooded hills behind the fort, but since the day they'd visited the reservation he'd never offered to let Percy ride his horse again. "You get to ride a horse all day?" he said. "Can I come too?"

Mandy smiled at him. "I'm sorry, Percy, but I don't think so. We may be going into fairly rough country, and I don't think it would be appropriate to bring you along."

"But I can ride better than you can," Percy pointed out. He'd learned to ride a pony at boarding school, while he'd never even seen Mandy on a horse!

"I can ride when I have to, Percy. Drew—I mean Captain Robelard—is going to find me a sidesaddle and—"

When Percy heard Anna cough, he glanced her way, and saw she was grinning. He was astounded. He'd grown very fond of Anna, but he'd never imagined that she knew how to laugh.

Mandy looked startled too. "What's so funny, Anna?" she asked.

Anna tried to look sober, but she couldn't seem to contain her pretty smile. "You have asked the captain to take you across the desert like a man, but you expect to ride perched on the side of the horse like a city woman. He will never take you seriously if you act like that."

"Well, he'd hardly consider me a lady if I rode astride!" Mandy replied indignantly, unable to suppress a smile of her own. "Is it true that some of the women out here actually do that?"

Anna's fleeting grin faded as she said, "I have never seen a sidesaddle in a Yokuts village, but we all know how to ride."

Mandy flushed. "I didn't mean—"

Anna waved a hand. "Some of your women learn to ride like men because they are less concerned with looking delicate than staying alive. If you want to survive in California, you must think the same way."

Mandy looked confused. "I didn't ask for a lady's mare, Anna. It was Captain Robelard's idea. And we're not crossing the desert, just going up into the mountains a little way."

"It is more than a little way to Fishback Creek," Anna corrected her. "I've often gone manzanita berry picking up there. I am surprised that the captain does not prefer to question the settler by himself."

Now Mandy looked determined. "Oh, I'm sure that's what he'd prefer, but I don't want him to question anyone alone. I'm the one who came here looking for Rodney. I may need some help, but I'm not about to turn over something this important to the Army."

Percy always felt good when Mandy talked like that. Sooner or later, she was going to find Rodney. He'd never doubted it. If only somebody would get him a pony like Salt Hair's pretty pinto, he'd gallop up to Fishback Creek in a flash! He was tired of waiting for the grownups to track down his brother. If Mandy didn't come up with some information soon, he was going to have to go looking for Rodney on his own.

Now Anna said, "Mrs. Larson does not ride anymore, but I do not know if she has any old dresses for riding."

Mandy shook her head. "No, she already told me she

gave them to her daughter long ago. She suggested that I borrow something from Mrs. Harris, but Mrs. Harris is a great deal bigger than I am."

To Percy's surprise, Anna said sharply, "Do not wear her dress."

Mandy looked startled. "Why?"

Now it was Anna who looked embarrassed. She seemed to be struggling for an explanation, and the one she finally gave sounded odd to Percy. "I do not want Jonathan near her."

"But, Anna," Percy pointed out, "it's only fabric."

"It would smell of her," she retorted, hugging Jonathan to her tightly as she marched out of the room.

Percy turned back soberly to Mandy. "I didn't mean to upset her."

"I know you didn't, Percy. Don't worry about it."

"But I like Anna. I don't want her mad at me."

"I'm sure she isn't mad. There's probably something else bothering her."

Mandy's comment reminded Percy of the last time he'd seen Anna upset, when they'd talked about somebody stealing the Yokutses.

"You promised her you'd try to help the Indians, Mandy," Percy reminded her. "You haven't talked to Major Larson yet."

"I'll talk to him when the time is right," she answered vaguely.

Percy knew Mandy well enough to realize when she was sidestepping a question, and he wondered why she was backing off now. "Mandy, it's really important. What if somebody stole Anna?"

He was sorry he'd said the words the moment they burst out. It was a thought too terrible to contemplate.

*   *   *

"Have you ever been to the captain's quarters before, sir?" asked Lieutenant Isley as he strolled along to the Harrises' house next to Drew.

Drew shook his head. "No, I haven't, but I'm certainly looking forward to it."

"So am I, sir."

It occurred to Drew that they were doubtless looking forward to the evening for very different reasons. Isley was a lonely young man who was probably delighted to spend time with his fellow officers, especially with the added bonus of home-cooked food. Drew, on the other hand, looked at the evening as an opportunity to study his potential suspects with a closer eye at a time when they were sure to be off guard. It also gave him a chance to spend more time with Mandy.

Granted, he saw her nearly every day, but their time together was circumscribed by the restraints of his duty as an officer and a gentleman. Ever since he'd foolishly given Mandy a glimpse of his true regard for her and she'd smartly set him down, he'd been rigid in his courtesy, determined to make his conduct unimpeachable. Sherwood had assigned him the task of helping her search for Potter, and it would be unforgiveable to make her uncomfortable during those daily journeys.

But his restraint had done nothing to lessen Drew's keen interest in Mandy Henderson; in fact, it had made the secret flames burn hotter. Day by day he smelled her sweetness, admired her courage, envied her determination. And he also realized that she no longer spent hours extolling the virtues of Rodney Potter. She had come to California to find the man, or at least to lay to rest any guilt that she had not waited for him long enough. She was still going through the motions of the search, but it seemed to Drew that her resolution was waning.

If Drew had believed that Potter was alive, or that Mandy truly ached for him, he would have silenced his own feelings for her forever. But he did not believe he was invading another man's territory, not when that man was dead. In his mind he saw Mandy as a single woman, free to respond to any man she might choose. And in the long days they'd spent together, there had been moments, entirely too many moments, when Drew felt certain that he made her pulse quicken.

She made his body throb.

As he and Isley strolled across the grounds, Drew heard a commotion in the men's main barracks that sounded like a party that had gotten out of hand. "Is this typical, Lieutenant?" he asked the other man.

Isley shook his head. "No, sir. I believe it's a bachelor party for Sergeant Ryan. He's finally gotten the go ahead from his girl."

"A long courtship?"

"A difficult one. She's a local rancher's daughter. Apparently she's been stalling him for a very long time. When he got his transfer orders, he went to tell her goodbye and she broke down and cried." Isley shared the other details of the story with no sign of pleasure in his voice. "I guess Ryan is one of the lucky ones."

Drew wasn't quite sure how to respond. Most of the time Isley seemed to be a capable officer and a solid man, but from time to time his conversation turned quite bitter. Bitter men, Drew had learned to his regret, were sometimes unpredictable.

"It's hard being married when you're a career officer," Drew said, hoping to get Isley talking about his personal life.

But the other man said coolly, "I wouldn't know about that, sir. Sometimes I feel as though I'm married to a stack of manifests."

It was an odd comment. "Married to the Army" would have been a more likely phrase for a military man. Drew wondered how many hours of every day Isley spent doing his job and whether he did all the work at the quartermaster depot or sometimes worked in his own quarters as Harris did. Did he ever return to the warehouse after dark, the way Johnson had once returned to Sherwood's office?

Or could there be somebody else involved? Drew himself had slipped inside Isley's office one night to get a copy of the official manifest record book and had found nothing amiss, and he'd returned it without anyone the wiser. Could somebody else at the post have done the same thing? Somebody so obvious, or so unlikely, that Drew hadn't yet considered him?

The Harrises' door opened just as they reached the house. Inside, right behind Mrs. Harris, stood a beautiful light-haired woman in a stunning crimson dress. Drew took a deep breath as Mandy turned to face him, and after that he forgot about everything else.

"I hear Doctor French won't be joining us this evening because of the trouble out at Ben Hayward's ranch today," Lieutenant Collier commented as Dorn, the Harris's big striker, began to serve the first course of rock-fish soup.

Mandy had no doubt that this dinner party had required a tremendous amount of preparation. Earlier, Lucinda had explained to her that a post event was never a mere social engagement. It was always a display of military decorum and an exercise in command. Even in this farflung outpost, where no housewife could ever hope to have all the necessary ingredients for her favorite dish, she was expected to put on a party worthy of the best establishment in Washington.

"I understand there was a shooting," said Drew, his eyes on Mandy. The truth of the matter was that his hungry gaze had never left her since he'd first entered the house, and it had been an effort to keep her own gaze from constantly drifting back to his.

Drew looked absolutely magnificent this evening. He was wearing his dress uniform, complete with gold bullion epaulettes and shining sword, and his gloves all but gleamed with whiteness. But it wasn't his gloves Mandy was watching now. It was his thick, dark hair, the strong cut of his jaw and those temptingly full lips that weren't quite smiling. Day after day she surreptitiously studied his fine, firm profile, and day after day his expression was veiled. But tonight he was making no effort to hide his appreciation of her. Her fashionable crimson satin dress, with its box-pleated skirt, its pagoda sleeves and its baby-smooth bodice, was having its intended effect.

"Another shooting?" asked Lieutenant Markson as Dorn set a steaming bowl before him. "It seems there's always some sort of trouble out there."

"Was it a white man this time," asked Betty Sue Harris, "or another Indian?"

Under his breath, her husband said, "Why do you always think it's another Indian? They're not the ones who cause most of the trouble around here."

Betty Sue gave him an icicle smile that made Mandy wonder if he'd be allowed to sleep in his own bed tonight. In fact, since Mandy had first arrived, the tension between the Harrises had been palpable. Mandy barely knew the captain, but by now she knew his wife well enough to be glad she wasn't in his shoes. Betty Sue could whittle a person down to size with very little provocation, and she seemed quite provoked with her husband now.

"What about the Tule River uprising?" she badgered him. "I suppose that was the work of white men?"

Mandy hadn't heard of the Tule River uprising, but the Tule River was close enough that the mere notion of trouble there gave her goosebumps. Actually, just being in this house made her pretty edgy. Betty Sue always brought a certain tension with her when she entered the Larsons' household. That same tension seemed to permeate everything in this home.

"The Tule River uprising was only a couple of years ago," Betty Sue began, "and it was the most horrible—"

"Five or six," her husband interrupted impatiently. "It was a good five or six years ago and it wasn't nearly as bad as some of the Indian trouble we've seen in other places."

"The Yokutses all went crazy and nearly killed us in our beds!" Betty Sue insisted. Then she turned to Lieutenant Watson, a quiet young man assigned to ordnance, and said, "You were here, Lieutenant. Tell Miss Henderson all the ghastly details."

With a nervous glance at Captain Harris, he nodded. "It was a difficult situation, ma'am, that's for sure. But with the First Dragoons headquartered here, I'm certain it won't ever happen again."

For the first time, Lieutenant Isley spoke. He was a plain, pudgy man who always looked a little sad, and Mandy felt a bit sorry for him. "I hear it was a very bad time, Miss Henderson," he said quietly, "especially for the local civilians."

"What happened?" Mandy couldn't help but ask. "The Yokutses seem so friendly." A sudden vision of Anna's primitively clad grandfather flickered through her mind, and she wondered if he'd ever been a warrior. He was certainly too old—and too sweet-tempered—to go on the warpath.

"There's only so much a man can take," Captain Harris explained, his grim gaze on his wife. "When he reaches his fill he doesn't much care about the consequences."

For a moment the table was taut with tension. Then Sherwood Larson spoke. Although his voice was soft and easygoing, nobody present could fail to hear the tone of command.

"What the captain means, Miss Henderson, is that the Yokutses had been slaughtered by the local settlers for years and were starving to boot. They rose up in sheer desperation."

"Now, Major," chided Betty Sue, "surely you don't think there's any justification for Indians taking white lives."

Mandy watched several pairs of eyes flash in surprise

and indignation. She'd spent enough time on Army posts to know that nobody contradicted the commanding officer, not even the lady of the house. But Betty Sue did not appear to be cowed by Sherwood's rank anymore than she took heed of Lucinda's.

Now Sherwood said, "Justification, no. But sometimes there is an explanation. And some of the trouble we've had throughout the West could have been avoided by some better decisions on the part of the decisionmakers at the other end of the country."

Mandy found herself meeting Drew's eyes across the long expanse of table. She remembered quite clearly his description of the time he'd avoided bloodshed with the Sioux. She also remembered the conversation that had followed. He'd called her a rare jewel, and she'd shivered inside and turned away from him.

She was shivering tonight, and she knew she'd have to turn away again if Drew showered her with flattery, but it would be harder than it had ever been before. There was something about his smile this evening that was making Mandy tremble, something about his dimples that was making her glow. His blue eyes were bright with longing. He couldn't seem to keep from staring at her. Even when she turned away, she felt his hungry gaze at her back.

Mandy did her best not to look at Drew while Dorn produced broiled hare, a saddle of elk and a dozen fresh-killed quails. Captain Harris demonstrated his adroit carving skills while Betty Sue maintained a running commentary on the latest shenanigans in Washington. After voicing her strong political views—she predicted bloodshed in the Senate in six months if Abraham Lincoln was elected—

she proceeded to bray about her husband's hunting prowess, the efficiency of her striker, and the skill of her amazing cook. Once Lucinda's eyes met Mandy's with a glance that said she did not approve of such self-aggrandizement, but she smiled at her hostess anyway.

Mandy, for one, was glad when the meal was over and they all strolled out to the porch for some air. It was a sterling California night. The bracing scent of pine owned the fort, and the evening breeze was cool and gentle. She took a seat on a crude mesquite bench and courteously chatted with everyone but Drew. He didn't seem to be mingling this evening, but instead spent a good half hour in private conversation with Captain Harris and the major.

Mandy told herself it didn't matter, since she saw Drew every day, but somehow she knew she wanted a private word with him this evening. His expression at dinner had told her he thought she looked beautiful tonight, but she wanted to hear him say it.

"I hope we didn't frighten you, but I think a woman's safer when she knows the truth," Lieutenant Isley said to Mandy.

With a guilty start, she jerked to face him. Had they been talking? Had she simply forgotten he was there? Or was he so lacking in social graces that he thought it was appropriate to start into the middle of a conversation with a person who hadn't even acknowledged his presence on the porch?

"I always prefer to know all the facts in a difficult situation," Mandy answered, hoping her inattention had not offended him. "I didn't expect things to be easy when I decided to travel out here."

Isley tried to smile, but the expression looked odd on him. "Oh, it's not too bad here at Fort Tejon. In fact, I'm told it's heaven compared to Fort Mojave."

"Because it's in the desert?" Mandy asked courteously.

"Because of the *kwanamis*." He gave her a meaningful look that erased any doubts about the innocence of his comment. Someone had clearly told him about her quest, and he, like all the others, probably believed that the *kwanamis* had killed Rodney. There were times, more times than she wanted to admit, when Mandy was starting to believe it herself.

Uneasily she glanced at Drew, who was still chatting with Captain Harris. "Unfortunately, Fort Mojave is my next stop, Lieutenant," she told Isley stoutly. "That's the last place I'm certain anyone saw my fiancé."

Isley gave her that tolerant, sympathetic look she'd often seen in the eyes of people faced with someone who was clearly crazy. "Miss Henderson, the Mojave Desert is hot enough to bake a man to death in half a day," he warned her.

"Every place has its dangers, sir. I understand the snow is quite fierce up here in the mountains."

"The snow is the least of it. The earthquakes are what cause the greatest damage."

"Earthquakes?" Mandy had heard of such a thing, but it was not an experience she had any desire to sample firsthand. "Do they shake the ground right here at the fort?"

He nodded gravely. "We had a terrible quake here just a few years ago. The fort sustained a lot of damage, and one of the Indian villages was levelled to the ground. I wasn't here then, but Captain Harris was. He's not a man to shake in his boots, Miss Henderson, but I'll tell you he looked pasty when he talked about it. I think the earthquake scared him more than any of his battles with Indians. And he's had an exciting career, unlike yours truly who's had seven singularly boring years."

Mandy wasn't sure how to respond to Isley's dark comment. Like Drew, he seemed concerned about her safety, but Drew always sounded determined to protect her from any danger. Isley recounted life's troubles as though they were entirely beyond his control.

Even though she was facing Lieutenant Isley, Mandy knew the instant Drew walked up behind her. She felt his presence with every nerve in her body. Her disappointment was acute when Drew failed to touch her, even casually, as he joined the conversation.

"I hope you've been enlightening Miss Henderson regarding the dangers of life in California," he said to Isley. "She needs to know how things really are out here."

"Life is dangerous anywhere," Isley said sadly, then excused himself and headed back toward the parlor.

"Did I say something wrong?" Drew asked.

"I don't think so, Captain," she assured him. "He was growing a bit morose before you joined us."

Drew stepped a little closer and faced her squarely. "I would also be morose this evening if I thought I'd never have a chance to get close to a woman as beautiful as you."

Mandy tried to glance away as propriety required, but she found herself unable to do anything but smile as she soaked in his flattery. *I wore this dress just for you,* she wanted to confess, suddenly realizing that it was true. She pushed away the suspicion that it might have been more appropriate for her to dress in black, or at least a sober gray. But that would mean she was in mourning once again, this time for Rodney. And she wasn't. At least, not yet.

"You've been quiet this evening, Miss Henderson," Drew observed as he sat down beside her on the bench. By now most of the group was drifting inside, and one or two men had even left for the evening. Mandy knew that she should go in as well. Sherwood and Lucinda might be ready to take their leave soon. "Is everything all right?"

Mandy wasn't sure how to reply to that. The tiny whisper of unease that had lurked in her mind increased in volume. "I guess it bothers me that I'm enjoying myself so much this evening when I'm almost . . . on the edge of mourning."

Drew's blue eyes deepened with a curious blend of relief and sympathy. "Mourning is not forever, Miss Henderson. If you'd just allow yourself to accept the inevitable and feel your grief, you could start recovering. That's hard to do until you face the fact that Rodney Potter is dead."

It was Mandy's habit to lash out at him in anger whenever he hinted at Rodney's death, but she couldn't feel much anger with Drew tonight. "I have no proof that he's dead, Captain," she managed to protest. "And until I do, I have to believe he's among the living."

Drew sighed deeply. As his body shifted, his knee brushed against Mandy's. The simple contact made her shiver with a feeling that had been new to her before she came to California. Nowadays it was her steady companion. Every time Drew touched her, this vague, unfulfilled longing grew more intense.

"Tying up loose ends is one thing," Drew said patiently, "but pushing away the present in order to cling to the past is—"

"How am I pushing away the present, Captain?" she demanded guiltily, determined to ignore the quivering sensation generated by the proximity of his manly thigh. "I have no present. I have nothing but a glimmer of hope that a miracle will take place and some semblance of my old life can be resurrected. You seem to want to deny me even that."

For a long moment, Drew studied her face. Then he did something he'd never done before. He lifted one gloved hand and touched Mandy's cheek in what could only be termed a lover's caress.

Her eyes flashed, but she could not turn away. She knew she should rebuke him firmly, but the words would not come. She was suffused by a singing sensation deep within her, a place where no man had ever been.

She'd wanted Drew Robelard almost since the day they'd met, but always they'd danced around their feelings. Now there was no mistaking what he was asking for. Worse yet, there was no mistaking what she ached to answer. For a moment she felt almost overwhelmed by her longing for him.

"What I want, Miss Henderson"—Drew's low voice broke the spell—"is to replace your flickering dream with a reality that's even better."

At once Mandy jumped up, dislodging his hand. She could not, would not, allow herself to be faithless to Rodney! "I'm not sure what you mean, Captain," she lied a bit breathlessly, "but I must remind you that I am engaged to a man whom you promised me you'd do your very best to locate."

Drew stood up beside her, his body warm and terribly male as a single long-legged step closed the space between them. His thighs pressed against her hooped skirt and his hands slid sensually over her shoulders as he reached out for her again.

"I promised to find out how he met his end, Miss Henderson," he whispered in a voice that was unabashedly husky with desire. "I never promised to step aside for him."

7

An hour later Drew marched back to his quarters trying to decide if he'd made a terrible mistake. He had spelled out his intentions so clearly that Mandy had quickly backed away. She had not exactly fled back to the Harrises' parlor, but she'd given him no chance to press his suit.

Neither, he noted hopefully, had she truly pushed him away.

He was trying to work out what might yet happen between them tomorrow when a man with carrot-colored hair materialized out of the darkness in front of his quarters.

"Good evening, Corporal," Drew managed to say without revealing his surprise. He saluted quickly, then invited Johnson inside. He didn't know just what Johnson had come to tell him, but it seemed that discretion would be better than public conversation. "At ease," he instructed the stiff-spined boy.

Johnson did not look the tiniest bit relaxed as he started to speak in a high-pitched, squeaky tone. The colorful southern chatter Drew had often heard him use with his fellow enlisted men was nowhere in evidence this evening.

"Sorry to trouble you, sir, but I wanted to report that I found a sidesaddle and a well-trained lady's mare as you instructed. I rented her from a miller about four miles from here whose wife is pregnant and unable to ride. He says the horse is as steady as they come."

"Did you ride her yourself?" Drew asked, even though he intended to check the horse out personally in the morning. When he'd asked Mandy about her riding experience, she'd been a bit vague, and he intended to keep a close eye on her until he was certain of her ability.

"Yes, sir, just as you told me. She has a very smooth gait and a soft mouth."

Drew nodded as he wearily took a chair. "And you tried her with the sidesaddle?"

Johnson blushed. "No, sir. I'm a man."

"Corporal, a sidesaddle's a real challenge for a horse. It's not enough that the mare's gentle if she's not accustomed to a lopsided saddle and a billowing skirt, especially if we have more of the wind we had today."

Johnson's Adam's apple bobbed. "I'm sorry, sir. I never thought of that. If you want me to go back and—"

"No, it's too late now. I'll check her first thing in the morning. Thank you for procuring the animal." Drew considered his words a dismissal, but Johnson stood his ground. "Is there something else, Corporal?"

Johnson swallowed awkwardly, looking like a lost child. For a moment Drew wondered how close that description was to the truth. Most of the recruits were from poor families, cities or farms, who'd never been more than a few miles from home before they'd joined the Army and been shipped to the end of nowhere. It was a rare recruit who managed to boost himself to Corporal in a year or two. Drew wondered how Johnson had done it.

"I found that missing letter about Miss Henderson's missing fiance, sir," the young man began uneasily. "It was filed with the other reports. After I reviewed them, I started thinking that—"

"What other reports?"

"Of *kwanami* attacks on settlers and local Indians. Our job is to go after anybody who causes trouble with the local populace, sir. We have records of any kind of trouble."

"And?"

"The *kwanamis* were all over the place last summer, clear into the fall. We had at least a dozen attacks reported to us between June and November. The odd thing is, the attack on November second took place sixty miles north of the reservation, and the attack on November third took place out in the Mojave a good two days from here."

Drew scowled. "What are you saying?"

"I'm saying, unless the *kwanamis* have two bands, they couldn't be in both places at the same time. I think somebody else might be causing trouble and trying to make it look like Indians."

"Who would do that? More to the point, why?"

"Well, sir, if you don't mind my venturing an opinion—"

"Go ahead."

"Before the fort was built, there was a lot of trouble with outlaw gangs in this area. Some of these old ranchos have everything a man could ever want to steal, not only gold and horses but religious artifacts from Spain."

Drew nodded and listened more intently.

"The Army doesn't go out looking for outlaws unless some sort of trouble has been reported. On the other hand, we know where to look whenever Indian trouble flares up. What if somebody thought it would be easier for white men to drift around unnoticed if any trouble was blamed on the *kwanamis?*"

Drew pondered the notion. It was a sound idea, and not one likely to come from the gawking boy that Johnson sometimes appeared to be. There was another side to Johnson, one that alternately impressed Drew and made him uneasy. It was the reason he'd already checked Johnson out thoroughly, but he'd come up with no tangible reason to distrust him. He'd finally come to the conclusion that Johnson was an old-fashioned breed, honest and pure. With maturity and polish, he might turn into one of those rare officers that moved up from the ranks. "So you think Rodney Potter could have been killed by white men."

"Isn't it possible, sir?"

"Of course it's possible. The question is, why?"

"Why?" Johnson looked crestfallen.

"I mean, the band of hoodlum Indians is out to kill anybody who's white because they're at war. But white men usually have a good reason to kill white folks they don't even know."

"Well, sir, Rodney Potter probably looked like a gentleman. Outlaws might think he had money."

It was good an explanation as any, but Drew wasn't sure it would help him. "We're still no closer to tracking down Rodney Potter," he pointed out.

Johnson seemed to slump. "I'm sorry, sir. I thought it might help. I've been going over the old records ever since supper."

"I appreciate all your hard work, Johnson. I think you've done enough for tonight."

Johnson saluted as Drew dismissed him, then marched off with the tiniest bit of a boyish bounce in his stride.

Drew spent the next hour trying to make some sense of everything he'd learned about the missing supplies, but he knew he was no closer to the answers. He'd hoped that spending time in Captain Harris's quarters would help him understand the man, but all he'd learned was that Harris's wife could be a bit testy. It was Isley whose behavior intrigued him. His view of life seemed distinctly sour.

Still, Drew could see why Sherwood was loath to accuse either officer. Both were good soldiers, and once the official finger of suspicion pointed in the direction of either man, his career would be ruined. Drew understood why Sherwood's predecessor had simply chosen to look the other way.

But Drew had seen the faces of those rib-thin Yokuts children, and he knew he never could.

*   *   *

When Salt Hair appeared at the Larsons' back door late that night, his proud young face wordlessly proclaimed to Anna that he had met the Yokuts test of manhood and had left his boyhood behind. She knew he would never again come to her in tears or do her bidding. He was a man now and would confront life on his own.

She did not embarrass him by commenting on the obvious change in him. Instead, she walked outside to sit on the porch steps beside her son without the hug they would have shared when he was a boy. As usual when the house was sleeping, no one realized that Salt Hair had slipped past the guards to join her. Because he was Anna's son, he was always welcome here, but he crept into the fort secretly just to keep in practice. One never knew when he might need the skills of a Yokuts warrior.

"I have come with two messages, Mother," Salt Hair whispered in the darkness. "Grandfather says to tell you he has asked the others about the missing white man. No one has heard anything. No one has heard from the Hiding Ones either."

Anna was not surprised that no one had heard anything about Rodney Potter, who was surely dead, but she was worried that no one had heard from the Hiding Ones. Granted, the various bands of Yokutses who lived throughout the valley did not gather together as freely as they once had, but a message of such importance would surely have reached the reservation sooner or later. If some word did not come soon, she might have to attend the *lonewis* to find out something for Mandy, who was slowly becoming Anna's friend.

At night sometimes they talked about Mandy's life in Boston and Anna's teenage years on the reservation . . . and her childhood on her father's ranch. Mandy knew things about Anna that even Mrs. Larson did not. It was no secret that her father was a white settler whom the Yokuts had taken in when they found him injured, but Anna had rarely found a way to bring him into the conversation. Besides, her memories of her father were not always happy ones. He'd made her feel cherished as a tiny child, but when he and her mother were killed by cattle ranchers for defending her people, all the joy in her simple world had vanished. She and her sister had survived only because Grandfather had taken them in.

"I have worse news," her son now told her darkly. "Last week a group of women went up to the berry patch by Fishback Falls. You remember, the one the settlers have not yet stripped bare?"

Anna nodded. She knew it well; in fact, she'd intended to go collecting manzanita berries there herself, but it had simply been too far away to carry a burden basket and Jonathan's cradleboard as well.

"They have not come back. We have looked everywhere for them. Grandfather is certain they have been snatched by slavers. He does not want you to pick berries there again."

Anna fought a rush of unexpected tears. She wasn't sure whether she was more upset that more of her people had been taken or more touched that her grandfather had been so quick to think of her. No one outside her own family, she was certain, would have bothered with such a message. They no longer considered her a true Yokuts since she'd started taking jobs off the

reservation a few years ago and coming back to visit
wearing white shoes and dresses.

"I will look elsewhere for my berries," she promised
her son. "And I will tell the major about the Missing
Ones."

Salt Hair made a disparaging noise only used by
Yokuts men. "You told my grandfather we could trust
the bluecoat chief, but he has done nothing for us."

Anna swallowed hard. She too felt betrayed by
Major Larson. Of all the white men she had known
since her father's death, he had struck her as the most
honorable, yet his promises, also, had been like smoke.
He had done nothing to help find any of the Missing
Ones.

Sadly, she spoke the truth. "He is white, Salt Hair.
For him honor is not what it is to a Yokuts man like
you."

Salt Hair touched her shoulder almost the way he
might once have done. "Mother, I do not understand
why you stay here."

"I have told you many times. I am needed by the
little one."

"He is a white baby you are paid to care for. No
more and no less. I do not know why you keep calling
him my brother. Someday the major and his wife will
go away like all the Army people do. I know it is not
easy to keep distance between yourself and this child,
but it is something you must do."

Anna was not sure how to answer. Yesterday afternoon she had overheard Mrs. Harris badgering Mrs.
Larson again about her care of Jonathan. Apparently
she had discovered that Anna kept Jonathan's skin soft
with powdered grains of soapstone in the Yokuts fash-

ion. In Anna's presence, Mrs. Larson usually defended her, but she spoke quite differently when she didn't know that Anna was in the next room.

"There's only so much you can teach an Indian, Betty Sue," she'd heard Mrs. Larson say. "We're lucky we've managed to train Anna to serve us as well as we have. She was a lot more Yokuts when she first came to us, but she's coming along rather nicely."

"Nicely?" Mrs. Harris had scoffed. "Why, Lucinda, underneath that raggedy dress, she's little more than an animal. And she talks as though Jonathan is hers. Even if she doesn't do him harm, aren't you afraid she might run off with him?"

There had been a long, tense silence before Lucinda had replied, "Don't be ridiculous. Anna would never do such a thing."

Anna took heart until Mrs. Harris had added darkly, "I guess not. She knows the First Dragoons would hunt her down like a mad dog."

The part of Anna's soul that was white and longed to fit in began to shrivel. Then she heard Mandy's voice ring out strong and clear, "Mrs. Harris, that's a terrible thing to say. Anna's not some wild animal. She's a bright, compassionate woman, and a highly respected member of this household."

"Almost a member of the family," Mrs. Larson added stoutly.

After that Anna had fled, because she could not bear to hear what else Mrs. Harris might have to say.

Now she said to Salt Hair, "This is my place now. Wherever my baby is, I must be."

Salt Hair studied her for a long, quiet moment. "You are not coming back to the reservation?"

"No. I will keep sending the money, but I do not think I can live there anymore." Although they had discussed her situation many times before, it occurred to Anna that tonight Salt Hair was asking about her plans with far more interest than usual. "Why do you ask?"

She could not see his face clearly in the darkness, but she could hear the uncertainty in his voice as he whispered, "Because I cannot live with Grandfather forever, now that I am a man."

At first Anna could not answer because she did not understand. And once she did, she still had no words to give him.

"You are already courting someone?" Yesterday he'd seemed like a child to her. She wanted to tell him he was far too young to marry. But he'd completed the jimson weed ceremony with honor. It was not her place to question his decisions now.

"Once while I was hunting, I saw a girl who lives with a band north at the base of the mountains. Now that I am ready, I will go see her again."

He didn't need to tell her more. Oh, there were rituals to be carried out and gifts to be exchanged, but in the end, if her family accepted him, he would go to live with her family in the Yokuts way. And if he did, there would be no one to live with Grandfather. He was too feeble to go live with another band, even if it had been the custom to follow a great-grandson, and he was much too old to live alone in his familiar hut.

In the old days, no elderly Yokuts had had this problem. There was always a daughter, a granddaughter, a wife. But now so many of their people had been slaughtered and so many had died of disease. Salt Hair had come to her because she was his mother. He would always do his duty to his *shaugh-num-uh*, but Anna knew that this domestic responsibility fell to her. Her cousins and aunts had been filling in long enough.

"We will have to think of something," she promised.

The baby she'd once suckled at her breast rose to his full height, dwarfing Anna with his new manhood. There was a new forcefulness in his voice as he commanded, "We must make arrangements soon."

Mandy was relieved beyond measure when she patted the black mare at the stables the next morning. Jessie had a kind look in her eyes and she made no attempt to flinch away when Drew helped Mandy into the saddle. She felt a bit ridiculous in her short-hemmed skirt, one obviously not designed for riding, and hoped she wasn't showing too much ankle.

If Drew noticed her odd outfit, he didn't say so. He was too busy asking her about the length of her single stirrup and the way she held her reins. He assured her that he and Corporal Johnson had tested the horse and were certain she was reliable. In fact, it seemed to Mandy that the horse was all Drew could talk about this morning.

After his unexpectedly intimate proclamation on the Harrises' front porch, she wasn't sure whether to be relieved or insulted. Right from the beginning, she'd felt that she and Drew were moving toward some kind of understanding that could fill her life with great guilt or joy. Last night he'd stated his intentions clearly. But she'd rejected him, the stiff set of her shoulders belying the melting hunger of her heart. She was not at all certain she could keep herself a safe distance from him this morning.

Soon after they left the stable area, Drew squeezed his horse into a brisk trot, then heeled him into a canter. Mandy had hoped for a little more time to warm up, since she'd only ridden a horse at a canter maybe half a dozen times in her life. She bounced about, holding on to the saddle horns with her knees for dear life, as she desperately prayed for a miracle. None came. For at least a quarter mile, Drew cantered close beside her, but he did not stop.

It was not until she was breathing hard that he pulled up and studied her with an infuriating grin. "Miss Henderson, I must say I'm impressed."

"With my riding?" Mandy asked incredulously.

"Hardly. I'm impressed with your valor. Your riding skill is so elementary I can't imagine how you managed to stay in the saddle, but you never begged for mercy."

Mandy glared at him. She was sweating in a most unladylike manner and was more than a little bit afraid. It was hard to see any humor in the situation. "When you suggested we take mounts today, I didn't realize that I'd have to pass a test."

"Surely you didn't think I'd take a lady from back east into rough country without some assurance she knew her way around a horse? Even a skilled horseman can get into trouble, Miss Henderson, let alone one who—"

"Captain, I won't pretend that my riding experience is extensive, but I won't get any better just sitting here."

Drew laughed. "You haven't had enough? You're ready to spend the whole day like this?"

She was not inclined to share his laughter, nor to melt at the sight of his dimpled grin. She wasn't at all sure why Drew was in such a playful mood this morning, but she knew she'd be in trouble if she allowed herself to soften toward him.

"I'm here to look for some sign of Rodney, sir, and I'd appreciate a little respect," she said crisply.

Drew sobered at once. The beautiful smile faded from his lips, and though Napoleon had not moved, Mandy felt as though Drew had galloped a hundred miles away from her.

"I assure you, Miss Henderson," he said gravely, "that my respect for you could be no higher."

Mandy couldn't meet his eyes, and she certainly couldn't answer. Fresh tension wrapped around her, tying her to Drew with a potency that made her shiver.

Why was it so hard to remember Rodney when she was with this man? Why did he awaken parts of her that had slumbered all her life? Mandy wondered how she'd ever find the strength to banish him from her heart.

"Captain, may we proceed to our destination?" she suggested in self-defense.

Briskly Drew turned away from her. "At once, Miss Henderson," he promised. Then he clucked to his horse, setting off at a steady pace that led them straight up into the mountains.

It was another beautiful day, and Mandy secretly knew that she could not have thought of a more wonderful way to spend it than riding beside this sometimes surprising but always virile man. Despite the rocky

beginning to their morning, Drew made her feel at ease
by pointing out local sites of interest that they passed—
boarded-up mines, a burned-out ranch, an occasional
abandoned Yokuts hut. He also told her the local
names of the magnificent flowers that dotted the hills:
buttercups and baby-blue-eyes, tidy-tips and red maids,
evening snow and fairy lanterns. They provided a festi-
val of color that would melt an artist's heart, and each
new bloom they spied helped to soften Mandy's.

"The road to Fort Mojave leads out of this valley,"
Drew told her as they jogged slowly through a widen-
ing pass. "The mountains open up on either side and
the Tehachapi Pass keeps getting wider until it reaches
the desert floor. The fort is due east from here." He
gave her a chastening look. "I don't mean to make it
sound easy to get there, Miss Henderson. Once a person got out in the desert, he'd be hopelessly confused
by the blinding sun, the world's driest winds and the
utter monotony of the desert landscape. An inexperi-
enced desert traveller would be lucky to live till the
first sundown."

"Still trying to scare me, are you, Captain?" she
asked, trying to keep her tone light.

"I hope I don't have to," he said seriously. "By now
you surely understand the gravity of a desert crossing."

Mandy didn't answer. She understood the dangers
of searching the desert for a missing man, but it was
still something she knew she had to do. More than ever
now. Drew had almost convinced her that Rodney really was dead. And when he was his most charming,
Mandy almost wanted to believe she was free to reach
out to him. Nothing she faced in the desert was more
frightening than that.

She was grateful when they reached the settler's hut late in the morning. Her knees were exhausted and sore from the effort of gripping the saddle horns, and there wasn't a square inch of her back that didn't hurt. She was not about to complain, though. She'd come on this journey to question this stranger herself, and despite her physical discomfort, she had no regrets.

But when Drew called out a cheery hello at the house, there was no answer, just the distant yipping sounds of coyotes. He tried again at the barn but came up empty there, too. While Mandy slowly trailed behind him, he circled both areas and found nothing but a noisy flock of chickens, a very hungry team of horses and a bellowing unmilked cow. The coyotes sounded closer now. Finally he dismounted and checked inside the barn, then opened the door to the one-room hut and looked around.

Mandy stayed mounted, since she was afraid she might never get back up if she got down, until Drew returned and studied her gravely.

"I'm not sure what's happened here, but I feel quite certain something's wrong," he finally told her. "Whoever lives here is a poor but careful man. Everything is neat and tidy even if it's been mended a dozen times. A man who takes such good care of his harnesses doesn't let his horses go hungry or show such indifference to the distress of a milk cow."

"What do you think we should do?" Mandy asked.

"I'm going to feed the livestock before we go, then ask Major Larson to send somebody back up here tomorrow. If there's no sign of the settler by then, we may have to take some further action." He studied her for a moment, then asked, "I don't suppose you know how to milk a cow?"

Mandy couldn't help but grin. "I grew up in the city, Captain. I can whip up the best currant ice cream you ever tasted, but . . ."

He smiled back in a way that made her wish she'd met him years ago in her mother's parlor, before the disaster of the fire had led her to become engaged to Rodney. Her mother would have loved Drew!

"Never mind. I'll take care of it," Drew said cheerfully, oblivious to the train of Mandy's thoughts. "But we'll be here long enough that you might want to get down."

Slowly he walked over to Mandy, his eyes meeting hers as he reached up to help her dismount. He'd lifted her up and down a dozen times as they'd travelled about in the carriage, and she'd always managed to ignore her body's keen response to his hands. But today, everything was different. It had been different ever since last night.

Mandy felt a sudden rush of warmth as Drew placed his right hand on the small of her back, and she wondered if Drew felt it too. Instead of lifting her quickly from the saddle, he let his fingers linger at the base of her spine in a motionless but intimate caress.

She could not deny it. The heat of Drew's hand left her breathless. The white-hot flame of arousal was so sudden, so intense, that when Drew started to speak again, it took Mandy a moment to decipher his husky words.

"Do you want me to help you?" he repeated, bracing the front of her waist with his free hand.

His voice was so soft she could barely hear him, so

beguiling that she realized she had no strength to stop him from doing anything he wanted to. Never in her life had she felt a man's fingerprints sear her skin so flagrantly. Never had she felt this wanton, irresistible need to take his hands and push them ever so slowly . . . down.

Mutely, Mandy nodded, knowing that in another second, Drew would lift her from the saddle and lightly set her on the ground. She also knew that if she gave him the slightest clue to her potent feelings, he would hold so close that she could not help but brush against him, breast and hip and thigh. She closed her eyes against the rush of anticipation.

Mandy took a deep breath and tried to think of Rodney's face, but it would not come into focus. She struggled for an image of her home in Boston and Rodney's house next door, but all she could see was her bed at the Larson's house. But in her romantic vision, Anna, Percy and Jonathan were not in the room; Drew's sword and boots lay on the floor.

She had barely kicked her foot from the stirrup and loosened her knees from the horns when Jessie snorted and spooked to one side. An instant later the mare reared, almost crashing into Drew. Already half out of the saddle, Mandy managed to tighten her knees just as the barnyard peace was shattered by the growls and snarls of the coyote pack, which sounded quite nearby.

It all happened too quickly for her to think. One moment she was practically in Drew's arms, and the next Jessie was running full speed away from the settler's hut with Mandy holding on for dear life. Instinctively, she hollered at the horse, which only heightened Jessie's terror. The mare scrambled straight up the hillside, crashing through high weeds and low branches, ignoring Mandy's feeble efforts to pull back on her bit.

Jessie must have run a quarter mile when Mandy heard the gunshots. A fresh wash of panic, even greater than the first, shook her so badly she could hardly hold on. She wanted to scream for Drew, but she couldn't find her voice. Besides, she didn't dare. What if he was fighting for his life and she distracted him? Was he shooting at the coyotes or was somebody else shooting at Drew? Or had he been seriously injured when he'd been kicked by her horse?

It was the thought of Drew hurt and bleeding that sobered Mandy. With the sudden sure knowledge that her own life was in danger and his could be too, she realized that she had to take control of this runaway horse.

She seized the reins with all her might and pulled back, calling "Whoa!" but Jessie paid no heed. The terrified mare kept galloping at breakneck speed until she tripped over a rotting stump half-buried in the brush. As she started to fall, twisting her body in fright, Mandy flew out of the saddle and landed in a thorny patch.

The mass of weeds and briars broke her fall but ripped her dress and scratched her skin clear through the fabric. The wind was knocked out of her, and she lay helplessly as Jessie struggled to her feet and bolted again.

Mandy was still gasping for breath when she heard Drew's horse galloping up the ridge. "Mandy? Mandy, where are you?" Drew called.

The naked panic in his voice made her heart turn over. This was no sense of official duty. This was a terror born of love.

For the first time she realized how hard these weeks had been on Drew. How cruel she'd been to him! She'd pretended not to notice his feelings for her because her own guilt was overwhelming. But she knew this man. He was not the type to play with a woman. He was reaching out for Mandy for the same reasons he always tried so hard to pull back. Whatever he felt for her was deep and abiding. And, right or wrong, she felt the same for him.

As Napoleon galloped up beside her, Drew swung off almost before the horse came to a stop. He dropped to his knees and touched Mandy's face, his eyes frantic for assurance that she'd sustained no damage.

"You're not hurt? Nothing's broken? Nothing twisted in the fall?"

Mandy couldn't answer; she just shook her head. Without thinking she threw her arms around him and sobbed against his chest.

"What happened?" she whispered, the words breathless and choked. "Who was shooting at you? Oh, Drew, I thought you were dead!"

He clung to her tightly and rocked her as though she were a child. His arms were so strong, so protective, so unbearably masculine. All the terror of the last few moments vanished. Mandy felt as though a long, frightening journey had ended; at last she'd come home.

"Nobody shot at me," Drew soothed her, his lips tenderly brushing the top of her head. "Jessie was spooked by that pack of coyotes, and I just fired to scare them off. It never occurred to me that you'd think you were left without protection."

Mandy looped her arms around his neck more tightly as he pulled her closer. "Is that all you think you are to me, Drew?" she cried. "A big man with a gun?"

She couldn't see his face because hers was buried in the scratchy blue wool of his uniform, but she heard him swallow a deep, choking breath.

"Mandy," he pleaded urgently, "I never know for sure what you're feeling. All I know is what you mean to me. I'd die before I'd let anything happen to you."

It was not an idle promise; passion rang through his voice. As he tenderly wiped away her tears, a fresh note of anger crept into his self-chastising tone. "This is my fault. I knew you weren't up to riding in the hills. I should never have let you leave the stables this morning. I should have insisted on giving you riding lessons there."

He pulled back just far enough to see her face . . . and for Mandy to see his. His eyes were full of something she'd never seen in them before. Not just anger, desire, or resolution.

His eyes were full of love.

"And to think you were planning to ride across the desert when you first came to the fort," he whispered hoarsely.

It was the moment he said "desert" that Mandy abruptly remembered Rodney. With a belated wash of guilt, she also remembered the carnal thoughts rushing through her heart just before Jessie had run off with her. She remembered the way Drew had touched her so enticingly; she remembered her body's answering erotic pulse. Even now, giddy with panic, she still reeled with that thundering need.

In desperation, Mandy knew she had to escape before she abandoned every vestige of honor, for herself and generations of the Hendersons. She'd made a promise to herself, to Rodney and to Percy. She had no business lying on a California mountainside in Drew Robelard's enticing arms.

If he kissed her now, she knew she couldn't fight him any longer. She was far too confused and rattled to keep from giving in.

With all the strength she could muster, she declared, "I still have to cross the desert, Captain. I just need a little more practice on a horse."

He froze so suddenly that she could feel the muscles of his arms knot up. Hurt and disbelief lashed across his handsome face, followed by a flush of shame.

"You still intend to cross the desert?" he asked incredulously. He pulled back so quickly that Mandy had to brace herself to keep from falling. "You are still determined to find this dead man?"

Ashamed of so many things—her tears, her inept riding, her near capitulation to Drew's passion— Mandy vowed weakly, "Of course, Captain Robelard. And I would thank you to refer to my fiancé as merely missing."

For one terrible moment, Drew just stared at her as he slowly shook his head. His eyes, full of torment, demanded that she yield to him, demanded that she cling to him once more. The need to do his bidding hurt so much that Mandy could hardly breathe or swallow. But somehow she remained where she was.

She battled fresh tears as Drew slowly stood upright,

holding one hand down to her in perfect, frigid courtesy. "Might I help you up, Miss Henderson?" he asked acerbically.

She took his hand and clumsily found her way to her feet, aching to press herself against him. But Drew released her the moment she was standing and briskly announced, "If you are uninjured, we can return to the fort."

Mandy couldn't face him as she pointed out in a small, shaky voice, "My horse is missing."

"So she is, Miss Henderson." His voice grew colder every time he growled her name. "We'll have to double up to ride back."

Mandy stared at him in dismay. She couldn't imagine sharing a saddle with Drew, feeling his pelvis press against her hips for mile after achingly intimate mile. She couldn't think straight when he was close to her. After all that had happened this morning, if she had to spend hours touching him like that. . . . .

"I can't ride your horse, Captain," she protested. "He doesn't have a sidesaddle."

"Don't be ridiculous, Miss Henderson." By now she could hardly bear the way he kept savagely repeating her name. Was it only a few moments ago that he'd so tenderly called her Mandy? "Back east you can indulge the luxury of female propriety. I should think you'd have learned this morning that out here what matters most about the way a woman sits a horse is whether or not she can hang on."

"I wouldn't have fallen off if it hadn't been for those—those coyotes," Mandy burst out, unable to harness her surging emotions. "Why were they hunting there anyway? Wasn't it awfully close to a house?"

"They weren't on a hunt, Miss Henderson. They were drawn by the scent of something that had been killed before."

"A deer?" Mandy asked.

"No."

Drew's tone was so curt that Mandy knew she should not press him, but the strain of silence was too much. Discussing the coyotes seemed safer than anything else she might think of to say.

"What were they eating?" she pressed.

Drew seized her waist a bit roughly and more or less tossed her up on the horse. "It doesn't matter."

Each raw syllable sliced Mandy to the core. "I'm just curious. I don't know why you won't tell me."

Drew glared at her. "I'm trying to protect you, Miss Henderson, though Lord knows why I bother! You just don't get it, do you? Your life is in peril out here."

Mandy fought the urge to cry all over again. She was frightened and upset, and she longed to feel Drew's arms around her once again. Why, oh, why couldn't she either find Rodney out here or manage to forget him? Why did she have to keep aching for Drew and pushing him away? Was she destined to spend her whole life this way?

"The coyotes were tearing up the carcass of a man," Drew snapped. "A very dead man who was once as alive as you."

"The settler?" Mandy blanched. She felt sick to her stomach and very, very faint. She gulped a breath of air before she could ask, "How did he die? What happened?"

"I don't know!" Drew thundered. "And that's the goddamn point! He could have been killed by a thousand things, the same thousand things that killed Rodney Potter."

Mandy covered her face with both hands, hating the tears that streamed down her cheeks almost as much as the lump of guilt that still lived in her heart. "Rodney's still alive," she whispered unconvincingly. "And I'm going to find him."

"Like hell you are," Drew growled, intimately wedging his thighs against hers as he swung up in the saddle behind her.

8

By Sunday afternoon, Percy was feeling acutely bored with life at Fort Tejon. As far as he knew, nobody had done a thing to look for Rodney since Captain Robelard had gone to Silverton the day after he and Mandy had returned from Fishback Creek. Ever since then she'd been busy sewing a new dress for the wedding reception they were holding at the mess hall next weekend after some sergeant got married. At least Percy got to go this time instead of being stuck in the nursery with Jonathan. He was very fond of Anna, but he was too old for a nanny. He was also too old to sit around the fort when he could have been off looking for his brother.

He'd been sitting on the corral fence for half an hour, idly tossing stones at the gatepost, when he heard the sound of hoofbeats at the north end of the fort. He glanced around only because he had nothing better to do. But once he saw what was coming through the

gates, he turned to look again. Captain Robelard was
riding that fine big bay he'd let Percy ride home from
the reservation. Tied to his saddle was a long rope, and
at the other end was a shaggy gray pony.

Percy held his breath as the captain rode toward
him, letting his weary horse find his own pace.
"Howdy, Percy," he called out. "Want to help me with
the horses?"

Percy was so curious he could have died, but he
wasn't about to ask the captain outright why he was
leading a pony just the right size for a boy who was
almost eight. Maybe it was a pack animal, like a Mexican
burro or an Army mule. Maybe there was some other
boy at the fort that the captain thought deserved a pony.

But the captain was grinning from ear to ear as he
dismounted. "Anything exciting happen since I've been
gone, Percy?" he asked.

"No, sir," Percy answered seriously. "No word about
my brother." He studied Captain Robelard with care
before he asked, "Did you find out anything about
Rodney, sir?"

The captain's weary face sobered. He squatted down
to face Percy eye to eye. "No, Percy, I'm sorry. I asked a
lot of questions, though. All I can tell you is that I'm
certain he never got as far as Silverton."

Percy studied the ground. He'd never expected Rodney to be in Silverton in the first place.

"So, I'll be looking for him between here and Fort
Mojave, Percy. I can't promise you good news, but I'm
determined to turn up some trace of him."

"I'm sure you will, sir," Percy answered. His eyes
strayed to the pony again. She had friendly eyes and a
pretty head. The poor thing's coat looked seedy and her

ribs stuck out too much, but nothing seemed wrong with her that good food and regular grooming wouldn't fix.

Captain Robelard stood up and ran a kind hand over the pony's back. "When I saw this pony in Silverton, she reminded me of one my little brother and I used to own."

"Oh?" Percy wasn't sure what to say.

"A miner was using her to haul his supplies. Not fit work for a creature like this. I told him to get a burro or a mule."

"And he gave her to you?" Percy asked in wonder.

Captain Robelard smiled. "Not exactly. But I did persuade him to part with her. And now that I've got Daisy, I don't know what to do with her. She's too small for me to ride, and my little brother isn't . . . here."

Percy's heart began to beat like crazy.

"If somebody doesn't ride her every day, she'll get wild, and then what good will she be to me? She needs somebody small and lightweight, but quiet and kind."

Percy stood up as tall as he could. "Maybe I could help you out, Captain. I'm about the right size."

Captain Robelard looked him over as though Percy had presented a new idea he hadn't thought of before, but Percy wasn't fooled for an instant. "I guess maybe you are at that. Do you think you have time to ride? She'd need somebody to work with her every day."

Percy thought he'd burst. "Oh, yes, sir, I could do that for you!"

"Even while I'm gone across the desert? I wouldn't want you to forget about Daisy while I'm away."

"No, sir! I'll ride her as long as you want me to, every single day!"

Captain Robelard smiled again, and Percy didn't

care at all that his leg had been pulled. The captain had brought the pony just for him. Percy was sure of it.

"Captain, thank you, thank you, thank you!" he finally burst out.

Captain Robelard laughed out loud and patted his shoulder. "You're more than welcome, Percy. Just one hitch, though. We've got to get permission from Miss Henderson."

"Oh, I'll go talk to her right this instant!"

He was about to bolt across the grounds toward the house, but Captain Robelard put a friendly hand on his shoulder. "No, I think you better let me do that. You ought to take care of the horses now, and I've got some other things I need to say."

Mandy looked just the way Drew remembered her— thick soft hair, smooth white skin, beguiling curves caressed by a pretty peach frock that flowed majestically over her crinoline. Drew wondered if she was so dressed up because she knew he might be back today. Her eyes were unreadable, as always, but he thought he had seen a sudden sparkle in them when she first spotted him. He wasn't about to lay any bets on her feelings, though. More than once he'd been dead certain he read passion in those sweet gray eyes only to have Mandy pull away.

Drew had had a perfectly good reason to go to Silverton, since it was the mining town Sherwood had suggested as a possible lead on the Yokuts slave trade, but he couldn't lie to himself about the reason he'd suddenly taken a trip up into the mountains. After Mandy had snatched that heartwrenching moment of hope away from him at Fishback Creek, he'd desperately needed to get away from her long enough to sort things out. But all he'd learned in Silverton was that he wanted Mandy more than ever.

He certainly had no proof that Mandy wanted him. Still, Drew found himself desperately adding up each tiny clue: the look in her eyes when he'd found her tangled in the brush, the urgency of her hands when she'd clung to him, the way she'd tossed aside proper etiquette and called him "Drew." Wasn't it possible that she returned his potent feelings? Wasn't it likely that her sense of duty to Rodney Potter was all that made her push him away? Wasn't it time to lay his cards out on the table? He'd already proved to both of them that his frustration had become so great he could no longer keep acting like a disinterested gentleman.

"Good evening, Captain," Mandy greeted him coolly, avoiding his tense gaze. "I trust you had a safe trip."

"I came back whole, Miss Henderson." Drew longed to greet her with a bouquet of heartfelt words, but her reserved demeanor nipped that notion in the bud. It was obvious that he'd have to proceed with great caution. "I also came back with a Percy-sized pony. He's out at the stable bedding Daisy down for the night. I intended to ask your permission before he knew anything about it, but he saw me ride in."

A strange look, half-happy, half-concerned, flitted across Mandy's lovely face. "You brought him a pony, Captain? That's terribly kind of you, but I can't possibly afford—"

Drew shook his head. "It's a gift, Miss Henderson. No strings attached." He couldn't afford it either, but the moment he'd spied the overworked, underfed pony, he'd made the purchase without a second thought.

"But when we go home—"

"Let's cross that bridge when we come to it. The pony needed a better home than the one it had, and that boy was desperately in need of a pony."

Actually, he thought Percy needed a great deal more than a pony, but at the moment, a pony was about all Drew could provide. He hoped it wouldn't always be that way. He was thirty-two years old, more than ready to start a family of his own . . . and starting to think about starting one with Mandy. If he could ever persuade her to return his passion, there was room in his heart for an adopted son. Percy's stalwart courage and his desperate need to prove his youthful manhood in the Yokuts way touched Drew, reminding him of how he'd ached to prove himself at Percy's age.

He was pleased and surprised at the shakiness of Mandy's voice when she answered, "Captain Robelard, you are very kind." It was obvious that she was struggling to control a host of other feelings.

Mentally he sorted through a dozen things he could say to keep her from pulling away from him again, but none of them seemed to fit the situation. Instead he did what he'd longed to do since the moment he'd walked in the door. He reached out and took her hand.

This time Mandy didn't fight him. She didn't even look surprised. She just held on tightly, blinking her eyes. "He's so lonely, Captain. So lost. So frightened."

So are you, Drew longed to say. Instead he murmured, "Everybody needs somebody they can count on, Miss Henderson. I hope you feel you can count on me."

As her gray eyes flashed up at him, he knew she could read his potent feelings. It was pointless for her to keep pretending that she didn't know how much he wanted her. Surely it was becoming more evident every day.

As Drew stepped closer, he could see that Mandy quivered with the effort of rejecting him once more, but still she turned away. Every fiber of his being protested. Why did she make it so hard for herself? Why did she make it so hard for him? Somehow he willed himself to silence as she took a deep breath, then crossed the room to stare silently out the window in the direction of the stables far across the creek.

"Were you able to find out anything about my fiancé in Silverton?" she asked with dignity.

It was a good question, if somewhat belated, but the fact that she asked it now bothered Drew. How could he ever convince her to give the future a chance if she still refused to face the past?

"There's been no sign of him there."

Her shoulders slumped. "He could not have just vanished when he departed from Fort Mojave. Someone must have seen him since then."

Drew crossed the room and stood behind her, fighting the need to take her in his arms. "People vanish in the desert, Miss Henderson. I spent six years in New Mexico Territory, and it happened all the time."

"I don't need to hear this," she answered shortly. "Major Larson gave me the same speech this afternoon."

Drew had a hunch that her stubbornness stemmed from more than her loyalty to Rodney Potter, or even little Percy. His death was all tied up with the loss of her family, and Drew suspected that it was the anguish of their loss, rather than Rodney's, that made her feel guilty about the possibility of celebrating life again.

"I don't know what else to tell you but the truth," he said wearily. "I vowed to find some trace of Potter's last days for you and Percy, and I won't give up until I do. But that's all I'm ever going to find, Miss Henderson. The sooner you accept that, the sooner you can get on with your life. And then that sad little boy can do it, too."

Her voice grew strained. "Major Larson has flatly forbidden me to go with your supply train to Fort Mojave. Unless you can change his mind, I'll have to find another way to get there."

A sudden surge of alarm all but suffocated Drew. Hadn't she yet laid that crazy dream to rest? He'd assumed all that talk about crossing the Mojave after her fall had been her way of escaping from his arms. He couldn't believe she was still considering such folly. "Miss Henderson, I beg of you, don't even consider it," he pleaded. "Percy needs you desperately. You'd be committing suicide."

She turned around abruptly, so abruptly that her hooped skirt twisted awkwardly against his legs. Mandy flushed and tried to step back, but the wall was too close. She looked trapped and frightened as she faced him instead.

Drew could have moved, and he knew that as a gentleman, he should have. But he was exhausted by his mountain journey and frightened for this woman he was growing to care for so deeply. His powerlessness infuriated him. He finally had her close enough to listen to him, and he was not about to let her slip away.

"Please help me, Captain," she pleaded in a husky tone. "Convince him I won't be in the way. I'll be invisible. I'll learn to ride better, or walk if I have to. I'll even cook for you and the men if—"

"Miss Henderson—" Drew suddenly found himself touching her fine, high cheekbone "you could not be invisible if you covered your head with a pillow sack. Every night I see your beauty with my eyes closed."

Mandy lowered her gaze and licked her lips, but she did not pull away. A web of passion suddenly spread out its tendrils between them, ensnaring Drew so totally that he could not even consider escape.

"I don't care about any inconvenience your traveling with us might present," he said, "and neither does Major Larson. We both just want you safe." His fingers slipped into her hair as he whispered, "You don't know how the thought of you getting hurt out there haunts me."

"You can protect me," she whispered.

He shook his head. "I can protect you by keeping you here."

His thumb slipped over her lower lip, then her chin. Her eyes widened in alarm as he moved even closer, but she still didn't stir. If she'd wanted to escape, she would have done so by now, he was certain. He'd never have a better chance to tell her the truth.

"You're very, very special to me, Mandy," he murmured, deliberately using her given name. "I'd do anything at all to protect you."

He was so close he could smell the fine and fragile scent of her body, and his need to embrace her almost overpowered him. She was quivering now, but did not seem able to pull away from him.

Her voice was low and husky as she confessed, "It's not protection that I want from you."

"I know." He tipped up her chin until her tempting lips were just inches from his own. "Let me give you more."

She closed her eyes tightly. "I don't think you understand," she pleaded.

Her voice was so soft Drew thought he'd imagined the words. "Yes, I do."

"I have an obligation."

"Only to Percy," he answered, trying to say the blunt words in a gentle tone. "And I've got room in my heart for him, too. Pushing me away won't bring back Rodney. It won't bring back your family or your home. Would your parents want you spend the rest of your life mourning? Would they want you to be so terribly alone?"

The pain on her face wounded Drew. Tears slipped silently from beneath her closed eyelids, but this time she offered no denial.

He cradled her head and pulled her close, so close he could feel her heartbeat thud against his own chest. "I don't want to hurt you, Mandy. I want to take the pain away."

At last she opened her eyes, gray eyes that shone with love and anguish. She wanted him; he knew it. Every line of her body told him she was his.

"Mandy, have mercy," he begged her, unable to hold back the long-hidden words a moment longer. "Can't you see that I'm in love with you?"

He would have kissed her then, but suddenly she pressed her face against his neck. He hugged her tighter, ready to rejoice for just an instant before he realized that her whole lithe body had sagged against him in a motion filled with defeat, not passion.

"Drew, please don't," she whispered.

"It's too late for me," he told her truthfully, his heart hammering in his chest. "Isn't it too late for you?"

He heard Mandy swallow back a sob, then murmur something almost too soft for him to hear. But he did hear. Dropping his arms, he left her without another word.

"Rodney" was all she'd said.

It took some doing for Mandy to get Percy into his stiff new shirt for the wedding party on Saturday night. In the past few weeks, he'd grown accustomed to wearing casual clothes and he squirmed a bit at the notion of putting on his suit and spats. Although it was a bit aggravating to wrestle with him, she was secretly glad to see him acting like a normal boy instead of a little man forced too soon into adulthood.

His wiggling seemed to be the only thing normal about this odd day. Mandy had only seen Drew a few times in the week since he'd returned from Silverton, and each time they had been with others and she'd managed to keep her conflicting feelings at bay. Mandy wasn't sure she could conquer them this evening. She'd barely conquered them the last time they'd been alone in the same room.

In hindsight, she was beginning to believe that Drew might be right that her devotion to Rodney was an extension of her love for her family, but that didn't change anything. She couldn't erase the lifetime of experiences that bound the Hendersons and the Potters just because she was sexually attracted to Drew.

She tried to tell herself that desire was all she felt for him, an ignoble need a strong woman could override. But the truth of the matter was, she suspected she was already more than halfway in love with Drew.

"Aren't you a picture!" Lucinda sighed as she studied Mandy's new dove gray gown and tugged just a little on the collar. "You'll have those young soldiers going wild."

Lucinda had generously given Mandy her choice of several bolts of fabric she insisted she'd never use. Mandy had sewn up the least colorful one, explaining the process to a very curious Anna. She'd also explained that gray was more suitable than crimson for a lady whose fiancé was missing, since it was also appropriate for half-mourning, those awkward months when the worst of a woman's suffering was over and she no longer felt the need to dress in black. Secretly, Mandy knew that half-mourning was what she felt for Rodney now.

Now, Mandy struggled not to blush at Lucinda's compliment. "Lucinda, you know I'm engaged."

Lucinda's knowing eyes met hers briefly. "Yes, dear," she said.

Mandy's feeble protest sounded artificial to her own ears, and she was sure it sounded the same to Lucinda. She was still determined to find Rodney and to care for Percy, but she'd always known that her feelings for Rodney were not those of passion. Passion was not something she'd ever missed before.

Tonight her emotions were breathless and swirling, dangerous ones for a woman who claimed loyalty to a man who most likely lived only in her imagination. There was no way she could avoid seeing Drew at this wedding party, and no way she truly wanted to. Mandy tried to steady herself as she walked sedately with Lucinda and the major to the mess hall, but she felt edgy and excited. She couldn't seem to stop herself from seeking out Drew the moment she entered the hall.

But there was no sign of him in the gaily decorated building, though the place was already filled with officers, enlisted men and their families. Mandy had helped the other women fill the plain mess hall with flowers, and both Lucinda and Betty Sue had brought out their best china for the affair. Their household cooks, along with their official Army counterparts, had outdone themselves this evening. The mingled scents of hoecakes, tea biscuits and sasparilla mead wafted tantalizingly around the room.

The Fort Tejon band was assembled in the corner, playing rowdy versions of military marches that one could almost dance to, and Lucinda assured her that later on a small group of violinists would render music appropriate for waltzing.

The rest of the Army community was a sight to behold this evening. All the officers were in their best dress uniforms, complete with dashing plumed hats, gold bullion epaulettes and sabers. Even the lowliest private looked scrubbed and shiny-faced. Betty Sue looked almost regal in her flounced pink paisley gown as she greeted each man effervescently. Although she did not actually stand in Lucinda's rightful place, she did push her husband quite close to his commanding officer.

The bride, dressed in a white ruffled gown bedecked with a string of tiny pearls, was already glowing beside her new husband when Mandy greeted the Harrises.

"Don't eat so much you get sick, Percy," she warned the small boy as he started to trot directly toward the heavily laden tables without so much as a glance at the bridal couple. "Remember what happened at last year's Christmas party."

"I bet Anna doesn't tell Salt Hair stuff like that now that he's a man," Percy grumbled.

Mandy flashed him a tolerant look. "Salt Hair is a little older than you are, Percy," she pointed out. "And at least you've got a pony now."

Percy's moment of pique vanished. "You bet I do. She's the fastest horse that ever lived, Mandy! Captain Robelard's teaching me to ride Indian style. Wait till you see what I can do!"

Mandy felt a moment's jealousy. She'd love to have Drew give her riding lessons, but after their last fiasco he'd refused to take her anywhere on his quests for information. Mandy was determined to ride Jessie again, since she would need to learn to ride better if she was ever to conquer the Mojave, but even after Jessie had wandered home from the mountains, Mandy hadn't found a good time to broach the subject with Major Larson. He'd nearly had apoplexy when she'd asked for permission to join Drew on the trip to Fort Mojave.

"I hear the youngster is doing quite well on Daisy," said a quiet voice beside her ear.

Mandy turned at once to meet the sober eyes of Lieutenant Isley. He was wearing his dress uniform for the occasion, but even with his saber he never looked as dignified as Drew.

"Good evening, Lieutenant," she greeted him kindly, noting that, as usual, the plain young man was alone. "I didn't realize that Percy's exploits were the subject of post gossip."

"Hardly gossip, ma'am. But Captain Robelard and I are both housed in bachelor officers quarters and we share meals when he is not otherwise engaged. He's quite proud of what the young boy can do."

Percy's chest swelled up like a peacock's. "The captain's a fine teacher, sir."

JOIN THE
TIMELESS ROMANCE READER SERVICE AND GET FOUR OF TODAY'S MOST EXCITING HISTORICAL ROMANCES FREE, WITHOUT OBLIGATION!

Imagine getting today's very best historical romances sent directly to your home – at a total savings of at least $2.00 a month. Now you can be among the first to be swept away by the latest from Candace Camp, Constance O'Banyon, Patricia Hagan, Parris Afton Bonds or Susan Wiggs. You get all that – and that's just the beginning.

PREVIEW AT HOME WITHOUT OBLIGATION AND SAVE.

Each month, you'll receive four new romances to preview without obligation for 10 days. You'll pay the low subscriber price of just $4.00 per title – a total savings of at least $2.00 a month!

Postage and handling is absolutely free and there is no minimum number of books you must buy. You may cancel your subscription at any time with no obligation.

GET YOUR FOUR FREE BOOKS TODAY ($20.49 VALUE)

FILL IN THE ORDER FORM BELOW NOW!

YES! *I want to join the Timeless Romance Reader Service. Please send me my 4 FREE HarperMonogram historical romances. Then each month send me 4 new historical romances to preview without obligation for 10 days. I'll pay the low subscription price of $4.00 for every book I choose to keep — a total savings of at least $2.00 each month — and home delivery is free! I understand that I may return any title within 10 days without obligation and I may cancel this subscription at any time without obligation. There is no minimum number of books to purchase.*

NAME_____

ADDRESS _____

CITY_____STATE____ZIP_____

TELEPHONE_____

SIGNATURE _____

(If under 18 parent or guardian must sign. Program, price, terms, and conditions subject to cancellation and change. Orders subject to acceptance by HarperMonogram.)

GET
4
FREE
BOOKS
(A $20.49
VALUE)

"I don't doubt it, young man," said Isley. Then he glanced at Mandy. "After what happened in the mountains, ma'am, perhaps you should be taking some riding lessons, too." The moment the words were out of his mouth, he colored slightly. "No disrespect intended, Miss Henderson. I only meant that after a spill, it's important to get right back in the saddle, especially if the rider hasn't had a great deal of experience."

Over the last hard months, Mandy had learned to take opportunity when she found it, and she had a hunch she was looking at it now. "I would be happy to improve my riding skills with a capable instructor, Lieutenant, but I'd hate to impose on anyone."

"I'd be honored to assist you with your horsemanship, Miss Henderson," Isley offered at once, "if you'd care to join me when I'm off duty."

If he realized that he'd been manuevered into helping her, he gave no sign. In fact, he looked both pleased and astonished when Mandy accepted his offer. With a cautious smile, he offered to get her some sasparilla and enjoyed a glass himself.

After another few moments of desultory conversation, he asked, "Would you do me the honor of this dance?"

Mandy had mixed feelings about dancing with Lieutenant Isley, but courtesy forbade her to refuse. As she moved into his stiff arms, she was reasonably hopeful that he would not press her for too many dances this evening, and reasonably certain that he had not misread her eagerness for riding lessons as romantic interest.

"Do you have these parties often?" she asked him pleasantly.

Isley shook his head. "Not often enough for the men.

Unless there's trouble, there's not much to do on an Army post. I hope the new bride won't regret her decision. Sergeant Ryan has never brought her here before and I imagine he's going to spirit her away rather quickly tonight before she realizes what she's in for."

Mandy pondered the odd tone of his statement at such a happy occasion. Most of the time he seemed like a nice young man, but sometimes his bitterness was disconcerting.

"She certainly seems like a pretty girl," she observed. "And I'm sure she'll be happy to support her husband's career in any way she can."

She considered the other Army wives she knew. Lucinda, she was certain, would be happy living anywhere with the man she loved, and Betty Sue most likely would find some reason to complain about any profession her husband might choose. As Mandy thought of Drew's pride in his commission, she realized that she would have no complaints about garrison life if it meant she could make a home for him.

Flushing as she realized the embarassing train of her thoughts, Mandy said quickly, "Mrs. Larson tells me that many wives are quite happy with garrison life."

"Miss Henderson," Isley replied in a low, dour tone, "Nobody is truly happy with life in the Army."

She was saved from searching for a suitable reply when Isley stepped on her toe and spent several moments apologizing profusely. Although he remained polite to her, he looked continually more unhappy as they danced. Once the music ended, he said gravely, "You must forgive me for being such a poor companion this evening. I think this wedding has me thinking about all the choices I didn't make when I was younger. I'll be over it in the morning."

"Of course you will, Lieutenant," she assured him, relieved when he thanked her for her company and then excused himself.

Two other officers asked her to dance before she could return to Percy, who was still devouring hoe cakes at the table. She had almost reached his side when she realized that he was eagerly recounting a recent adventure to Drew. Percy had found a "bear nest" high in tree about a mile from the fort. It wasn't a bear's nest at all, he explained, but rather a platform built by Yokuts hunters where they could lie in wait for a bear without taking the risk of being attacked by one while sleeping.

"I'm really proud of the way you've learned to handle yourself as a frontiersman," Drew praised him, clapping one gloved hand on the boy's shoulder. "It usually takes a great deal longer for a boy from back east to learn to handle a horse and a gun."

Percy's chest visibly swelled as his shoulders straightened. "I'm doing my best, sir."

"I know you are." Drew's smile was warm, almost tender, even before he glanced up and spotted Mandy. "Good evening, Miss Henderson. You look"—he seemed to have trouble finding the right word— "exceedingly memorable this evening." His eyes met hers in a mute but heartfelt question.

Mandy knew what the question was, and the answer he was looking for; she knew the answer she longed to give. But nothing had changed. Prudence had dictated her behavior the last time they'd been alone, and prudence must dictate her behavior tonight.

She took a deep breath to steady herself. "Thank you, Captain. You look quite elegant yourself." With his boots freshly blacked and his medals glistening, Drew looked positively princely. All of the men looked well-turned out tonight, but none had Drew's proud carriage or his magnificent shoulders. Mandy's breath caught in her throat just looking at him.

He gave her the faintest hint of an embarrassed grin. "I trust you enjoyed your dance with Lieutenant Isley?" A drop of jealousy seemed to lace his tone.

"I enjoy dancing, Captain."

Drew took her reply for an invitation, which Mandy secretly had to admit that it was. A moment later he'd excused himself from Percy with the same courtesy he'd have extended to a superior officer, and offered Mandy a white-gloved hand.

She knew, from the first moment that she slipped her own fingers into Drew's, that she was playing with a forest fire this evening. A jolt of need brushed the fine nerve endings of her fingertips, and a second jolt, greater than the first, rocked her when he slid his arm around her waist. When she cautiously placed her hand on his shoulder, she realized that it wasn't dancing she was in the mood for. She would have welcomed any excuse to get this close to Drew.

"I want to thank you for being so kind to Percy," she told him, hoping to keep the conversation on an even keel. "He's so desperate for male attention. He misses his brother terribly."

When Drew pulled her a little closer, the sudden tautness of her nipples reminded Mandy of how very close he'd come to kissing her the last time they'd been alone. His voice was low as he answered, "I know just how he feels, Miss Henderson, and it's a pleasure to buck him up. He's a fine young boy, and you have every reason to be proud of him."

Mandy smiled.

Drew smiled back. It was a beautiful smile that started out quite soberly and ended in a rakish grin. His fingers splayed out across her back, sensuously stroking the smooth gray velvet.

"What shall we talk about this evening?" he asked boldly. "Other than the beauty of your dress and the effect it has on me."

Mandy fought a pleased blush. "Captain, I'm not at all sure that's an appropriate topic of conversation."

He grinned and pulled her closer. "Come now, Miss Henderson. Surely you know it's the perfect color for your eyes and it shows off your complexion. The skirt sways just enough to draw attention to your tiny, touchable waist—"

"Captain, please!"

Now he looked at her soberly. "Am I really embarrassing you, or is that just your Boston upbringing speaking?"

"I suppose you're more relaxed about propriety in the South?"

He shook his head. "I doubt that. I suspect that I've simply tired of the chase and perhaps you haven't yet."

Mandy felt a strange, sinking sense of alarm in the pit of her stomach. She had barely admitted to herself how much she wanted Drew, and he was telling her he was tired of her? She should have been relieved, but she didn't feel the tinest breath of relief.

"You don't need to waste your time with me if I'm boring you," she said stiffly.

Drew grinned again, much wider this time. Both dimples deepened. "Never that, Miss Henderson. I was simply trying to make a point."

Mandy knew she shouldn't rise to the bait, but she couldn't help herself. "What point is that, Captain?" she asked with a saucy smile of her own.

He laughed out loud, then gestured toward the bride and groom who were dancing at the opposite end of the room. "I understand that Sergeant Ryan gently courted that girl for over two years. He begged for her hand in marriage, but she would never commit herself to him. Then he suddenly got orders to go to Fort Wilmington. He went back to the ranch to tell the girl goodbye. He'd given up on marrying her by then."

Drew chuckled. "He was on his horse and riding out when he turned around and found her running after him, begging him not to leave her. She sobbed, she kissed him, she told him she couldn't live without him."

Mandy wasn't sure what the point of the story was, but she knew Drew had told it for a reason.

"What had she been waiting for?" she asked.

"I don't know. It doesn't matter. The point is that if she'd waited any longer, she would have lost him." His eyes met hers meaningfully before she could glance away.

The dance ended on that note, and Mandy knew it was time to escape from Drew. This conversation was getting far too personal. She didn't know where it was leading but she knew where she secretly wanted it to go.

Drew didn't seem willing to release her. Briskly, he ushered her outside the stuffy building, one hand firmly supporting her arm. To any watching eyes, it merely looked like a courteous gesture, but courtesy didn't begin to describe Mandy's awareness of the pressure of his elbow against the side of her breast.

She knew she should be trying to make casual conversation, but she couldn't seem to think of anything safe to say. In her mind the story of Sergeant Ryan's bride still lingered.

"I don't think I'd take any risks with a man I loved," she said thoughtfully, eyeing the moon that was just starting to rise. "Marriage is hardly a business investment where a woman sells out to the highest bidder."

"No?" Drew asked, his voice low and beguiling. "I think a lot of people look at it that way."

Mandy didn't reply as Drew failed to release her arm, but neither did she pull away.

By now she knew she was in trouble. Beneath her layers of small clothes, her skin was achingly hot. They were strolling farther and farther from the others. If Drew tried to kiss her, she wasn't at all sure she could deny him again.

"The Apaches are quite precise about it," he commented, tucking her hand securely around his elbow. "They literally buy their brides with an exchange of gifts."

"Really?" At this point any topic of conversation seemed safer than thinking about the large male hand surreptitiously caressing hers. "What's a typical price?"

"Several horses." Drew's eyes met hers as they came to a stop. "You're worth a great deal more to me than a Shetland pony."

Both touched and alarmed, Mandy asked indignantly, "Is that why you gave that horse to Percy, Captain? Just to try to get close to me?"

At once his dimples vanished. "Absolutely not. I got him that pony because the pony needed a boy and I've never known a boy who had a greater need for a horse."

Mandy was ashamed of her accusation, but she didn't want to say so. What she wanted was a safe way to break the rising sexual tension. Carefully she suggested, "What he really needs is his big brother."

"Or a *shaugh-num-uh.*"

They shared a grin. Drew was still standing far too close, but at least he didn't look angry. "Why are boys so eager to grow up?" Mandy asked him. "Don't they know the trouble that awaits them?"

"Poor Percy's had all the trouble he needs already, Miss Henderson. He can't enjoy being a boy, so maybe he figures if he could grow up a bit, he might be better equipped to deal with life's disasters."

"I've done everything I could for him," Mandy responded a bit defensively. "Until I find Rodney—"

"Miss Henderson, you're not going to find Rodney," he said, his voice losing some of its warmth. "Not alive. I don't think you're doing Percy any favors pretending that you will. If you really want to help that boy, you need to start thinking about how you're going to take care of him when you give up this wild goose chase. And it seems to me that marriage is—"

"Captain Robelard, I'm going to marry Rodney."

Duty forced her to say the words, but they sounded stilted and ludicrous to Mandy's ears. Who was she trying to fool? Drew was surely right. Poor Rodney was dead and she had no hope of ever seeing him again. Why couldn't she shed her guilt and do what Drew wanted? When he stood this close, it was all she could do not to tremble. If he confessed his love for her once more, she wasn't at all sure she could push him away again.

As Drew's eyes met hers with fresh impatience, the air was clean and crisp, rich with pine, and the whole mountainside seemed bathed in starlight. Mandy waited for a long, tense moment, but he did not try to kiss her. Instead he glanced back toward the noisy mess hall, where they could hear toasts being made to the bride and groom.

"It's too bad that the wedding had to take place at the Catholic Church in town," Mandy said, unable to bear the awkward silence. "I would have loved a chance to see an Army wedding here."

"I'm sure that would have been Ryan's choice," Drew told, his voice low and husky near her ear. "There's nothing more splendid that a full military wedding. But he did what any man worth his salt would have done in his position. He deferred to the wishes of his bride."

Mandy smiled. "You think all men do that, do you, Captain?"

He gave her another beguiling grin. "The Zuni have a custom that always intrigued me," he murmured seductively. "When they marry, the man weaves a blanket for his woman. He has to do all the work himself, and once he puts that blanket around his bride, no one can ever take her away from him."

By now he stood so close that Mandy didn't dare lift her chin for fear her lips would be pressing his. She didn't dare straighten, either, for fear her skirts would brush Drew's thighs. Desperately she tried to remember why she simply could not yield to this man, but all thought abandoned her. She tried to breathe but she couldn't seem to do that either.

"How would you feel if a man wove a blanket for you, Miss Henderson?" Drew asked in a sultry whisper.

Mandy swallowed hard. In her mind, she could see a thickly woven blanket draped around her shoulders, as Drew's hands pulled the ends together across her naked breasts.

"I would be touched," she could not help but confess, "if I truly loved him."

For a long moment, awareness quivered potently between the two of them. Mandy knew they were in such dangerous waters that she must swim away before she was scuttled by the tide, but a curious languor had settled over her muscles. She could not seem to make the slightest effort to escape.

"I would be touched if a woman accepted a blanket that I made for her. Once I wrapped it around her shoulders"—Drew leaned so close that his breath fanned her throat—"I would never, ever let her go."

Mandy could hardly breathe. Her need for Drew's touch was unbearable. She was in trouble, terrible trouble, and she shivered with apprehension and delight.

"Are you cold?" he whispered, the simplest words imbued with sensual implication. "Would you like me to get you a warm, woolen shawl . . . or a blanket?"

Mandy's eyes flashed open as she realized the symbolic blanket Drew had in mind.

"Zuni marriage blankets aren't made of wool," he said, his voice as soft and compelling as the scrape of a violin's bow. "The man weaves it of strips of rabbit-skin. It's soft and warm when he wraps it around his unclothed bride."

Mandy was shocked at Drew's blunt language, but she couldn't deny that she felt a thrill of anticipation at the vivid words. She knew what he was doing: hoping to conjure up an image of herself, quite naked, wrapped in a blanket that was half rabbitskin and half-Drew. Against her will she saw him roll on top of her in a tiny Yokuts hut, heard herself sigh and pull him close. The picture was too clear, too beautiful, too unexpectedly erotic. Suddenly she felt an embarrassingly potent flush of need between her thighs. Remembering the day they'd shared a saddle, she longed to feel Drew's body pressed urgently against the most intimate portions of her own.

Was he truly thinking of marriage? Mandy asked herself. Or was he just thinking of one sizzling, sensual night? Surely her answer must be the same either way. But if he actually wanted to marry her, to give a home to Percy ...

"No Captain, I don't want a shawl," she forced herself to say, remembering the lonely little boy she'd left inside. "I'd like to go back to the party now."

For a long, tense moment Drew's magnificent blue eyes met Mandy's, begging her to reconsider. The pain and need she read there all but undid her. But somehow she found the strength to close her own eyes and wait until Drew slowly stepped away.

The night was still for an achingly long moment before he offered her his arm in his usual courtly fashion. As she steeled herself against the warmth of his touch, she desperately summoned up her fading image of Rodney Potter and the hazy memory of the promise she'd made to him. If she could only hold on until they reached the mess hall, she just might make it through the night without letting Drew know how very much she wanted him.

Percy was jounced half-awake by the sound of boots crunching over rocks and leaves, but he was too sleepy to rouse himself. The arms that held him were muscular, tender and secure. They reminded him of Rodney's, and all the times Rodney had found him sleeping and carried him up to bed. There was love in these arms, too, love like a brother's, and after all he'd been through in the past hard years, it felt awfully good to Percy to feel loved just then.

Mandy's voice came to him, soft and low and remarkably happy. "It's awfully good of you to carry him, Captain. He's completely tuckered out."

"It's been an exciting night for all of us. He held out as long as he could."

Percy didn't want the captain to think he was a baby; he might change his mind about helping him become a man. As he struggled for consciousness, he started to feel embarrassed. Nobody should be carrying him. He was almost eight years old. He should walk on his feet like a real man.

As he heard the Larsons' front door open, he found the strength to say, "I'm awake, Captain. You can put me down."

He opened his eyes and looked up at the strong brown face. There was no censure there. "Are you sure, Percy? I don't mind carrying you upstairs."

Percy nodded. "I was sleepy before, but I'm fine now."

Slowly the captain lowered him to the ground, but

the look on his face gave Percy the feeling that he rather liked carrying him. Percy didn't want to admit that he rather liked it, too.

"Goodnight, Captain," he said with a grateful smile.

The captain touched his shoulder in a gesture that made him feel more like a well-loved boy than like a respected man. "Goodnight, Percy. Sleep well." A strange look came into his eyes then, a look that reminded Percy of the expression he'd sometimes seen in his own father's when he was especially pleased with him. Slowly, Captain Robelard suggested, "Tomorrow, if you like, we can talk about that ceremony you've been wanting."

"Ceremony?" Percy repeated sleepily.

"Your coming of age ceremony." The captain's voice was low. "There's a 'Boston Boy' version of Salt Hair's jimson weed training that I happen to be familiar with. Instead of a sweat bath it involves a campout in the hills and pre-dawn hunting. I'd be proud to be your *shaugh-num-uh* counselor, Percy, if you've no one else in mind."

Percy could hardly believe it. He'd mentioned the Yokuts manhood ritual to the captain several times, and he'd always responded by offering to teach him something new. But he'd never come right and offered to do a white man's version of the jimson weed ceremony before. "Oh, Captain! That would be wonderful!"

This time the captain shook his hand, as though he were already a man. "We'll start making plans at once. A man needs a good a night's sleep before he undertakes anything important, so you go hit the hay."

Percy thanked him once more before he started up the stairs, expecting Mandy to say goodnight and follow him. And she did lift her skirts the tiniest bit so she wouldn't trip on them as she took the first step. But then she turned to the captain and said in an oddly husky tone, "Just give me a moment, Captain Robelard, and then I'll be back down."

Percy couldn't imagine why she didn't just say goodnight now and be done with it, but he was too tired to figure it out. All he wanted to do was crawl into bed and pull the covers over his head, and when he reached his pallet, he did just that. Anna lay on her own pallet close to his, but she seemed to be asleep. The only sound in the room came from the softly snoring baby.

Percy mumbled goodnight to Mandy, then gave himself up to sleep. He was drifting off again when he felt Mandy kiss his cheek and whisper how much she loved him. Then he heard her footsteps on the stairs as she hurried back to Captain Robelard. They'd been together most of the evening, dancing and laughing with their heads and hands quite close. Percy couldn't imagine what she still had to say to him.

9

The sounds of the night surrounded Drew with a soft medley as he waited downstairs for Mandy. Back at the mess hall, voices were still raised in song and warmed by laughter. The air was graced with the scrape of the bow and the peal of a piccollo. Outside he could hear chirping crickets and a single full-throated toad.

Drew listened to the swish of Mandy's skirt as she closed the door to the room where Percy slept, then descended to the main hallway. As she approached him slowly, her face bathed in the dim light from the candles in the wall sconces, he realized that he was having trouble breathing.

Mandy did not speak until she reached him, stopping a discreet yard or so away. Her voice was not quite steady as she whispered, "Thank you for carrying Percy, Captain."

"Drew."

He watched her swallow hard. "Captain, I—"

"Drew," he repeated firmly.

She clutched her hands tightly together. "I don't think it's seemly to—"

"Mandy, stop. There's no point in pretending any longer. This is special between us."

Her eyes flashed in alarm, but she offered no more protest. She looked so helpless, so distraught, that Drew was almost sorry he'd pressed her.

"Drew," she whispered, "I am engaged to another man. You must remember that."

He shook his head. "You were faithful to him while he lived, and you have long clung to his memory. But he's gone now, Mandy, and you have your own life to live."

"He's not gone! He's just—"

"He's *gone,*" he repeated, daring to touch her clenched fists.

Mandy took a step back, dislodging his hands. "Even if that were true, you're assuming that I—"

"That you feel the same way about me that I feel about you." He'd seen proof in her eyes, heard it in her voice. She trembled every time he touched her. He refused to leave this house again until Mandy admitted that she loved him.

Mandy flushed. "Please, Captain, I—"

"Drew, dammit!" he burst out. "How long are you going to keep playing this ridiculous game?"

"It's not a game! I have told you and told you that I am not interested in any man but Rodney."

He took a step closer, so close that the hilt of his saber brushed her gown. "Tell me again."

By now she was backed up against the bottom stair.

She didn't face him, but she didn't run. For a long, tense moment, raw awareness tingled between them. Then she laid both hands on his chest in a nameless, ambivalent plea as she whispered, "Please, Drew."

Her touch made him tremble, yet somehow made him whole. With infinite care Drew cupped her face and tilted it toward him. "Please what?"

He felt her quiver. She struggled for breath. "Please let me go."

Drew couldn't bear to release her, but he refused to kiss her against her will. "Are you afraid of me?" he asked softly, his fingertips brushing one of her enticing silken curls. "Are you afraid I'll force you to do something you don't want to do?"

Mandy's eyes were big and troubled. Her breasts brushed against him as she struggled for composure, but she couldn't seem to steady herself. "No," she finally confessed, "I'm afraid you'll tempt me to do something I'll sorely regret."

Drew might have pulled back then, but Mandy's eyes were too big, too bright and too inescapably hopeful.

"Mandy," he breathed.

She closed her eyes as he stroked her cheek. He could still feel her fingertips against his chest, but her strokes were light, almost caressing. By no stretch of the imagination was she pushing him away.

Drew took a step closer, so close that his legs brushed intimately against hers. Mandy moaned ever so slightly when he slid his free hand around her waist.

"Mandy," he breathed again.

She raised her chin the tiniest amount as her crinoline pressed against him. "Drew, I—"

He claimed her lips with his before she could offer

another protest, before she could say words that would force a gentleman to go. A sudden wash of heat wrapped itself around him. He knew the exact instant it wrapped itself around Mandy, too.

Her fingertips suddenly curved against his chest, bunching the coarse wool of his coat. She flattened herself against him so quickly that Drew could feel her taut nipples and her womanly, yearning thighs. He gasped as he cradled her head and pulled her closer, deepening their kiss.

She kissed him back. She gave him everything he asked for, answered every question, matched the fire of his own desire. He'd ached for this strong woman almost from the moment he'd met her, and he'd desperately hoped she'd ached for him too. Until this moment, he had never been sure.

For a long fiery moment, Drew was oblivious to everything but Mandy. There was no future, no past . . . just the potent woman in his arms. A tornado of physical need swelled up inside him, blinding him to everything but Mandy's urgency.

When she wrenched her mouth from his, he felt as though he'd been tossed in the air and fallen on his head.

"No!" she cried, pushing him away. "No, Drew! Let me go!"

Stunned, Drew dropped his hands, but he could not move. "Mandy, what's wrong? You can't tell me that wasn't what you wanted!"

She covered her face with both hands. "I'm not blaming you," she said in a tiny voice he hardly recognized. "I'm just asking you to . . . go away."

"Go away? Mandy, if that's how you tell a fellow to get lost, then—"

"Drew, don't you understand?" She grabbed his shoulders and met his eyes with an aching earnestness that broke his heart. "I want you. I can't deny it. But I'm betrothed to another man!"

"A man who's dead!" It was a cruel way to say it, but he was too upset to mince words.

"You don't know that! Neither do I! And I *want* him to be alive, Drew, even if you don't! I love Rodney Potter. He's the best friend I ever had."

He stiffened. Almost angrily, he took her hand. "Did you ever kiss Rodney the way you just kissed me?"

Mandy wheeled away, but she did not answer.

"I've listened to the way you talk about this man, Mandy, and I don't think you were ever in love with him at all. He's a brother to you. That's fine. But it shouldn't stop you from loving another man. Even if Rodney were still alive—"

"Stop it! He is alive! He *is*!"

"Mandy, he won't live or die based on how you feel about me. Living in misery won't bring your family back! Can't you just give in to your feelings?"

She straightened then and met his eyes squarely. "If you were lying in the desert somewhere, Drew, injured and maybe dying, how would you feel if I forgot about you and fell in love with somebody else?"

As Drew watched her gather her skirts together and sweep briskly back up the stairs, he realized that she'd asked the one question for which he had no answer.

"Have you had a chance to speak to Sherwood yet?" Mandy asked Lucinda the day after the wedding.

It had rained in the night, and the cloudy day precisely matched her mood. At breakfast, in desperation, she'd pleaded with Lucinda to convince her husband to let her accompany Drew to Fort Mojave. It was a last-ditch effort which could not possibly succeed, but she'd run out of options. Worse yet, she was running out of motivation. Last night she'd almost forgotten Rodney entirely when Drew had pulled her into his arms.

It was a cataclysmic event that she could not afford to repeat. Whatever Drew wanted from her, she could not give it to him until she knew, without the tiniest bit of doubt, that there was no way she could honor her previous obligations.

"I tried, dear," Lucinda said quietly. "I'm afraid you'll have to rely on Drew."

Mandy didn't respond at once. Last night's searing kiss had proved beyond doubt that Drew was no longer an impartial observer doing his duty as an officer and a gentleman. She could no longer trust him to keep his promise to her. And while she didn't doubt his love for her, she knew he had every reason to hope that Rodney was dead.

Mandy had tossed and turned in her bed all night long, silently asking Rodney for forgiveness. She had never imagined that the power of the force of nature could cause her to yield to Drew so completely, for even a heartbeat. She could not imagine what strength of will she'd have to summon to keep it from happening again.

"You couldn't convince him?" she asked Lucinda. "You couldn't make him see how much this means to me?"

Lucinda's eyes met hers across the parlor. "No, dear, I didn't even try. The problem was, I couldn't convince myself that I should."

Mandy sank lower into the stiff willow-bottomed chair. "Lucinda, I can't just sit here. I can't—"

"I can't let you wander out on the desert and die, dear." The words were absolutely firm. "I haven't been an Army wife for forty years for nothing. I know what's out there. I know the price you'd have to pay."

Mandy wasn't sure what to say to that. What would Lucinda say if she knew that Mandy's alternative plan was even more dangerous than going with Drew? One way or another, she had to search for Rodney. She'd completely run out of options. If she couldn't cross the Mojave with the dragoons' best scout, she'd scare up one of her own.

Anna was crossing the compound late in the afternoon, Jonathan securely in her arms, when she saw Captain Robelard approaching. At first she averted her eyes, expecting him to ignore her as she passed, but to her surprise he stopped and addressed her directly.

"Good afternoon, Anna. How are you?"

She studied him warily. It was rare for white people outside of the Larsons' house to speak to her, although a couple of the laundresses chatted with her now and then. Just an hour ago one of them had told her alarming news: Mandy had asked the post sutler how she could find a scout to take her to Fort Mojave! It was obvious that she was growing desperate to find somebody to help her cross the desert. It was equally obvious that Anna would have to find a way to stop her.

After the wedding party last night, Mandy had come upstairs in tears. She had not confided her problems to Anna, but she had asked dismally, "Have you ever wanted something so desperately you thought you'd die if you couldn't have it, but you couldn't because of how desperately you wanted something else?"

Anna understood, because that was the way she felt about stealing away with Jonathan. She ached to do it because she was so afraid she might lose him one day, but she couldn't because she loved him too much to deny him his future. It wasn't too hard to guess that Mandy was equally torn between wanting to find Rodney and falling in love with Captain Robelard.

"Hello," was all Anna could bring herself to say to the captain who was smiling at her now. He had never mistreated her, but she had no reason to trust him, either. The fact that Mandy secretly yearned for him did not change the fact that he was white.

He stepped forward to touch Jonathan's cheek. "Miss Henderson tells me that no one in the world could take better care of the major's grandson, Anna. She always speaks of you with the highest praise."

Her eyes flickered up to his briefly. "He is a good baby." Her grip on the little one tightened. She didn't like it when the white people talked about the way she loved the child. It heightened her fear that some day they'd take him away from her.

Now the captain looked at her more seriously. "Anna, Miss Henderson tells me that some of your people are missing. She wants me to find out why they've disappeared."

"We know why they've disappeared," Anna burst out, surprised at the sudden rush of words. "We don't know why the Army does nothing to stop the miners."

She looked away, ashamed of her display of feeling. She had heard nothing new about the Hiding Ones, and after Salt Hair's last report on the slavers, she was more afraid than ever that they had never made it to the mountains. Until the *lonewis* ceremony next week, she could not learn anything new about them. Nor could she find out anything new about Rodney Potter.

"Anna, I want to help you," the captain said. "I want to help your people."

She did not answer. Her eyes merely bored into him with the truth as she knew it. He couldn't really want to help. He was white.

He held her gaze for a long moment. To her surprise, he repeated his lie. "I want to help your people whether you believe it or not. But we can discuss that later. You can come talk to me whenever you have something to say. In the meantime, I need your help, along with a vow of secrecy."

"My help?" It was an odd thing for a white officer to say.

He nodded. "There's something I want to make in the Indian way. In some places it's a man's job, but among the Yokutses I believe it is a woman's task."

Now she was intrigued. "What do you want me to make?" she asked, instinctively rocking Jonathan as he started to squirm.

"A rabbitskin blanket," the captain answered, his neck suddenly as bright as flame. "But I don't want you to make it for me, Anna," he clarified. "I just want you to teach me how."

It had not been easy to arrange for a meeting with Big Charlie. In the first place, Mandy didn't want either Drew or the major finding out about it, and in the second place, she was not about to track him down in a saloon. The only other place she expected him to visit was the sutler's, and it was there that she had made plans to meet him this afternoon.

The sutler's store was a busy place where local folks, as well as military families, went to buy everything from flour to harnesses. Mandy had gone there for Lucinda several times and had gotten friendly with the sutler, Joe Crawford. He'd cheerfully passed on her message to Big Charlie without asking any questions, and now, as the burly mountain man blotted out the opening to the dark building, Joe discreetly vanished into the back of the store.

"I understand you're lookin' fer me," Charlie boomed out. "Got some business in mind, I hear tell."

Mandy was loath to get too close because of his odor, but she held her ground as she said, "I'm looking for a seasoned scout to take me to Fort Mojave. I understand you've had experience crossing the desert between here and there."

He gave a yellow-toothed grin. "Ain't no part of that desert I don't know, ma'am. I remember in '56—"

"If I decide to hire you, you'll have time to tell me all about your colorful experiences, Mr. Charlie," Mandy interrupted, having been warned of his propensity to blabber. "What I want to know is how long it will take to get there, what supplies we would need and the amount of your fee."

He leaned back on his heels and slipped both hands in his ragged pockets. "How many of us are going?"

Mandy blanched. She couldn't very well take Percy with her on this risky mission, but she couldn't imagine going anywhere alone with this unappealing fellow. She wasn't even comfortable right here in the sutler's store.

"I'm not certain yet," she hedged. "You still haven't named a price."

He looked serious for a moment. "Fifty dollars, and that's a bargain. You won't find nobody else to do it for less than that."

Mandy didn't know if that was true. She only knew that if she paid this man fifty dollars and she didn't find Rodney, she wouldn't have much left to take care of Percy.

"I'll need to think about it, Mr. Charlie," she said slowly. "And I'd like to talk to some of your references."

"References?" His smile turned grim. "I done some scoutin' for the cavalry at Fort Apache when Captain Harris was out there. You can talk to him."

"I'll do that," Mandy answered, wondering if she could extract some information out of Betty Sue under the guise of casual gossip. If she asked the inquisitive woman about Charlie directly, she'd probably guess what Mandy had in mind and go straight to the major or Drew.

"When you be wantin' to head out?" He plucked out a chaw of tobacco from a dirty leather pouch and jammed it in the side of his mouth.

"I'm not sure yet, Mr. Charlie. Why don't we discuss that next time we meet."

"Fair enough." He studied her for a long, intense moment. "I'll be back here tomorrow around two."

Mandy shivered as he elbowed by her and pushed through the door. She waited until he had time to vanish, then walked out into the bright sunlight herself. She felt unclean, somehow, just from spending time with the mountain man. How could she survive a private journey with him?

She was still examining that question as she crossed the pretty stream that danced its way through the fort when she suddenly found herself face to face with Drew. She didn't know what building he'd been inside, but she had the definite feeling that he'd come out solely to talk to her. She hoped he hadn't seen Charlie. If

Drew realized that she'd talked to the old scout, he was sure to lecture her.

The instant her eyes met his, Mandy felt herself blush deeply. It was the first time she'd seen him since that fiery kiss they'd shared after the party, and she couldn't suppress the sudden rush of sensual need triggered by the mere sight of him.

Drew pulled off his hat and bowed slightly. "Miss Henderson." Then his voice dropped a note as he asked, "Or may I still call you Mandy?"

She tried to stiffen her spine; she tried to act sophisticated and haughty. She tried to pretend that she'd never kissed him and never wanted him to.

It was a wasted effort. The first words out of her mouth revealed everything she was feeling. "I don't know what to say to you, Drew."

His smile was slow but cautious, and it broadened when she said his name. "Say you're glad to see me. Say we're still friends. Say you've reconsidered your obligations to a dead man whom you once loved dearly but who surely would not want you to spend the rest of your life alone."

Mandy swallowed hard and stared at Drew's dusty boots. "I'm glad to see you," she said hesitantly. "And I hope we're still friends. But nothing has changed in regard to my commitment to Rodney."

There was a long silence, so long that Mandy finally had to lift her gaze to Drew's. His eyes were blue and full of feeling. His strong hands crumpled the edges of his hat.

"I hope you don't think I was just feeling carefree because of the party last night," he finally answered soberly. "I've tried to tell you more than once how very much I care for you."

Mandy tried to find an answer. She could not possibly reach out for him, but neither could she push him away.

"Drew," she finally admitted, "you surely know that I . . . I am not at all indifferent toward you."

The strain on his face lessened slightly. "And you surely know," he said as if it were a promise, "that I'm prepared to wait for you."

It was almost ten the next evening when Drew pulled up a chair beside Big Charlie. The Prairie Schooner was nearly empty, no girls were dancing, and the few men present were chatting in muted tones. Drew wasn't sure he could ease into a conversation with the blowhard casually, so he decided to come right to the point.

"I hear you've been approached about a private scouting mission," he said softly, taking care that no one else could hear. It was a precaution Mandy had apparently not exercised when she'd talked to Charlie yesterday.

Charlie grinned in a display of yellow teeth. "I take work where I can get it."

It wasn't the answer Drew wanted. He'd hoped the rumor Corporal Johnson had reported had been false, but he knew that Mandy might well have been desperate enough to seek help on her own. He suspected that she'd gone to Charlie in a desperate attempt to alleviate her guilt for kissing Drew.

He ached for the woman, and he'd made the decision to let her know. Hindsight showed him he'd been wrong to rush her.

Tensely, he asked, "Do you have any idea what I would do to a man who took a woman out into the desert and left her to die alone?"

Charlie's eyes narrowed. "Who said anything about leaving her to die? She wants to go to Fort Mojave. I can take her there."

Drew leaned forward. "No, you can't. Nobody can. She's going to stay safe and sound right here."

Charlie shifted restlessly. "We was talking lots of money, Captain. It ain't fair for you to interfere with a honest man trying to feed hisself."

Drew knew it was true, though he wasn't sure just how accurate the term "honest" was when applied to Charlie. He figured the man would do just about anything for the right price.

"How much did she offer to pay you?"

Charlie shook his head. "That's between me and the lady."

Drew stood up abruptly and towered over the big man. "Now it's between you and me."

Charlie's lips pulled back in a snarl. "Don't crowd me, Captain. I got as much right to be here as you do."

"No, you don't. You're a civilian with no ties whatsoever to the Army, and you've outlived your welcome at this post."

Now Charlie stood up. "You ain't got no right to throw me out. We ain't on Army property, and even if the Army sticks its nose in here, it's the major's call."

It was a moot point, but Drew didn't take time to argue about it. Sherwood would back him up on this for Mandy's sake, but he preferred to take care of it himself without dragging his old friend into it.

"Honest work for honest pay," Big Charlie whined. "That's all I'm asking."

"And all I'm asking is for you to tell the lady that you've had a change of heart."

Charlie's eyes narrowed again. "If somebody else was to pay me what she offered, I reckon I'd come out the same."

Drew grimaced. It was a lousy deal, but better than risking a major incident that was sure to upset Mandy. And she was already upset with him because of the kiss. He had a long way to go before he dared to present her with the wedding blanket he was determined to weave by himself. "I'd say that's fair," he reluctantly conceded.

"Yeah?" The yellow teeth stuck out again.

"Yes. But only if it's a bargain between gentlemen. Nobody else has to know."

Anna waited until Mrs. Larson was alone in the parlor and not likely to be disturbed. Mandy was upstairs with Percy, the major was out and Mrs. Harris had gone home. She delivered the sweetly cooing baby, then sat down on a stiff rawhide chair. Normally she left Jonathan alone with his grandmother during their special time, but today she had something on her mind.

"Mrs. Larson," she said carefully, "I would like to ask your advice about something."

The kind blue eyes met hers with interest. "Of course, Anna. I hope nothing's wrong."

"Not with me," Anna assured her. "I am very happy working here."

Mrs. Larson smiled at her. "And we're very happy with the work you do. You are absolutely wonderful with Jonathan."

Anna could not restrain her shy smile. It felt wonderfully warming to know that she had pleased Mrs. Larson. "It is easy to be with my baby," she admitted softly. "Sometimes it is hard to talk right to the other people who come to the house, but I am trying, Mrs. Larson. I am trying to act more white for you."

An uneasy expression flitted over the other woman's face, but Anna wasn't sure if it was because of her confession or because she'd slipped again and called Jonathan her baby.

"I know you're trying, Anna. I appreciate that. So does the major. I think that having Mandy here has been good for you."

Anna nodded. She wanted to tell Mrs. Larson that Mandy was her friend, but it seemed too presumptuous. Besides, she might have imagined the growing kinship she felt with the white woman who shared her room and often shared her private feelings when the children were sleeping late at night. Mandy had even offered to help her make a new dress and teach her how to sew, but it was possible that she was only being kind.

Carefully, she said, "It is Mandy I want to speak to you about. I think she needs my help."

"Your help?" Mrs. Larson asked, a whisper of surprise brushing her usual straightforward tone. "What exactly do you mean?"

Anna had to be careful now. She did not want to give away Mandy's secrets, but neither did she want her to die in a futile search of the Mojave for a man who was already dead. She wanted her to open her arms to the blanket-making white man who loved her and was still alive.

"She is growing desperate for word of her fiancé. I am afraid she will try to cross the desert. I do not want her to die that way."

Mrs. Larson's arms tightened around her grandson, and Anna knew she was thinking of her daughter, Sarah

Beth. Anna did not know all the details of what had happened to the girl. It was enough to know that Mrs. Larson had loved her dearly and she'd been murdered by Indians. Every now and then Mrs. Larson looked at Anna as though she couldn't quite recall that the Yokutses were nothing like the Apaches. Right now was one of them.

Quickly she said, "When we went to the reservation, my grandfather told her that our people would come from everywhere to the *lonewis*." When Mrs. Larson stared at her blankly, Anna added, "The dance of the dead. It is like a white man's funeral, but it is a funeral for all those who have gone before, especially those we have lost in the same year. It is a sad time at first, but it makes us feel happy in the end after all our tears are shed."

Mrs. Larson stared at her thoughtfully as she rubbed Jonathan's back. "And you think Mandy would benefit from some sort of healing ritual like that?"

Anna shook her head. "I think Mandy would admit the truth about her fiancé if I could bring her news about his death."

Mrs. Larson considered her words in silence.

"My grandfather will be there, and Salt Hair, too. They can ask questions for me, but I think I could ask better questions myself. Salt Hair does not know Mandy, and he . . . he has no use for white people, Mrs. Larson. Forgive me, but it is true."

Mrs. Larson nodded; it was no surprise. Salt Hair visited the house often, but he avoided the Larsons whenever he could.

"My grandfather is quite frail. The week will be hard on him. If someone says something, he might remember it later, but he will not spend his time asking questions the way I would."

Mrs. Larson stood up quickly, bouncing the baby over her shoulder so rapidly that Anna was afraid she'd wake him up. "And you want to go to this . . . Indian ceremony to ask questions about Rodney Potter? Is that what you want to do?"

Anna didn't like the hesitant tone in Mrs. Larson's voice, but it was too late to back down now. "I do not truly want to go the *lonewis* this year, Mrs. Larson. It is no longer"—she fumbled for the words—"the right place for me. But if you agree it would help put Mandy's heart at ease, I would be willing." In the ensuing silence, she added, "Of course I would never take Jonathan away from the fort without consulting you."

Mrs. Larson wheeled around. "Take Jonathan! To a week-long spectacle of wild heathen dancing?"

Anna lowered her eyes as though she'd been slapped in the face. "I would not be dancing. I would not stay for a week. I would only go to ask questions." In sudden defiance, she foolishly added, "I could have taken him along for a day without asking you and you would never have known. But I thought it might make you uneasy, so I asked for permission first."

"Uneasy?" Mrs. Larson took a deep breath and hugged Jonathan so tightly that he squeaked and opened up his eyes. At once he reached for Anna. Mrs. Larson ignored his outstretched arms. "Anna, let me make it clear to you that I do not want Jonathan anywhere near a group of Indians! Betty Sue says she can't imagine how I can even—"

She broke off then, but Anna knew what she'd been about to say. *Betty Sue says she can't imagine how I can even allow one in my home.*

Deeply hurt, Anna snapped, "I am not an Apache,

Mrs. Larson. I have never done harm to anyone."

A terrible silence fell on the room, broken only by Jonathan's low crying. It hurt Anna to listen to him, but she didn't dare hold out her arms.

Mrs. Larson tried to rock him for a long, tense moment, then abruptly reached out and handed him to Anna.

The baby quieted at once, and after a moment, Mrs. Larson started talking.

"Please forgive me if I hurt your feelings, Anna," she said in a voice filled with remorse. "I know who you are, and I cherish the way you care for my grandson. I just have so much hurt and fear left inside me after what happened to Sarah Beth that I have trouble, sometimes, thinking clearly."

"I understand," Anna said, grateful for the apology. She was still hurt deeply, but there was no point in saying so. At the moment all she wanted to do was make sure that Mrs. Larson was not upset enough to dismiss her.

The old blue eyes were full of anguish now. "It doesn't help any that I spend so much time with Betty Sue," she lamented, almost speaking to herself. "But you have to understand, Anna, that life in the Army would be unbearable for women if we didn't have each other. Nobody's perfect. Betty Sue has her faults, but she's there when I need her, and she's the only other officer's wife here. If I ever told her what I thought of her high-handedness, I'd be all alone."

Again Anna was silent, but she longed to say that she was here, too. When Mrs. Larson was lonely, she could talk to her.

Mrs. Larson sat down again, her eyes focused on the baby. At last she said, "I think you're right about Mandy needing more information before she does something foolish, and I think you might be able to learn something at the . . . whatever it's called. I think you should go, Anna—without Jonathan, of course. I'll have Sherwood arrange for a horse and escort for your journey."

Anna shook her head. "I would be grateful for the horse, but I cannot go with a soldier. None of us can reveal the location of the *lonewis* to anyone who is not a Yokuts."

Mrs. Larson said, "I thought you were going as a spy for Mandy."

Anna rubbed the baby's back. "I want to help a friend who is white," she said softly, "but that does not mean I would betray my people."

"I see," said Mrs. Larson. Then she stepped closer and took back the sleeping child.

As Anna left the room, she wasn't sure whether she'd failed or succeeded in her mission. She was going to the *lonewis* for Mandy, but she would have to be away from Jonathan several lonely days. And she had not, despite her best efforts, managed to convince Mrs. Larson that her desire to help proved that she belonged in this white household. She'd only made herself feel like a traitor.

As she thought of her grandfather, who might soon be left alone alone in the brush hut she'd helped him build, Anna wondered how long she could live in this awkward situation. Salt Hair had failed to win the first girl he'd chosen, but now he was talking about another one. Sooner or later, Anna knew she would have to make a choice between Grandfather and Jonathan, between her family's needs and her own. Like a dandelion in a windstorm, she felt herself disconnecting. She could not go on forever feeling half-Yokuts and half-white.

* * *

"How dare you!" Mandy raged at Drew the moment she cornered him near the flagpole the next evening. She tried to keep her voice low so that the soldiers nearby wouldn't hear their business, but her sense of betrayal was so keen that she was on the edge of losing all control. "I thought you were a man of honor. You promised to help me find my fiancé. But first you try to convince me he's dead, then you try to seduce me. When that doesn't work, you thwart my private plans to locate him!"

Drew's face turned gray. She didn't need to ask if Big Charlie had been lying. She had gone to see him to say she'd decided to make other plans, since she'd decided overnight that travelling with Big Charlie might be almost worse than setting off across the desert on her own. But before she could speak that he wouldn't be able to take her to Fort Mojave. His change of heart had been so dramatic, and so smug, that she'd realized at once something was wrong. It hadn't taken much pressure to get him to reveal his deal with Drew.

"Mandy, let's step into Major Larson's office," Drew said quietly, his tone hard as iron. "I don't think we need to discuss this in front of the whole post."

"We have nothing to discuss, Captain Robelard. You are a snake. I know it and you know it. There's nothing more to say."

Drew's lips tightened as he gripped her arm. "We'll step inside," he ordered in a tone that reminded her he was an officer in the U.S. Army.

She was too angry to speak again until they climbed the rude stairs, passed a startled looking guard and stepped inside the major's office. It was after supper, and the office was dark. Even when Drew lit a candle, she could barely see his face.

"Before you start hurling accusations around, don't you think you might want to ask me what really happened?"

"I know what happened." Mandy was too hurt to deal with details. What did they matter anyway? All that mattered was that she might never get to Fort Mojave . . . and that she'd been betrayed by Drew. "You bribed or bullied that man not to take me to find Rodney! You'll do anything to convince me that he's dead. I wouldn't believe it before, even when I thought you were a man I could respect. What makes you think I'll believe it now?"

Drew slammed one fist down on the table. Mandy winced in the face of his anger.

"I'm going to tell you what happened. Just once. You can believe it or not. I don't give a damn."

Mandy would have barked back at him but she couldn't find her voice.

"I heard you'd gone to see Big Charlie. I knew what you had in mind. I also knew that Charlie couldn't find his way out of a rathole. If I knew you were charging across the desert with that buffoon, I'd lose my mind."

The pain in his voice hurt her, but that didn't change the facts. "It's my life, Drew. Mine and Rodney's. You had no right to intervene."

"I have every right to try to keep you alive."

"You're trying to keep me from finding Rodney."

"I'm trying to keep you from ending up like him!"

Mandy felt a gust of shame, for she knew he was telling her the truth. She herself had decided that Big Charlie was not a reliable guide. If Sherwood Larson had found out her plans, he might have warned off the mountain man, too. But that didn't change Mandy's guilt and desperation.

"I can't just sit here, pretending you're searching for clues when I know I can't trust you," she burst out. "One way or another I'm going to cross the Mojave. I've got to exhaust every possibility or I'll never be able to live with myself!"

The ensuing silence hovered in the dark office so long it seemed to take on a life of its own. Drew's body was tightly coiled and his hands were balled into fists. Before Mandy had been frightened by his vehemence. Now she desperately wished he would say something . . . anything at all.

"Drew?" she pleaded softly. "Drew, please talk to me."

For another endless minute he stared at her, his eyes as dark as midnight. When he finally spoke, his words were brusque and bitter. "Why should I bother? You've made it quite clear you won't believe anything I tell you."

Mandy knew she'd hurt him deeply, and she longed to ease his pain. She hadn't been entirely fair in her accusations. She stifled a ghost of suspicion that part of her anger really should have directed at herself. She was the one who'd betrayed her own code of honor. She was the one trying to expiate her guilt. "I didn't say I didn't believe you, Drew," she told him gently. "I only said—"

"That I'd break my word to you. That I'd ignore evidence of Rodney's survival or even manufacture proof of his death."

"I never said—"

"When the woman I love says she's lost all respect for me, then I've got nothing left to say," Drew said curtly. Marching to the office door, he closed it with a bang behind him.

10

About the last thing Drew wanted to do the next morning was go to see Mandy to request permission to take Percy on the overnight hunting trip he'd promised him. But Percy had made it clear the last time they'd talked that he was counting the minutes until they could go, and Sherwood had just received word that the long awaited supply shipment for Fort Mojave would reach the post sometime tomorrow. The camel train, accompanied by Drew, Captain Harris and Lieutenant Markson's company of dragoons, was scheduled to depart a few days after that.

When Lucinda answered his knock on the door and ushered Drew inside, Mandy looked up from her sewing tensely. She said hello, but she did not meet his eyes as he courteously refused Lucinda's offer of afternoon tea and biscuits. Instead he stood stiffly a few feet from Mandy's chair as though she were a superior officer who'd recently pulled rank on him. At the moment, it seemed like an apt comparison.

"I'm sorry to disturb you, Miss Henderson," he said tightly, "but I must speak to you about Percy. I promised him I would prepare a manhood ceremony akin to the jimson weed initiation Salt Hair recently undertook. He seems to be looking forward to it."

Mandy concentrated on her stitching. "I'm sure that Percy realizes you have other responsibilities, Captain Robelard."

Drew got the message. She didn't want him near her and she didn't want him near the boy. Under other circumstances, he would have honored her request, but he had more important things to consider than her hurt feelings.

"Miss Henderson," he said tersely, "I am not in the habit of breaking my word to children."

Her eyes flashed up at his.

"I've just received orders to prepare to leave for Fort Mojave in three days' time, and it will be weeks or even months till I return."

He didn't add the obvious, that he was a soldier heading into enemy territory, and might not come back at all. At least he wouldn't be leaving a woman waiting for him the way Rodney Potter had done. Mandy had made her position only too clear on that front.

"I don't think he should have to wait that long. I'd like to take him hunting overnight in the mountains before I go. Naturally," he added crisply, "I will do nothing without your permission."

"Is that a new policy of yours, Captain?" Mandy asked sharply.

Lucinda shook her head in disapproval. "Mandy,

Drew has been very generous with his time with Percy and the boy desperately needs a father figure. I don't think—"

"He has a big brother who loves him and he remembers his own father quite clearly. I'm not sure it's in his best interest to grow attached to a soldier who just happens to be wandering through a few weeks of his life."

Drew clamped his jaw so tightly he thought he'd break a tooth. He remembered only too painfully Mandy's accusation that he was using the boy to get close to her. He was willing to do a lot for Percy, but he'd gone just about as far as he could go.

"I will tell Percy your feelings on the matter, Miss Henderson," he said acidly. "You can deal with him when his hopes are crushed." As her cheeks flamed, he added, "For good measure, why don't you take away the pony also? After all, I gave it to him, too."

"Drew!" This time Lucinda turned on him. "Mandy is a guest in my house and I won't let you talk to her that way."

"Yes, ma'am," Drew replied, instinctively pulling himself to attention.

"I won't have you treating me like an officer's wife instead of an old friend, Drew Robelard," Lucinda said tartly. "Now you apologize to Mandy and apologize to me."

He felt like a child called on the carpet. For a moment he toyed with stomping out of the house, but he knew none of it was Lucinda's fault.

Reining in his temper, he said, "I'm sorry, Lucinda, if I offended you. I did not mean to be rude."

Now her bright blue eyes looked sad and frustrated.

"I know you didn't, Drew. I shouldn't have snapped at you either."

She took his hand, as though he were one of her own sons, and squeezed it firmly. Then she turned to Mandy. "I don't know what's wrong between the two of you, but I suggest you patch it up. In the first place, it's not fair to Percy to miss out on the little fun in his young life just because you're mad at Drew. Besides that, Drew's going to be gone for a long time. You're going to eat your heart out if you don't mend your fences before he rides away."

On that note she strode briskly out of the parlor, leaving Drew to deal with Mandy by himself.

He stood at parade rest, not quite facing her, waiting for her to speak. The cool morning breeze ruffled the curtains and brushed a few loose strands of her hair. Mandy had stopped sewing, but her eyes were still on the tablecloth in her lap. When she finally glanced up at him, he was surprised to see that her eyes were wet with tears.

At last she said softly, "You may do whatever you think best with Percy. He very much enjoys his time with you."

Drew waited, but Mandy said nothing more. "I'd like to ride out with him this afternoon and make camp in the mountains," he finally replied. "We'll go hunting in the morning and come back by late afternoon."

"That will be fine, Drew."

He didn't know whether her use of his first name was intentional or just slipped out, but it touched something deep inside him. He still loved this woman, damn her! In spite of everything, he desperately wished he could find a way to break down all the barriers between them. The kiss they'd shared had been glorious and inevitable, but her resulting distrust of him had been too high a price to pay for it.

Slowly Mandy rose and turned to face Drew, a grim sort of sorrow clouding her lovely gray eyes. "What time should I tell Percy to meet you at the stable?" she asked stiffly.

"Four o'clock. I'll take care of our provisions, but he should prepare his own mount and bring his canteen."

"I'll tell him, Captain."

Drew felt a sagging sense of hopelessness as she used his title once more. Had it been an accident when she'd called him Drew before? Was there no hope that she might soften enough for one of them to make the first move to heal this breach?

Belatedly, he realized that Mandy had dismissed him and he had no good reason to continue standing in the parlor. He struggled to think of a way to prolong their conversation, a way to wash away the hard feelings of the day before, a way to recapture what they'd lost. But it was Mandy who'd made so many accusations, Mandy who'd made it clear he'd lost her respect. All he'd done was try to save her life and confess unwisely that he loved her. To speak of his feelings now could only make things worse.

"Good day, then, Miss Henderson," he said quite formally.

She nodded, just once, without quite meeting his eyes, then purposely picked up her sewing.

Drew took a deep breath as he turned and left the room. Who was he kidding? He still loved Mandy Henderson, loved her desperately, and he was a long, long way from giving her up. She might be mad at him, but she still felt something for him, or her eyes would not have filled with tears when he'd spoken to her so harshly. He knew she wasn't just fighting for Rodney Potter's memory. She was fighting for her own set of values, her own self-worth.

Drew marched across the compound, certain that he had only two choices now. He had to forget Mandy altogether, which he wasn't at all sure he could ever do, or he had to produce Rodney Potter . . . alive and kicking. Man to man, Drew might yet have a chance to win her. He was sure to be defeated by a ghost.

It was still quite dark when Percy woke up the next morning. The captain was shaking his shoulder, covering his lips with one finger to remind him of the need for absolute silence. Percy threw off the veil of sleepiness and rose at once. No matter what, he was determined to meet whatever challenges came his way today.

Captain Robelard picked up his musket, then handed a slightly smaller one to Percy. Last night he'd told Percy that he'd be entitled to keep it once he shot his first buck. Percy was determined to go home with the buck and the long gun.

The night before had been exhilarating and exhausting. They'd hiked for miles up the pine-studded canyon, first on horseback and then on foot. The captain had taught Percy how to set up camp, how to picket the horses, how to make fire in the wilderness. He'd shown him how to whittle funny little men out of dry oak twigs and how to cook beans in the dark. Then they'd talked about hunting in the morning and all the things

Percy would have to remember. When they set off at dawn, the captain had warned him, they could not talk. Deer could hear and smell humans under almost any conditions. They must blend into the forest completely.

They didn't wear antlers and deerskins like the Yokuts hunters did, but they both wore weathered boots and heavy leather jackets that had seen a lot of wear. Underneath, the captain wore a tired old uniform, but Percy wore a baggy pair of pants and a cotton shirt that the captain had found for him along with the other clothes. Percy revelled in the comfort, and pushed from his mind the certainty that when he returned to the fort, Mandy would made him take a bath.

Mandy had been acting very, very odd the day before. Actually, she'd been acting rather strange for several days now, but she'd looked almost frightened when she'd told him he was going to spend the night with Captain Robelard. She'd fussed over him so much that he'd finally snapped, "Geez, Mandy, how am I supposed to become a man if you keep treating me like a little kid?"

To his surprise she'd started to cry. "I want you to grow up, Percy," she'd assured him. "I just want you to be careful in the mountains. I love you so much."

He knew Mandy loved him, and he'd thought she trusted the captain, too. But he hadn't seen the two of them together since the night of the wedding, and every time Percy had tried to talk about the captain since then, she'd cut him off. Lately she hadn't even wanted to talk about Rodney.

Percy felt a moment's guilt as he realized that he hadn't been thinking much about Rodney lately, either. When he was with the captain, he didn't feel all alone anymore. Oh, he knew he hadn't been alone before, but Mandy was, after all, a woman. It wasn't the same as learning how to hunt from a man.

Percy followed the captain in utter silence for an hour before he spotted a rack of antlers through the nest of deep pines. He knelt down and braced himself, as the captain had taught him, while the captain nodded his approval and stood to one side.

Percy could feel the flare of excitement running through him. He was going to do it. He was going to shoot this deer! He was going to prove to everybody that he was as much of a man as Salt Hair.

He fired. The musket slammed into his shoulder so hard it knocked him flat. His face flamed as he heard the deer thunder across the mountainside. Struggling to his feet, he fought back tears.

Mandy, he knew, would have cuddled him and told him he was just a little boy, after all, and he wasn't old enough to go hunting anyway. For a minute, he wondered if it might be true.

Then he heard the captain say, "No man ever gets the first deer he sights in the morning, Percy. Let's go find another one."

Percy shook off the leaves and wiped away the tears. The captain hadn't given up on him! He slowly stood up, retrieved his fallen gun, then scrambled after his *shaugh-num-uh*.

Salt Hair's directions to the *lonewis* were accurate, and Anna arrived on her Army horse without difficulty. She'd been afraid to travel in her old deerskin dress in case she encountered a slaver, so she hadn't changed

until she'd come within sight of the Yokuts campfire.
But she still carried a knife that the major had given
her with the quiet warning to keep an eye out at all
times for strangers. She'd been heartened by his concern, but his worry had only intensified her own sense
of danger.

She was surprised at how stiff the hide felt compared to the supple cotton dresses she was used to
wearing. She was also surprised at how big her Army
horse looked compared to the Indian mustangs in the
tule-rope corral. There were so few horses and so
many people! Most of them had walked to the *lonewis,*
some as far as a hundred miles. She wondered how
many of the Hiding Ones had made it down from the
mountains.

As she announced herself to the Yokuts watchman
and entered the gathered circle of mourners, some lifting up the Yokuts high-pitched grieving wail, she realized sadly that her old dress was no longer enough to
make her feel as though she belonged here. It had been
several years since she had truly been in mourning, and
Mrs. Larson had trimmed her long hair so it hung neatly over her shoulders even when it wasn't pinned back.
Most of the other Indians' faces were dark with
graphite clay, but Anna's was unblackened. New
mourners could not bathe or change their clothes until
the *lonewis*—no matter how many weeks might pass—
but she had washed herself just that morning.

She found the Winatun, seated grandly in the center
of the convivial chaos, greeting people from everywhere, accepting offerings of food and designating
campfire locations. The singers were already in cos-
tume, their faces black and white-spotted, their stom-

achs black and white-striped. Even though the Hohuno would not perform until tomorrow, he was already dressed in the smooth skin and feathers of a fish crane. He looked like an owl with those feather horns on each side of his head and the two large pieces of abalone shell gleaming roundly just above his eyes. Anna remembered as a child being absolutely terrified of him.

Now, as she stood alone in this circle of traditional Yokutses gathered at their most sacred ceremony, she felt terrified again. Had only a year passed since she'd attended her last *lonewis*? Had she given up her roots so easily for the sake of regular food and smooth cotton dresses? Was she trying to act white solely for Jonathan? Or was she being called by another source of her ancestry, the voice of her stronghearted white father? He had taught her from birth that good people come in all varieties, but her life had been so hard since his death that when she'd met the Larsons she'd had to learn the lesson all over again.

Anna felt a shiver as she realized she could never feel at home again on the reservation. She hoped the Larsons would take her with them when they left Fort Tejon, but when she remembered the look on Mrs. Larson's face the last time she'd talked about her daughter's death at Indian hands, she knew there was no good reason to believe that they would. And even if that miracle happened, how could she live with herself if she abandoned Grandfather?

Her uneasiness grew as she moved from fire to fire asking questions. No one had heard a word about a missing white man, and no one cared about one, either. Many of the Hiding Ones had not yet arrived, and their situation was of far greater concern to the gathered Yokutses than that of a solitary white stranger. They were irritated and suspicious of Anna's inquiries and let her know it, too.

At sundown, when Salt Hair and Grandfather finally arrived, Anna felt a sharp gust of relief. But as she greeted them with fresh gooseberries she'd lovingly collected in her burden basket, she knew she was only going through the motions. She was a white woman now, and she would never again find peace as a Yokuts squaw.

Mandy could see the difference in Percy the minute he walked in the door the next afternoon. If the purpose of a *shaugh-num-uh* ceremony was to turn a boy into man, or at least send him in that direction, then Drew's makeshift version had surely done it. While Percy didn't exactly swagger into the Larson's house, his shoulders were thrown back and his bootheels rang out forcefully on the wooden floor.

Behind him, looking tired and wary, marched Drew.

He met Mandy's eyes directly as he nodded with the briefest of hellos. For a long moment she couldn't help but stare at him, fighting the urge to throw her arms around his neck. But she didn't dare, for different reasons than the ones which kept her from hugging Percy.

She'd had plenty of time to think about Drew since that terrible fight in the major's office, but she still wasn't sure how she could fix the rift between them. Drew didn't want a simply apology for her ire or her accusations. What he wanted was a confession of her feelings for him . . . and a promise to give up her search for Rodney.

It would be so easy! When she stood so close to Drew, the desire to yield to him was almost unbearable. Mandy had thought she knew where her duty lay, but Drew had been right when he'd said that turning his love aside would not bring back her family. If Rodney was truly dead, was learning to care for Drew Robelard so disloyal?

She wished that Anna would return with word from the *lonewis* before the camel train left for Fort Mojave. If she knew that Rodney was still alive, she could find the will to keep fighting Drew; and if she knew he was dead, she could make her peace with him. But Anna had only been gone two days, and the *lonewis* was supposed to last through the weekend. Mandy was afraid her anguish would last the rest of her life.

"Good afternoon," squeaked Percy, his voice as deep as he could make it.

She stifled a grin. "Good afternoon, honey. Did everything go well?"

He straightened up until he looked an inch taller. "Yes, it did. We brought home enough venison to feed all of us tonight."

Now she did allow herself a smile, but a proud and grateful one. "That will be a welcome relief from Army beef, Percy."

For the first time, Drew spoke. "I think you should know he shot it himself."

Mandy's eyes met his briefly, and she found herself unable to face the defeat she read there. "Thank you for teaching him how to hunt, Captain. I'm sure that will be a useful skill while we're out here."

"A man needs to be able to provide for his family anywhere, Mandy," Percy told her, in words she was almost certain were a paraphrase of Drew's.

"I'm sure that's true," she replied, wondering if hunting was a skill Rodney had learned on his journeys. As she recalled, he had never much cared for guns.

"The deer is outside on my horse. I'll bring it around to the kitchen if you like." Drew's voice was stiff and unyielding.

Mandy longed for him to soften toward her, to give the slightest hint that he'd forgiven her for her unjust accusations, but his spine was even straighter than Percy's. Over and over again she could hear him saying, *When the woman I love says she's lost all respect for me, then I've got nothing left to say.* Drew Robelard was a man whose essence was honor. When she'd accused him of breaking faith with her, she'd speared his Achilles' heel. He was still wounded and angry, but he hadn't taken back his confession of love for her. Only to herself could Mandy admit that she loved him, too.

"That would be kind of you, Captain," she said tensely. She would have said something else, anything to ease the hurting, but Drew tipped his hat to her smartly, shook Percy's hand and marched away.

For a moment she was tempted to follow him, but suddenly Percy, a little boy again, was clinging to her hand. "Can you believe it, Mandy? I shot my own deer! Captain Robelard showed me how to set up a tent and start a fire. He taught me what roots were safe to eat and what trees were too tall for a bear to climb. He even taught me to clean my own gun, Mandy. I know how to do everything safely now, so you don't have anything to worry about." By now he was wriggling like a puppy. "I never had so much fun in my whole life!"

Mandy was thrilled to see him so joyful. She hadn't seen him smile like that since before the fire. "I'm so glad you had a successful ceremony, Percy. It was certainly kind of Captain Robelard to help you."

"I think so, too, but when I tried to thank him he said I was the one doing him a favor."

"Doing him a favor?" Mandy asked curiously, her suspicions raising again. "What do you think he meant by that?"

Percy stiffened. "I'm not sure I'm supposed to tell you. It was something that sort of slipped out. You know, while we were talking man stuff."

Mandy felt a fresh surge of anger welling up inside her. Had she been right on the night of the wedding party when she'd accused Drew of using the gift of the pony as a means to soften her heart toward him? Had Drew arranged this hunting trip just to wiggle back into her good graces?

"Percy, I want you to tell me exactly what he said," Mandy ordered, "and I want you to tell me right now."

"Yes, ma'am." Percy slumped. "He said he was doing all the things with me he'd always wanted to do with his own little brother when it was time for him to become a man."

It was not at all the answer Mandy had expected. "Captain Robelard has a little brother?"

Percy shook his head. "Not any more. He died when he was my age. Of cholera, I think. Or yellow fever. Anyway, the captain rode fifteen miles across a mountain all by himself in the middle of the night when he was nine trying to get a doctor to save him. But his pony, a shaggy gray one like Daisy, stepped in a snake hole and broke its leg, so Captain Robelard had to run the rest of the way on foot. Once he got there, his feet were so swollen he couldn't put shoes on for a week, but he was too late anyway. By the time the doctor got to his little brother, Eddie was already dead." Percy blinked at her from behind his round glasses. "The captain says he still has dreams about Eddie sometimes. He cried about him more than once when he was a kid, he said. That's why he's trying so hard to find Rodney, Mandy. He knows how much it means to me. And he knows how much it means to you."

Mandy had no reply for those innocent, heartfelt words. She felt unbearably selfish as she realized how much she'd told Drew about her own life and her own problems and how little she'd inquired about his own. She'd accused him of using Percy for his own ends and deliberately trying to block her from finding Rodney. No wonder he'd been so angry. She couldn't blame him for not forgiving her.

But then again, she hadn't asked for his forgiveness. She had not apologized. She had told him to leave her alone, to forget that he'd kissed her, to wipe from his memory the way she'd shamelessly pressed against his thighs.

Tomorrow he'd lead a caravan across the very desert route where Rodney had disappeared. If Drew vanished also, Mandy would have to live with the memory of the anger he'd taken to the Mojave with him.

It was a possibility that frightened her even more than the likelihood that she'd never see Rodney again.

When the troops assembled the next morning, it was not yet dawn. The horses were restless, eager to be off, and the camels were making a din to wake the dead.

Drew himself was too tense to be eager, too depressed to even notice he was tired. The few moments he'd spent with Mandy at the Larsons' yesterday had just about shredded his pride. It was one thing to tell himself that he'd given up on courting her and would outgrow his love for her in time. Looking into her sad and lovely eyes was another matter altogether. It was better for both of them, Drew decided, that he would be gone for a good long time.

Drew expected another shipment of Yokuts supplies to arrive in his absence, but he'd left Sherwood instructions to keep a close eye on Lieutenant Isley if it did. Isley had the easiest access to the manifests, and and his bitterness worried Drew. He didn't talk like a man who was determined to keep an untarnished military record.

Captain Harris seemed content enough with his light paperwork duties and his free time for hunting, but Drew wanted to keep an eye on him, too. Sherwood had assigned Captain Harris to join the supply train to Fort Mojave ostensibly because he needed field experience, but mainly to eliminate one suspect in case any more thefts occurred. For a multitude of reasons, Drew had eliminated Corporal Johnson from the list entirely, though he still reluctantly felt the need to watch Abu.

Drew had just mounted up when bright-eyed Johnson scampered toward him, scratching at an acne scar on his neck. "Sir? I hate to trouble you, but Miss Henderson would like to speak to you before you leave the fort. I told her you were very busy, but she insists."

Stifling his sudden sense of dread, Drew glanced back at the main barn, where Mandy stood woodenly in front of the adobe wall. She looked as proud and stubborn as ever, but there was something almost fearful about her tense expression. He didn't want to look at her; he didn't want to see her pain. He'd decided there was no hope in loving Mandy and he'd been doing his damnedest to thrust her from his mind.

"I imagine she's got some question about how you're going to find word of her fiance, sir," suggested Johnson.

"No doubt," Drew replied. For just a moment he considered refusing to speak to her, but he knew he couldn't turn his back on Mandy and just ride off.

"Tell her I'll be there as soon as I can."

"Yes, sir."

It took Drew a good ten minutes before he could break away, and by then the camels and mules were pulling out of the fort. Mandy still stood by the barn, eyes wary and watchful as she waited.

Drew rode up close beside her, but he stayed mounted. "Miss Henderson," he said cooly, tipping his hat.

"Good morning, Captain. It was good of you to see me." Her voice was quiet and subdued. Her eyes were puffy, as though she'd spent a good portion of the night crying.

"How can I help you this morning, ma'am?"

She took a step closer to his mount. Her words seemed practiced, almost forced, but emotion throbbed beneath them anyway. "You can tell me you forgive me for speaking out of turn the other day," she said in a dark, husky tone. "I was angry and upset. I said things I didn't mean and that I deeply regret."

Drew's gaze met hers only briefly. "We all speak out of turn sometimes, Miss Henderson. No harm done."

It was the right answer, but it didn't seem to be

enough for Mandy. She took a step closer and laid one hand on his gelding's side. Startled, Drew glanced at her again, realizing that with the adobe wall behind her, no one could see her fingers as they slowly closed around his boot.

"Please, Drew. Don't ride off like this."

His heart did a somersault as she said his given name, but he didn't dare answer.

"I know you'll do everything you can to find Rodney. I know I can trust you. I'm so sorry I accused you of . . . well, of anything."

Drew took a deep breath. He knew what was motivating her apology. He was heading into the same desert that had claimed her fiancé, and she was afraid it might claim him also. She didn't want to live the rest of her life remembering that they'd parted in anger. In spite of how badly she'd hurt him, he wanted to spare her that, too.

"It's all right, Mandy," he assured her. "It's all right between us. Over and done."

Her eyes flashed up at him with such joyful relief that he felt like a cad for having made her suffer. He wanted to reach out to her, to hold her or even kiss her goodbye, but he didn't dare. He wasn't sure what she wanted, and he wasn't sure that Napoleon blocked everyone's view. He was also a long way from being willing to risk inflaming his still-smoldering feelings.

"I'll find out what happened to Rodney, Mandy," he vowed, determined to finish the job he'd set out to do. "I swear it."

"I know you will," she whispered. "I believe in you."

Drew swallowed hard, unbearably moved by the

passion in her voice. He knew he had to go, but he thought he'd die if he had to leave without knowing how she felt about him now. He didn't think he had the strength to ride off without touching her.

And then Mandy saved him. She leaned against the horse and reached for his hand with both of hers. Closing her eyes, she pressed his palm against her silken cheek.

"Come back, Drew," she begged him. "Come back to me."

Drew fought a sudden swelling in his groin. Was this real? Was Mandy finally reaching out for him? Had she finally decided to accept Rodney's death?

He didn't have time to analyze the situation. Mandy had come to him this morning, and not just to apologize and say goodbye. If he'd been staying at the fort he could have made her wait, or even spent some time making up his own mind. After all, he'd already decided to forget her. It was prudent. It was wise.

But neither prudence nor wisdom entered into his feelings at the moment. Mandy had just admitted that she longed for him. There was only one thing to say.

As he cupped her face with barely banked hunger, Drew pleaded, "Promise me you'll wait for me. Promise me you won't take any chances."

She nodded once, eyes swimming, before she fiercely kissed his palm.

Drew swallowed hard as he slipped his fingers deep into her hair and pressed her face against his booted leg. He was dying to reach down and kiss her; he didn't think he'd ever wanted to touch a woman more desperately. Never had he been more loath to ride away.

"I won't disappear out there, Mandy," he vowed. "I'll come back for you, believe me."

She started to sob. "Be careful, Drew. I couldn't bear to lose you. You don't know what it's cost me to keep on pushing you away." Her eyes shone with love for him. "It'll all be different when you come back. I promise."

It was not until Drew galloped off a moment later that he remembered that he was not the only man Mandy had promised to wait for.

He wondered what she'd do if Rodney Potter came back first.

11

When Anna saw Mandy, she didn't need to ask what had happened. The shadows that had haunted her pretty face for so long had vanished. There was still a ghost of fear, and maybe a hint of guilt as well, but her eyes shone with the joy of a woman who knows she's cherished. Anna's eyes had not shone like that for many years, but once she had been cherished, too.

She had learned nothing new at the *lonewis* that might help Mandy, but she had learned a great deal about herself. Although she often felt out of place at Fort Tejon, she had come to belong there. Even with the closest members of her own family, she no longer felt entirely at ease.

Anna had stayed as long as she could bear the ritual, which had once been so dear to her, and now seemed so very strange, but by the third day, it was obvious that many of the Hiding Ones were not coming. Those who arrived reported rumors of slavers working more diligently than ever, and much white man's sickness among those bands that still hid in the hills. The reservation Yokutses reported that more of them had been stolen lately, almost out from under Lieutenant Cox's nose. He sent his men out on daily sweeps of the area, but they never seemed to catch the slavers. Nobody felt safe anymore.

Anna hadn't felt safe herself riding back to the fort alone. She'd been too proud to ask her son to travel with her, but he'd joined her silently when the time for leaving came. They'd had a good trip, stopping to share a meal at an abandoned Yokuts hut, one of the many hidden ones that all Yokutses used as way stations when travelling far from home. There, he'd brought up the subject of Grandfather again.

"You can see he needs someone with him," Salt Hair said softly. He did not need to remind her of how totally the *lonewis* had sapped Grandfather's energy. "I do not know if I can make him come with me to a new place."

"Have you found the right woman yet?" Anna asked.

Salt Hair's eyes lit up with a curious expression. "I did not think I had, until last night. But then I met one of the Hiding Ones."

"Is she going back into hiding?"

Salt Hair nodded. "Yes, but she told me where she is going. She has told nobody else."

Anna did not need to ask any more questions. Her heart was full of joy for Salt Hair and fear for herself. She did not know what to do for Grandfather. She only knew that the Hiding girl had given her heart to Anna's son.

*   *   *

"Nothing?" Drew asked Lieutenant Markson when he reported to the temporary officers' quarters they'd been alloted at Fort Mojave. Like Drew and Harris, Markson had spent the day asking questions about Rodney Potter. "Nobody's heard a word about them?"

Markson shook his head. "Nothing since the survey party left here in October. But I did find out the name of the Chemehuevi scout they hired to guide them. I'm told that Best Horse was newly married and well-respected by our people and his own. I hoped we could talk to him, but since he left with Potter, nobody ever saw him again. After his band came here looking for him, the locals figured he was dead."

Beside Drew, Captain Harris said, "Well, we've done all we can do. Now that the men are rested, I think we should start back home. Don't you agree, Lieutenant?"

Lieutenant Markson, outranked by both of the other men, stiffly replied, "My orders from the major were to accompany the camel train to Fort Mojave and perform any other search and rescue operation that Captain Robelard might command. I think the animals could use another day at rest, sir, but my men are prepared to execute the captain's plans."

It was a subtle rebuke of Harris, who had a habit, Drew had noticed, of ignoring the chain of command. He often made a proclamation which sounded like an order, undercutting Drew's authority or bypassing the lieutenant when he pushed around the men.

Now Drew said carefully, "I've never been married, Harris, but I hear it sometimes makes a soldier a bit too eager to return to his own fireside."

Harris's handsome face split into a laugh. "That's

rich, Captain. If only you knew!" As Drew stared at him wordlessly, he recovered himself. "The major made it clear that you were in command, Captain Robelard. I did not intend to challenge your orders. I was merely venturing an opinion."

"And that opinion is?"

"Well, sir, I simply feel that we've spent enough time asking questions about a dead civilian who has no ties to the Army. I find it hard to believe that Miss Henderson's curiosity is worth so much trouble."

She's worth everything to me, a voice within Drew countered. He wondered how the other men would feel if they knew his personal stake in carrying out this promise. That last sweet scene with Mandy had told him what he'd needed to know: with words and without, she had promised to love him for all time. They had not had time to speak of marriage then, but words were no longer necessary between them. She surely understood that his talk of the Zuni wedding blanket had not been idle chatter. Drew was certain she would marry him before he returned to Washington if he could only bring back the proof she needed to put any lingering doubts about Rodney's death to rest. Not just her doubts, but Percy's.

"Lieutenant Markson, we'll leave the camels here with Abu and ride out to the Chemehuevi camp tomorrow and talk to Best Horse's people," Drew said. After all, his orders embraced more than solving the Yokuts problem and checking out the camels. Sherwood had also commanded Drew to find out the truth about Rodney Potter. "Perhaps the Indians will know something that hasn't come to the attention of the Army."

"Yes, sir. I'll prepare the men."

As the young lieutenant saluted and disappeared, Captain Harris reiterated his opinion. "I don't understand your thinking, Captain. We're heading deep into *kwanami* territory for no good reason. Potter's dead and we all know it. We've talked to everyone who knows anything at Fort Mojave. Isn't that enough information to take the girl?"

It might have been enough for Drew if the civilian woman had been anyone but Mandy. But he'd promised her he'd do his best, and he'd be damned if he'd fail to keep that promise. The Chemehuevi scout was his last lead, and he owed it to Mandy to check it out. When he took her for his woman, he did not want there to be any lingering doubt for either one of them.

The days lagged for Mandy once Drew set off for Fort Mojave. She was still deeply frustrated that she had not been allowed to make the journey herself, not only because she so desperately missed Drew but because she was quite certain that no matter how hard he tried to find some trace of Rodney, there might be some tiny clue which might elude him. There were things she knew about Rodney Potter that she wouldn't think to mention, things that might be triggered by his handwriting or one of his belongings.

Her anxiety was no longer just for Rodney. Now she was worried about Drew as well. Fort gossip buzzed with the story of a recent attack by *kwanamis* on a Chemehuevi band, and the Army track to Fort Mojave cut through the southern tip of Chemehuevi country. Mandy didn't think she could live with herself if Drew vanished in the Mojave. She already grieved for one man. She couldn't bear to grieve for two.

But she also knew that she'd be in a terrible quandary if they both returned. She had not meant to make a commitment to Drew before he'd left the fort; she'd only meant to apologize so they could part on good terms. But something had happened when she'd seen the anguish in his eyes that morning. Quite suddenly nothing had mattered to her more than letting Drew know how much she loved him. For an instant, Rodney Potter had simply vanished. Only now that Drew was far away could guilt and sanity return.

But she refused to look back, refused to indulge in self-flagellation. She had always known that Rodney must be dead. There was no other reason why her life-long friend would not have sent some word. She realized now that holding on to Rodney had been a way of clinging to her family, just as Drew had said. She had refused to face the future because it held nothing but despair; all her joy had been in the past.

Now Drew had changed all that.

Night after night she found herself flushed with desire for him; day after day she wandered through the stables, hoping for some gossip among the men that hinted he might be on his way back. Poor Hadj, who had been left behind with a sore back and moved to the horse stables for the duration, looked as lonely as Mandy, and she'd taken to smuggling him pieces of sugar pine bark when no one was looking. Few things at Fort Tejon were considered stranger than regarding a camel as a friend.

Mandy had other friends to warm her life as well. She and Lucinda grew increasingly closer, and she was enjoying the time she spent teaching Anna how to sew. Almost daily Mandy rode with Lieutenant Isley, who'd proved to be a very good instructor. Although Percy insisted that his *shaugh-num-uh* had taught him everything he needed to know, he was happy to come along with them.

Lieutenant Isley was a quiet man, always courteous, though sometimes boring. He also seemed to be looking for something, though she couldn't begin to imagine what. He had a disconcerting habit of wandering off whenever she and Percy stopped to rest, usually within a mile of passing some old barn or abandoned Yokuts hut. Drew had often done the same thing, but Mandy had never questioned him since she assumed it had something to do with his secret search for the missing Yokutses. More than once she was tempted to ask Lieutenant Isley if he was working on the same project, but Drew had told her to mention it no one, so of course she never did.

As time went on, her list of questions to ask Drew grew longer and longer. She wanted to ask him about the Yokutses, and she wanted to asked his advice on helping Percy accept the fact that he'd never again see his big brother. She wanted to ask him how he could survive so many weeks without a single kiss or rapturous hug. She wanted to ask him if it was unseemly for a woman to ache so sensually for her man.

But each day passed with no word from Drew.

It took a good two hours of formalities before Drew got to talk to the Chemehuevi chief with only an interpreter present. The dragoons had looked uneasy riding into an Indian camp, but Drew felt safer here than he'd felt on the desert. Lieutenant Markson's men were highly trained, but there weren't very many of them.

They were deep in *kwanami* country now, and for the past two days Drew felt quite certain that they were being followed.

"We are trying to find some men who were led into the desert by a Chemehuevi scout named Best Horse," Drew explained. "We are told he was a trustworthy man who always did his tribe proud. But no one has seen him since he left Fort Mojave, and no one has seen the other white men."

The chief nodded as the interpreter repeated Drew's words. He spoke in a low, steady tone that was slightly disapproving.

"He says that that Best Horse was a good warrior, one of his best. He would be alive if he had not tried to help the white party," the interpreter relayed.

Tensely, Drew questioned, "Does the chief have some proof that he is dead?"

Again there was an exchange before the interpreter said, "When Best Horse did not return when he should have, the chief sent several men to follow the trail Chemehuevi scouts always take toward the mountains. They found a feathered war party pike painted in the way of the *kwanamis*. They found the shell necklace Best Horse's new bride made for him. They found many bodies."

Drew's stomach tightened. This was the news he had prayed for, but somehow he could not rejoice. He didn't want to give up Mandy to Rodney Potter, but he hated to tell her that her worst fears were well founded. He hated even more to tell Percy that his brother was dead.

"White bodies?"

The chief nodded.

"How many?"

"He does not know for sure. Some had been cut into pieces by human hands, some strewn about by the wolves and coyotes. His guess is that there were six or seven. There is no way to know for sure."

Drew swallowed back his bile. He couldn't count the number of dead men he'd seen in his career, but he always felt fresh grief for each and every one. "Can you show me where they are buried?"

The chief shook his head. "Best Horse has been laid to rest in the way that befitted a Chemehuevi warrior. The white bones were left where they were."

Drew fought back a rush of anger. He knew that many white men looked on Indian dead with the same indifference. Still, he had to say, "We would like to bury the white bones our way."

There was a lengthy dissertation by the chief before the interpreter said, "He will tell you where he found Best Horse, but he will send no men to guide you. He has lost one good man to the *kwanamis* for white men. He will not lose another one."

"How long have you been in the Army, Lieutenant?" Mandy asked Isley one balmy morning as they slowly jogged their horses through a field of purple clover. The hillsides were covered with fivespot and popcorn flowers, glistening with dew. Up ahead scouted Percy, his gun in its boot just in case he found anything worth hunting, though Mandy hoped he wouldn't try to use the gun.

"Too long, Miss Henderson," Isley replied without a smile. "I was commissioned right out of West Point."

"So you always wanted to be a soldier?"

"Believe it or not, I did," he said drily. "I wanted excitement and glory, and I thought I'd find it in the Army."

Determined to cheer up her glum companion on this magnificent spring day, Mandy said, "You must feel quite proud of all you've accomplished, sir. Your career must be quite gratifying."

He gave her a look that was quite daunting. "Gratifying, Miss Henderson? One promotion in seven years? A decade spent moving from one fort in Hades to another in hell? No one to share my days and nights with? Does that sound gratifying to you?"

Mandy wished she could think of something to say to brighten his outlook on life. She could guess why dull, chunky Isley had found both promotional and marital opportunities limited, but she wondered if his negativism didn't bring some of his bad luck on himself. She was still searching for just the right way to word her question response when Jessie abruptly veered sideways with a snort.

At first, Mandy was too angry to be frightened. She had gone riding almost daily in Drew's absence to prove to herself and to him that she could control her horse if coyotes, or some other trauma, ever spooked the animal again. But suddenly Jessie was trembling and twitching almost explosively, and Mandy's efforts to calm her down seemed to be of no avail.

Suddenly she realized that the lieutenant's horse was rearing, and Isley was struggling to keep from being unseated as well. The pines that flanked the mountain path were shaking back and forth, and the ground beneath Mandy was wobbling too. It was like trying to swim in thick pudding. Never in her life had he felt more confused and disconcerted. In her panic, she forgot everything she'd ever learned about riding a horse.

Far away, Mandy heard Percy screaming. "Percy!" she shouted back in terror, desperate to find him as she saw his riderless gray pony streaking past her. Her mare broke free of Mandy's death grip on the reins at the same moment and tore after the pony. Mandy wasn't sure if she were more relieved or frightened when she lost her seat entirely and flew to the ground.

"Percy!" she screamed again, struggling to rise to her feet. But she couldn't get her legs free of the long tangled skirts, and the ground refused to stop shaking.

Out of the corner of her eye she realized that lieutenant Isley, though silent, was struggling desperately for control of his terrified horse. The animal's eyes were bloodshot and its ears were laid back. Isley kept pulling on the reins, but the gelding was thrashing so violently that one hoof banged over and over again against a huge black oak trunk.

Then, quite suddenly, the earth stopped moving, and so, after a minute, did the horse. The world was a silent and solid place once more. The restoration of sanity was so perfect that Mandy hated to break the peace, but she couldn't stop herself from screaming for Percy again.

He didn't answer, but she heard him crying from behind a grove of trees. She struggled for breath as she stood up and ran toward the little boy, feeling a lightning bolt of panic deep in her heart. "Honey, are you all right?" She raced toward him as rapidly as her bruised legs would allow.

Percy just kept sobbing, even when Mandy reached him. "I want to see Rodney," he cried as she took him in her arms. Mandy had heard him ask for his brother a thousand times, but never with such raw anguish.

"We're going to find him, Mandy, aren't we? We're going to find Rodney and go home?"

Mandy hugged him as hard as she could. "Of course we are," she lied. "We'll all be back in Boston in no time at all."

Suddenly the glory of the sunny day had vanished. Even if Drew came back safe and sound, Mandy knew that they could not marry quickly. Percy was still a lifetime away from accepting his brother's death, and until he did, she couldn't imagine how she could tell him she was in love with Drew.

It took Drew five long weeks to return to Fort Tejon, but all in all it had been a productive trip. He'd learned a great deal about how efficiently a camel train crosses the desert and he'd learned that in battle, Abu was worth his weight in gold. With courage that nobody had expected, Abu had strangled a *kwanami* who'd been about to club Drew's head.

It had been a horrible night when they'd found the bodies and stayed up burying the widely scattered bones. As the Chemehuevi chief had said, there was no way to prove exactly how many men had died in that lonely patch of sand, let alone who they were, and that might have been true even if the Army had gone looking for Rodney sooner. But Drew had found several items that might mean something to Mandy, and he'd given them to Abu with orders to keep a close eye on the camel who packed them home and deliver them directly to the major's quarters as soon as the detail arrived.

"Are you happy now, Captain?" Captain Harris had chided Drew after they'd sustained serious injuries at the hands of the *kwanamis*. No one had been killed, but two dragoons would always carry scars from arrow wounds. Only Harris had complained, however, and he was the only one who had not taken part in the battle since he'd been out hunting at the time.

Throughout the journey, Harris had shared his meat freely with the men, but he'd complained about any other form of work. He certainly had shown no leadership abilities, nor the kind of creative thought usually necessary in either a good officer or a good crook. Once they'd started back across the desert, Harris had pushed Drew to keep the detail moving. Even though the men were tired and on some occasions the horses needed an extra day's rest, Harris was eager to get back home. Drew doubted that the man was dying to return to Mrs. Harris, and it was less likely yet that he urgently missed performing his duties as an adjutant. Possibly he was just afraid of another Indian attack, but more likely something vital awaited him at Fort Tejon. The possibilities intrigued Drew.

As he rode toward the post with his small, weary contingent, he watched Harris's body grow tense and eager in the saddle right about the time that Big Charlie ambled into view. It was the first time Drew had seen the unsavory scout since he'd warned him off of Mandy, and he found it interesting that he managed to arrive at the stables just in time to wave to Harris when he failed to acknowledge any of the other dragoons. Drew didn't know if there was any connection between Harris and Big Charlie, but it was a possibility he couldn't afford to overlook. The potential linkup between the two offered excellent possibilities for the theft of Army supplies and Yokuts slaves, and Drew figured that if the two men had to catch up on business, they'd do it very soon.

Drew knew he ought to tail Harris, but he didn't dare do it himself. Harris would spot him in an instant. He needed somebody trustworthy with a knack for melting into the woodwork.

Drew didn't have a lot of choices. He told the first private he came across to go get the major's aide-de-camp. Less then ten minutes passed before Johnson showed up, his carroty hair sticking out uncombed from beneath his battered cap.

"How did everything go, Captain?" Johnson asked after they'd exchanged salutes. "Did you have any trouble with the camels?"

"Not with the camels, corporal, and I don't have time to tell you about the other kind. Were there any problems here?"

"Well, we had a small earthquake that shook everybody up. Old Hadj just kept chewing his cud, but the horses all went crazy. Miss Henderson and the boy were out riding, and they both were thrown."

Drew's stomach rolled in panic. "Were they injured?"

"No, sir. Just some bruises."

"Were they alone?"

"No, sir. Lieutenant Isley was with them."

"Lieutenant Isley?" One of his chief suspects? What on earth was Sherwood thinking of! Drew had difficulty concealing his dismay from the sharp-eyed corporal.

"Lieutenant Isley is a superb horseman, sir. He puts in many hours riding off duty on his own."

"If he's such a good horseman, why did Miss Henderson and the boy have trouble with him as their escort?" Drew snapped unfairly.

"I don't think there was much he could do about the earthquake, sir," Johnson pointed out. "They had to walk a good four miles back to the fort because their horses ran off and his came up lame."

By this time Drew's need to see Mandy was growing almost out of control. It wouldn't be dignified to gallop across the compound and seize her in his arms, but once he saw her, he was afraid that might be exactly what he'd do.

Forcing himself to attend to the business at hand, he dropped his voice and said, "Corporal, I have an assignment for you that requires absolute discretion. You are not to breathe a word of it to anyone."

Johnson looked surprised and gravely flattered. One nervous hand tugged on a pimply ear. Tensely, he said, "Yes, sir. I'll carry out your orders unless the major countermands them."

Drew was heartened by his loyalty to Sherwood. "He won't. I don't do anything without his knowledge and consent, Corporal, rest assured."

"Neither do I, sir," Johnson answered gravely.

"This time you're going to have to discuss it with him later. I sent for you at once because I don't have much time. Captain Harris just dismounted and started off across the compound. I presume he's going home. But I don't think he'll stay there all evening. If he leaves his quarters, or admits anyone, I want to know about it. Follow him wherever he goes and report to me first thing in the morning."

Johnson's eyes opened wide. "You want me to spy on the major's own adjutant?" he whispered. "Are you sure the major knows?"

Drew placed a comforting hand on the corporal's thin shoulder. "He knows enough already, and he'll know the rest as soon as I make my report. If you're uneasy, Corporal, you can make your report to both of us after reveille." Though no one was within earshot, Drew still kept his voice low. "Just make sure that nobody else knows you have any interest in the captain's activities. Do you understand?"

"Yes, sir," Johnson said unhappily. "I'll follow him wherever he goes."

They exchanged salutes, and Johnson turned and started to saunter casually in the direction of the Harrises' quarters. Relieved that he'd dealt with an unpleasant situation judiciously, Drew handed Napoleon's reins to the nearest private, who happened to be Dorn, Captain Harris's big striker.

"I want him groomed, grained, and watered," he ordered. "I'll be back to check on him later."

"Yes, sir," Dorn promised as he started to untack Drew's weary bay.

With a quick glance around the stables to make sure that he was no longer needed, Drew struck out for the Larsons' house, glad that it was late enough in the afternoon that he was more likely to find Sherwood there than in his office. But even so, Sherwood was going to have to wait a few minutes for Drew's report. His first order of business was kissing Mandy. Then he'd tell her that her long quest was over.

As he jogged up the front porch steps, two at a time, he spotted Mandy on the other side of the open door. Tears were running down her face and she was breathing hard. Reaching out to grab his hand, she tugged him out of sight of the soldiers milling around the parade ground. Drew pulled her into his arms and kicked the front door closed.

He didn't bother to ask if she was alone. At the moment, he didn't even care. He'd waited for this potent moment for far too many hot days and even hotter nights. If he didn't feel her body crushed against own he knew he'd simply explode.

Drew's embrace was so fierce that he was afraid he'd give her bruises, and she clung to him so hard he could feel her nails clear through his heavy woolen uniform. Electrified with need, he pressed her against the wall of the house, his lower body seeking hers.

"Mandy, Mandy, how I ache for you," he growled.

Mandy kissed his neck, then his throat, as tears kept running down her face. "You came back alive," she burst out with a sob.

"I promised you I would," he reminded her. "I love you so much, Mandy."

He kissed her then, his lips claiming hers with all the hunger of the long, empty weeks, and she kissed him back with equal fervor. It was everything he'd dreamed of throughout his long desert journey. Only now that it was over could he admit, even to himself, that he'd been afraid it would never happen. He'd feared that in his absence, Mandy's guilt would reclaim her.

But there was no guilt in the soft female flesh that molded to his hard male body, no restraint in the desperate crush of desire and need. After half a dozen flaming kisses, Mandy pulled away for just long enough to drag him through the parlor door.

The curtains were drawn, and the room was empty. Drew wanted her so much that wasn't sure he could restrain himself from taking her right there and then.

12

When Mandy pulled Drew into the dimly lit parlor, she knew that no one was in the house, but she also knew that somebody might come home at any moment. The Larsons had taken the carriage to see some civilian friends at a nearby ranch and would not return until supper. But Percy was riding in the hills right behind the fort, and Anna had only taken the baby out for a stroll. Mandy never knew when to expect sudden appearances of the cook or the striker.

All she was sure of was that she could not have endured another minute without feeling free to press her body intimately against Drew's. It seemed to her that she'd spent half of her life waiting to give herself for him. She knew this was neither the time nor the place for her complete surrender, but she knew she didn't want to wait any longer.

She felt him tremble when she lifted her lips once

more to his. A moment later his tongue teased open her mouth and stroked the wet heat inside. As Drew wrapped his arms around her, his body, hard and hungry, pressed against her softness, inciting her yearning in a way she could barely control.

She had wanted Drew almost since the day they'd met, and now that she had finally given up the struggle to keep her feelings under wraps, there was no way she could fight him.

"Oh, Drew," she murmured. "You will never how very much I've missed you."

"I love you, Mandy," he vowed as his fingers sent majestic shivers up and down her back. "Don't you ever doubt that. I'm going to love you for the rest of my life."

He kissed her again, even more urgently this time. Mandy felt the fire that drove him, rose to it, surged against him as his grip tightened. As her hands lifted to stroke his half-bearded chin, her body seemed to swell and open with a newfound kind of hunger. It was shocking and explosive, but in Drew's arms it felt exactly right.

She couldn't speak, couldn't put her surrender into words. Drew's hands slipped lower, unleashing a powerful wave of desire at the base of her spine. She pressed herself against him, wrenched by the sensations that swept through her.

"Mandy, you are everything I have ever wanted in a woman," he confessed with a groan. He knotted his fingers in her hair as he urgently bent to kiss her again, and this time his lips triggered something deep within her that made her go wild. When he moved his hands to the top of her dress, she felt a rush of sudden ardor. She thought she would burst when his palms dropped lower yet. She could not stifle her tiny cry of need.

When Drew's fingertips closed over her nipples and gently squeezed, Mandy moaned. By now she was far too aroused to think clearly. The beginning and end of her world was Drew. She felt helpless, bound hand and foot, unable to do anything but press against him.

He kissed her again. He kissed her lips, her throat, her ear. Then he pressed his hot mouth against the uppermost curves of her aching breasts until she gasped out loud. Everywhere he touched her she felt tiny stars of magic twinkling. She didn't stop him when he wrapped his arms around her once more and tugged up her full skirt.

"Mandy," she heard him murmur. "I've never felt like this in my life. You can't imagine how desperately I want you."

"Yes, I can," she whispered back. "I want you just as much."

He groaned with a desperation that thrilled her to the bone. His hands battled her layers of petticoats and pantalets as he ground his hips against hers. Despite the wads of fabric, she could feel him, hard and urgent, almost parting her thighs. Mandy stifled a crazy, feral desire to climb up on top of him.

"Drew, please," she heard herself begging, not quite certain what she was begging for. She'd lost track of the whereabouts his hands, of his lips, of his body. He seemed to be inciting her everywhere. She was clinging to him desperately, wanting to please him but not quite sure how.

And then, with a suddenness that shocked her, Drew's hands vanished from beneath her clothes. Mandy reeled with shock and unmet need until he caught and held her chastely.

By then she knew why Drew had released her, why his face was embarrassed and grim. The curtains were drawn but she could still hear the odd noise coming in through the window. It was the rusty-hinge creaking sound that heralded the arrival of a cranky camel.

Mandy gasped for breath and shuddered once more as Drew pulled aside the curtain and looked out beyond the front porch. She could see Ila, heavily laden, and Abu holding her lead rope. They were headed right toward the Larsons' front door.

Percy was never allowed to ride alone beyond earshot of the fort, so he heard the general uproar that signaled something exciting was happening. At once he pressed his heels against his pony's sleek sides and short-loped back toward the Larsons'. If the captain had returned with news, Percy knew he'd go straight to the major's house. And if there was some other trouble at the fort, Percy wanted to be with Mandy.

He'd almost reached the house when he spotted the white camel. Daisy spooked, but he rode her firmly, proud that this time she hadn't dumped him in her fear. His own panic was sharply rising, though. There had to be some reason that Abu and the camel had come right up to the house, something that might have to do with Rodney. Desperately he scrambled through the door.

"Mandy! Mandy, why's the camel here? Is Captain Robelard back? Did he find my brother?"

He heard a muffled call from the parlor as he tried to open the door, but it didn't swing open right away when he turned the knob. By the time he called out to Mandy again, he was a little miffed.

When Captain Robelard opened the door, it was dark in the parlor, so Percy couldn't see his *shaughnum-uh's* face very clearly, and he looked funny with a few days' growth of beard. Percy couldn't see Mandy very well either. It was pretty dim in the parlor, and she was standing in a corner near a wall.

"What's wrong, Captain?" Percy blurted out, all but paralyzed with fear. "Why are you and Mandy here in the dark? Why is there a camel outside the door? Did you find my brother, Captain Robelard?"

He waited a thousand years for the captain to take a step toward him, to bend down to face him, to slowly shake his head. "Percy, I'm so sorry," he said softly.

Percy's lower lip began to wobble. "You mean you didn't find anything?" he asked as bravely as he could.

The captain shook his head. "No, son, that's not what I mean. We found some things that belonged to your brother."

"You did?" Suddenly the fear became fresh hope. "You found out where he is? Or at least where he was last? Oh, Captain, what did you find? Can I see it?"

The captain patted his shoulder as he nodded slowly. "Yes, you can see what we found. I told Abu to keep everything safely loaded on the camel so it didn't get mixed in with our supplies at the warehouse." He took Percy's hand, something he'd never done before, and led him out the front door toward Ila as though he were a toddler.

"We found some clothes, Percy. We also found some letters that Mandy wrote to your brother, and we found this theodolite. Do you know what it's for?"

Percy didn't care about the letters. He didn't care about the clothes. But he knew that Rodney's theodolite was his most precious possession. About the only

time he'd ever yelled at his little brother was the time
Percy had accidentally knocked it on the floor.

He took a step closer to study the instrument Captain Robelard held in his hands. He could see the long
mark on the top that had happened way back then. But
he could also see all sorts of other cuts, some like
scratches, some like the teethmarks of tiny animals.
The wood was badly faded and splintered at the ends.

Percy stared at the captain in confusion. "This looks
like Rodney's theodolite, but it can't be. He treats it like
a baby, sir. He'd never let it get all cut up and sandy."

He felt a sharp pinch in his stomach, a feeling worse
than anything he'd ever felt before. It didn't get any
better when the captain tightened his grip on his hand
and squatted down once more.

"Percy, I know you loved your brother dearly. And I
don't doubt that he worshipped you. He would have
come home to you and Mandy if there had been any way
at all he could have done it." His lips were tight, and he
looked unhappy. "But he was a brave man with a dream,
son. Sometimes brave men set out to do something that
fate won't let them do. Rodney wanted to map that savage desert, but his dream didn't come true."

Percy stared at the captain blankly. He knew what
he was trying to say, but he could not believe it. The
captain was his friend. Why would he say something
that wasn't true? "You found some things. You know
he started off across the desert. You don't know what
happened after that," he accused. "You don't know
where he went."

The captain looked positively sick to his stomach
now. It was Abu, for once unsmiling, who said to
Percy, "We found the bodies, small friend. At least we

found the bones. We buried them in the desert. The captain himself took the time to carve your brother's name on the mesquite cross."

"No!" The word came out of Percy in a howling rush. "*No!* You don't know what he looks like! That's why Mandy wanted to go! It wasn't him you buried." He turned on Captain Robelard and tore loose his hand. "You had no right to put his name on that cross. You buried someone else!"

Wildly, Percy looked up at Mandy, who had joined them on the porch. She was studying the camel, and she looked absolutely gray with shock.

"Mandy, tell them they're wrong! Tell them Rodney's just missing! Tell them he isn't dead at all!"

Slowly Mandy's eyes met his with a look he'd never seen in them before. She looked full of pain, but somehow full of anger, too. And full of something that Percy didn't understand and could not name.

"Let me see the letters, Abu," she whispered. "Give the theodolite to Percy."

The camel driver pulled the bulky instrument off the white camel and did as she asked. Then he stepped up on the porch and handed her a leather packet.

Mandy's hands were shaking as she pulled out one sheet of paper. It was deeply weathered and worn. Percy couldn't read it at a distance, but when Mandy held it up, then closed her eyes and covered her face, he knew the worst.

"No!" he screamed again, hugging the theodolite as tightly as he longed to hold his brother. "Mandy, tell them it's not true!"

But Mandy was crying, deep down crying, and he knew there was nothing she could do.

"Percy, honey, let's go upstairs," she said in a trembling voice he'd never heard her use. "Honey, you're not alone. I'll always be right here with you."

Tears were streaming down Percy's own face now. Clutching the theodolite, he ran to Mandy and pressed his face against her side. "He can't be dead, Mandy. Tell them it's a lie."

When Percy felt Mandy's hands cradle his head as though he were a baby, he started to bawl like one. He'd thought Captain Robelard was his friend, but what friend would try to make him believe Rodney was dead?

"How could you?" he shouted at the captain.

Captain Robelard reached out to touch his arm with one hand; with the other he reached for Mandy. It was just the way Rodney had reached out to hug them both the last time he'd said goodbye. "Please don't hate the messenger," he pleaded. "If there's anything I can do—"

Mandy pulled Percy closer in a way that almost pushed the captain's hands away. "You've done what you came to do, Captain," she said crisply. "At least all you're going to do today."

When she turned and hurried back into the house, Percy had the feeling she was even more angry with the captain than he was. And Percy never wanted to see him again.

"Another shipment of food for the reservation arrived while you were gone," said Sherwood.

He and Drew were sitting together on the porch a few hours after Drew's fiasco with Mandy and Percy. Sherwood, rocking his grandson, had already expressed his dismay at the *kwanami* attack and his relief that Drew had finally put the Rodney Potter issue to rest.

"I checked the manifest the instant it arrived," Sherwood continued, "and I rode out to see Lieutenant Cox a few days later. According to him, only about two-thirds of the supplies reached the reservation. When I returned I checked Isley's manifest again, and this time it matched up with Cox's numbers."

It took Drew a great deal of strength to focus on the Yokuts problem with the memory of Mandy's icy farewell still uppermost in his mind, but somehow he managed. "Since Harris and Abu were both with me, I guess the finger of suspicion points at Isley."

Sherwood nodded sadly. "I'm afraid it does, Drew, but we still can't prove anything. I imagine the circumstances clear Abu, but Harris could still be masterminding the thing and having somebody else juggle the books. He's good at getting other people to do his work."

Drew's eyebrows raised. "You must have been talking to Corporal Johnson."

"Well, the boy never complains, I'll give him that. But with Harris gone, I expected things to stack up. The truth of the matter is that everything ran quite smoothly. It became quite obvious who'd been doing most of the work."

Drew gave Sherwood his own impressions of Harris's performance on the journey, then mentioned the impromptu assignment he'd given Johnson. "I don't think I would have sent him if I'd known you had another theft in my absence. Or else I would have had him tail Big Charlie. But it's too late to call him off now. I have no idea where he's gone."

"Well, he might turn something up. You never know."

"I wonder if I should have given him more information," Drew said thoughtfully. "Once he's given an order, he's as tenacious as a bulldog. If Harris is involved in this, Johnson might get in over his head."

Sherwood changed the baby's position and patted his small back. "Surely you can't imagine that Johnson is in danger from one of my officers, Drew."

"One of them is stealing from the government and may be trafficking in people, Sherwood. It's time to face the truth."

Sherwood looked quite solemn. "I'll face the truth when I have proof."

Drew shook his head. "The truth isn't always enough for people. Even when they beg you for it, digging it up is a good way to make them hate you."

He didn't feel like explaining himself, and mercifully, Sherwood didn't press him. Drew knew why Percy was mad at him, but he knew that in time, Percy would forgive him. The boy would see that it wasn't Drew's fault Rodney had died. He'd risked his life to bury him.

But Mandy was another story altogether. She wasn't angry with him because he'd brought back proof of Rodney's death. She was angry because he'd started making love to her without telling her everything he knew.

He had never planned to withhold the truth from Mandy, but from the moment he reached the fort, he'd been consumed with the need to see her, to claim her, to celebrate the fact that she'd promised to love him for life. Until Abu had shown up with that damned camel, Drew had forgotten his earlier command. Compared to his reunion with Mandy, Rodney's death had ceased to matter to him.

But now he kicked himself for letting the heat of

passion cause him to forget, for even a minute, how much Rodney's death meant to Mandy. Just because everyone else but Percy had long since accepted the inevitable didn't make the hard reality any easier for her to bear. Drew had intended to break the news to her gently and give her time to grieve, but somehow it had all gotten away from him. He wished he could find a way to ease her pain.

Sherwood came up with the idea of setting a possible trap for Isley now that they'd narrowed things down, but neither he nor Drew could think of the best way to arrange one. After several minutes of tossing ideas around, Sherwood suggested that it might be worthwhile for them to confide in Anna.

"When all this started, she was still so hostile toward whites that I was afraid she'd go straight to her people and they might take matters into their own hands," he told Drew. "But she's changed so much since Mandy's been here that I think now she might trust both of us enough to keep our secret."

Drew didn't mention that Anna was already keeping a secret for him. Before he'd gone to Fort Mojave they'd conferred at length about his wedding blanket, and he'd shot enough rabbits during the trip to have plenty of rabbit skins to work with by the campfire at night. By following Anna's directions, he had a crude but warm blanket that was nearly done. He only needed her advice to finish off the edges. By the time he finished it, he hoped Mandy would have forgiven him.

Sherwood was still making suggestions for forcing Isley's hand, but Drew lapsed into a morose silence, feeling the profound frustration of his failure to achieve his goals at Fort Tejon. Oh, he was ready to write up a report on the camels—they did their job, but they'd never work out in the long run if the men couldn't be persuaded not to hate them—but he'd made precious little progress on the bigger problem here. Worse yet, he felt paralyzed by his inability to comfort Mandy.

As Drew tried to think of a way to ease her pain, he drank in the evening sounds of an Army post settling down for the night. Here and there a horse neighed or a cow lowed. A short bark of laughter would ring out from the barracks. Far away in the hills the coyotes began to howl. It was an eerie sound, even when it came from a unified pack. At the moment, he felt more closely akin to a solitary wolf, howling his own forlorn song.

"Drew, what's troubling you?" Sherwood asked.

Drew was startled. It was rare for Sherwood to question him so directly. "About the thefts, you mean? Or about the camels?"

Sherwood shook his head. "Neither. There's something personal eating at you, unless I miss my guess. Are you blaming yourself because you couldn't find better news for Miss Henderson?"

For a moment Drew stared blankly at his friend, amazed he hadn't yet figured out the truth. Or maybe he had figured it out, or most of it, and was trying to give Drew the benefit of the doubt.

He wasn't at all sure how much he ought to tell Sherwood, or how much the man already knew. Had Mandy spent these last long weeks in silence? If she hadn't told the Larsons that she loved him, she hadn't told anyone.

"You have all the facts regarding the mission, sir," Drew said, avoiding answering Sherwood's question. "I'm still a bit perplexed as to why the Chemehuevis found a feathered pike with the bones. The *kwanamis* who attacked us dropped their staff and kept coming back for it long after it was obvious that we could hold them off. Two braves lost their lives trying to retrieve it.

"If they left a pike when they attacked the survey party, my guess is that all the *kwanamis* were dead or that one or more of Potter's group was still returning fierce fire. It wouldn't be the first time a man has been fatally injured and took a long time to die." He paused a moment before he added, "It's also remotely possible that one of the men survived."

"Quite remote, Drew." The old man wrapped the baby's blanket a little more closely around his tiny shoulders before he asked, "But it troubles you?"

Drew pondered that a moment, then shook his head. He had never believed that Rodney Potter was still alive—at least not alive and wanting Mandy. Now he had no doubt whatsoever about what had happened. He'd told Percy the truth as gently as he was able. Potter had been exactly the sort of man Mandy had believed he was and he'd been doing exactly what he'd been assigned to do. He'd simply had the bad luck that had savaged so many fine men in this wild land. He was dead, and that should have been the end of it.

But Rodney still stood between Drew and his dreams because his death still haunted two people Drew loved. "What troubles me," Drew admitted, "Is that when all is said and done, Potter's death may not change a thing."

"For Miss Henderson?" asked Sherwood. "Or for little Percy?"

"Both," he confessed. "As long as they're still grieving for that dead man, I don't know how I can start a new life with the two of them."

* * *

Anna found Percy in his bed after supper, clinging to Mandy's hand. She was sitting beside him while he cried, alternately telling him that it was time to accept the fact that Rodney was dead and admitting that it was very hard for her to believe it.

Neither one had much to say to Anna, but tonight she didn't mind. They had both loved this man she had never known, and she knew that each could give the other special comfort. But she also knew that Percy was a little boy who leaned very heavily on Mandy. Sooner or later Mandy would need a grown up to help ease the pain within her. And Anna didn't think Mandy would be able to bring herself to go to Captain Robelard tonight.

It was very late when Percy finally fell asleep on his pallet, hugging the clumsy theodolite as though it were a doll. Anna didn't know what a theodolite was, but she knew it had belonged to Percy's brother, and watching him cling to it made her hurt for the child.

By candlelight, Mandy sat on her bed and read her old letters to Rodney, each and every one. Her face was so pale that Anna was sometimes afraid she would faint. She did not speak when Anna sat down on the bed beside her, but Anna could tell that Mandy knew she was there. Her grandfather had not said much when Anna's sister had been stolen, but she was always grateful for his silent healing care.

It was much, much later, in the middle of the night, when Anna heard Mandy waken. She listened to her sighs, then to her tears, and finally she heard her dress and go outside.

Anna did not follow her at once, and even when she did she hung back until she was certain that Mandy was not going to the captain's quarters. But she walked the other way, out toward the stables, as though she might be thinking of a very dark ride. Anna followed silently, her knife tucked into the pocket of her skirt. No one would hurt her white friend while she was watching.

When Mandy reached the stable, she tried to call her pretty mare to her side, but Jessie simply stared at her indifferently. There was a desperation in Mandy's voice as she called the beast. Anna was quick to note the change in her.

She moved closer yet as Mandy tried again, but the horse continued to ignore her. A sound like the creak of a rusty hinge turned Mandy's eyes to the far corral where Old Hadj was tossing his head. She moved toward him quickly, and as the big camel nuzzled her—looking for sugar pine bark, no doubt—Mandy hugged his head.

Anna waited silently until Mandy's body was shaking with the explosion of pent-up tears. She waited until the sounds of mourning tinged this long-feared night. She waited until she knew that grief had lanced the wound.

Then she silently walked up behind Mandy, rustling a single twig so the white woman would know she was not alone. Mandy whipped around, eyes frightened and opened wide. When she spotted Anna, she closed them again with a new spate of tears.

Anna had learned to forget that Jonathan was white, and she never thought of it when she rocked him while he cried.

She didn't think of it while she rocked Mandy, either.

*   *   *

"Well?" Drew asked the carrot-haired corporal when he reported to his quarters while it was still pitch dark the next morning. "Did you find out anything?"

Corporal Johnson looked even more embarrassed than usual. "Well, I, uh, found out where Captain Harris was headed in such a hurry," he reported. "He rode out to a ranch a few miles this side of the reservation."

Drew's interest quickened. "And?"

"A young woman greeted him at the door rather, uh, affectionately."

"Affectionately?" Drew was surprised he hadn't seen it coming. He'd been so focused on his investigation that he hadn't given a moment's thought to any other reason why Harris might want to keep his private activities under wrap.

"Well, they stood in the doorway and kissed for quite a while, sir. I only watched because you told me to. When things got, uh, more personal than that, I decided it would be all right if I just stayed close enough to the captain's horse to hear him when he got ready to leave."

"And when was that, Corporal?"

"Around four A.M., sir. The captain returned to the post just in time for reveille."

Drew shook his head. Another woman? That was all? Drew was almost sympathetic, since life must be hell for Harris married to Betty Sue, but neither could he condone the other man's behavior. He took a woman's honor quite seriously. If he ever pledged himself to Mandy, it would be for life.

At the moment he wasn't sure just where things

stood with Mandy, and many aspects of their future troubled him. He'd tried to talk to her again before he'd left the Larsons' house last night, but she'd sent her cold regards and said she wasn't up to seeing anyone. Drew was deeply torn. He knew she was hurting, and angry or not, he longed to comfort her. But he could hardly order her to accept his love and comfort when she was already so distraught.

Nor could he pretend that he wasn't hurt himself at the way she'd rejected him so brusquely. His love for Mandy was great, but he wasn't sure he could spend the rest of his life fighting to gain her devotion. In hindsight, he knew he'd made a grave mistake not waiting to claim her until after she'd buried her grief for Potter once and for all.

But he hadn't waited, and neither had Mandy. Circumstances had prevented the ultimate consummation of their relationship, but they'd bonded in every other way that counted. At least Drew had. He understood that she was in shock and might need a day or two to put things in perspective, but if she still refused to see him after that, he'd have to face the possibility that whatever she felt for him might never be enough.

The afternoon after Drew came back to Fort Tejon, Mandy sat stiffly on her bed, too tired to move but unable to rest. Anna had been a great comfort to her in the night, and the worst of the great shock had receded. But she still had Percy's feelings to contend with, along with her own guilt and outrage.

She was no longer angry with Drew, but she was still steaming at herself. Drew should have told her about

Rodney the instant he'd arrived, but she'd hardly given him a chance to speak. She had thrown herself in his arms in a wanton fashion unbefitting to any lady. She could forgive herself for that: she loved Drew and she planned to marry him soon. But she had not even bothered to ask him if he'd learned anything about Rodney before she'd dragged him into the parlor. And that, she realized sadly, was something she would never be able to forget.

But neither could she forget Drew, or the way he made her sizzle. How desperately she wished she could separate her desire for him from her crushing guilt!

Rodney had never touched her intimately, and now he never would. She had never longed to feel his hands on her breasts, but she would have given herself to him willingly within the dutiful bounds of marriage. She had truly loved Rodney, in a different way than she loved Drew, and his loss would cloud her life forever. Drew seemed too jealous to understand that, and for that, she wasn't sure she could forgive Drew.

She ached to go to him, but she still felt too confused and wounded. What was there to say? Underneath the layers of shock, Mandy knew she still loved him. But sometimes love was not enough to conquer guilt's demons. At the moment, she could only cope with Rodney's death by pushing Drew away.

She'd found no resolution to her whirlwind of feelings when Lucinda came into the room and sat solicitously down on the bed beside her.

"Mandy, dear, Drew is downstairs again," she quietly reported. "He looks like he's been ridden hard and put up wet. Are you sure you won't see him today?"

Mandy shook her head. "Tell him . . . tell him I'll see him soon. I'm just not ready yet to—"

"Assure him you still love him," Lucinda finished gently.

"He told you?" Mandy asked in surprise.

Lucinda shook her head. "No, dear, you did. In every move, in every glance, almost from the first day you arrived at this fort. Since Drew returned, even Sherwood has figured it out. We discussed the matter last night. We don't want to interfere, dear, but don't forget we're here if you need our help."

Mandy covered her face with both hands. "Oh, Lucinda, I am so ashamed. I would never have let my thoughts stray to another man if I'd been certain Rodney was alive. I swear it. But by the time I met Drew, it had been so long. It seemed so hopeless. I almost felt as though I were alone."

"My dear, you were alone. And you still are, as far as Rodney goes. You have nothing to be ashamed of. Drew is a fine man, and if I'm any judge at all, he's hopelessly in love with you. It seems to me that you should rejoice in this miracle."

"Rodney's death is not a miracle!" Mandy burst out in a fresh wave of guilt.

"Don't misunderstand me, dear. That's not what I meant. I'm only saying that since he is gone, God rest his soul, it's wonderful that you have someone else to love you and little Percy. Your young man's death is tragic. Pushing Drew away out of some misguided sense of guilt would only make it doubly so."

Mandy studied the twinkling blue eyes and tried to believe her. "I let him kiss me," she confessed.

Lucinda smiled. "If that's all that's ever happened between the two of you, Mandy, you have even less to feel guilty about than I imagined."

Mandy colored deeply as she remembered that she'd shared far more with Drew than a few sizzling kisses. Just yesterday she'd been ready to give him anything he wanted.

"When a young lady is planning to marry a man, I see no harm in a few discreet kisses," Lucinda assured her, not pressing for details. "And I do believe, my dear, that your feelings toward Drew are definitely the marital kind." Kindly, she patted Mandy's hand. "You do love him very much, don't you?"

Mandy closed her eyes. She couldn't speak, but her silence answered the question.

"Don't make him suffer too long, dear. Even if you need a few days to yourself, at least send him a reassuring message. Life is short out here in the west. I've watched more than one young woman grieve because she let her young man in blue ride off to do his duty carrying the weight of her anger."

Lucinda's voice dropped as she warned, "That's a hard thing to forget if your young man can't ever ride back."

When Anna reached the captain's quarters, he was working on the blanket, laboriously tugging the last few slender strips of rabbitskin through his warp of twine. She was touched by the knowledge that even now, while Mandy refused to speak to him, he continued this special project undaunted. Another man would have spent this hard night at the Prairie Schooner. This one had sent for Anna to check on the progress of his wedding gift.

She was almost ready to correct the angle of his

stitches when the captain said quietly, "Anna, I told you before that I wanted to help your people."

"You told me you wanted to make Mandy happy by showing your concern."

The captain's mouth opened in surprise, then closed prudently. "I think you misunderstood."

Anna did not answer. Bit by bit, she was learning to trust the captain, but she was always slow to give her trust.

Captain Robelard studied her carefully, then asked, "Do you want to help me, Anna? Do you think you can? Frankly, I'm running out of options. I want to make sure that all the supplies get to the reservation from now on, and that means I've got to find out who's been stealing them."

Anna pondered his words, his sincerity, and his love for Mandy. She wasn't sure why he wanted to stop the thefts, but his offer was more than she'd received from any other white man. She wanted to protect her people. She also wanted to do whatever she could to impress Major Larson with her willingness to help the Army.

The truth of the matter was that she was finding it easier and easier to fit into the Larsons' household these days. It helped that Mandy was teaching her to sew in the white fashion and had even shown her how to put curls in her hair. It helped that Mrs. Larson seemed more comfortable when she stayed downstairs with the baby and often included her in the women's conversation. When Anna had first come to the post, she'd had to work hard at remembering to speak English. Now she was speaking it without thinking, even when she was alone with Jonathan.

"I will help you if I can, Captain," she said slowly, feeling guilty that she'd made no progress toward finding a good solution for her grandfather's situation once Salt Hair married. "But I do not know what I can do."

Captain Robelard smiled, then gestured for her to sit down. "I need to tell you some things that no one on this post knows but the major. The safety of your people depends on your absolute silence. You may not discuss what I'm about to tell you with anyone but him."

Anna would not have listened at all if he'd told her to keep a secret from the major.

"Do I have your word?"

Anna did not answer him directly. "I will always do what is best for my people," she replied. It was far too late for anyone to bring back her sister, but she would do anything to help protect other Yokutses from a similar fate.

He nodded. "Officially, I was sent here to study the camels, as you know," he told her, discreetly keeping his voice so low that even she could barely hear him. "But that is only half of my job. I have another secret task. Major Larson sent for me to help him find out who is stealing the Yokutses' supplies and people. I have been studying the situation and eliminating suspects one by one."

Anna was not quite sure she believed him, but she liked the sound of his words.

Swiftly he told her what he'd learned so far and what he suspected. "I'd like to set a trap with a special shipment of food destined for the reservation," he confided. "But I don't know how to flush out the thieves. I've had no luck finding out who's stealing the goods, and I haven't been able to locate where they go once they're out of the fort. I've looked everywhere, but I can't find a trace of evidence."

Anna pondered his confession, mutely rethinking his

activities since he'd arrived at the fort. Yes, it made sense that he'd been checking things out. That would explain why he'd gone to so many odd places with Mandy when he never believed she'd find her fiancé.

Now, she said simply, "You have looked in the places where a white man would hide supplies. Have you tried thinking like an Indian?"

"No, I haven't. Think for me, Anna. What am I missing?"

It was an odd question, one which caused Anna to realize that she could not think like a Yokuts with the ease of her youth. It had been a long time since she'd lived in a brush hut or scraped hair off a deer hide, longer yet since she'd boiled gruel in a tightly-woven reed basket. With a start, she realized that she had no desire to do any of those things again.

Then, as an idea struck her, she said slowly, "We always build our houses where it is sheltered. Sometimes they are hidden from a white man's view."

The captain's eyes narrowed. "You may be on the right track, there, Anna, but I don't think they'd hide goods in the village on the reservation. What I had in mind was—"

"The Army ordered us to put our village on the reservation," she interrupted. "Where do you think we lived for centuries before you white men came here?"

The captain tensed as he leaned forward. "Are you telling me there's another village? A secret village near the fort?"

She shook her head. "No secrets, just empty houses. Most of the willow-frames were taken by their owners when they moved, and most of those abandoned have fallen down. But there are still a few."

The captain gave her a wide and earnest smile. "And

you could tell me where to find these hidden Yokuts houses?"

Anna faced him squarely. "You could never find them by yourself. I will have to show you."

Nightfall the next day found Drew ensconced in a Yokuts hunter's "bear nest," high atop the forest floor north of Fort Tejon. He was entirely hidden from anything or anybody for miles around, but he could see the land between the fort and the reservation perfectly. This afternoon he had found a dozen barrel-sized indentations on the dirt floor of the eighth abandoned hut Anna had led him to, and he was quite certain that since the whole garrison had been told that Major Larson would take fresh supplies out to the reservation tomorrow, somebody would try to move the goods by morning. All he had to do was wait.

Unfortunately, he was hardly in the mood to spend the night perched in a tree twiddling his thumbs, especially under a sky that threatened to rain. He needed to ride, ride hard, for about ten hours until he was too numb to think or feel. Instead he spent some time while the moon was full finishing up the last of the rabbitskin blanket for Mandy, then tucked it away in his saddlebag.

That afternoon he'd gone to the Larsons' house again to speak to her, and again she'd refused to see him. At least she'd sent him a note this time, begging him to understand what a difficult ordeal she was going through. She hadn't said she loved him, but she'd pleaded for a little more time. It was not a note that promised a joyful family future, but at least it acknowledged that they shared something special.

Drew had considered writing back a reassuring answer, but he hadn't done it yet. He knew he ought to tell her that he loved her, that he wanted to marry her, that he'd give her all the time she needed to sort things out. But he knew that was only half-true. He was not a patient man, and he'd already waited far longer than he'd hoped to.

He wanted Mandy Henderson in his arms, in his bed, in his life. He wanted to adopt little Percy. He wanted to put all memories of Rodney Potter behind them so they could get on with their lives. But Mandy had made it only too clear that forgetting her fiancé would not be easy; all the time in the world might not be enough. Drew wanted his wife's entire heart, not just the leftover parts that did not belong to Rodney.

All night long he crouched in the bear nest, struggling to stay awake, his admiration for Yokuts hunting skill soaring. The sun was just starting to rise when he first heard the sound of hoofbeats. One horse and three pack mules moving fast, running straight for the hut. Through the branches he could see a glimpse of a big bearskin coat like the one Big Charlie always wore. Drew stifled a brief moment of triumph. He had evidence at last! Of course he still didn't know who the inside man was, but now that he'd caught Charlie red-handed, he didn't think it would take much to make the mountain man spill the information.

Drew couldn't say he was surprised that Charlie was low enough to be part of this scam. He was only surprised that he had the intelligence to steal right out from under the Army's nose.

He knew that Charlie would not be easy to capture

without a gunfight, and that was something he didn't want to risk. Aside from the fact that Drew was in no mood to die, he didn't want to kill Charlie, either. At least until he could interrogate the scum. He wanted to know who was behind the thefts—who had tarnished the blue uniform he wore so proudly—and that meant he had to take Charlie by surprise. Once the mountain man reached the hut and started unloading would be the best time.

As Charlie let his horse pick his own pace though the cluster of trees surrounding the abandoned hut beyond the bear hut, Drew lowered himself, flat and tense, against the sheltering branches.

13

Mandy rose later than she'd intended on Saturday, but Lucinda and the major were still eating breakfast when she reached the kitchen. Percy sat at the table, too, but he made no pretense of enjoying his food. He'd been silent and morose since Drew had told him the truth about Rodney. Mandy was still feeling numb as well.

"Good morning, everyone." Her tone was not bright, but at least she thought she sounded in control. During the last two days she felt as though she'd shed the bulk of her tears for Rodney. She'd also shed more than a few for Drew.

"Hello, dear girl. How did you sleep?" Major Larson asked kindly as she reached the table.

Mandy managed to smile. "Better than the night before."

Lucinda passed her flapjacks and bacon, taking time

for a gentle pat on the shoulder, before her husband said, "Miss Henderson, I don't know if you have plans to ride this morning, but I'm afraid I won't be able to loan you an escort today. Most of the suitable men are going with me, except for Drew and the officer of the day. Please don't stray too far into the mountains if you and Percy go off alone."

"I can take care of her," Percy vowed in a trembling voice.

"Why is everyone so busy, Sherwood?" Lucinda asked.

"We're delivering a new shipment to the reservation. With those *kwanamis* about, we need a lot of men."

His comment struck Mandy as odd. The *kwanamis* had attacked Drew's small contingent a good three days' ride to the east, and they couldn't possibly come through the pass to reach Fort Tejon without being spotted. She had not given Drew much chance to confide any special plans to her, but she assumed that he was still working on a plan to protect the Yokutses. She wondered why he wasn't going with Sherwood. If he wasn't ill, he must be working on something here at the fort that was terribly important.

Possibly she could find the courage to talk to him today. She didn't know what to say to him, but she knew she'd already stretched his patience as far as she dared. If she didn't make amends soon, Drew might decide she just wasn't worth the trouble. And the one thing Mandy was now absolutely sure of was that the only thing worse than losing Rodney would be losing Drew.

"Can we go with you again?" Percy wanted to know.

Sherwood shook his head. "I'm sorry, son, but it's

too dangerous. Besides, it looks like it's going to rain."
When he saw the corners of Percy's mouth droop, he
said kindly, "I'm not even letting Anna go, and she
takes every opportunity to see her family."

"She'll have time enough with them when you retire,
Sherwood," Lucinda said almost sadly. "Poor Jonathan
was miserable when she went to the *lonewis*. I don't
want him to suffer through that again until it's absolutely necessary."

Despite her own despair, Mandy felt a sharp pang
for Anna. She knew her Yokuts friend desperately
hoped to earn a permanent place in the family the way
Mandy's lifelong housekeeper had done. She would be
devastated if the Larsons went back home without her.

Carefully, Mandy suggested, "I think she'd be more
than willing to go anywhere with you, Lucinda."

Lucinda did not meet her eyes. "I've considered that
possibility, Mandy, but Betty Sue has pointed out that
Anna just wouldn't fit in back east. Besides, her family
is here."

"Part of her family," Mandy corrected, not at all certain how Anna would cope with her aging grandfather's
situation if the Larsons did offer to take her along. "But
I think you underestimate her loyalty. Not just to
Jonathan, but to both of you."

Lucinda flushed and glanced at Sherwood. He
looked away. They were both silent for a moment
before Lucinda said gravely, "Sarah Beth had an
Apache nanny for Jonathan when he was first born. She
was with them when Sara Beth was killed."

Lucinda rarely talked about her daughter, so Mandy
had not heard this detail before. Gently she asked,
"And the nanny was killed also?"

A dark anger clung to the edges of Lucinda's quiet words. "The Apache nanny abandoned Jonathan and ran off to join her own people. It was an eighteen-year-old wounded private who found that terrified infant." Tears flooded her old blue eyes. "He hadn't a clue how to feed a nursing baby, but somehow he kept Jonathan alive on what he could find until they were rescued."

Mandy didn't dare speak in the ensuing silence, but Percy could not hold his tongue.

"Anna would die before she would abandon Jonathan," he declared stoutly. Bristling with loyalty, he pressed, "Mrs. Larson, you know she would."

Slowly, Lucinda nodded. "Yes, Percy, I know she's devoted to him." In a softer voice, she added, "But as Betty Sue says, when push comes to shove, you never know quite what to expect from an Indian."

The major cleared his throat and downed the last of his coffee. He made a few more comments about the likelihood of rain on this unseasonably cloudy day, then stood up and said to Mandy, "I know this is a difficult time for you, Miss Henderson, and I don't want to belabor your misfortunes at every meal. You and Percy need to pick up your lives and carry on in whatever way you see fit. I just want you to know that you are more than welcome to stay here as long as necessary while you sort things out."

Mandy knew she had to choose her words with care. Percy was clearly not at all ready to consider any long term plans that did not include Rodney. He certainly was not ready to hear that Mandy had pledged herself to the man who'd brought the news of Rodney's death. Percy adored Drew, and Mandy was sure that in time, he'd make the adjustment happily, but he was a small child who had lost every member of his family in this past year. She refused to rush him, but she wasn't sure she could ask Drew for much more time.

She was struggling to come up with just the right reply to Sherwood's comment when Percy burst out, "Don't you talk that way, Major. Don't you try to make me think my brother's dead! We knew he was in trouble or we would have heard from him by now. But those bones in the desert just mean that his friends were murdered, and he's all alone hiding out somewhere now! We've got to find him. He needs us more than ever! He—"

"Percy!" Mandy cut in, horrified at the shocked look on the kindly major's face. "We are guests in this home. Under no circumstances will I allow you to talk to Major Larson that way!"

Percy's face colored and his eyes filled with tears.

Sherwood looked stunned, but he remained absolutely silent.

Lucinda said softly, "We understand why you're upset, Percy. This is a terrible time. All Major Larson was trying to say is that you're both welcome here, no matter how long you need to stay."

Mandy flashed her friend a grateful look before she said to Percy, "You will apologize to the major. We will discuss this situation privately."

Percy's small shoulders trembled as he stared at the table. He took two deep breaths before he mumbled, "I'm sorry I yelled at you, Major."

Then, in a very small voice, he added, "But you said my brother was dead."

* * *

Percy was silent as Mandy's mare trotted out of the stable next to his. She was angry with him, he knew. But he was mad at her as well. She was acting like all the other people they'd met on this long journey. She'd started talking as though Rodney was dead.

She waited until they were well away from the confines of the fort before she slowed Jessie down and said, "Percy, I know you're very upset about your brother, but I cannot allow you to speak that way to our host. Major Larson has been very good to us. If it weren't for him, we still wouldn't know anything about Rodney."

"It wasn't him," Percy stubbornly persisted. "It was Captain Robelard who took you out looking for him. He's the one who found the theodolite."

"And he's the one you accused of lying to you, Percy. You owe the captain an apology, too."

Percy took a deep breath. He was still a bit miffed at the captain, but he really missed him, too. It wasn't like his *shaugh-num-uh* had tried to be mean about Rodney. He'd just gotten his facts all wrong.

Mandy sighed as she steadfastly jogged forward. The sky was pretty dark and Percy was sure it would rain before the day was over. He just hoped the storm would hold off till they got back to the post. The major was likely to get soaked going out to the reservation, but Percy was so mad at him that he didn't much care.

"Captain Robelard has done everything he possibly could for us. I'm afraid I also treated him rather badly when I got the news. What if we went to apologize to him together?"

Percy sort of liked the idea; it wouldn't be so bad if Mandy had to say she was sorry, too. "All right," he finally agreed, "but only if he takes back what he said about my brother. He had no right to say that Rodney was dead."

Mandy pulled her horse up close to his and studied him for a long, thoughtful moment. Then she laid one hand on his shoulder. "Percy, you know I loved your brother very much. You know I love you. If there was any chance at all that Rodney was still alive, I'd spend the rest of my life looking for him."

Percy shrugged away from her. "You think he's dead, too," he accused.

There was a long, dark silence before Mandy answered, "Yes, honey, I do."

Sudden rage, desperate and blinding, erupted in Percy. He wanted to run, to kick a rock, to shout until his lungs would burst. Instead he slammed his heels into Daisy's ribs, ignoring Captain Robelard's rules about never taking out your anger on your horse. But the startled pony had barely bolted forward when she jumped, then bucked in an odd sort of frenzy. Percy flew off over Daisy's head and came down hard on something that felt more like quivering quicksand than solid earth.

"Percy!" Mandy shrieked, not in anger but in panic.

And then he realized that her horse was running too, not toward him but away from him, and the trees and rocks beyond the mare were shaking as though a great wind was pummeling them.

He knew at once what was happening; he'd had this terrible scare before. But the last time the earth had buckled, it had been brief, finished almost before it had begun. This time it seemed to go on and on forever.

Jessie seemed determined to go on and on, too, running in panic toward the dense trees. The minute she swerved to avoid one, Mandy fell off the wildly galloping mare and hit the ground on her back. Although the dirt bubbled up around her and rocked back in forth in waves, Mandy herself lay very, very still.

Percy screamed her name as he tried to crawl toward her, but even though his arms and legs were pumping wildly, he could not seem to move.

Anna was in the kitchen when the shaking started. She was unable to find her feet, unable to reach the stairs. Her baby lay upstairs in his wooden cradle, screaming. As the windows cracked and later shattered, his tiny voice called out to her. He did not call for his grandmother or his young white mother who'd been killed by Apaches. He was still too small to speak, but Anna was certain he called her name.

She found him whole, red-faced, still screaming, when the shaking subsided long enough for her to race up the stairs. She clung to the child and rocked him fiercely. She must get him calm. She must convince him that everything was normal. Then she would have to look for Mandy and Percy, Mrs. Larson and the major, all of whom she suddenly realized that she held quite dear. Worse yet, she'd have to wait for news from the reservation. She'd seen a Yokuts village levelled by an earthquake before.

A moment later Mrs. Larson rushed into the house, hollering for Jonathan. Anna yelled back that the baby was fine but she was worried about the rest of them. Mrs. Larson cried, "Stay with the baby, Anna, no matter what! I'll see what I can do."

Anna thought it was an unnecessary order. Nobody could have pried her away from Jonathan. But she understood his grandmother's panic. It was almost as great as her own.

The post was in chaos when she hurried outside with Jonathan, afraid to stay indoors in case the shaking started again. Bloody soldiers rushed with water to bloodier soldiers who lay on the ground. The laundresses were tearing clothes for bandages, trying to clean out wounds. One of them was sobbing hysterically over a young private whose head had been split open by a collapsed beam by the guardroom.

It took Anna a moment to realize what was different about the fort. It was missing things. Some of the buildings were lopsided now and some were nonexistent. Only a pile of rubble sat where Captain Robelard's quarters had stood.

Anna swallowed back a surprising well of panic. While it was possible that he was still hiding in the Yokuts bear nest she'd found for him in the mountains, it was also possible that he'd already returned to his quarters by now and lay buried beneath the pile of adobe bricks.

Captain Harris was shoveling the rubble while he shouted orders to the men. His wife stood beside him, barking her own commands to passing officers, until he ordered her to go to the hospital and help Mrs. Larson.

Belatedly, Anna remembered that Major Larson had left for the reservation that morning and wasn't due back until nightfall. In the meantime, she couldn't bring herself to take the risk of confiding Captain Robelard's whereabouts to anyone.

She could have gone to look for the captain herself,

but she didn't want to take Jonathan anywhere when the world could tremble again at any second. Besides, how could she take one of the Army horses? All of them were neighing shrilly, stomping the ground and generally acting crazy. The only beast at the post who was likely to remain calm during an earthquake was a camel, and as far as she knew, only Old Hadj, whose back was just about well, had not yet returned to the distant camel stables. The rest of the herd was on its way to the reservation, where her grandfather and her dear son might be fighting for their lives.

It was a terrible choice to make, but Anna knew she could not leave Jonathan, let alone risk taking him with her on a camel, to make sure they were all right. Surely Salt Hair would come to her the first moment that he could, and in the meantime, he would take care of Grandfather.

Guiltily she clutched the baby to her chest more tightly. If she could not help her first family, maybe she could help her second one. There *was* one other person she could trust with the captain's secret! Mandy had risked everything to find a man who was dead. Surely she'd take a gamble to find one who might still be among the living.

But Mandy had been out riding during the earthquake, and Anna did not know if she'd survived.

It seemed like hours that the earth trembled and shook with a ripping sound that made Mandy wonder if God had rent his primeval garden with a hoe. But when it was over, when the earth settled into its rightful place again, she realized that the whole thing couldn't have lasted more than a minute or two.

Percy was shaking, clinging to her, falling to his knees beside her on the ground. "Mandy, Mandy, are you all right? Can you hear me? Mandy, don't die! Mandy, I'm so sorry."

Mandy was still dizzy from her fall and not quite certain whether or not anything was broken, but she managed to hug him tightly. "I'm fine, Percy. It's going to be all right. I'm just a little wobbly."

He was sobbing now, all of his rage over Rodney's death flooding him with the earthquake's terror. "Oh, Mandy, is this my fault? Is God punishing us for what I said to the major?"

"Of course not. It's just one of those accidents of nature, honey. It's got nothing to do with us."

He trembled for another minute, struggling to control his tears. Mandy didn't rush him. She just held him tightly, waiting for him to cry it out.

At last he straightened a bit, still kneeling on the ground, and asked, "Is Daisy all right? And Jessie? They just went crazy."

"Earthquakes frighten horses. Remember what happened the last time?"

"That was just a little one. Not like this."

"Well, that's true, but the horses were very uneasy. Corporal Johnson said Old Hadj kept chewing his cud like nothing had happened."

Suddenly Percy's eyes met hers. Mandy knew what he was thinking. They'd been together out here, far from the fragile old buildings. How was everybody back at the post?

"Mandy, do you think they're all right?" he asked in a whisper.

As Mandy got to her feet, she realized that she didn't

know the answer to the question. She didn't know if she and Percy were all alone in the world again. Lucinda was somewhere inside the fort. So were Anna and the baby. So was Drew.

She took Percy's hand and began to run. The earth cooperated by not moving, but the undergrowth seemed full of terrified creatures that were all bolting this way and that, and she nearly tripped over a careening jackrabbit. By the time they reached the post, Mandy's terror had multiplied by leaps and bounds. Human cries of terror and dismay filled the dust-choked air. Most of the buildings looked unshaken, but there was a pile of rubble where Drew's quarters used to be.

In the instant that she saw the pile of broken adobe, Mandy knew she'd buried Rodney Potter. Her grief for him was cold and tired and ready to be laid to rest.

The grief that seized her now was as sharp and fierce as the stab of a red hot poker.

By the time Drew regained conciousness under the steady pummeling of a thundershower, he was a mess. The right side of his head, which had hit the ground when the earthquake had shaken him out of the tree, had a lump on it the size of a small rock. His knee was so badly bruised and twisted that it hurt to walk. Most of the front of his body was covered with mud, the same mud which tugged at his boots as he trudged through the muck back to the tree where he'd tied Napoleon.

When he found no trace of Napoleon, Drew wasn't really too surprised. Any earthquake bad enough to shake a man out of a tree was surely bad enough to terrify a horse into breaking loose, especially one who'd had most of the night to get bored and restless enough to untie himself.

Still, the missing horse left Drew in quite a quandary. In the best of circumstances, it was a day-long walk back to the post on foot. With the sky pouring buckets and the thunder getting closer, it was obvious that a limping soldier needed to find somewhere to hole up and wait out the storm. The nearest shelter Drew was sure of was the abandoned Yokuts hut where he'd found evidence of hidden barrels.

Even that would be a long walk and a painful one, but he didn't think he had much choice unless somebody happened along this isolated road. And the only person he'd expected out here today had already come and surely gone while he'd been unconscious under the tree. Drew wondered if Charlie had seen him in the bear's nest or heard him fall. If he had, the chase was over, and he had lost his prey.

He had walked a quarter mile, maybe more, before he heard the noise of something coming up the trail. He knew at once it wasn't a horse or a mule, because the sound was all wrong. The animal's legs were hitting the ground in the stride of a lope, not a trot, but the speed was slow and the gait was awkward. At first he thought the horse was grossly overloaded, or possibly lame. But just before the lumbering beast came into view, he realized there was another explanation.

Somebody was riding a camel.

In the whole time he'd been at the fort, Drew had never seen anybody but Abu voluntarily mount one of the beasts. And though he'd checked Abu off his list of suspects, it suddenly occurred to him that there was one other man at Fort Tejon who got along well with camels: Corporal Johnson, who knew entirely too much about Drew's plans.

The speed of the creature worried him. Somebody was pressing it for all it was worth. There was panic, even urgency, in such a rider.

From his spot in the bushes near the edge of the road, Drew watched the camel approach in the heavy downpour, puzzled by what appeared to be a flapping saddle blanket. An odd oversight from any soldier, even a green one. And then, with a jolt, Drew realized it wasn't a saddle blanket at all, but a woman's dress.

He stood up straighter in shock and wonder, as he watched Mandy gallop toward him. All righteous indignation about female riding propriety seemed to have left her as she grappled with the square box saddle that perched high atop Old Hadj's hump. She'd barely managed to sit a lope the first time Drew had taken her riding, but he knew nothing could shake her from her mount this time. Her lush brown hair, usually so tightly pinned at her nape, had battled loose from its pins and now flowed in the rainy wind. Her gray eyes were dark with a brand of determination that could never be denied.

In that moment, Drew knew she was his for life. She could weep for Rodney Potter, but her guilt could not outlast Drew's love for her. He would wait forever. Sooner or later, she would turn back to him.

He stepped out in the road and waved his hand, not quite sure that either Mandy or Hadj could see him in the stormy darkness. When the camel didn't slow down, he called out, "Mandy? It's Drew! Pull up."

And then, like a rainbow after an endless storm, the panic in her face turned magically to joyful disbelief. Drew didn't know why she was out here all alone on a camel, didn't know what she was rushing toward or who she was running from. But he knew that nothing in this world had ever felt more right to him than the feel of Mandy's body as she threw herself off Old Hadj and quite literally collapsed in his arms. Weeping unabashedly, she clung to him.

"I love you, I love you, I love you!" she cried out against Drew's chest as he gathered her closer. She was sobbing so hard that he tightened his grip on her just to keep her from shaking. "Oh, Drew, I was so afraid I'd lost you. I never thought I'd see you again."

He would have answered with an outpouring of the feelings swirling in his heart, but suddenly Mandy's lips captured his. She'd kissed him before, with hunger and remorse, but never had she kissed him quite like this. It wasn't a tentative kiss or a hopeful one or one tinged with remorse. It was a kiss that signalled the end of Mandy's old world and the beginning of the new one. It was a kiss that cried out her need to be Drew's woman, now and forevermore.

This time he didn't need to ask whether memories of Rodney Potter still weighed her down with guilt. Mutely she answered all of his questions as she slid her hands under his soaking shirt until her urgent fingers singed his skin.

14

It was the rain, ultimately, and the resulting complaints from Old Hadj, which caused Mandy to loosen her fierce hold on Drew and give some thought to shelter. She was still far too upset and relieved to be embarrassed about the way she'd greeted him. He looked terrible. Not just muddy, but battered and bruised. She longed to ask him what had happened, but there was no time for that now. All that really mattered was that he was alive and she'd had one last chance to let him know she loved him.

"I was on my way to an old Yokuts hut near here," Drew told her quickly, one hand still warm around her small waist. "I don't know that it's waterproof, but it's got to be better than standing out here like this."

Mandy nodded briskly. She let Drew help her mount, then eased down on Hadj's neck while Drew dragged himself up on his hump. It wasn't easy to mount a camel without a block, she decided, and there definitely wasn't enough room on the beast for two. But Hadj lumbered along, despite his creaking sighs and moans, until Drew pointed out the hut up on the next ridge.

Even at a distance, Mandy could see why the location had been chosen. The trees around the hut were dense, providing a rich canopy above it, and a nest of rocks provided a wall that blocked most northern wind and rain. The hut was definitely too small for a camel, but the rocks and low limbs gave Hadj enough shelter that she wasn't worried about him weathering the storm.

While Drew unsaddled the giant beast, Mandy hurriedly gathered some brush to fill a gaping hole on one side of the hut. Inside it was fairly dry, except for the section near the hole. With the saddle blanket to sit on, it wouldn't be a bad spot to wait out the storm.

When Drew dragged in the box saddle a moment later, he thrust it to one side. "Not bad as a chair, or at the very least a backrest," he observed. He didn't toss the blanket down right away, however. Instead he folded it carefully and held it in his hands.

"It's really pretty cozy in here, Drew," Mandy said cheerfully. "I'm not sure I'd want to raise a family or entertain a superior officer, but it will certainly do for an hour or two."

Drew clutched the blanket a bit more tightly, but he did not speak as he studied the hard packed earth. Outside the wind grew a little louder. She could hear the rain pounding on their thatched roof.

"Drew, what is it?" she finally asked.

"It's empty. He must have realized we were on to him. He might even have seen me fall."

"What are you talking about?"

He gestured to the floor of the hut. "If you look carefully, you can see that barrels have been stored here, and not by the Yokutses who used to live in this place, I'll wager. I saw Big Charlie heading this way with three heavily laden mules just before the earthquake. I was sure he was hauling goods to stack in here. I can't believe he got away."

"Drew, it's not your fault," she said, touched by how easily he now confided what had previously been secret Army plans. She felt no surprise that Charlie might be implicated, just chagrin that she'd ever considered trusting him. She should have put her trust in Drew all along. "Nobody can fight an earthquake," she assured him. "Besides, if you actually saw Big Charlie with the goods—"

"I saw Big Charlie and three mules which could have belonged to anyone. I can't prove he was carrying Army goods. And I sure as hell can't prove that Lieutenant Isley was giving him inside information."

"Lieutenant Isley?" This time Mandy was surprised and more than a little disappointed. She felt a rush of sadness for the bitter young man. He'd been kind to her, in his dull, plodding way, and she didn't want to believe he could have been stealing from the Indians. "Are you sure it's Isley?"

"I don't know who else it could be. I took Harris with me to Fort Mojave, but the reservation shipping manifest was still doctored while I was away. Isley's the only officer who sees the paperwork besides Harris."

"Nobody else?"

Drew studied her thoughtfully. "Well, Sherwood's aide has access to everything Harris does, but I'm convinced that Corporal Johnson isn't involved in any of this."

"Why are you convinced?" she asked.

Drew looked troubled. "Well, I guess I don't have any hard proof of that, either. But I've checked out his record and talked to the men about him. Everybody says he's just what he seems to be—a green, good-natured patriot who always does a great deal more than his job requires."

"I like him, too, Drew, but that doesn't mean he couldn't be capable of finding an easy way to earn some extra money. There's something about him that doesn't add up. I mean, at times he seems so full of corn pone, but other times he seems like a very bright and capable young man."

Drew nodded. "I know, that puzzles me, too. But I think he's just a bit uneven. Still growing up. He doesn't have enough confidence to trust his instincts yet."

Mandy pondered this a bit before she said, "You're probably right. Anna's like that, too. She's trying so hard to fit in, to become more white, and when we're alone she's so relaxed. But she's still quite guarded with Lucinda. She learned to sew almost overnight, but she's still afraid to risk mending Sherwood's socks for fear she'll do it wrong."

After a thoughtful moment, she added, "Drew, I'm still convinced that your culprit isn't Lieutenant Isley."

"What makes you so sure?"

"I don't know. He just doesn't act . . . well, smug enough to be pulling the wool over your eyes. He seems sad and troubled."

"That just means he's got enough Army blue left in him to feel guilty."

"Maybe. But I think it's more than that. Besides, I'd

rather it be Captain Harris. He's not so bad, but I'd like to strangle his wife sometimes. I'd love to see the look on Betty Sue's face when he was towed away in chains."

Drew shook his head. "Somehow I think she might enjoy it. Seeing him humiliated, I mean."

Mandy chuckled. "I think you may be right. She's very ambitious for him, but for every word of praise about him as an officer, she makes at least two disparaging cracks."

"Was Harris there at the fort this morning?"

Mandy nodded. "Anna said he was giving orders to dig out the pile of adobe bricks that used to be your quarters. He seemed quite concerned that you might be trapped underneath the rubble. Since you'd ordered her to secrecy, she didn't dare tell him where she thought you'd gone. That's why she sent me."

Drew's lips tightened. "I need to return to the fort, Mandy. I'm surely needed there."

"Yes, you are, but if you try to ride Hadj back in this storm you'll probably get lost or hurt or show up too exhausted to do anybody any good. Let's just rest here until the rain slacks off."

He nodded, but he didn't look convinced. "Won't somebody be missing you?"

Mandy shook her head. "Anna knows where I am, and I told Percy to stay put when he tried to come after you himself. It'll be a while before Lucinda realizes that I didn't report to the mess hall with the others when she told me to."

Drew grinned. "Obedient as always, I see."

Mandy laughed. "In my position, what would you have done?"

Then he grew quite solemn. "Followed you to the ends of the earth."

His gaze took in her wet dress, clinging to her almost indecently, before he said, "I suppose we could ask for a wedding ceremony that left out obedience from the vows. If you started breaking one you'd be more likely to break the others."

Bravely, Mandy's eyes met his with all the turbulent emotions she longed to lay to rest. "If I promise to love you for the rest of your life, Drew Robelard, that's a vow I won't be breaking."

Drew's expression changed to one of hope and joy. There was a long silence in the hut while Mandy tried to read his heart. As she remembered all the tense moments between them, all the false starts, she suddenly knew that for all the chaos back at the post, the earthquake had brought a minor miracle. Right now they were alone with no chance of interruption. Right now she could give herself to Drew completely. Once they exchanged private wedding vows, there would be no questions left unanswered.

Drew mutely stroked the shabby camel blanket in his hand, then held it out to her. When Mandy gave him a puzzled look, he asked, "Do you remember the Zuni wedding blanket custom I mentioned at Sergeant Ryan's party?"

She nodded. It was a beautiful custom, and Drew had told her about it in a way that had given her many sleepless nights spent dreaming of cuddling naked beneath such a blanket with him.

"I made you a wedding blanket, Mandy," he now confessed. He looked half-proud, half-sheepish. "It's woven from strips of rabbitskin."

Tears filled Mandy's eyes. Drew had actually woven her a blanket? After everything she'd put him through, did he really love her that much?

"I finished it last night, but Napoleon ran off with it," he reluctantly informed her, "and I might have to make another one." He was still holding the camel blanket out to her. "In the meantime, this will have to do."

Mandy took a deep breath and pondered her choices. She could refuse to take the blanket, so Percy could cling to his hopeless dream a little longer. Or she could do what she'd been dying to do for weeks—give herself irrevocably to Drew.

Over and over again she'd pushed him away; in a few hours the storm would let up, and Drew would ride off again. Earthquake, *kwanamis,* or chasing Big Charlie, he'd be rushing back into danger. This time she would not leave him wondering how things were between them. She would become Drew Robelard's woman before he rode off again.

Slowly, Mandy reached out for the old blanket and draped it around her damp shoulders. She ached to look at Drew, but somehow found she couldn't. All she could do was tremble and wait.

He stood still so long that Mandy wondered if he'd changed his mind, or she'd misread him altogether. Then he swept away her cloud of anguish when he tenderly laid one hand on her cheek and made her face him.

His eyes were blue, a wild and hungry shade of blue, and his lips were moist as he pressed closer. "Mandy," he whispered unsteadily, "are you absolutely certain?"

She knew it was a question she could not take lightly, and she carefully searched the hidden corners of her heart. Two days ago, even last night, she might have hesitated. She might have been haunted by guilt, by propriety, by Percy. But the earthquake had changed all that.

"I love you, Drew," she said simply. "I want to be your wife."

Drew closed his eyes as he seized the ends of the blanket and tugged Mandy closer. "You *are* my wife, from this moment on," he vowed in a deep and husky voice. He kissed her once, with tender urgency. "We'll have the wedding as soon as we can get a chaplain out to the fort. If you want to wait to give yourself to me till then, I—"

"Drew," she interrupted, "I want to give myself to you right now."

Mandy knew her eyes were shining, and in Drew's eyes she read the same quivering newfound trust. They'd crossed a line together, and there could be no turning back. They weren't separate people anymore. They were a couple vined together by the pain of the past and the joy of the future, chained together by a fresh knot of love.

Drew waited half a startled second, surely no more, before his lips claimed Mandy's with a desperate, joyous kind of passion. There was nothing subtle about the way he reached for her this time, and nothing hesitant about the way she clung to him.

"Mandy," he murmured against her tingling throat. "I love you so much. You're worth every moment of agony you've put me through."

She kissed him again, her eager lips seeking the heat of his. "I'm done pushing you away, Drew."

Once more his lips seared hers, and this time his

warm hand also seared her breast. Instinctively, she pressed against him, rejoicing in the magic of his urgent fingers. Her nipple rose and tautened as he tugged on it, inflaming her with keen erotic hunger.

He kissed her again, his tongue claiming hers this time, and Mandy shivered with the power he had to move her. When Drew's free hand slipped around her back, then lower, her whole body writhed with need.

Boldly, he slid his hands down over her hips, then stroked the parts of her where the quivering was greatest. By now he was trembling too, his low moan a plea for the same sweet anguish. She knew what he had in mind when he tossed the camel blanket and his long coat on the ground, making an impromptu wedding bed. At once Mandy dropped to her knees, then stretched out on the coat and held both hands up in urgent invitation.

In an instant, Drew was straddling her on the blanket, his sensual heat potent and overwhelming as he ripped her chemise down to her waist and sucked her need-swollen nipple. Clenching his hair, she cried out her pleasure. After that Mandy couldn't tell just where he touched her because her whole body was steaming. Every intimate part of her shivered with the impact of Drew's hands, Drew's lips, Drew's thighs.

In a haze of desire she felt him untangle her wet clothing and slowly pull it off, piece by tantalizing piece, while she grabbed frantically at his. It took forever to battle the buttons and ties, long underwear and pantalettes, and Mandy thought she would lose her sanity before she was entirely naked.

As Drew's knees corraled hers, she lifted her hips, desperately trying to merge with him. Her need was a wild thing, achingly alive, as she mutely begged him to cover her bare body with his. His skin was hot and slick as his flat stomach dipped down to tease hers, hotter yet when his manhood parted her pulsing thighs.

When they finally joined in a frenzy of love and hunger, Mandy had no questions, no regrets, no lingering doubts about the life she'd left behind. Outside, the storm raged on without mercy, but inside the brush hut danced the sun.

When the storm finally blew itself out, Drew and Mandy convinced Hadj to brave the mud and started back to the fort. Drew still had a lump on his head and some pain in his knee, but other than that, he felt fit as a fiddle. Euphoric. He felt, in every sense of the word, like a man on his honeymoon.

He had always known that something wildly special brewed between himself and Mandy, but always he'd had to fight to keep her from holding something back. Today all that had changed. She had given herself to him totally, unshakably, without the tiniest hint of shame or regret, and he knew that her motivation had been far more than her potent sexual hunger. Mandy had deliberately given a part of herself to Drew that she'd never given to any man, not even Rodney. She could never take it back.

When they reached the fort, where Captain Harris, all things considered, had things running pretty smoothly, Drew was afraid his pride and blissful satiation would show on his face for every man to see. He was so proud of Mandy he could burst, but he didn't want to embarrass her, and he knew she wouldn't want anyone to know what happened until they were legally wed. It couldn't be too soon for Drew.

He knew Lucinda and Sherwood would understand if they married right away—before he had to return to Washington—and he didn't much care what any of the other officers thought about it. The only person whose feelings in the matter troubled him was Percy.

He spotted the little boy before they reached the stables. He was wearing his best box suit and running, almost hysterically, toward Mandy.

As she slid off the groaning camel, Percy threw himself in her arms. His tiny face was awash with tears.

"I'll be good," he promised between sobs. "I'll do whatever you say. Just don't leave me, Mandy! I'm so sorry I was rude."

Mandy clutched him tightly, and Drew wished that he could too. He and Mandy had mended their fences, and he longed to patch things up with Percy too.

"Percy, darling, I would never leave you. Never! I told you I was going to look for Drew."

"But you didn't come back. I thought you got hurt out there. Or that you were so mad at me you didn't want to come back at all."

"Percy, how could you think such a thing! We're family. We're forever."

Drew thought it was the perfect opportunity for her to say that he was about to become family, too. But she didn't even mention him.

He felt so extraneous, standing there beside Old Hadj, that he was relieved when Abu trotted up to him and said, "Ah, Captain! Old Hadj has rescued you." The Arab threw his arms around the shaggy beast's neck in unabashed relief.

"He did his job like a good trooper, Abu," Drew had to admit, planning to make Hadj's oblivion to the earthquake a footnote to his report. "He delivered under fire."

Abu grinned toothily. "You have been good to Old Hadj. And Old Hadj never forgets."

The camel driver's comment triggered Drew's thoughts of Lieutenant Isley, who'd once reported having so much trouble with this docile animal. If the supply thefts involved the camels, Isley could hardly be involved in the actual removal of the goods. But Big Charlie had been leading pack mules. Were the goods transferred to the mules from the camels, or directly from the warehouse at the fort?

"Where are the rest of the camels, Abu? And the men who left this morning for the reservation?"

"The camels are all back in their corral, and so are most of the horses, including Miss Henderson's and Daisy. But so many went wild in the earthquake that we could not find them all. Two of the men are missing, too."

"Missing?" Drew asked sharply. "Killed? Wounded?"

Abu shrugged. "We do not know. We only know that after roll call when the supply detail returned, they were gone."

"Who are they?"

"Lieutenant Isley"—he could not restrain a grin—"and Corporal Johnson." Now he sobered in obvious sympathy. "I hope nothing has happened to the corporal. He has always been good to my camels."

Drew wasn't quite sure how he felt. It was possible that Isley and Johnson had been injured. But. Surely the other men would have found them by now if that were so. It was more likely that they were both in the theft business together and had decided that the earthquake would be a good time to simply vanish. There was so much damage to the small community that it was likely that many people would never be found.

But Drew found it hard to believe that Johnson had been laughing up his sleeve at him all along. It was more likely that the ever-vigilant Johnson had seen Isley acting suspiciously and decided to tail him as he'd tailed Captain Harris. He'd never explained his reasons to Johnson, but the boy might have pieced it together himself. Half of Drew was glad he hadn't shared any secrets with Johnson, but half of him was afraid of what might happen to the young corporal if he stumbled on something the thieves could not afford for him to see.

And then it occurred to him that if Mandy was right, it could have been Isley who'd taken off after Corporal Johnson if he'd noticed something amiss. Corporal Johnson had surprised Drew time and time again, especially with his ability for sleuthing. Wasn't it possible that he could organize things with the big mountain man and juggle the Department manifests?

Drew knew he had to talk to Sherwood at once. It would be hard to explain to Mandy, but all he had time for was a quick change of uniform before he got back in the saddle and started searching for the missing men.

As the camel driver headed off with Hadj in tow, Drew turned back to Mandy and Percy, who were still tightly hugging each other. Finally, Percy opened his eyes and spotted Drew. Slowly, he disengaged himself from Mandy and took a step in Drew's direction.

"You're all right, aren't you, Captain?" he asked

with a heartwarming concern that more or less dispensed with the need for an apology. "Mrs. Harris said she was certain something terrible had happened to you, but I told her I knew you'd be all right. I know that the earthquake didn't hurt Rodney, either."

It was obvious, from the look on Percy's face, that he meant what he said. He seemed to view Drew as indestructible. He viewed his brother the same way.

As he glanced at Mandy, standing stiffly behind the boy, Drew didn't need to ask what was on her mind. She loved him; she'd proven it beyond all doubt. Desire for him still danced in her eyes. But she had a prior commitment to this courageous young boy. He'd been through a terrible time and he was still a long way from coming to terms with reality. He wasn't ready to hear about Mandy's marriage to Drew until he accepted the fact that his brother was dead.

Anna waited all night by the window for some sign of Salt Hair, but it was not until dawn that she caught sight of him slipping through the *loy-yo* on the far side of the mountain. The posted guard did not see him, and neither did anyone at the house. Nobody saw Anna, either, as she laid Jonathan over her shoulder and silently padded down the stairs.

Despite her agonizing concern for her Yokuts family, she had felt a surprisingly keen bond with all the white people at the fort today. Her fear for the captain and the major had surprised her, as had her joy that both were safe again. Mrs. Larson had checked in with her several times and actually hugged her twice.

Never had she felt more certain that she had finally

found her place. Surely the Larsons would never leave California now without taking her with them! It was more than Jonathan that drew Anna to them now. The Larsons had become her family, and she never wanted to live as an Indian again. Somehow she would find another way to meet her obligation to her grandfather when Salt Hair married.

It wasn't easy to thrust away her worries about both of them. The earthquake had been devastating, and several local civilians had not survived it. Jonathan was safe, but, until now, Anna had had no such assurance about her grandfather or her other son. As she watched Salt Hair sidle closer, she fought to keep from running down the stairs and hugging him. He was a man now and would not permit such coddling.

He was also, she realized the moment she slipped out on the porch and got close enough to touch him, a warrior who had just lost someone terribly dear to him. Anna could not stifle her sharp cry at the sight of his black-painted face and his singed hair clinging chaotically to his scalp. He only had one relative besides herself whose death would require such a dark display of mourning.

The sudden pain that gripped her was so fierce it stole Anna's breath. Instinctively she broke into the high-pitched Yokuts woman's grieving wail. Guilt added to her terrible sense of loss. If she'd been willing to do her duty, might she somehow have saved Grandfather?

Her panic doubled an instant later when a woman's voice, angry and bold, called out from the Harrises's doorway, "Guard! Indians attacking! It's the major's house!"

In an instant, Jonathan was crying and soldiers were running toward the porch. Reeling with grief, it took Anna a moment to realize that it was her own shrill cry of agony that had sounded the alarm. One look at Salt Hair's blackened face had finished the picture for an ignorant observer who feared the worst. With a fresh jolt of fury, she realized that Mrs. Harris was still hysterically shrieking for the dragoons from her porch.

Salt Hair wasn't taking any chances. At breakneck speed, he started running toward the sheltering brush of the nearby mountains.

"Don't shoot! Don't shoot!" Anna screamed as the soldiers poured out of their barracks like wolves after a fleeing hare. "He is my son!"

Then she turned on Mrs. Harris, who was egging on the sleepy dragoons. She was fully dressed, but there was no sign of her husband. "Look what you have done!"

"Don't get uppity with me, Anna," the woman shouted as she strode across the grounds to the Larsons' porch. "This is an Army post. If an Indian comes slinking in here after dark in warpaint, he can expect to get shot! Especially if he's trying to steal the major's grandson."

"Who's trying to steal Jonathan?" Lucinda called out, her voice high-pitched and terrified, as she bolted down the stairs in her night clothes with her half-dressed husband right behind her.

Anna planned to tell her what had happened. In fact, the words were already halfway out of her mouth, when Mrs. Larson reached her and seized her grandson almost violently with both shaking hands.

There was no way Anna could misread the panic in

Mrs. Larson's eyes. She wasn't afraid that some nameless Indian had tried to cause trouble or seize her
grandchild. She was afraid of what *Anna* might have
done.

The blow was crushingly deep, but Anna knew she
would have to deal with it later. First she had to get the
major to listen to her long enough to call off his soldiers who were chasing her son. Their guns were
already booming.

She blocked him before he reached the porch steps,
literally throwing herself against his chest. "It is my
son, Major! He has done nothing. He came only to tell
me that my grandfather is dead." The words tasted bitter, so bitter they were hard to speak. "You must help
him."

He stared at her as though she were a stranger. "Is
he armed?" he demanded as Jonathan started to cry.

Anna straightened, awash with fresh anger. "Of
course he is armed. He is a Yokuts warrior. But he did
not come to cause trouble. He came to tell me that—"

"Try not to kill him," the major ordered a soldier
running by. He had to repeat the command, raising his
voice, because the baby was making so much noise.
"Spread the word to the other men."

It was a beginning, but it was not enough for Anna.
"Why do you have to chase him at all? He has done
nothing. He means no harm to anyone."

"He is an Indian who's snuck past my guards,"
barked the major. "No Army officer could let that
pass."

Anna fought back the urge to tell him that Salt Hair
had done it a dozen times already. Instead she said,
"Would not an Army officer go tell his own mother if

her grandfather had died? We are a family in mourning. Would you punish us for that?"

He gave her an apologetic glance. "I'm sorry about your grandfather, Anna, but I can't avoid my obligations. I've given orders for him to be brought in alive, but at the very least I'll have to question him. There must be some reason why Mrs. Harris raised the alarm."

Anna's heart swelled with rage. "She hates my people! That is all the reason she needs!"

She knew she'd gone too far, but she was past all thinking. She was bleeding inside—for her grandfather, for her son—and suddenly she felt surrounded by the enemy.

"How dare you!" Mrs. Harris bellowed. "Major, surely you're not going to let that Indian speak to me like that!"

Sternly Major Larson said, "Anna, you will apologize."

Trembling with grief and fury, Anna shouted, "My grandfather is dead. My son is running for his life when he's done nothing. This woman had insulted me day after day when I have never done her any harm. And you are asking me to apologize to her? It should be the other way around."

Mrs. Harris began to berate Anna once more, but Anna did not stay to listen. Instead she marched back to Mrs. Larson, who was holding the screaming baby.

As she always did when Jonathan was too upset for Mrs. Larson to calm him, Anna reached out for him and waited for Mrs. Larson to place him in her arms. She knew it was a risk. Mrs. Larson was still scared and upset with her, but Anna's own agony was so great she could hardly endure it. Knowing her baby was frightened as well was more than she could bear.

Suddenly she realized that Mrs. Larson was still clinging to Jonathan, pressing his sweet face against her neck. She did not look at Anna. Her jaw was firmly set.

"Let me take him upstairs," Anna said, unable to prevent the words from sounding like an order. "It is not good for him to be so upset."

Mrs. Larson's grip on the baby tightened. His squalls intensified.

Despite the anguish inside her, Anna realized that she was in terrible trouble. There could be no worse time to challenge Mrs. Larson, especially when Mrs. Harris was still present, but she knew that if she could not persuade Mrs. Larson to give Jonathan to her now, she might never hold him again.

"Please," she said more gently. "You know I can calm him down."

When Mrs. Larson's eyes met hers, they were dark with panic.

"I think we should all go upstairs and calm down," Mandy said softly from somewhere near the major. Anna had not even realized that she had joined the group, but she was profoundly moved that her friend was trying to help her.

Now Percy said, "I don't understand why they're chasing Salt Hair. They never did when he came before."

"That was when they knew he was coming to visit," Mandy answered, the tone in her voice willing the boy to silence.

Anna felt another wash of gratitude. But her pain was overwhelming, and gratitude was not enough.

"I'm waiting for that apology, Lucinda," said Mrs. Harris.

"Anna, we're waiting," the major prodded.

She did not face him. She could see nothing but her baby's bright red face, hear nothing but his desperate screaming. She reached out to touch his tiny shoulder, hoping that her fingertips would reassure him.

Mrs. Larson jerked back as though Anna had touched the baby with a dagger. When her eyes met Anna's this time, they were wild. "I will take care of my own flesh and blood," she said coldly. "Jonathan will sleep with me tonight."

"Lucinda, I'm not sure that's wise," the major countered. "You know how he gets when he's—"

"He will sleep with me!"

Suddenly the tiny porch grew silent. Anna felt her legs go wobbly, as though she were being rocked by an earthquake once more. Would she have to grovel to Mrs. Harris to make things right with Mrs. Larson? She would do anything for Jonathan. Maybe even that.

Desperately she begged, "Let me sit right beside you and hold him until he's calm. Then you can sleep with him if you still—"

"The decision is made," Mrs. Larson declared with a tone as icy as Mrs. Harris's. "You were just the hired help. I am his grandmother, and I'll take care of him from now on."

A claw of pain gripped Anna's heart as she watched her hysterical baby vanish up the stairs with the white woman she'd foolishly believed had come to care for her. She felt light-headed as she realized it might be the last time she would ever see either one of them.

15

"*I want you* to tell Captain Robelard exactly what you told me," Sherwood ordered Corporal Johnson in the privacy of his office at four A.M. The soldiers had searched the hills in vain for Salt Hair, but after two weary hours, all they'd discovered was Corporal Johnson. To be more accurate, he'd heard them and announced himself, a distinction which he'd already brought to Major Larson's attention twice.

Drew himself had spent the afternoon circling every inch of soggy ground between the abandoned Yokuts hut and the place the supply train had been when the earthquake struck, searching for some sign of Isley or Johnson. He'd never found any clear sign of either man, but he had come back with one of the horses. It was not Napoleon.

He was concerned about the horse, but he was also concerned about the painstaking gift to Mandy that

Napoleon carried rolled up behind his saddle. Now, more than ever, he wanted her to have it.

She had given herself to him unequivocally, and he was no longer afraid that she'd still change her mind. But he was worried about Percy. Drew cherished the boy, and he'd already suggested to Mandy that the two of them legally adopt him. Unfortunately, they didn't have much time to wait for him to accept his brother's loss before they revealed their wedding plans to him. Drew wanted to marry Mandy before he headed back to Washington, especially if there was any chance that she could be embarrassed by an early birth of their first child.

Now he sat across from Johnson and did his level best to read the man. Once, he'd found the corporal's behavior highly suspicious. Later, his trust had been absolute. Now, he tried to hold all judgments in abeyance until he found out exactly why Johnson had been absent without leave for so many hours. As far as he knew, nobody had yet seen any sign of Lieutenant Isley.

Johnson looked scared, his Adam's apple bobbing, but there was a surprising anger in him as well. "I was having a rough night out there when our men showed up, Captain," he said defensively. "I'd already had to hold off two wolves. I expected somebody to come out looking for me, but I didn't expect to come back here to get the third degree."

"I searched for you all afternoon, and Captain Harris had sent troops out looking for you in the morning," Drew informed him, wondering where Harris had slipped off to tonight. He'd never appeared during all the trouble at the Larsons. He was not on duty, but with the earthquake still leaving the garrison a bit shaken, it seemed an odd time to spend the night away from the post.

"I appreciate that, sir," Johnson replied, looking somewhat mollified. "And I'm very sorry to be absent without leave, but it couldn't be helped. I'd have been back sooner if my horse hadn't pulled up lame. After he slipped in the mud and pulled a tendon, I decided to wait until morning to walk back to the fort."

"We aren't concerned with why you were delayed returning, Corporal," Sherwood said rather sternly. "I want to know why you left this post without permission in the first place."

Johnson swallowed hard again. "I was trying to do what Captain Robelard wanted, but he wasn't here to ask. And you were off with the supply train, sir. With secrecy so important, I didn't have a choice."

"You could have followed your orders," Sherwood barked.

The corporal hung his head. As always, Drew found himself perplexed by this young man. At times, he was so gauche it was hard to believe he'd survived several years in the Army. At other times, his capacity for clear thought and dedication was impressive for one so green.

After a moment, Drew said, "Go ahead and tell us what happened, Johnson."

Johnson glared unhappily at Sherwood before he explained to Drew, "I never knew just what it was you thought Captain Harris had done, sir, but I knew there was some good reason you had me tail him. The same day, you got a real funny look on your face when I mentioned Lieutenant Isley, so I was sort of keeping an eye on him for you, too. When I saw him at the stables acting sort of strange, I was sure you'd want me to follow him."

"There could be a thousand reasons why an officer

leaves this post, Corporal," Sherwood growled. "It is hardly your place to second guess him."

Drew glanced at Sherwood, wishing he'd restrain the chastisement until he got some information out of Johnson. He still wasn't sure whether Johnson had shown great industry or grossly overstepped the bounds of military obedience and respect.

He asked carefully, "What was odd about his behavior, Corporal?"

"He kept looking around like he hoped nobody would see him. And then he took off in the same direction as the camel train, and the major had only left with the food for the reservation about ten minutes sooner. I figured he would have left with the others if he was supposed to go, and if he had an urgent message, he would have sent an enlisted man."

Johnson looked hopefully at Drew for any sign of approbation. It was a clever deduction, but Drew wasn't about to tell him that until the interrogation was through.

"Please go ahead, Corporal," he said.

Johnson looked pleadingly at Sherwood again, but managed to continue. "He headed straight to the widow's house. The place where I found Captain Harris."

Drew had to admit that the news took him by surprise. He'd never found any reason to believe that Isley and Harris were in on it together. Was it possible that Harris's relationship with the widow wasn't just romantic? Her location was perfect for smuggling goods from the nearby reservation or the fort. It was so well hidden that Drew had never located it himself.

"And?" Drew prodded.

"First he looked around the barns, then the lady

stuck a shotgun out the door and asked what he wanted. He told her he served with Captain Harris and she invited him inside. He stayed for maybe twenty minutes, then headed north."

"Did you talk to this woman, Corporal?" Drew asked.

"No, sir. I didn't think that would be my place. I just wanted to keep an eye on the lieutenant, especially when I saw the pace he was keeping."

"Riding hard?" asked Sherwood.

"Hell bent for leather, sir."

Drew's eyes met Sherwood's. He knew what the major had in mind.

"Go see if you can pick up his trail, Drew."

"Yes, sir." He saluted because Johnson was in the room, then turned to go.

Johnson rose to follow him, but Sherwood stopped the boy. "You're confined to the post until further notice, Corporal."

"But, sir"—his face flushed an unbecoming shade of scarlet—"I can lead the captain straight to the house."

"Make him a map. And do it quickly."

Johnson opened his mouth, as though to protest further, then prudently changed his mind.

Ten minutes later, Drew was in the saddle, heading north before dawn's first light.

Percy got up at daybreak and ran to the stables, eager to avoid the Larsons' breakfast table. Things were so tense in the house he felt itchy just getting out of bed, but Mandy said they had to stay there even though Anna had left with a broken heart in the middle of the night and Mandy's search for Rodney had come to an end. He'd told her that her search might have ended, but his had just begun. Mandy had gotten mad at him then, and said he had to accept the way life was.

He did not feel like accepting anything this morning. He didn't want to believe that Rodney was dead or that Captain Robelard was gone again or that Anna had vanished forever. He was tired of loving grownups who simply disappeared. And he was tired of listening to Jonathan, who'd been screaming ever since Mrs. Larson had snatched him away from Anna.

As Percy charged into the stable yard, the guard gave him a cheery hello. How many things had changed since he'd first arrived here! In the beginning he'd hardly been able to ride a borrowed horse, and Captain Harris had snarled at him. Now he had a pony of his own and everybody knew that Captain Robelard was his special friend. In fact, the captain was one of the reasons that Percy had no intention of leaving Fort Tejon. No Yokuts brave ever wants to live very far away from his *shaugh-num-uh*.

He was rubbing Daisy's ears and thinking about his hunting trip with the captain when he noticed that a pretty pinto pony was outside the corral, sticking its head between the slats of the fence. It was obviously hungry. Just as obviously, it didn't belong to the Army, but it acted like it had been there before.

Suddenly Percy knew where he'd seen that horse before. It belonged to Salt Hair! Surely it was the horse Salt Hair had ridden here last night when he'd come to see Anna. If the horse was near the fort, then Salt Hair had not been able to return to where he'd hidden it. And Poor Anna was still on foot even if she'd found her son.

What if she hadn't found him at all? Or what if she'd found him dead? She was out there, somewhere between the fort and the reservation, all alone and thinking that no white person in the world cared a fig for her.

Percy was sick of watching his loved ones disappear. He was tired of being told to hold still and do nothing while it happened. He'd come to California as a little boy, but Captain Robelard had changed all that. He could ride a horse, make a fire in the woods and shoot a musket. And he could remember, if he worked at it, the right road to the reservation.

Mandy dreaded getting out of bed. She had not slept since Anna's heartrending departure, and she doubted that Lucinda and Sherwood had either. When she did finally drag herself up and met them at the breakfast table, they both looked quite exhausted and morose. Still, Lucinda politely greeted Mandy and Sherwood handed her a sealed envelope that contained a brief but passionate note from Drew. He had to leave on Army business, it said, but they could marry as soon as he returned. He'd already telegraphed Washington with a request to arrange for married quarters instead of his former bachelor's room.

Mandy wished she'd had a chance to reaffirm her vows made in the tiny hut before Drew had ridden away, but Sherwood assured her that he'd left before daybreak. After the shabby way she'd treated him the last time he'd returned from a long journey, she couldn't blame him if he felt apprehensive about leaving. This time she vowed to make his homecoming a truly joyous occasion. She would welcome him back as her husband-to-be in front of everyone. And that meant that, ready or not, she would soon have to share their imminent wedding plans with Percy.

In the meantime she had another obligation, one she was not sure how to fulfill. It wounded her unbearably that Anna had been sent packing, virtually in disgrace, for no other reason than being part Indian.

"What are you going to do?" she asked Lucinda when she couldn't stand the silence anymore. Surely, now that Lucinda had calmed down, she'd regret her terrible words of the night before. "She left on foot in the middle of the night without weapons, without food, without water. She wouldn't even wear the dresses you'd given her, or the one I helped her make, for fear she'd be accused of stealing. She put on that ragged old deerskin she wore to the *lonewis*."

Lucinda studied her gnarled hands. "I can't have someone work here who fails to show respect."

"Respect!" Mandy snapped. "Lucinda, you sent her away for no greater reason than your own pride."

"My pride!" Lucinda's old blue eyes were flashing. "I want to protect my grandson. That's the beginning and end of it!"

"That baby loves her more than he loves you. If you'll be honest with yourself, you know that's part of it."

Lucinda's face grew red.

Before she could speak, Sherwood stepped in. "Miss Henderson, I've extended to you every kind of hospitality I can offer, with few questions and fewer demands. I do not mean to be discourteous, but I cannot allow you to upset my wife."

For a long moment, Mandy could not speak. She owed these people so much. They were good folks in so many ways! It was only where Anna was concerned that Mandy found their behavior unforgivable. Sternly, she reminded herself that Lucinda's response last night had been triggered not by prejudice so much as fear.

Cautiously, she answered, "I did not intend to appear ungrateful, Major Larson. I am well aware of the debt I owe to you. I only hope that I can repay it someday."

"In the Army," he said slowly, "it's a debt you can repay to the next soldier's family who needs your help. You'll come to understand this better as time goes on."

It was the first time ever that Sherwood had acknowledged Drew's love for Mandy, and she knew it was time for her to confirm that Drew's marriage plans were hers as well. But she wasn't about to talk about something as precious as her love for Drew while Sherwood was glaring at her and Lucinda was steaming.

Besides, she had to share the news with Percy first.

Now that she was alone in the mountains, Anna did not try to stop her hot tears from flowing. Her beloved grandfather was dead, her manchild was missing, and her baby had been snatched from her arms forever. How desperately she'd longed to tell him goodbye! But she'd been given no chance to hold Jonathan privately, and even if she had, the tension between Anna and his grandmother would have confused him terribly. It was better to leave as she had, before any more terrible moments, with only her digging stick and her herb basket. She had taken nothing of the white world with her, and she had not left a trace of her Indian self inside the once-beloved white house.

The fact that the soldiers had not found Salt Hair did not worry her; in fact, it meant that he surely was still alive.

An injured Yokuts warrior had a dozen ways to hide from white pursuers, and Anna knew just where to look for him. It troubled her, as she began her laborious climb throughout the mountains, that she had shown Captain Robelard many of the places where Salt Hair was most likely to hide. He had never given her any reason to distrust him, but then again, neither had Major Larson. Until last night. And she knew without question that the captain's first loyalty would be to the major. Hers must be to Salt Hair.

It was not until she had almost reached the third abandoned Yokuts hut that she first sensed the danger. In her grief and anger, she was not as alert as she should have been, and her months of living as a white person had dulled her senses. When she heard the sound of a man's low moan, her first thought was that she'd found Salt Hair, lying in pain inside the hut, dying or severely injured.

Swallowing back her mother's fear, Anna started to run toward him, only vaguely aware that she now heard other sounds of people, far more people than one Yokuts man.

The warning voice within her, the Yokuts one, called out to her a moment later. She froze, then melted behind a massive oak. Her instincts were right. There were a dozen people near the hut, and she was right to hide until she was certain they were Yokuts Indians.

But they were not all Yokutses. Three of them were white. So was the big, burly man in the bearskin who suddenly appeared behind her. The one who had a gun.

It was full daylight by the time Drew reached the last place Corporal Johnson had seen Lieutenant Isley. It was evident from the hoofprints that he was not trying to hide his trail. He was moving north and moving fast.

But Drew was moving faster. By ten the trail revealed that he was not more than an hour behind his quarry. The sun had just reached its zenith when he heard hoofbeats and saw the dust up ahead.

He didn't have time to sneak up silently. If Isley didn't realize someone was after him now, he'd know it soon enough. Then, if he was guilty, he'd waste no time in running.

Drew still felt guilty about leaving Corporal Johnson back at the post instead of bringing him along as a guide. In a sense the boy had been found guilty without a trail, but Drew couldn't afford to take any chances. Whoever was in charge of this operation was very crafty, and it had to be someone that Sherwood trusted.

At one point, the dust abated and there was silence up ahead. But a few minutes later, the dust doubled in intensity and the hoofbeats increased to a gallop.

Drew spurred his weary mount to full speed. He was so intent on catching Isley that it took him a minute to realize that Isley had doubled back and was now heading in his direction. Drew tugged out his Colt revolver and hoped he wouldn't have to shoot him.

But as Isley galloped toward him, Drew could see that he was reining his horse with his left hand and holding his right up in the air. He seemed to be calling for Drew's cooperation, or, at the very least, his silence.

Drew pulled up warily and faced his fellow officer. He didn't want to believe Isley was a threat to him, but what other choice did he have? He watched the lieutenant for any sign of trouble, but he could detect no malice in the young man's eyes.

When Isley reached him, his face was red and his horse was panting hard. "By God, Captain, am I glad to see you!" he called out. "I knew somebody was on my tail and I thought it was another one of them."

"Them?"

Isley gestured with his head toward the mountain. "The slavers. They've got at least a dozen Yokutses up there in an old hut on the other side of the hill. I couldn't get close enough to see if they have any of our supplies, but I'd be surprised if they're not part of the ring."

"Ring?"

"Ring, Captain. Don't pretend you don't know. You've been trying to find something wrong with my manifests ever since you got here. I finally decided I had better figure out what it was for myself before I got court-martialed for something I hadn't done."

Startled, Drew chose his words with enormous care. "Tell me what you know, Lieutenant. Then tell me why you haven't shared this information with me or the major sooner."

Isley shook his head. "We don't have time for finger pointing now, sir. All I know is that when the last reservation shipment came in, we had a whole lot more food than we had by the time we loaded up those camels, but the manifest showed no discrepancies at all."

"You're the one who keeps the books, Lieutenant."

"Yes, dammit, I am, but I didn't doctor anything!"

"Nobody else sees the records but Harris, Johnson and the major, and Harris was off with me the last time Yokuts supplies were stolen."

"Don't you think I know that? Don't you think I've wracked my brains trying to figure out who's been making me look like a thief?"

"You've got a theory?" Drew asked.

Isley shook his head. "All I've got is one piece of information you might not know. Captain Harris takes office records home to work on them from time to time when he gets backed up." He added bitterly, "Hunting can cut into a man's paperwork time."

Sherwood had said the same thing, but it hadn't seemed particularly important to Drew at the time. "But Harris was gone the last time this happened."

"So were the books."

"What?"

"I'm telling you, while you and Harris were off in the Mojave, the record books were taken out of the office overnight. They were back in the morning, but I know exactly where I put them and what I'd just written down. At first I thought maybe you'd taken them again"—he almost smiled at Drew's look of surprise—"but then I remembered that you were gone. They were moved ever so slightly to the right, and when I checked, the flour barrels were reduced by about one-third. The same thing happened the night before last."

Drew was stymied. "Can you prove it?"

Isley's face reddened further. "As an officer and a gentleman, I give you my word."

Drew had no reply to that. He wanted to believe Isley, but if he did, who was lying to him? There was nobody left but Harris, and if Harris had somebody working with him who was slick enough to doctor the books while he was gone, he wasn't about to admit it.

"Look, Captain, we can argue about this later. Right now we've got to get over that mountain and capture these slavers before they get away. If we're going to launch any sort of a surprise attack, we need to circle around them and come in the back way."

It only took Drew a moment to decide. If Isley was lying, then he'd surely find a way to keep Drew from returning to the fort alive no matter what he did. If he was telling the truth, then this might be Drew's only chance to catch the slavers, not to mention save a number of Yokuts Indians.

"Do you recognize any of the people?"

Isley shook his head. "I couldn't get that close. But I saw at least one blue uniform and one big bearskin coat."

"The kind Big Charlie always wears?"

Isley nodded. "I couldn't see his face, but all my instincts tell me he's our man."

Instantly, Drew spurred his horse in the direction Isley had pointed. All his instincts told him the same thing.

Percy had never intended to go so far. Riding Daisy and leading the pinto pony, he'd thought he'd catch up with Anna quite quickly. But Anna hadn't stayed on the main road. She'd veered off up into the mountains.

He'd spied her from a great distance. At least he thought it was her up there on the hill. He'd started to follow her, or at least go the direction where he'd seen her last. He was too far away to tell what happened, but when he heard her cry out, he froze in the saddle. But he slammed his heels into Daisy's ribs when he heard gunfire.

He was still a good half mile away from where he'd heard the scream when he saw a big Army horse bearing down on his right. He recognized Captain Harris instantly. He looked mad at Percy. He also looked tired and messy, like he'd been out all night.

Remembering the morning he'd yelled at Percy for being in the stables, Percy remembered that he'd yelled at Salt Hair, too. Now Percy was miles from the fort and leading Salt Hair's pony. As the angry captain caught his reins and pulled him over, Percy felt a shiver of fear.

"What the hell are doing out here all alone?" Captain Harris shouted. "I heard gunfire. When I saw your little pony up ahead, I thought you were hurt."

"It's Anna who's hurt," Percy answered. Whether the captain was a nice man or not, he *was* an Army officer, and Percy knew he needed help. "We don't have time to talk! We've got to go save her!"

"Who's Anna?" Captain Harris asked. "I thought Miss Henderson's first name was Mandy."

"Anna's the Larsons' nanny!" Percy told him, amazed that he could live so close and not know.

"The Yokuts woman?"

"Yes! Now we've got to go!"

Harris didn't look particularly alarmed. "All right, I'll go check it out. But you stay right here and don't get into any trouble."

He released Percy's reins and started jogging up the hill as though he had all day. Percy didn't. He dropped the pinto's lead rope and galloped right on by him.

The captain hollered as he chased him, and at first it seemed like a race. But when the screaming started again, followed by dozens of shots, the captain's attention turned away from Percy. Together they charged up the hill.

In all his dreams of western excitement, Percy had never expected anything like this. He wasn't dreaming or playing make-believe. Anna was in trouble. Somebody could get killed.

By the time he reached the source of the gunfire, everything was crazy. There were a bunch of Yokuts fighting white men hand to hand. He knew two of them: Captain Harris's striker, Private Dorn, and the mountain man they called Big Charlie. Percy wasn't fond of either one of them, but he knew he should take their side over that of Indians. Yet Anna was hiding behind a tree, throwing rocks at Private Dorn, and that pretty well decided things for Percy.

And then he saw there were some soldiers who seemed to be taking the Yokutses' side. Captain Harris had already reached the clearing and started firing, but Percy couldn't tell who his bullets were aimed at for the life of him. All he knew was that suddenly he was close enough to recognize one more person dressed in Army blue. Captain Robelard was lying on the ground without his musket, and Big Charlie was towering over him with a gun.

Nobody had paid any attention to Percy; he knew to them he was just a little boy. But when he heeled Daisy a dozen galloping strides to Big Charlie's side and thrust his musket in his face, he had never felt more like a man.

16

Drew never knew if Percy would have killed a man for him, because a moment later, Charlie had ducked a bullet that Captain Harris sent flying toward his head. Between Percy, the three officers, and the Yokuts, the battle was over fairly quickly. The bullet lodged in Isley's thigh would require some medical attention, but unless infection set in, he wouldn't lose his leg. Big Charlie roared like a lion when they tied him to a horse, and Dorn glared at Harris like a man possessed.

"I want to know exactly what's been going on here," Harris shouted at his striker. "What's your role in all of this?"

Dorn spit at him. "If you're too stupid to figure it out, why should I help you?"

"Maybe because you value your life."

Dorn shrugged. "I don't reckon it's of much use to me now."

Drew was inclined to agree with him. It was obvious that Big Charlie had been in charge of selling the slaves and stolen supplies, and had hired the two men Drew didn't recognize. But Dorn had been the missing link for which he'd searched in vain. He'd studied Harris's office, never his house. The striker spent so little time there each day! How could he have had access to Harris's books? And how could he have the experience to know how to juggle them? He was an ordinary enlisted man and nothing in his bearing or deportment gave any hint that he might be educated.

"Are you telling me that Captain Harris knew nothing of your activities?" he now demanded.

Dorn laughed. "Captain Harris don't know which end is up. That runty corporal runs his office, and the missus runs his house."

Harris's handsome features darkened with rage. "That's a lie! I meet all the obligations of my command!"

"Hell, you ain't even at the post often enough to know what's going on. You'd be court martialed by now if Johnson didn't cover your behind. Maybe you'd learn more if you kept your nose to the grindstone instead of catting around at night."

By this time Drew was hopelessly confused. It wasn't Harris and it wasn't Isley, and he couldn't believe Dorn had masterminded this whole thing by himself!

But Drew had more important things to worry about at the moment. Percy was uninjured, but he was shaking like a leaf in Anna's arms. Drew crossed the clearing to them quickly, touching her shoulder as he knelt down before the little boy he hoped would choose to be his son. "Percy, are you—"

He got no further before Percy threw himself in

Drew's arms. The moment of manhood had vanished, and it was a very frightened little boy who clung to his neck. As he gathered Percy closer, Percy buried his wet face against Drew's blue wool. "I thought he was going to kill you, Captain! Rodney's gone and Anna was leaving, and I was so afraid I was going to lose you, too!"

Drew hugged him tightly, feeling a bit misty-eyed himself. "You're not going to lose me, Percy. Not ever. I'm your *shaugh-num-uh* for life." As Drew kissed the top of his head, he added, "I couldn't be prouder of you if you were my own flesh and blood."

Percy started to cry again, but this time, it seemed to Drew, it was because he was so happy. After a few minutes the child quieted enough for Drew to set him down. He still held Percy's hand, though, while he turned to Anna.

"Are you all right? And Salt Hair?"

She nodded. "But there are several people here who have the white man's sickness. It is the reason the slavers caught them unaware. They came down for the *lonewis* but could not make it when the sickness struck. They have been here since then, hoping they would not be discovered, hoping they would not give it to the other Yokutses."

Drew didn't know what to say. Even if he could get a doctor to look at the sick Indians, there was very little medical science could do to help them.

"I think we should put some of Lieutenant Cox's men on guard right here until they recover, Anna," he said softly. "If we take them to the reservation, they could infect everyone. If we take you back to the fort right now—"

"I am not going back. I am not wanted there."

"Anna, we can straighten out this misunderstanding."

"I have not misunderstood anything. Both Mrs. Larson and the major made their feelings quite clear."

It was another quandary for which Drew had no solution, and the weariness of the last few hectic days was catching up with him. He had to return these thugs to the fort and let Sherwood help him sort out the mess.

"Captain, I know I can trust you to take Percy back to Mandy. I must also trust you to deliver a message to her from me."

There was a gravity in Anna's tone that alarmed Drew, but he had no idea what sort of a message it would be.

"Of course, Anna. I owe you so much. If there's—"

She shook her head. "I have important news for her, and for Percy." Her gaze took in the sniffling child. "But for your sake, I wish I did not know. Please forgive me, Captain. I must speak the truth, and you must, too."

By now Drew was feeling decidedly uneasy. What on earth had Anna so upset?

"These people know many of the Hiding Ones. Some are still in the mountains. They have heard . . . they have heard stories that did not reach the *lonewis* because so many of the mountain Hiding Ones did not go."

Drew's stomach tightened, but nothing in his weary mind could possibly have prepared him for Anna's next statement.

"This winter a group of Hiding Ones saved a white man's life."

"What white man?" Percy demanded, eyes suddenly aglow. "It was my brother, wasn't it?"

Anna did not answer him, but now she took his hand. "There was a white man that some Hiding

Yokuts hunters found out last year where the mountains meet the desert, just as the first snow came. He was shot with arrows in several places, and was unconscious and bleeding freely. Some of them said to leave him for dead, some said to put him out of his misery. But some of them said he deserved their help because he'd taken the arrows that would have found them if they had been the first to encounter the *kwanamis*."

Anna met Drew's eyes, then quickly looked away. "They made a travois and carried him up into the mountains with them, treating his wounds in the old way."

Percy leaned toward her, looking almost breathless. "It was Rodney! He's alive, just like I always told you!"

Drew fought a sudden wave of nausea. Could he possibly be right? Percy had always been certain that his brother was alive. And Mandy had been certain too, until Drew had seduced her into believing otherwise. But he hadn't trumped up any evidence or misled her in any way! He'd sincerely believed that Rodney Potter was dead, believed it with every ounce of his soul. Quite suddenly he realized how desperately he still hoped it was true.

"For a long time he did not know where he was, and even when he did, he could not move much. They nursed him through the time of deep snow and he gradually got better. He seemed grateful and acted kind to them, but still they could not let him leave until they broke camp to go to the *lonewis* because he might give away their secret location. When the time came, one of the men led him down to a mining town where he could find help to get to San Francisco."

Anna reached out to touch Drew's shoulder in a gesture of comfort she had never offered him before. "I am told that in Yokuts the white man called himself Maker of Baskets, Captain. The kind made of clay."

It was almost midnight when Mandy was awakened by a noise in the parlor. On some other night, she might have rolled back over and tried to go back to sleep. But not tonight. Not when Drew and Rodney were duelling in her heart. Not when her whole future hung in the balance.

Quickly she threw a wrapper around her shoulders and slipped across the floor. She opened the door just a crack, but it was enough to hear Drew. Enough to feel the pulse of his crushing anger.

"I don't give a damn if it's the middle of the night, Sherwood!" he boomed. "I'm going to talk to Mandy this instant if I have to charge up those stairs!"

"Drew, don't be absurd. I know you wanted to marry this girl, but her fellow is still alive. She's thrilled and that little boy is absolutely delirious. You gave your word to her as an officer and a gentleman that you'd find her man. You did the best you could. I believe that. You had every reason to believe he was dead. But now you know better."

"I didn't say he wasn't alive. I said I had to talk to Mandy."

"I already sent a telegraph to the Presidio."

"I don't give a damn what you did. Besides, after the earthquake, who knows how long it'll be before a message gets through? How do you even know he'll make contact with the Army?"

"Well, that's a problem I haven't figured out yet, but there is no other authority up there. Everything's still in chaos here, Drew, and I need you to help get things back in order."

Mandy knew that was true. When the detachment that Sherwood had sent out in search of Percy had encountered Harris and injured Isley with the prisoners, the dragoons had brought them back while Drew had stayed with the Hiding Ones until reinforcements arrived from Lieutenant Cox at the reservation. Harris had reported what he knew, including the news that some of the Yokutses claimed they'd rescued and detained Rodney Potter. Oblivious to all the trouble he'd caused by disappearing, Percy had greeted Mandy with the delirious news about Rodney. It was not until much later that she learned that the boy had saved Drew's life.

By that time, Mandy had been emotionally exhausted. It had taken her sometime to realize that a black cloud hung over the wonderful news. Her joy at learning that Rodney was alive had left her breathless for a good five minutes. It was only after that she'd realized that her entire future with Drew was jeopardized by the miracle.

"I still don't know who to blame for the trouble, Drew," Sherwood growled. "I can't believe that Dorn was acting on his own. I've grilled Harris thoroughly and he won't be shaken. He seems embarrassed that all of this was going on under his nose, but the damn man doesn't look the least bit guilty. Now we've got to figure out who was giving orders to Dorn."

"We can figure that out tomorrow, Sherwood. I've got to talk to Mandy tonight." Drew's anger had subsided; it was raw agony Mandy heard in his voice now.

"I'm not even sure she's willing to see you, Drew. Under the circumstances, it would be most awkward. Even if she consented to be your wife, it's obvious that—"

He broke off abruptly as he spotted Mandy in the doorway of the parlor. She hadn't bothered to get dressed, but she held the wrapper chastely about her. She was sure Major Larson meant well, but he only knew the barest outline of the story. Drew had every right to demand to see her. And in spite of everything, she longed to speak to him herself.

"Major, I appreciate your valiant defense of me, but I'd appreciate a few moments alone with Captain Robelard."

Sherwood exhaled deeply. "Miss Henderson, a gentleman would wait until morning to address you."

"Captain Robelard is under no obligation to prove himself to me, sir. I am well acquainted with the quality of his character." She said the words as gently as she could, because she knew it was the only thing she was likely to say tonight that would give Drew any comfort.

Sherwood glared once more at Drew. "Call me, Miss Henderson, should you be in need of any assistance," he finally offered, bristling as he left the room.

When the door to his upstairs bedroom closed, Mandy forced herself to meet Drew's eyes. He looked haunted and hurt, and she couldn't think of a thing to say to ease his pain.

He didn't ask her what she knew or how she'd discovered it. It was obvious that all he wanted to know was what she planned to do.

"I gave you a blanket, Mandy," he finally said.

Mandy swallowed hard. "I promised to marry Rodney, too."

"You never gave yourself to him."

Hot tears stung her eyes. "Drew, I'm thrilled that he's alive. Can't you understand that? It doesn't mean that I don't love you."

"Mandy, I wish this man no harm. If you can look me in the eye and promise me you'll tell him the truth, then I can rejoice in the fact that he's alive, too."

"The truth?" she repeated, no longer sure what it was.

"Yes, the truth. That you loved him like a brother, you waited for him, you searched for him, you buried him, and then you gave yourself to me. You are no longer free to marry him."

Mandy swallowed hard and looked away. "I gave him my word, Drew."

"You gave your soul to me."

He crossed the room and pressed so close that she could feel his sweet breath on her hair. "Are you really so fickle, Mandy? So free with your words, your kisses, your body? Are you going to tell me it meant nothing?"

Her eyes flashed with anger. "Drew, you know that's not true! I love you. When I promised to marry you, I felt nothing but joy. I never doubted that it was a dream that would come true."

"It still can. It's not too late." His voice was hoarse and low.

"I've got to talk to Rodney. I've got to see how he's feeling, what he's been through."

"What about how you're feeling and what you've been through? If this fellow is really the epitome of manhood you claim he is, won't he want what's right for you?"

"Of course he will. And he might . . . he might understand. But I have to ask him, Drew. I have to tell him everything before I can take one more step with you."

"When I gave you the blanket," he reminded her, fiercely tugging her into his arms, "I told you there would be no turning back. My love for you isn't a quilt you can just roll up and tuck away whenever it's inconvenient!"

He leaned down to kiss her roughly, but Mandy turned away. "No!" she pleaded. "Not like this, Drew. Don't rob me of my memories. Don't steal the love I gave you."

She felt the corded arms around her tighten and knew he was doing battle with himself.

"Damn you, Mandy," he finally whispered hoarsely. "I deserve better than this from you."

"I know you do," she whispered in anguish. "Oh, Drew, I'm so sorry. I never expected anything like this. Please forgive me."

But Drew seemed to have used up all of forgiveness where Mandy was concerned. There was no softness in his eyes, no mercy in the hard set of his jaw. His parting words were cold and sharp, and they cut to Mandy's heart.

"You vowed that you would be my wife forever. I took you at your word. But I was never more than a substitute for Rodney, was I? Just somebody to keep you warm until your long dark night was through."

As Drew marched out of Sherwood's house, he saw the lantern burning at the Harrises' quarters next door. He was far too tired and too angry to wrestle with the Yokuts problems again tonight, but he didn't want to go to bed yet, either. He'd been stabbed in the back, and Harris had, too. Harris knew Dorn's activities better than anyone. Somewhere, if he delved deeply enough, he was bound to find a clue.

Drew was ready to knock on the Harrises' door when he remembered that Harris was not likely to be there tonight. In the awkward exchange of information up in the mountains, Drew had told Harris about his investigation and Harris had revealed several secrets of his own. He'd known nothing about the thefts because he had his mind on other things lately. He admitted that he had, unfairly, let Johnson carry the bulk of his load.

Harris had been trying to leave his shrewish wife without destroying his career, and he escaped from the fort nightly because he could not bear to be the object of her private displays of hate. After last night's fiasco with Salt Hair, Harris didn't think there was any point in trying to hide what most of the garrison knew by now: He spent his nights at the widow's house unless he was on duty. Over and over again he'd asked Betty Sue to leave him, but she'd refused.

The man was in a quandary of his own making, but Drew felt some sympathy for him regardless. At the moment, he was all too keenly aware of how it felt to be at the mercy of an unfeeling woman.

He could not believe that Mandy had ever loved him. If she'd said she had to see Rodney Potter and explain the situation to him in her own way, he could have endured that. But she'd made it clear she still believed her duty to Potter came before her duty to Drew. She still planned to marry Potter if that's what he wanted her to do. She wasn't willing to fight for Drew, and that meant they had never had a love worth saving.

Instinctively, he ducked when he heard a door at the Harris house open, hoping he hadn't frightened Betty Sue into another round of midnight hysterics. But Betty Sue did not appear on the front porch. As Drew listened, he heard stealthy footsteps creeping down the back stairs.

Drew followed Betty Sue's flowing skirt through the

darkness in total silence. She veered to the west, away from officers' quarters, up to the hills. Was it possible that the captain wasn't the only Harris to have another companion, he asked himself? If so, would Betty Sue really be bold enough to try to rendezvous with her lover tonight? With the whole post in an uproar, it seemed like an imprudent thing to do.

But as Drew followed Betty Sue, she melted into the trees along the north end of the fort, then started to work her way back toward the east. She passed the hospital, where wounded Isley was quartered tonight, then the bakery. Drew waited tensely, but she did not go inside. Instead she kept on moving until she reached the guardhouse.

She stood outside in the chilly night air for several moments before she crept yet closer to the unheated prison and stood beneath one of the tiny windows. In a voice raw with fear, she whispered, "Dorn? Where are you?"

Drew released a silent breath. Not matter what Harris's striker answered, Drew knew he'd finally stumbled onto the final clue.

"Captain! Is it true? Are you going north to bring my brother back?" Percy was running so hard that it was hard to get the words out of his mouth, but Captain Robelard was already on his horse and heading away from the stables. He pulled up and glanced at Percy over his shoulder, but Napoleon kept prancing, eager to be on his way.

"Yes, it's true," the captain said, without even a little smile. Usually he had a big one for Percy. "I figure that if I were him, I'd be heading for the first steamer to leave the dock in San Francisco to get back to you and

Miss Henderson. Since nobody knows just where he is, it seems like the best way to find him is to go look myself."

Percy wasn't hearing anything new. Mandy had told him the same thing over breakfast. But she hadn't said anything about Captain Robelard being upset with him. He couldn't draw any other conclusion from the captain's grim demeanor.

"Captain?" he asked quietly, hanging his head. "Whatever I did to make you so mad at me, I'm really sorry."

He couldn't remember doing anything to make the captain mad, but he must have done something. He'd never seen Captain Robelard so tight-lipped before. And the captain had seemed really proud of him since he'd used his musket to save his life.

To his surprise, the captain sighed heavily, then swung down out of the saddle. He bent down in front of Percy and took his small hand.

"Percy, I want you to listen to me."

Studying his dusty shoes, Percy nodded.

"You are a splendid youngster. You saved my life, and that's something I'll always be grateful for. You've had to become a man too soon with your brother gone. But that's all over now. Rodney will be back with you soon, and you can put all these months of suffering behind you."

It was an odd speech, and it didn't make sense to Percy. Captain Robelard sounded as though he was going away forever, not just going to fetch Rodney. "Captain," he asked, "aren't you coming back with him?"

The captain patted his arm and slowly straightened. "Oh, I imagine I'll be here for a day or two. But by then you'll be too busy welcoming Rodney back to spend much time with me."

His gaze drifted back to Major Larson's house, and his shoulders drooped a bit lower. "I just wanted to say goodbye to you, Percy. It's meant a lot to me, getting to know you. If I ever have a son someday, I hope he's just like you."

Percy was astounded, and deeply touched. Suddenly overcome with the swirling emotions of the last few days, he threw his arms around Drew's waist. Fighting tears, he whispered, "If I ever have another father, I hope he's just like you."

The captain hugged him tightly before he stepped back. His face was still grim as he said goodbye and hurriedly remounted. He turned toward the Larson's house once more, his gaze on the second-story window.

Percy thought he saw the curtains flutter in Mandy's room before the captain's heels pressed his horse.

If anyone had told Mandy, months before, that the waiting could grow any harder, she would have insisted it could not be so. But knowing that Rodney was alive only shifted the balance of her agony. She was relieved and grateful, even euphoric, to know that he had not died, but those joyous feelings could not counteract the anguish of the price she'd had to pay for that knowledge.

It was possible that Rodney would no longer want her, or that, even if he did, he might find it in his heart to let her go. But Drew had told her she'd made her choice and it was too late to change her mind. Even if she begged and pleaded, it didn't seem to her that there was anything she could ever do to make things right between herself and Drew. And after all that had happened, she didn't see how she could ever make things right with Rodney, either.

She didn't want to think about what it would be like to make love to Rodney now that she'd given herself to Drew. There was even a chance that she was carrying his child. The prospect had not worried her when she'd expected to be his wife so soon, but now it darkened the heavy shadows that already hung over her future. She still loved Rodney as much as she ever had, but now she knew the difference between surrender to a lover and platonic love for a friend.

Nothing seemed to be right at the Larsons' household, either, since Anna had run off in the night. Jonathan was always cranky, Sherwood was silent as a stone, and every few hours Lucinda would burst into tears. Mandy knew that she'd taken Betty Sue's betrayal rather hard, but she didn't think her grief was entirely because she'd been hoodwinked by her white friend. It was the loss of the other one that so sorely grieved her.

For two days the whole post had buzzed with gossip about how Betty Sue Harris had directed the theft of the Yokuts supplies by juggling the record books her husband brought home, and later by smuggling them out of the office herself. As her ambitious career plans for him had fallen short and he'd grown discontented, he'd found other companions and left her more frequently at home. Finally she'd decided to wreak revenge. Not only had she arranged to steal the supplies and make money selling Yokuts slaves, but she'd made sure that all the evidence would point to her husband once she ran away with a sizeable profit. She just hadn't counted on Drew.

He hadn't tried to hog all the credit for himself,

though. He'd added Corporal Johnson's research and Lieutenant Isley's legwork to his report, and the major said they'd both get some sort of official token of gratitude. Mandy had gone to the hospital to see Isley, who was mending nicely. After years of feeling sorry for himself because he'd failed to win the hand of the girl he'd wanted, taking a bullet had made him re-evaluate his life. He'd decided he wasn't really cut out to be an Army officer and was planning to resign his commission. He hadn't decided on his next career, but he was determined to choose something that would bring joy to his life.

Mandy wished she could bring joy to Anna, who'd done so much for her. Fort Tejon had been too unsettled for her to approach Sherwood about an escort out to the reservation, but she intended to go see Anna as soon as possible. It was the very least she could do for her.

"I'm worried about Jonathan," Mandy said to Lucinda one afternoon as she rocked the fussing baby. "He's just a different child than he was when I first got here."

Lucinda stiffened. "I'm doing the best I can, Mandy. I'm too old to stay up all night with a crying baby and I'm too unsettled to hire another nanny right now. I appreciate your help, but if it's becoming a burden ..."

"That's not what I meant, Lucinda. I'm delighted to have a chance to repay all your kindness. But it's obvious to me that Anna's absence is terribly hard on Jonathan."

Lucinda's gnarled old hands tightened. "I can't help that. Anna doesn't work here anymore."

"Lucinda, you know it's not that simple."

"She told Drew she'd never come back."

"Lucinda!" Mandy berated her. "I think she'd come back if you asked her to. She loves this baby. She loves *you.*

You broke her heart. She believed she was part of the family. She hoped to stay with you after Sherwood retired."

Lucinda didn't seem to have an answer. Instead she snatched Jonathan from Mandy as she mumbled, "Well, it's too late now."

"No, it's not. If you apologized, I'm sure she'd forgive you."

Suddenly those flashing major's-wife eyes darkened. "Mandy, you're coming dangerously close to overstepping the bounds of friendship here," she warned softly.

Mandy straightened her shoulders. "And you're dangerously close to making a mistake that will haunt you for the rest of your life." Before Lucinda could argue further, Mandy said, "You know what's best for Jonathan. You know what's best for Anna." She paused, then spoke the words she felt she had to say. "And most of all you know what's right. Don't let Betty Sue influence you."

Lucinda took off her spectacles and glared at Mandy. "I know that I can't live with the fear that something is going to happen to my grandson. It's not Anna I don't trust. It's the fact that she's an Indian. I tried and tried to forget it, Mandy. You must believe that. For a while there, she almost seemed to be turning white. But when I heard Betty Sue scream that an Indian was stealing that precious baby, I forgot everything I ever knew about Anna."

"I understand that," Mandy said gently, reaching out for Lucinda's trembling, blue-veined hand. "But don't you think, with love and patience, you could learn to trust her all over again?"

* * *

The full heat of summer had come to the reservation, and Anna found herself longing for the cooler air of the mountains. And that wasn't all she missed of her life at Fort Tejon, of course. She missed the soft cotton clothes, the comfortable house and the conversation of Mrs. Larson and Mandy. But above all, she ached for her baby son.

It was a physical thing, the hurt she felt for Jonathan. Every time she heard a baby wail, she thought she heard him crying out to her. He would not understand why she had left him. He would not understand that she'd had no choice.

The worst of it was that while her grandfather had been alive, he had always wanted her to return to the reservation, and Salt Hair had begged her to do so when it was time for him to take a wife. But now Salt Hair was getting married and Grandfather was dead, and there was no one to welcome Anna to her old home.

At least, since her grandfather had died outside in the quake, no one had burned her hut. Empty and cheerless, it still sheltered her. Most of her old neighbors were not unkind to her, but neither did they rejoice in her return. They were busy rebuilding their lives since the earthquake, and, because the slavery ring had been broken, joyfully reuniting with the Hiding Ones. Anna was glad for the others, but she had no heart for rejoicing.

Of all the wounds she felt, the worst, perhaps, was the knowledge that she had been lying to herself for months about her role in the Larsons' household. She had believed that the major had truly come to respect her. She had believed that Mrs. Larson had taken her into her heart. Mandy had proven to be her friend right to the end, and dear little Percy had saved her life. But they would both be leaving soon with Rodney Potter. She had never expected them to be a permanent part of her world.

She had never expected the Army to imprison Betty Sue Harris for theft of military property, either, and Anna had to admit that she'd rejoiced when she'd heard. She'd always assumed it was her Yokuts blood that made her despise the heartless woman. Now she knew it was her human instincts. Mandy had never liked her either. But Mrs. Harris's situation didn't do much to help Anna's own.

She was staring blandly into the boiling basket of her grandfather's hut, stirring the acorn mush that her mother had taught her to make so many years ago, when she heard the creak of a wagon and the clip-clop of hooves. She knew the others would rush out to see who had arrived. Anna did not want to know. Worse yet, she did not want to face a white person wearing shabby deerskin.

When the hoofbeats stopped, the sounds of heavy boots clomped on the hard earth. Still, the only voices she heard were Yokuts, calling for her to come outside. When at last she did, she was not prepared for the sight that greeted her.

Her friend Mandy was there, eyes shining with concern. Little Percy threw himself forward and plastered himself against Anna's side. Standing behind Mandy stood stern Major Larson, looking embarrassed but curiously determined. Mrs. Larson, clutching Jonathan, stood very close to his side. Jonathan was sleeping, but Anna was rocked by his cherub's smile. Oh, how desperately she missed her tiny son! How hard it was to keep her hands by her sides!

Anna hugged little Percy, but she did not meet his eyes. She did not study Mandy or the major or even her precious baby. She knew who had broken the unspoken vow of friendship that had made the Larsons' house her home. She knew that only one person could ease the searing pain inside her.

A thousand years seemed to pass before Mrs. Larson finally stepped forward and handed Jonathan to Anna. Her heart twisted painfully as she pressed her face against his sweet, warm neck; she could not hide her tears. The baby tugged on her hair with both puny fists and cooed. Anna's smile was so wide she was afraid her face would split. In another moment, she might be cooing, too.

Slowly she found the courage to look again at Mrs. Larson, the white woman she'd trusted, the one who'd broken her heart. She knew that Mrs. Larson had come to beg for her forgiveness, but she could not give it until the right words were spoken.

The silence in the watching Yokutses grew absolute before Mrs. Larson finally started speaking. Her voice was low and shaky as she struggled with each word.

"Please forgive me, Anna. Nothing's been quite right since you left home." Mrs. Larson's eyes filled with tears as she confessed, "Jonathan misses you so badly. And truth to tell, dear, he's not the only one."

17

It was a brisk fall day, close to high noon, when Drew said calmly to Rodney Potter, "The fort is just over that next ridge. Miss Henderson's lodgings are at the officer's quarters at the far end of the parade grounds."

Rodney studied him curiously. "Won't you be taking me to see her?"

"I think it's a private time for your family," Drew said stiffly. "I think you'd all be better off alone."

Rodney was silent for a moment. Then he said, "Is it the only building, or should I—"

"It doesn't matter," Drew snapped. "They'll know you're here before you enter the gates of the fort. Percy will come running, shrieking like a banshee, and Miss Henderson won't be far behind."

To his further irritation, Rodney grinned. As luck would have it, he was a tall, pleasant-featured man

with an engaging manner that made it difficult for
Drew to dislike him and easy to understand Mandy's
passionate loyalty to him. He still limped slightly as a
result of his arrow wounds, but the Yokutses had cared
for him well and otherwise he seemed healthy. A dozen
times he'd told Drew how grateful he was to be alive.
Each time Drew had longed to tell him the truth of his
own love for Mandy, but the die was cast. Mandy had
made her decision, and both men would have to live
with it.

"I can't tell you how good it will be to see them. I
imagine Percy's grown."

"He's had to become a young man in your absence,"
Drew said tightly. "It would be a mistake to expect him
to go back to being a little boy."

Apparently Rodney couldn't ignore the tension in his
guide's voice, because this time he said, "I get the
impression that you're somehow blaming me for what's
happened, Captain. Do you think I just ran off and left
them?"

"Didn't you?" Drew asked. "You knew they had no
one but you. Couldn't you have found a profession
close to home?"

"Like soldiering, you mean?"

"I don't have a family, Potter," he said bitterly.
"Nobody cares were I work or roam."

"And if somebody did, would you leave the Army?"
Rodney pressed.

It was a hard question, one Drew didn't feel Rodney
had any right to ask. Would he leave the Army if
Mandy begged him? Maybe. But she no longer had the
right to ask anything of him.

The past ten days had been among the most difficult

in Drew's life. He'd managed, to a certain extent, to put Mandy from his mind while he tracked down Rodney Potter, finding the man just before he'd boarded ship. Then things had gotten even harder while he'd ridden side by side with his nemesis, trying to quell his passion for the woman they seemed to share. But Drew knew that his part in Mandy's life was nearly over, and Rodney's time had just begun.

"My personal life is hardly the question here," he told Potter. "As it happens, I'm assigned to Washington, D.C., and I plan to stay there quite a while. When you get things straightened out with the Sea to Shining Sea Railway, you ought to go back east yourself. Miss Henderson deserves a stable home in civilization after all she's been through, and Percy needs to be close to a good school as well."

This time Rodney bristled. "I hardly need you to tell me how to take care of my family, Captain."

"No? Then why have I been taking care of them for the past three months? Where the hell were you?"

It was an unfair question, one Drew wished he could take back, but he was feeling too raw to be reasonable. In half an hour, maybe less, Mandy would be in Rodney Potter's arms. Nobody, not even Rodney, knew what a sterling gift that was. And nobody knew the price Drew had paid to give it.

"It seems to me," Rodney said slowly, "that your interest in Mandy may not be entirely . . . official."

Drew glared at him. "It seems to me that your interest may not be *sufficient*. She's been counting on you but taking care of herself."

"I assure you, Captain, that won't the case in the future."

"I certainly hope not." He might have said even more, but at that moment a cry burst forth from the other side of the stables. An instant later a shaggy gray pony was galloping toward them so fast its legs were a blur.

"Rodney! Rodney! Is it really you?" Percy shouted at the top of his lungs.

Drew stopped his horse. He let Rodney gallop on ahead, and watched in silence, as the other man leaped out of his saddle and swept his baby brother off the pony in an embrace that sought to wipe out months and months of suffering. He whirled the little boy around and around and around, laughing and crying with as much glee as Percy. In spite of himself, Drew was happy for the boy. He had waited with the utmost of loyalty, the utmost of courage. He deserved the reward of a jubilant big brother. Only a small man would begrudge him his joy.

Still, it wasn't easy for him to nudge Napoleon on toward the fort, passing within two feet of young Percy. But Percy never even noticed Drew.

It was Corporal Johnson, green eyes sparkling, who knocked on the Larsons' door and shared the news. "They're here, ma'am! Down at the stables. Captain Robelard and your fiancé. Percy's already joined his brother."

Mandy had dreamed of this moment a thousand times, planned her behavior in a thousand ways. She had had one plan before she'd met Drew, another afterwards. But now Drew was back at the fort safe and sound, Rodney was alive and well, and her endless quest had come full circle. Suddenly nothing else mattered.

Mandy didn't even take off her apron. She just bolted out of the house and started to run. She had to pick up her skirts to keep from falling, and her stiff-heeled shoes gave her no traction on the rough parade grounds, but she kept right on going anyway. She'd barely reached the stream when she saw Percy's pony galloping toward her. Another horse, a big, strong sorrel, was keeping pace beside him.

Her heart somersaulted as she saw Rodney's face, weathered and worn as though ten years had passed. In his eyes she saw her brothers and her parents and the wonderful old house where she was raised. She felt warm and safe and whole again. Desperately she pushed aside the nameless pain that still lingered in her heart.

"Rodney! Rodney, are you really all right?" she called, still running toward him.

A moment later he was on the ground, pulling Mandy into his arms. He hugged her so hard she thought he'd break a rib, and she clenched him with the same relief.

"Oh, Mandy, I've been through hell. The worst of all was not being able to let you and Percy know I was alive. I knew you'd wait forever, but I never dreamed you'd come out here to find me."

"We had to," Percy chimed in, hugging them both as he dismounted. "We never, ever believed you were dead."

The circle seemed complete, and Mandy could not deny that she was deeply happy. But despite her joy at her dear friend's survival, she felt a gaping hole inside her as she realized that only half of her wanted to be here rejoicing with Percy and Rodney.

The other half wanted to run to the stables and give herself to Drew.

"Captain, I have not had the chance to thank you for putting an end to the abuse of my people," Anna said quietly as she stood at the door of Captain Robelard's temporary quarters.

He was standing by the window, fidgeting with the rabbit-skin blanket that he'd retrieved from his saddle-bag after Napoleon had drifted back to the post. He looked bleak and broken, and she wished there was something she could do for him. But she had seen Mandy's ebullient reunion with Rodney Potter, and surely Captain Robelard had seen it, too.

She was very happy for little Percy, but she was still not certain if she should rejoice or grieve for Mandy. Anna knew her friend cared for Rodney Potter, but she also knew that it was far too late for her to erase her love for Captain Robelard. There was not much Anna could say to comfort to this kind, brave man who'd helped her put her own life back in order.

"Captain, Mandy does not love this man the way she loves you." She spoke with conviction, because she knew she spoke the truth. Ever since the captain had gone to San Francisco, Mandy had looked even more tormented than she had when she'd first arrived in California. Then she had ached for a miracle. Now she ached for one of another kind.

His eyes met hers bleakly. "I know," he said with unmasked sorrow. "That doesn't make things any easier."

He stared at the blanket for a moment, then placed it in Anna's hands. "I have no use for this anymore, and I don't have room to take it back east with me anyway. I'm leaving in the morning. Why don't you give it to somebody who might need it when the weather turns cold."

Anna took the thick blanket, clumsily woven with the most enduring kind of devotion, and folded it carefully.

"I will give it to the one who needs it most," she promised.

"At the very least, I wish you'd come to dinner, Drew. Surely you'll want to pay your respects to Lucinda before you leave in the morning."

Drew tried to look cheerful, but the grief he carried made it hard to smile even in Sherwood's office. Briskly, he handed his old friend three notes he'd written an hour ago. To Lucinda, he'd said thank you; to Percy, he'd said he'd always be proud to be his *shaughnum-uh*. To Mandy he'd said he would always come to her aid if she ever needed him, and he'd always cherish the memory of the day he'd "married" her in the Yokuts hut.

It had been excruciating to watch her reunion with Rodney, even at a distance. She had not asked for Drew, nor sought him out, and under the circumstances, he could not blame her. Rodney probably suspected that he and Mandy were more than friends. Seeing them together for even a moment would undoubtedly have proved it. Drew didn't know how Mandy felt about him now, but he knew that time had cooled his anger. There was no room in his heart for anything but the aching emptiness of regret. He had forgiven her for the choice that duty had forced her to make, but he would never forget his love for her.

"I'm sorry, Sherwood, but tonight I'm quite certain I'd be poor company. Besides, you have other guests."

Sherwood didn't argue. He understood the situation as well as anyone could.

"I'm sorry it worked out like this, Drew."

"So am I. But there's nothing more I can do." He gave a twisted smile. "I came here to check out the camels and solve the supply thefts. I've got a promising report on those falsely maligned beasts and given the Yokutses all they can hope for. I think any officer could call that a success."

But even as he shook Sherwood's hand and said goodbye, he knew he would have traded his whole career for Mandy.

The first hours were ones of joy and celebration, of hugs and tears that seemed to bind Mandy not only to Rodney, but to her family and Rodney's as well. Lucinda fed him all afternoon, determined, she said, to get meat on his bones. Tenderly Mandy listened to his stories and held his hand. She realized, as she gazed on his beloved face, how terribly much she had missed Rodney—as she missed all of her brothers—and how totally she had once believed that she would never see him again.

It was the memory of that time of loss that made her even more acutely aware of how she'd feel when Drew left the post again. She'd missed him unbearably over the past few days, and she'd counted the minutes until she could see his face. But he'd vanished as soon as he'd delivered Rodney, and she'd not yet found a good excuse to go see him. Once she did, she didn't know what she could possibly say. Duty still dictated that she marry Rodney, but how could she just let Drew ride away?

It was not until after supper, as darkness fell on the fort, that Mandy found herself alone with Rodney. Lucinda had rather pointedly chased everybody out of the parlor so they could have some privacy. But they had not been chatting for more than ten minutes before Anna showed up at the door.

She was carrying two quilts and a thick rabbit-skin blanket, all folded neatly. Without preamble she said to Mandy, "I brought Mrs. Larson's best quilts so your guest will be comfortable in the bachelors' office quarters. But they are the quilts off of your bed, so I brought this other blanket for you."

Mandy studied the rabbit-skin blanket thoughtfully, wondering why Anna had brought it back to the fort with her and why, when she was finally melding into the household as more white than Indian, she'd chosen to bring it out now. She also wondered at how roughly it was made. She'd seen Anna's other handiwork with tule weaving, and it was precise and beautifully executed. This looked like a beginner's work.

It was Rodney who casually observed, "That doesn't look like the same style of rabbit-skin weaving used among the Yokutses I wintered with."

"This blanket is not made in the traditional Yokuts style. It is supposed to be Zuni."

"Zuni?" said Rodney. "Why, I thought the Zunis were a tribe in New Mexico Territory."

Mandy closed her eyes against the sudden sure

knowledge that she was looking at her wedding blanket, her priceless gift from Drew. With a jarring rush of remembered passion, she saw Drew in the Yokuts hut, Drew wrapping Old Hadj's saddle blanket around her shoulders, Drew wrapping his long, naked legs around her own.

"The Zuni men weave blankets for their brides," Anna told Rodney bluntly. "A white man asked me how to teach him to weave so he could make this one for his woman. He wanted to give her something of himself, a gift that could come from no other. Once he rejoiced because she said she would marry him, but now he has no use for the blanket because she decided to marry someone else."

Mandy felt the blood drain from her face. Drew hadn't told him that Anna had been helping him. Surely he hadn't told her to deliver the blanket in front of Rodney.

"He no longer needs the blanket, and he is leaving here tomorrow, so he asked me to give this special blanket to whoever seemed to need it the most." Anna stepped forward and placed the rabbit skin in Mandy's hands, then gripped her fingers tightly. "I think that person is you."

Anna left the room before Mandy could find her voice. She dug her fingers into the rabbit skin, longing to lift it to her face to conceal her threatening tears. She could not let Drew leave without telling him goodbye. And yet, if she saw him again, how could she possibly find the strength to do the right thing and marry Rodney?

She did not know how much time passed before Rodney crossed the parlor and slowly sat down beside her. Very gently, he took her hand.

"Tell me about the blanket, Mandy," he requested. "I believe Anna's not the only one who intended this gift for you."

Mandy's eyes flashed up at him. How much did he guess? How much should she tell him? How much did he have a right to know?"

"Mandy, we've been friends all our lives, and that's never going to change. Something important has happened to you since I've been gone. Some important things have happened to me, too. We need to talk about them before we can go on."

Mandy's eyes met Rodney's as she struggled for breath. She wanted to tell him the truth but she didn't want to hurt him. She wanted to tell him how deeply she loved him as a brother and a friend. She wanted to plead for Drew's forgiveness before he rode out of her life forever.

"I thought you were dead," she finally found the courage to tell Rodney. "Everyone said you were."

"I thought I was, too. A man can't go through what I've endured without changing inside, Mandy. He learns what's important and whom he owes debts to."

Mandy couldn't answer. Once she'd hoped that a miracle might occur, that there might be some way for Rodney to free her from her promise, but now it seemed impossible.

"Mandy, I spent several days alone with Captain Robelard. He did his best to behave professionally, but he couldn't hide the fact that he has very strong feelings for you."

Mandy swallowed hard and battled tears again. Somehow she found the strength to tell him, "After we'd looked for you so long, it all seemed so hopeless.

Everyone told me there was no reason to keep on waiting for you." She tried to face him directly, but it was more than she could bear. "He asked me to marry him, Rodney," she admitted in a low, strained voice. "During the time we thought you were dead."

Rodney's lips tightened for a moment. He released her hand. "And what did you say?"

Slowly, painfully, she nodded.

After a long pause, he said, "And Percy?"

"Drew wanted to adopt him. They had become very close."

Her eyes met his again. "Percy never believed you were dead, even when all the evidence proved it. I couldn't tell him I was going to marry somebody else as long as he believed you were still alive. So we were waiting until the time was right."

"And then I spoiled it all by turning up alive."

"No, Rodney, don't say that!" Mandy reached out to him blindly. "I was thrilled to learn you were still living. Ask Percy. Ask Drew! Ask anyone."

"I don't imagine Robelard was thrilled."

"He went to get you for me, Rodney. That was a far greater gift than the blanket."

"Do you really think he's planning to leave in the morning without you?"

Mandy started to cry. "Yes. I know he is. Before he went to San Francisco, he gave me an ultimatum. When I said I couldn't turn my back on my family obligations, he said goodbye."

"So what are you going to do?" Rodney barked. "Give up the man you really want and pretend you'll be happy married to me?"

Put so bluntly, it seemed to Mandy like an absurd

thing to do. Was it remotely possible that Rodney might see it as an absurd thing, too? Could she make him understand how desperately she loved Drew? And if Rodney were to release her from her vow, could she persuade Drew to give her one more chance to prove her love for him?

Slowly, painfully, she lifted both hands to cup her dear friend's face. "Rodney, since I was a little girl, you've always been my friend," she told him gently. "I love you dearly. I always will. I promised to marry you before I promised Drew, and if that's what you still want, I will."

Her tears were flowing freely now. Her voice was choked with sobs. "But if you feel about me the way I think you do, you don't need me as your wife to honor the debts our families owe each other. I'll always take care of Percy whenever you're away. I'll love you forever. I'll be your second home. But let me be your sister, Rodney, as I've always been. That little girl will always cherish you."

She stepped back, and straightened slowly. "But the woman I've become on this long journey will always belong to Drew."

Percy was already perched on his pony when Captain Robelard approached the corral the next morning. His face looked terrible, dark and furrowed, and his eyes were devoid of light. He tried to smile when he saw Percy, but it didn't seem to work.

"Hi, Captain!" Percy sang out cheerfully. "Isn't it a beautiful day?"

The captain gazed at the mountains, still wet with

dew, adorned with hundreds of wild orange poppies. "I guess it's a fine day for you, Percy. You're finally reunited with your brother."

The captain didn't sound quite as happy about it as Percy expected him to be. But Percy was happy enough for both of them. "I always told you he wasn't dead," he chirped.

The captain nodded. "Yes, you did. I guess we grownups should have had more faith in you."

Percy grinned as the captain reached out and shook his hand. Last night Rodney had patted him on the head, and he'd realized that Rodney didn't know that Captain Robelard had helped his little brother become a man.

Suddenly he remembered what he was doing out here at the crack of dawn. "Oh, Captain, I almost forgot. You're supposed to go to the major's house before you ride out this morning."

"Oh?" The captain didn't look too happy. "I believe I already said my farewells last night. And I left a message for you with the major, Percy. I would never have left without some sort of goodbye for you."

"Oh, I know, Captain. A *shaugh-num-uh* is for life. But we won't be apart very long, will we?" Before the captain could answer, Percy added, "All I know is that Mandy said to tell you she's almost packed and you're supposed to talk to my brother."

"Packed?" he said, seizing on the word with remarkable ferocity. "Your brother is heading out immediately? Doesn't he need a few days to just enjoy being with you?"

Now Percy smiled again. "Sure he does. That's why I'm going to stay with him in California for a while. Till summer's over, I mean, and I have to go back to school.

Then I'm supposed to go back east to live with Mandy."

The captain's face turned snow white. "Mandy's going back east to live?" he whispered. "Without your brother?"

"Well, he's going to come visit us from time to time when he's not out here making maps," Percy explained. "He told me that he'll always love Mandy and, you know, be her brother. But she explained that if you were leaving the post this morning, she was leaving, too. I begged her to wait awhile, but she told me that she'd have my room all set up and waiting by the time I got there. By that time she'll be married to you."

For the briefest of moments, the captain seemed to reel. "She told you she's planning to marry *me*?" he repeated in a choked voice. "No matter what?"

Percy nodded. "Well, actually she said she was afraid it might take a little doing to talk you into it, because for some reason she thinks you're mad at her. But you know how Mandy is when she makes up her mind, Captain, so you might as well just give in right now." Suddenly Percy sobered as a thought crossed his mind. "You do like Mandy, sir? I mean, enough to marry her?"

The captain didn't answer the question; in fact, Percy didn't even think he heard. He jumped into Napoleon's saddle and kicked the poor horse into a dead run. He didn't even bother to steer the bay toward the bridge across the post stream, just spurred Napoleon over it at one of the smaller squiggles.

Percy had never seen anything quite so extraordinary. The captain was always so quiet, so confident, so dignified! But now he was pressing his horse so hard that little Daisy, at a full gallop, couldn't catch up with him.

But Percy wasn't too far back to hear the captain calling out Mandy's name in a voice that was so full of hurt and joy it gave Percy goosebumps. As Captain Robelard neared the house, curtains fluttered in the upstairs window. A moment later the front door opened and Mandy rushed outside.

Right there, in front of God and everybody, she threw herself in the captain's arms. He gave her a kiss that would have started a fire without any flint or sticks to rub together, and Percy was too embarrassed to sit there watching the two of them start to burn.

He wasn't sure just what had happened with all the grownups since last night, but he knew that all of them seemed pretty happy. And he was happy too. He still got to live with Mandy, his big brother was still alive, and he wasn't going to have to say goodbye to his *shaugh-num-uh* forever. Now all he had to worry about was how to get his pony back to Washington.

Percy dismounted in front of the house, planning to ask Mandy if Rodney could borrow her horse. But he didn't have much luck getting her attention, because she was still clinging to Captain Robelard, hugging and kissing him like crazy, and Percy had a hunch she was going to keep on doing it for the rest of her life.

AVAILABLE NOW

SONG OF THE NIGHTINGALE by Constance O'Banyon
A mesmerizing historical romance from bestselling author Constance O'Banyon. This enchanting love story sweeps from the drawing rooms of London to the battlefields of Waterloo as a beautiful woman fights for her family's honor and finds her one true love.

LOVE WITH A WARM COWBOY by Lenore Carroll
When her boyfriend returns from a trip abroad with a Croatian bride, Barbara Door is crushed. She heads for a friend's dude ranch in Wyoming to find confidence, adventure, and love with a warm cowboy. A sassy, moving story for all modern women.

SWEET IVY'S GOLD by Paula Paul
Award-winning author Paula Paul brings the Old West back to life in this winsome turn-of-the-century romance about a feisty young woman who sets up a gambling parlor in a small gold-mining town in Colorado. Adventure and true love abound when she meets Langdon Runnels.

THIEF OF HEARTS by Penelope Thomas
From the author of *Master Of Blackwood* and *Passion's Child* comes a story of love and intrigue in 17th century England. Forced to flee her village home after accidentally killing a local squire in self-defense, Damorna Milfield seeks refuge in London. She is rescued by mysterious "Lord Quent," a charming but duplicitous man-about-town, who teaches Damorna the art of deception and love.

SUNBURST by Suzanne Ellison
A sweeping tale of love and adventure in the Mohave Desert and the Sierra Nevada. Bostonian beauty Mandy Henderson goes out west in search of her fiancé, Rodney Potter, who has disappeared while doing survey work for the railroad. Drew Robelard, a handsome army captain, is assigned to help Mandy find Rodney, but he actually has his own secret agenda.

PRIVATE LIES by Carol Cail
The lighthearted adventures of a young woman reporter who sets out to investigate her boss's death and ends up solving a different crime, discovering unexpected romance along the way.

COMING NEXT MONTH

SILVER SHADOWS by Marianne Willman
In this dramatic western of love and betrayal, Marianne Willman, author of *Yesterday's Shadows*, continues the saga of the Howards. Intent on revenge for wrongs done to his family, half-Cheyenne Grayson Howard unexpectedly finds love with a beautiful widow.

THE WAY IT SHOULD HAVE BEEN by Georgia Bockoven
From the author of *A Marriage Of Convenience* comes a story of drama, courage, and tenderness. Carly is reasonably happy with a stable marriage and three wonderful children. Then David comes back to town. Now a famous author, David had left twenty years before when Carly married his best friend. He'd never stopped loving Carly, nor forgiven her for leaving him. Yet, Carly did what she had to do. It was the only way to keep the secret she must hide—at all costs.

THE HEART'S LEGACY by Barbara Keller
When Céline Morand married the man she'd dreamed of for years, she thought the demands of love and duty were the same. But an unexpected trip to the lush plantation of her husband's cousin in Louisiana ends Céline's naiveté and opens her heart to a man she can't have.

LADY OF LOCHABAR by Jeanette Ramirez
In this beautiful, heartbreaking love story, Maggie Macdonald is but seven years old when Simon Campbell saves her life after his father's army has massacred her entire family. As fate would have it, they meet ten years later and enter into a forbidden love.

OUT OF THE PAST by Shirl Jensen
When Debbie Dillion moves to Texas to pick up the pieces of her life, she finds her dream house waiting for her. But soon Debbie wonders if she has walked into a living nightmare, where someone is willing to do anything to hide the past—even commit murder.

WHEN DESTINY CALLS by Suzanne Elizabeth
A delightful time-travel romance about a modern-day police officer, Kristen Ford, who would go to any distance—even to the rugged mountains of Nevada in the 1890s—to find her soul mate.

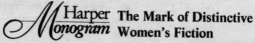 **Harper Monogram** **The Mark of Distinctive Women's Fiction**

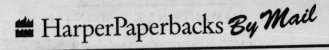